THOSE
WE
THOUGHT
WE
KNEW

ALSO BY DAVID JOY

WHEN THESE MOUNTAINS BURN

THE LINE THAT HELD US

THE WEIGHT OF THIS WORLD

WHERE ALL LIGHT TENDS TO GO

THOSE
WE
THOUGHT
WE
KNEW

A NOVEL

DAVID JOY

G. P. PUTNAM'S SONS
NEW YORK

PUTNAM
— EST. 1838 —
G. P. PUTNAM'S SONS
Publishers Since 1838
An imprint of Penguin Random House LLC
penguinrandomhouse.com

Hardcover ISBN: 9780525536918
Ebook ISBN: 9780525536925

Printed in the United States of America
1st Printing

Title page art: Shovel image © Tayfun Mehmed / Shutterstock

Book design by Alison Cnockaert

For Marie, whose spirit burns as fiercely
bright as anyone's ever born of this place

Let us take a knife
and cut the world in two—
and see what worms are eating
at the rind.

—LANGSTON HUGHES

THOSE
WE
THOUGHT
WE
KNEW

1

The graves took all night to dig. There were seven in all, each between five and six feet deep, dug by a dozen pairs of hands. Some of
the diggers brought gloves, and they took turns sharing them with
those who had not so as to try to keep their hands from breaking.
By the end, every hand was blistered and burning just the same.
Their fingers hurt to straighten. Their backs bent crooked as laurel.

It was the middle of summer, but on the mountain the air was
cool. Each time they swapped out of the graves to rest, their sweat
chilled their bodies and they welcomed that feeling, for the work
had nearly set them afire. Katydids wailed from the trees and it was
that sound that dampened the chomp and clink of spades digging
away at the earth, the labored breaths of those who drove their
shovels deeper.

Around midnight, campus police circled the parking lot once
making their rounds, but the diggers hid and were soon alone. The
dirt rose mounded at the heads of the graves, and when the digging

was done they shuttled back and forth from pickup trucks to carry buckets filled with river stones.

The young woman who'd planned this took the last of the work alone. She'd painted the river stones white and with them she slowly formed letters on the mounds of clay at the head of each grave. She took her time with this part, as if it were some sort of meditation. Holding each rock with both hands, she slowly turned them until they seemed to show her their place, and when the last was set, a word was spelled. Even in the blue glow she could read what was written, and with it finished she stretched flat on the grass to watch the last of pinprick stars dim and fade as first light blanched the sky.

Early on, she'd considered stretching black sheets over the ground to signify the open graves. But now that the work was done and her body ached, she was glad she had taken the tougher row. This was part of the story and now she knew the details intimately. She rocked forward and wrapped her arms around her knees. Red mud was caked to the legs of her overalls. She could feel the clay dried like a charcoal mask against her face where she'd wiped away sweat with the backs of her hands. She grinned and slowly closed her eyes, satisfied with what they'd accomplished.

When the first birds started to call, the people who'd helped her began to leave. All of them were White save her, and some shook her hand while others hugged her neck. A young man named Brad Roberts was the last to go. He was a graduate student at the school and had been a tremendous help all summer with everything she was doing. Over the last two months, they'd spent time together nearly every day. He walked over and stood by her side. "It's powerful," he said, placing one hand gently at the back of her arm. "It really is, Toya." His words filled her with pride. Once he was gone and she was alone, she slipped a folded piece of paper out of her back pocket. She opened the paper to a black-and-white photograph she'd printed at the library.

In the picture, nineteen men and women were gathered in front of a church. Most of the men wore mustaches and all of the women wore hats, every person dressed in their Sunday best. Her third-great-grandfather stood in the second row with his hand in his pocket, something she could tell because of the way his jacket angled across the waist of his slacks. He was tall and lean with a low brow that shaded his eyes, light-skinned compared to his wife, who stood beside him. Her third-great-grandmother had a white knitted shawl draped over her shoulders, a wide-brimmed black hat propped high on her head. In the woman's face, the girl could see her mother, traits that had carried down and were still traveling.

As she stood there studying the faces in the photograph, the faces of where and whom she'd come from, she couldn't help feeling like they were watching her, their flat stares reaching somewhere far back inside her. It was as if there were a closet at the back of her heart and that image, coupled with the smell of the dirt, had somehow opened a door she had not known lay closed.

She folded the photograph and slid it back into her pocket, then walked across the courtyard to a sidewalk by the road. A small bronze plaque had been placed there long ago to dedicate the ground, and it was this plaque that had led to this. Over the course of the summer, she'd stood here dozens of times and read what was written until the lines were memorized.

ON THIS SITE IN 1892 ELEVEN FORMER SLAVES
FOUNDED THE CULLOWHEE AFRICAN METHODIST EPISCOPAL
ZION CHURCH. THE CONGREGATION, CHURCH AND CEMETERY
MOVED IN NOVEMBER 1929 TO MAKE ROOM FOR THE
CONSTRUCTION OF ROBERTSON HALL.

The plaque, of course, did not tell the story. In truth there were eighty-six bodies and an amputated arm exhumed and reburied.

When she'd asked her grandmother about what had happened, her grandmother had said that as a child she'd been told that when they dug up the bodies, the hair of the dead had kept growing, a grisly detail she didn't know whether to believe or dismiss as some scary story intended to frighten children. Looking back, her grandmother thought it was most likely true. Her voice had trembled as she said this.

In a whole lot of ways, the young woman thought, pain had been passed down from one generation to the next, and that's what so many people never could understand unless it was their history, unless this was their story. For certain groups in America, trauma was a sort of inheritance.

The young woman turned from the plaque to the three-story building that stood in place of the church, the red brick walls warming in color as sunlight started to reach them. The courtyard and graves still rested in shade from a tall hedgerow of pines, and she walked with her hands locked together at her chest for one last look before going. The stones were brighter now and under her breath she read what they spelled aloud.

In the beginning, there was only the word.

2

That same night, seven miles down the road, the scene looked like a faded postcard from forty years ago. An '84 Caprice Classic wagon sat in the nightglow outside Harold's Supermarket. Harold's had been right there on that short stretch of road between Sylva and Dillsboro since the early seventies and never much changed its look. The parking lot was empty except for the Chevrolet. Streetlights filtered through the fog and shone off the blacktop to make the lot appear a solid sheet of dark blue glass.

A clerk working alone at the gas station across the road made the call. She said the first two times the man walked into the How Convenient he grabbed three tallboys of Busch Ice and paid cash. There was about an hour between each visit, another hour or so before he stumbled into the store for a third time. That last visit he gathered another three cans, emptied his pockets, and counted out a fistful of change. He wound up sixty cents shy and tripped toward the beer cooler to trade the tallboys for a forty-ounce High Life.

There was just enough left over for a couple loose cigarettes from a foam cup next to the register.

None of this of course was all that odd. A girl works graveyard at a filling station that sells more booze than petrol and she comes to see all sorts of folks waltz through that door. If it had been one of the usuals she wouldn't have batted an eye. But the thing was, she didn't know this man from Adam, and in a place like this a girl like her came to know every drunk in town. She took a smoke break after sweeping the store. Leaning against the wall by the stacks of five-dollar firewood outside, she could see the man across the street sprawled on the hood of his car cussing at the sky in front of Harold's.

Deputy Ernie Allison had been working nights all month for the Jackson County Sheriff's Office. Harold's fell within Sylva limits and was town police jurisdiction, but budget cuts had the Sylva PD low on patrol and Ernie wasn't doing much anyway. Tuesday nights were always dead shifts.

Town police were already on scene when he arrived, a single patrol car at the far side of the parking lot. Ernie cut his headlights as he veered through the empty spaces at an angle. He yawned and rubbed the heel of his right hand into his eyes, trying to shake himself awake. Running his palm from his forehead through his hair, he glanced at himself in the rearview mirror. His hair was trimmed low, his green eyes glassy and tired. As he pulled beside the cruiser, he lowered his window and looked across at a familiar face. Tim McMahan and Ernie had graduated in the same high school class.

Ever since they were kids, McMahan had been a drag. When they were seniors in high school, Tim ratted out the baseball team for getting stoned in the dugout after games. To this day, Ernie would've dreaded Tim's sidling up beside him at the bar, dreaded the drawn-out conversation, the you'll-never-guess-who-I-ran-intos, but despite all that Tim was decent police.

"You seen anybody?"

"Yeah, he's passed out in the back of that dinosaur." Tim motioned toward the station wagon that was parked in front of the store. The car was dark green with faded wood paneling and a crack running straight across the back glass.

"You try waking him up?"

"Figured I'd wait on you once I heard you check en route."

"I was bored stupid," Ernie said. "Couldn't hardly keep my eyes open."

Tim chuckled and smiled. "I bet I'd been asleep an hour." He grabbed an empty Mountain Dew from the cup holder and spit a dark line of snuff inside the bottle. "Radio went off I was watching the backs of my eyelids. I appreciate the backup."

"Not a problem."

The two cruisers crept side by side across the parking lot, one pulling tight to the back bumper of the Caprice while the other swung around to box the car in. Ernie stepped out and situated his belt on his hips. His legs were cramped from being in the car all night and he pushed up onto his tiptoes a few times to stretch his calves. Tim took the driver's side and Ernie the opposite, each sweeping his flashlight across the interior as they peered through smudged windows.

The rear seat was folded down and the entire back of the car was swamped with clothes. The man was shirtless and barefooted, lying flat on his stomach with a pair of black denim jeans painted to his legs. He had a black leather jacket wadded up and was hugging the coat with both arms under his head for a pillow.

Ernie glanced over top of the Caprice to see if Tim was ready. Tim took a step back, dug the wad of Skoal from his cheek, and tossed the tobacco into the parking lot. Turning his attention to the car, he rapped three loud cracks against the window with the head of the flashlight. The man didn't move at first but Tim pounded the glass again with his fist and the man groggily opened his eyes.

Ernie angled his flashlight straight into the man's face and he perked up on one elbow and squinted at the light, his face scrunched and puzzled. The man reached out and pressed one hand flush against the side glass to block the flashlight's beam.

"What the hell are you doing out there? Just who the hell are you?" He spoke with a funny accent, some sort of drawl from a deeper South.

"Jackson County Sheriff's Office," Ernie said. "I'm going to need you to step out of the vehicle."

All of a sudden the man whipped around and dug under the pile of clothes, and just as soon as he made that move Ernie drew his service weapon as Tim yanked open the far side door. Tim wrestled the man out of the car by his ankles and onto the ground where Ernie couldn't see from where he stood. There was a short commotion, two men grunting and snorting, then the ratcheted click of cuffs clinking closed. By the time Ernie made it around the vehicle Tim had the man on his feet.

"What in the hell you doing me like that for? I ain't done nothing!"

"What were you reaching for under those clothes?"

"My billfold, you son of a bitch. My license is in my billfold."

Ernie leaned into the car and pushed the leather jacket aside. Sure enough, a cheap nylon wallet was hidden under the jacket. Ripping the Velcro open, Ernie removed a Mississippi driver's license and studied the picture. William Dean Cawthorn had a head too small for his body, a long pencil neck, and a greasy mullet that lapped at his shoulders. Ernie tilted the license back and forth under his flashlight to check the hologram.

"You're a long way from Mississippi, Mr. Cawthorn." He walked around to the front of the station wagon and tossed the open wallet onto the hood. "What exactly are you doing in Sylva?"

The man stood up straight and shifted from foot to foot while Tim patted him down. He was tall and lean with broad shoulders. He jerked his head to the side and spit through the gap between his teeth. His torso was milky white, his arms and face sun beaten dark as leather. Road dust and dirt speckled his chest from where he'd wallowed across the blacktop.

"Tell me, why the hell you drug me out of that car like that? That fellow behind me about cracked my goddamn head open. Why don't you tell me what the hell for?"

"We both saw you reach under those clothes."

"I told you it was my billfold."

"But how were we supposed to know that?"

"Ahhhhh," he grumbled, and spit again off to the side.

The man kept trying to turn so he could get a better look at the officer patting him down. A couple tiny symbols were inked on his neck and arm like stick-on tattoos—a shamrock on the side of his throat, a crooked swastika centered on his right shoulder. He had bright blue eyes and brown hair, looked scruffy and unkempt. All of his facial features were mashed together, wide eyes sunk behind a nose that had obviously been broken, his mouth crammed under that beak like there wasn't a tooth in his head.

When Tim was finished searching the man's person he stepped around him and checked the license Ernie had tossed on the hood.

"All right, Mr. Cawthorn, I'm placing you under arrest."

"Arrest!" he squawked. "What the hell for?"

"Drunk in public. Vagrancy."

"Vagrant! I ain't no vagrant! I run out of gas and didn't have no place to go. Had a couple beers too fast and was sleeping it off. That's all. For Christ's sake, you going to arrest a man for sleeping it off?"

Tim began leading the man to his patrol car behind the Caprice. They were somewhere right around the rear tire when that long-legged son of a bitch spun around and kicked Tim square in the knee. After that it was off to the races.

The cuffs holding the man's arms behind his back kept him hunched forward as he sprinted across the parking lot barefooted. Ernie was on him in no time. He'd run the football all-state in high school and was still stocky and quick as a boar. He tackled the man from behind and rode him a few feet across the asphalt. Before Ernie could push himself up, Tim had his knee in the back of Cawthorn's neck, pressing his face into the blacktop. The man fought for a second or two, wrenching his body in every direction he could, but after that last burst Ernie felt him just sort of collapse and go limp. The man smelled like sweat and beer. He lay there spent and laughing.

"I just about had you," he said. He coughed and struggled to catch his breath. "Five more feet and I'd have had you."

"Five more feet and that Taser would've been pulsing fifty thousand volts. That's what five more feet would've got you." Ernie climbed to his feet and helped Tim lift the man from the ground by his elbows. Cawthorn was a good foot taller than Ernie and had five inches or so on Tim.

"You think a thing like that scares me?" The man's mouth was busted and there was blood dripping from his bottom lip as he smiled. Road rash reddened his chest and stomach where Ernie'd tackled him, the scrapes just starting to bleed. A long scratch ran from his hairline down the side of his face. "You think I ain't ever been tased? I'm from by-God Mississippi! Fifty thousand volts just gives us a hard-on!"

The man didn't shut up for one second as they led him to the back of Tim's patrol car and shoved him inside. Afterward, they stood there catching their breath and stared at each other, amused.

"Got a mouth on him, don't he?"

"And stretched out like the month's groceries."

"You all right?" Ernie asked.

"Yeah, I'll be fine," Tim said. "Kicked me in the shin like a little kid."

"Like that Charlie Daniels song." Ernie laughed and shook his head as they walked back to the Caprice. They still needed to search the car.

The station wagon stunk of soured clothes, stale cigarette butts, and empty cans of Del Monte canned peaches that lay on the driver-side floorboard. They had the rear gate and four doors open and the smell still burned their noses and eyes. Ernie took the back and sifted through the clothes. There wasn't much, but something funny caught his eye—a short stack of white fabric neatly folded and pressed. The rest of the vehicle was in disarray but here sat this one little piece of order. He grabbed the garment and held it up outside, the cloth folding out like a bedsheet.

Ernie studied a long white robe that stretched from where he pinched it at the shoulders to the ground. There was a circular patch over the right breast, a blood-drop cross that Ernie recognized from news stories and pictures. Another piece of cloth had fallen to the ground as he held up the robe. Ernie reached down and picked up a tall conical white hood.

Tim was busy searching the front of the car and had his knee in the driver's seat. He leaned back out of the vehicle to look. "That what I think it is?"

"Sure as hell ain't a Halloween costume."

Ernie draped the robe and hood over the top of the open door and walked around to the front passenger side to help Tim finish the search. The floorboard was crowded with empty coffee cups and food wrappers, Winston boxes and potted meat tins. He tried to open the glove box but it was locked.

"Toss me those keys."

Tim pulled the car keys out of the ignition and handed them across the cab. Ernie slipped the key into the lock and when the glove box fell open a blued snub-nosed revolver lay on top of the usual paperwork. The rubber grips had teeth marks pressed into them like a dog had chewed on the gun, a little Charter Arms .38 Special Undercover.

"What do you bet that gun doesn't pop?"

"I think I'd be buying your supper," Tim said.

The passenger seat was covered with sloppily opened mail—the corners ripped off envelopes, bills and credit card statements strewn about with disregard. Beneath the papers lay a black spiral notebook. Ernie grabbed the notebook and opened to a page bookmarked with a folded eviction notice. The page was headlined "Contacts," written out like a ledger with names and numbers scribbled in a column down the left-hand side.

What first struck Ernie were the phone numbers—every one with an 828 area code, then the prefixes 586, 273, 293, 743, running their way through the county from north to south. Ernie's eyes flicked to the names. He didn't know them all, but the second one took his breath. Holt Pressley was chief of police for the town of Sylva, Tim's boss, and his name and number were riding shotgun in this fellow's car. There were other names he recognized, a hotshot lawyer who got college kids off for DUIs and possession charges, an ex–county commissioner who'd been caught with his pants down. Those three names alone were high-profile men anyone in Jackson County would've recognized, and there they were in black and white without one bit of explanation.

Ernie tossed the notebook into the driver's seat. "Take a look at that."

"What is it?"

"Beats me. Says 'Contacts,' but take a look at those names."

"Jesus Christ. That's the chief's home number."

"Yeah, and his ain't the only one."

Ernie and Tim looked at each other. Neither knew what to make of what they'd just found, but Tim closed the notebook and tossed it back across the cab into the passenger seat where it had lain. Tim decided to take the gun into evidence, but he left everything else just how it was. He said it was obviously odd as hell, but odd wasn't breaking the law. This was his call and his arrest, and Ernie didn't argue. He wasn't even sure he'd have done anything differently had the shoe been on the other foot.

They questioned the man briefly about the revolver and he told them he had a concealed carry license in his wallet, that as far as he knew that license carried reciprocity, and that he'd locked the gun in the glove box before he cracked his first beer. Odds were he'd get the piece back when he was released, and truth was they didn't have much to hold him. A night in the drunk tank and he'd be back on the street.

3

The sun was up and a pair of crows cawed from the edge of the Justice Center rooftop as Ernie walked out at the end of his shift. He dragged his hands over his face and stretched his eyes at a bluebird sky. There was fog burning out of the valley and the mist rose gray as smoke against the mountains. Already a handful of laggards loafed around the parking lot with cigarettes dangling from the corners of their mouths and coffee cups in their hands while they waited for court dates and probation meetings or whatever clerk-of-court bullshit had brought them here.

A car door slammed and Ernie glanced over to see the sheriff making his way into the office. Sheriff John Coggins was finishing out his last term before retirement, and true to form he was still busting ass and cracking skulls like he had his entire career. He'd never been a man to take a day off and had worn a standard patrol uniform same as the deputies his entire time in office so as not to appear different from the men and women who worked for him.

Only over the past few months had he started to dress more casually, always wearing a polo shirt with the sheriff's office insignia embroidered on the breast, that and a pair of cargo khakis.

Truth be told, Coggins could have kept playing sheriff until he croaked if he'd wished. Past two elections no one had even run against him, knowing good and well the county loved him and a campaign would prove a waste of time and money. But despite his reputation, Coggins was ready to hang up his spurs. He was obsessed with turkey hunting and wanted to travel the country in his retirement to shoot a US Super Slam, bagging birds in every state except Alaska. It was the hardest feat in the sport, he said to anyone who would listen, only a handful of people having ever completed the task. At sixty-eight years old he knew the sooner he hit the road, the better.

"What you say there, Ernie? Shift go all right?"

"Pretty dead to be honest."

Coggins had a round face and a thick gray mustache over his lips. He had a warm complexion, wore an eight-dollar flattop cut by Lebern Dills, and had looked exactly the same for as far back as Ernie could remember. "Know how I know you're real police?"

"How's that?"

"'Cause you say that like it's a bad thing, like you're disappointed hell ain't break loose." Coggins grinned and patted Ernie hard on the shoulder. "Things'll pick up. Kids be back at the college before too long."

For a moment Ernie thought to tell the sheriff about the call, about the man they'd arrested in that station wagon and the notebook he'd had on his seat. The words were right on the tip of his tongue and it must've shown on his face, because there was a hitch in the sheriff's step as he started to walk away.

"You got something on your mind, Ernie?"

Ernie turned and looked the sheriff in the eyes. Coggins had a way about him that demanded a man look at him when he spoke, and that was an unsettling thing right then. What did he really know? There was no telling where those names came from or what they meant.

"No, sir," Ernie said.

"Well, all right, son." The sheriff slapped him hard on the shoulder again. "You be safe going home. Get some rest."

When Ernie left the Justice Center, he drove into town and ate breakfast at the Coffee Shop the way he did most mornings after a night shift. The food wasn't as good now that the owners had changed, but old habits proved hard to break.

The same old men who ate at the restaurant every morning were bitching about the temperature of their coffee just as they had every day before. One old man would die only to be replaced by another who looked and sounded like him, so that the image and the sound never altered all that much from year to year. Ernie appreciated the consistency of that white noise. He ate his hash and eggs and sopped up his grits with toast while the old men gave the waitresses a hard time, and when his plate was clean he slipped a ten under his coffee mug and didn't stick around for the bill.

No matter how hard he tried, he couldn't shake that man from Mississippi. How the hell a man like William Dean Cawthorn had wound up in a place like this was hard to figure. Sure, there was dope and crime like anywhere else, the latter almost always tied to the former, but Jackson County was still a hole-in-the-wall kind of place that you didn't land on by accident. That white hood and that notebook were tied together, and if Tim McMahan wasn't going to push that issue, if he figured he couldn't because of who he worked for, then maybe Ernie needed to pursue those questions himself.

The station wagon was exactly where they'd left it that night, but now other cars half-filled the lot outside Harold's, old women with fresh hairdos knocking grocery lists out early. He parked beside a gray Subaru Outback where a middle-aged mother was gathering reusable shopping bags from the back with one hand, a small child on her hip weighing down her other arm. Ernie wasn't planning to take anything from the car. All he wanted was a picture of that list.

He waited until the coast was clear and crossed the parking lot to the Caprice, opened the passenger-side door, and leaned inside. Envelopes covered the seat and the floorboard was still shin-deep with rubbish, but that black spiral notebook that had been there just hours before was not where they'd left it. He searched around quickly and shuffled through the filth, but deep down he knew the list was gone.

4

A mixed brood of laying hens followed Vess Jones through her garden. Hornworms were eating the tomatoes and squash bugs eating the beans, and the chickens fought and scratched to eat them both as the old woman plucked them from the vines and tossed them in the dirt at her feet.

Her hearing had been going for some time, and as much traffic as there was anymore, she often left her aids in the soap dish by the bathroom sink to keep from having to listen to all the road noise. That's where they were this morning, and so she never heard the patrol cars pull up to her house, nor did she catch the deputy's approach. He reached out and touched her shoulder, and she spun around and almost punched him in the nose.

"What in the world you sneaking around scaring an old woman like that?" She was barefooted and wore the same flowered house-dress she wore most days, a garment she called a duster. A wrap was knotted tight around her hair to keep the curls from falling flat, her trying to squeeze one more Sunday out of her last trip to the salon. For years she'd had her salt-and-pepper hair relaxed, then set in curlers.

"I didn't mean to scare you, ma'am, but is there a Toya Gardner here?"

"Toya? Toya's my granddaughter. What business you got with her? And what's he doing over there slipping around my porch? Who is that?" The old woman leaned around the deputy to get a better look. There was a middle-aged White man dressed in a black polo shirt and pleated slacks who was looking at the overalls she'd thrown across the railing earlier that morning. Vess had lived in this house for more than fifty years and not once in all that time had the law ever been there in any sort of official capacity. Their presence made her nervous.

Her granddaughter had come in just a little after daylight. Toya's overalls had been caked in red mud and Vess had made her leave them by the door to keep from tracking dirt in the house. Of course, nothing had seemed abnormal about this, about Toya's coming in late or being covered in clay.

Toya was an artist and had come to stay with her grandmother for the summer to do research at the university while she worked on her graduate thesis. For the past two months she'd snuck in all hours of the night, tiptoeing down the hall like a teenager breaking curfew. Her nights were spent digging through archives at the library, or working in an art studio she'd gotten permission to use, and that was likely where she'd been the night before. Vess hadn't asked. Truth was it was just nice to have someone else in the house for a change.

"That's Officer Daniels. He's with campus police."

The man by the porch picked up the overalls and held them up. "Do these belong to your granddaughter?"

She couldn't hear what he said, but caught the gist. "Those are Toya's."

"And is she in the house right now?" the deputy asked.

"Y-yes," Vess stuttered, stumped as to why they had come. "But one of y'all needs to tell me what this is about. Neither one of you have told me why you're here."

"We need to have a word with her about something that happened on campus last night. We think she may have been involved with an incident we're investigating."

"An incident? What are you talking about?"

"I think it's best if we speak to her, Mrs. Jones. Can we go inside?"

Vess squinted to focus on the silver name badge over the deputy's breast pocket. "Madden," she said. "You any kin to Bennie?"

"Yes, ma'am. That was my grandfather."

"I went to school with Bennie. Knew him all his life. Had three children, best I recall. A pair of twin girls, and a little boy. Catty, Grace, and—"

"Thomas. Or Tommy's what folks have always called him. That's my dad."

"I can place you now," Vess said. Navigating life here had always been a matter of placing people. Knowing who and where someone came from told you everything you needed to know. For Vess, it was also a matter of safety. "Believe it or not, I was there when your daddy was born. That's what I used to do—did a lot of things, really, but I was a midwife mostly. Helped Herschell Stillwell with house calls. You remember Dr. Stillwell? Died last summer. He was a good man. And so was your grandfather. Brought us a cord of firewood that summer your father was born. Good split locust, none of that dotty wood people sell nowadays."

"That sounds like him." The deputy half smiled. He was

toddling back and forth, antsy, from foot to foot, his black shoes shined to a polish. "You mind if we step inside and speak with your granddaughter?"

"You two just stay out here and I'll get her."

"If it's all right we'd like—"

"I told you I'd get her." The old woman crossed the yard and took a hard look at the officer by the porch. He was pale-faced with dark shadows around his eyes. Something about him felt off, and she didn't trust him. Vess snatched her granddaughter's overalls out of his hands and hung them back over the porch railing.

Toya was asleep in the rear bedroom and she didn't stir when her grandmother opened the door. The curtains were drawn shut and sunlight shone through them to cast the room in a hazy sort of green, like old bottle glass.

"Toya," she whispered, then raised her voice when the girl didn't stir. "Toya."

She'd only been asleep three or four hours. "What is it, Maw Maw?"

"There's two men outside say they need to talk to you. Police officers, Toya. You have any idea what for?"

Toya stretched her eyes, but it seemed more an effort to wake up than an expression of surprise. She sat up in bed and turned so that her feet were on the floor. There was a laptop on the nightstand and she leaned forward to grab it. "I'll be out in a minute."

"You need to put some clothes on."

"I will, Maw Maw. Just tell them I'll be outside in a minute."

"What's this about?"

"Everything's fine, Maw Maw. Nothing you need to worry about. Everything's going to be fine."

Coming back through the house, Vess felt in a tizzy. Her mind raced to figure out what was going on, why Toya hadn't even seemed shaken to hear they were outside. It was almost as if the girl had expected them. When she headed out the back door, both officers were waiting where she'd left them.

"So where is she?"

"She'll be out in a second."

The deputy who'd approached her in the garden nodded and told her that would be fine. Vess looked at the sky, where a murder of crows passed like ink over the mountain, and their presence struck her as a bad omen. Right as the last bird disappeared over the ridgeline, Toya opened the back door and stepped onto the porch.

The girl had a habit of wearing clothes so bright they hurt your eyes, and today was no different. She wore an ankle-length skirt that was dandelion yellow with a bright floral pattern, the fabric almost neon in the midday sun. A sleeveless white turtleneck hit her mid-stomach. The material was knitted and had a thick rolled neck that seemed overly stylish and out of place for Jackson County.

"Toya Gardner?"

"Yes," she said.

"Miss Gardner, you're going to need to come with us."

"Okay," she said without fuss. She had a flat look that seemed unbothered.

"Wait, what for? What is this about?" Vess couldn't figure out what was happening. It made no sense that her granddaughter was just going along with what they were saying as if she knew why they were there and what they wanted. It felt aberrant for her to carry no anxiety or hesitation, no fear.

Toya started down the steps, and her grandmother grabbed hold of her arm and stopped her. Vess came past to stand between her and the officers. "She's not going anywhere till somebody tells me what this is about."

"We've told you, ma'am." But if he had, her mind was spinning so fast she'd already forgotten.

"It's fine, Maw Maw," Toya said. She looked at her grandmother with a fearless certainty the old woman found hard to fathom. Toya leaned in and kissed her on the cheek. Vess could still feel her lips there on her skin as the girl stepped around her and walked to the officers with her arms straight out in front of her, her wrists held together for what she knew would come.

5

Sheriff Coggins stopped in his tracks as soon as he saw her. He was taken aback by how much the girl looked like her mother—the upward angle of her eyes, her high cheekbones and chestnut-colored skin. But more than anything it was an energy that seemed to radiate from her. One look and you knew the girl was hell on wheels.

The sheriff smiled as he crossed the interrogation room and pulled out a chair. She seemed out of place in a room like this, the painted block walls, a seat where people had done everything from lie about stealing catalytic converters to confess to murder. He considered leading her down the hall to his office, where things were more comfortable, where he'd be more comfortable, but then he just started to talk.

"I can't believe how much you look like your mother."

Toya had her hands pressed palm to palm. She was staring at her thumbs and huffed a sort of halfhearted laugh at what he'd said.

"You don't remember me, do you?"

She shook her head and briefly met his eyes.

"The last time I saw you was at your grandfather's funeral. Lord, you must've been . . . You couldn't have been more than—"

"I was in middle school," she said.

"Seems like that's forever ago."

She had sew-in braids pulled to the back of her head and tied into a messy overhand knot. Tracing her fingernails between two of the braids, she scratched her scalp but didn't respond.

"Me and him had a lot of fun together, chased a lot of turkeys. Lonnie used to call birds with a laurel leaf pressed between his thumbs like a blade of grass. Could cluck, cut, yelp, make any sound a turkey ever made with nothing but that leaf. You believe that? Used to drive gobblers mad. Lon," he said, and smiled. His vision dialed back and she was staring right at him. "You don't have a clue what I'm talking about, do you?"

"Not exactly," she said.

"I guess all you really need to know is that me and your family go back a long ways," he said. "I considered your grandfather a good friend and I'd say he'd have said the same about me. That's why I'm here, is out of respect for him. And respect for your grandmother. You understand?"

She nodded, but that was all.

"Speaking of, I just got off the phone with your grandmother."

"What did she say?" For the first time since he'd entered the room, she seemed eager to listen.

"She's worried sick like you'd expect. Asked me what happened and I told her. She wanted to know where you were, what was going to happen next. And to be honest I didn't really know what to tell her. I don't know how this plays out, what things will look like. She told me to look after you and I told her I would. Told her I'd do everything in my power. But that's the thing, see, there's only so much within my power. The law's the law and when it comes to that my hands are tied."

"Well, I appreciate you talking to her," Toya said. "And I understand the spot you're in. But I want you to know I'm not asking you for anything. I don't expect you to do anything for me."

"The thing is, that little stunt you pulled—"

"Stunt?" she interrupted. There was a sternness and agitation in her voice at the sound of that word. "That wasn't a stunt."

The sheriff started to speak, but she cut him off.

"Do you think it was a *little stunt* for that school to force my family to dig up their dead? Or a *stunt* for them to tear down and move the one place they had, the first place they'd managed to build on their own? That building had to have been the center of their universe. That church must've felt like gravity."

Coggins didn't know what to say. He didn't even know for sure what she was talking about.

"So, no, it wasn't a stunt, Sheriff." She situated herself in her chair and tightened the knot of her braids. "You ever wondered why they didn't move one of those other churches? There's two other graveyards on that campus. You ever wonder why they didn't move one of those?"

"I can't say that I have."

"They bulldozed a Cherokee mound and razed a Black church. Those are the things that school chose to move."

"I don't know anything about that," Coggins said. "That was a long time ago."

"Go sit with some of the people at that church and ask them to tell you the stories they grew up hearing. I think they'd feel differently. And that's why I want to make it very clear that this wasn't a stunt. It's like they say, an open wound cannot heal."

"I'd say you've opened it up pretty good."

"And I'd say it's been open the whole time," she said. "Just the people with the power to do something about it never bothered to look."

"How old are you?"

"Twenty-four."

"Jesus." Coggins chuckled. He leaned back in his chair, laced his hands together, and rested them on top of his stomach. "Twenty-four years old you ought to be at the beach somewhere. You ought to be out with your friends having the time of your life. You shouldn't even be thinking about things like this."

"That's a privilege I don't have."

"What's that supposed to mean?"

"I mean I've got no choice but to think about *things like this*. That's what I mean. And maybe that's something you can't understand."

"Maybe not," Coggins said. "But what I do understand is this. What you did has gotten you into a whole heap of trouble. Felony trespass. Vandalism. And what I'm about to tell you is something I don't tell many. Matter of fact, in all my years in this room, and that's been a whole lot of years, I can't recall having ever encouraged a single soul to do what I'm about to tell you to do, but you need to talk to a lawyer."

"If it comes to that I will."

"What do you mean if it comes to that? It's already come to that. Your grandmama's back at the house worried sick and you're sitting here with me."

"The thing is, Sheriff, I'd bet the shirt off my back that school drops the charges."

"And why in the world would they do that?" Coggins took a sip of coffee and waited for her to answer.

"Simple," she told him. "Optics."

He looked confused, not entirely sure what she meant.

"Because how would it look if they didn't?"

6

In the age of spin, the first news story hit at lunchtime, and by six o'clock the university had retaken the reins. "A learning opportunity and a chance for the school to finally make amends for a century-old mistake." That was easier to stomach. The chancellor said he was thankful Ms. Gardner had brought these issues to light. "An overdue day of reckoning," he said. And that was that.

Of course, Toya only heard this secondhand. The chancellor never came to the sheriff's office or sat down to discuss what making amends might actually look like. Instead, he told it to the cameras, everything they wanted to hear perfectly scripted and sealed with a dollar's worth of "deep regret" that folks would buy as sincerity. Lipstick and rouge. That's what the world was accustomed to seeing, the ugly made pretty with lipstick and rouge.

The email she'd sent that morning before walking outside the house to speak with the officers had detailed all of the history she'd uncovered over the course of the summer. It explained the work and what she was trying to do. Likewise, it explained that if they were receiving the email, she'd been taken into custody. This was sent to every paper and news channel across the region, and a few larger markets outside. She copied the chancellor, of course, as well as the university's director of communications.

Coggins got a laugh out of how perfectly she'd called it. He offered her a ride back to the house, but Toya felt like walking and downtown Sylva wasn't far at all. The Justice Center was less than a half mile from Main Street, a straight shot with a good sidewalk leading the way along a two-lane road busy with highway spill-off.

There was still an hour's worth of daylight, but it wouldn't last long, the woods already in shadow. Toya could still name some of the trees by their bark, most of these poplar, a few red oaks and hickories, though their trunks were strangled with vines and the darkness made them hard to read. It was a skill her grandfather had taught her when she'd visited each summer as a kid, he having always tried to put the land in her because he was scared to death the city would wash the mountains clean out of her blood.

Toya's mother had run off and left at eighteen, shedding the mountains she was from like a set of outgrown clothes. But Toya had always had a fondness for this place, the beauty of it, the sound. At night it felt like the sky was so close she could run her fingers through it, like dipping her hands in water, whereas back home in Atlanta she couldn't have counted a single star for the light pollution.

Cars thumped over a short bridge that crossed a narrow stretch of stream and she stopped for a minute to watch the water. There was some sort of hatch taking place over the surface, a steady wave of winged insects flying against the current so that the two things appeared to be moving in opposition to one another. From the corners of her eyes she saw a dark shape shift out of an eddy to center stream. The fish rose, sank back, and angled again into slack water, where she could make out its silvery sides through the glass. It was a medium-sized rainbow trout, maybe twelve or fourteen inches. "Dough belly," she said, not even really knowing what it meant, just something her grandfather had always called trout that weren't speckleds.

The traffic light just ahead turned green and the line of cars behind it began to move. Small planters lined the handrail of the bridge and Toya traced her fingers across the petals of pansies as she followed the cars into town.

When she was little, her grandparents would take her to Sylva on Saturdays to get ice cream at one of the tourist shops. Her grandfather would tell her what used to be there—a hardware shop, a soda fountain, a department store, a hotel—the names still visible against the brick, faded white paint hanging on like ghosts. The buildings hadn't changed, just the stores and the accents of the people who ran them. There were more cars and people than she remembered. The place was almost bustling.

The sun was setting now and the colors were stunning. Paintbrush clouds streaked a purple and orange sky behind the old courthouse. The building, which had been turned into a public library a decade before, was the landmark of the town, the image used on welcome signs and postcards. It sat at the top of a hill overlooking downtown. A four-column portico stood in classical revival style, its eave angling into a three-stage cupola. It struck Toya that in all her years of seeing that building she'd never once walked up to it, and in such light there was a sort of magnetism drawing her.

Up close, the hill looked even steeper than from a distance. Three levels of stairs scaled the grade and she counted them in her head while she climbed. As she neared the top, she could see a large statue on a pedestal, but with the light fading she couldn't make out what it was with any certainty. When she was finally beneath it and could see the monument for what it was, she felt like she'd been smacked across the face.

A patinaed copper soldier stood with his backpack high on his shoulders, his gaze fixed under a wide-brim hat, his rifle resting on its butt stock with his hands gripping the barrel as if it were a walking staff. The soldier, though, was above her field of vision. Her eyes were locked on the Confederate flag carved in granite. OUR HEROES OF THE CONFEDERACY, the base of the pedestal read.

She tried to swallow but it felt like something was caught in her throat. Her face was suddenly ablaze and her hands clenched so tightly that her arms began to shake. She walked a circle around the statue and on the back side there was a bronze plaque:

TO OUR VALIANT FATHERS

Champions of reconciliation with
justice of union with manhood,
of peace with honor; They fought
with faithfulness, labored with
cheerfulness, and suffered in silence.

TO OUR HEROIC MOTHERS

Spartan in devotion, Teuton in
sacrifice, in patience superior to either,
and in modesty and grace
matchless among womankind.

Working her way back to the front of the statue, she finally stared up at the soldier. Behind him the last of the light was gathered at the top of the courthouse. Lady Justice stood on the cupola, her sword and scales silhouetted against the sky, her eyes covered and blind. So many things were racing through Toya's head right then that she found it hard to make sense of what she felt. *Recon-ciliation. Justice. Grace.* The words sparked about her mind.

Words meant different things to different people, and unfortu-nately some of the most important words had seemed to lose meaning altogether.

Behind her the cars came and went, the tourists wandered past, and the streetlights flicked on to push against the night and its dark-ness. She closed her eyes and thought about what the sheriff had said just a few hours before, and what she had told him in return. Some people had no choice but to think about things like this. Every day was a stream of reminders and remembering.

7

William Dean Cawthorn's station wagon whirred and coughed like some worn-out war machine, one rattled bolt away from flying apart at the chassis. The fact that the Caprice had even made it from Mississippi seemed some act of providence, and his good fortune of late did not escape him.

No sooner had he lain down and closed his eyes in the drunk tank that night than the jailer had come clopping in to tell him he had a phone call. Half an hour later he was being ushered out the back, rubbing his wrists where the cuffs had worn him raw. He'd never spoken to the man on the phone before, but he knew the name from his list, knew that Slade Ashe ran the show. With a snap of his fingers, the charges were dropped. Even the revolver was returned. Willy Dean was cut loose and there was a motel within spitting distance of the police station with a room in his name.

This was as close to the red-carpet treatment as Cawthorn had ever experienced. He took a long shower and slept most of the day with the curtains drawn to black out the light. Late afternoon he walked the half mile to Harold's to pick up his car, and when evening came he drove to a ritzy community at the south end of the county where Slade had invited him for supper. In that falling sun, with those mountains all around him, he couldn't help thinking that for once he seemed to be holding a winning hand.

The watchman at the guardhouse opened the gates and the blacktop switched to brown macadam. The rooftops of mansions rose to form their own horizon. All the houses looked alike, three-story jobs with giant picture windows and patinaed copper roofs. They were board and batten, painted in a range of earth tones from red slate to olive, all blending into the landscape quite well despite their size. Slade Ashe's home was built like the others, but painted a deep bluish gray and with extensive rockwork along the foundation and a sprawling front porch that looked off toward a cliff face in the distance. Willy Dean stepped out of the car and slammed the door. He turned his back to the house and dropped his pants to take a leak.

"For God's sake, son!" Slade Ashe yelled from the porch. "Despite what you might've heard, we've got indoor plumbing in these mountains! Show a little couth!"

Cawthorn glanced back and saw no one. He threw up his hand as if to apologize but made no attempt to rush. When he was finished, he slicked his fingers through the sides of his hair and strutted like a crow toward the house. A double staircase of stacked red rock curved up to a full-length porch. Slade Ashe sat at the far end, where a spotlight of falling sun found its way through the trees. He was leaned back in a rocking chair with his feet propped on a small woven stool. A young Black woman, maybe mid-twenties, was on her knees polishing his boots with a rag.

"That'll be fine, Amelie," he said. "Just fine." He pulled his feet back and rolled up his pant legs so they wouldn't brush against the polish. "Go and see if the wife needs anything. After that I think we're good."

Cawthorn watched the woman as she tiptoed toward him. She was very dark-skinned and wore a black short-sleeve dress that hit her at the knees, white lapels down the front, and a white apron tied around her waist. Her hair was pulled into a bun.

"That's Amelie," Slade said. "French name. Every damned one of them from Senegal this year."

Willy Dean wasn't sure what he was talking about and he just stood there looking dumb and out of place as the woman disappeared into the house.

"The club brings in workers every summer. They get to come to America and build a little job experience, you know, working in the kitchen or on the course or housekeeping, and the folks in these houses get to feel good about themselves for providing that opportunity." Ashe leaned over to a side table and tonged two cubes of ice out of a bucket into a square glass. He poured himself two fingers of brown liquor from an ornate decanter. "But you want to know a secret, Mr. Cawthorn?"

"What's that?"

"Ever since I bought this house and been living amongst these generous folks, not one year have they picked a country where the workers didn't look just like that. They could get kids from any country in the world, but they don't." Ashe smiled and took a long sip of whiskey. He turned his head and squinted as if trying to discern some meaning from that far-off cliff face. "Have a seat."

Willy Dean crossed the porch and eased into the rocker beside him. There was only a small end table between them. Ashe was a short, stubby man who would've proven useless in a bar fight. He wore neatly pressed slacks and a dress shirt unbuttoned to the middle of a pale and hairless chest. He had a fat nose that was pitted like gravel and almost blue in color against the rosacea of his face. A waft of blond hair floated about his head, but his eyes glinted with malice and confidence and power. Willy Dean was rarely made uncomfortable, but there was something about Slade Ashe that had him by the short hairs.

"Me, though, I'm not like the rest of the people in these houses."

"How's that?" Willy Dean took an empty glass from the table and poured scotch until it spilled over the rim.

"Well, for starters, I'm *from* here," Ashe said. "I wasn't born into money and I didn't move to these mountains from someplace else. If my daddy was still around he'd have been out there pissing in the yard beside you." He lifted his glass as if to take a sip but pulled it away from his lips as he continued to speak. "The bigger thing, though, is this, Mr. Cawthorn, and this is important. I don't pretend like I'm doing that girl any favors. It isn't charity and she knows that the same as I do."

Willy Dean took a sip of whiskey and hacked as it hit his throat. The scotch was proofed hot and all smoke.

"There's ice if you want to cool that off. Don't look like you left much room."

"I'm good," Cawthorn said. He washed back half the glass in a failed attempt to short-circuit his nerves. Sitting in a place like this with a man like Ashe put him on edge.

"Mr. Cawthorn, I'm going to cut right to the chase if that's all right."

"All right," he said, then ran his tongue over his lips nervously.

"The goal of our organization might be the same as it's always been, but the mechanism's changed."

Once again Willy Dean didn't have a clue what he was talking about, but he nodded just the same.

"We're hell and gone from that adolescent bullshit you pulled down there in Mississippi. That's what I'm saying. The days of spray-painting slurs on churches or prancing around in rallies are behind us. The mechanism has changed. It's business deals. We're altering the political landscape. See, the thing about it is, all these people in these houses want the very same things we do. They just don't want to speak it aloud, and who can blame them? You get a lot more done in the peace and quiet. You get a whole lot more accomplished when there's not a thousand eyes watching every move you make."

Cawthorn leaned forward in his chair and rested his elbows on his knees. He eyed Slade closely while he spoke so as not to miss anything.

"White power's not just some catchphrase, son, some hollow slogan you get tattooed on your back. No, it's as real a thing as the shine on these boots." Ashe leaned back in his rocking chair and took a long sip of scotch. They were the fanciest boots Cawthorn had ever seen and his mind floated off as he tried to figure how much they'd cost. Ashe lifted his eyes to the rafters and tapped his knuckles on the arm of his chair. "White power is as tangible a thing as this chair I'm sitting in, as this house, see? You understand what I'm telling you?"

"I do." Willy Dean was just sharp enough to catch what Slade was trying to drive home, that he would need to toe the line so as not to cause any problems while he was here. The Klan was still willing to protect its own, but the last thing Cawthorn needed to do was overstay his welcome. He had nowhere else to go and the folks back home had made that clear. He filled his mouth with scotch and waited until the whiskey was stinging at the sides of his tongue before he swallowed. His eyes watered and he coughed hard into his fist to clear his throat.

Slade Ashe chuckled and leaned back with one hand rested on his stomach. "How's the scotch, son?"

"Tastes like a burnt-up house," Cawthorn said.

Ashe took a sip of his own. "Now, how in the world would you know what that tastes like?" He looked across that tiny space between them and winked.

Cawthorn cut his eyes to the floor and did not say a word.

8

Ernie was just old enough to remember when Caney Fork was gravel. He'd been a kid then, thrown in the truck as an afterthought when his father and uncles tore off for Ruff Butt to chase whatever game was in season. His uncle had been a fine wing shot. He was a ruffed grouse man, though he'd always called the birds pheasants. Some years his uncle had averaged nearly six flushes an hour afield, but now the birds were gone.

"I tell you what ruined this place," Ernie remembered him saying one time with a belly full of beer. "Pavement," he'd said, and looking back Ernie believed he was right.

The cars that passed showed where the people came from, and nowadays it was seldom here. People from Florida and Georgia had been coming for decades, but now the plates stretched farther. Colorado, Washington—they were likely to come from anywhere, and once they came they seldom left. The entire region had peddled tourism as some economic savior, never once acknowledging it as something equally extractive as timber or coal. Now that the people were here there wasn't the infrastructure to support them. And worse yet, the people whose families had been rooted to this place for generations were being priced out.

Ernie didn't think of this changing as good or bad, just as what was. The way he figured, there was no slowing it down, and there was damn sure no way to stop it. If a man wanted to keep living here and not lose his mind, he had to become indifferent. The history of all places was a story of displacement, and it just so happened he was witnessing the turning of a tide.

The summer air through the open window felt good as he drove. Bits of grass were stuck to his arms and face. His T-shirt was glued to his body with sweat. All morning he'd been weed-eating the bank below his house. The farm supply hadn't been open when he'd come home from his shift, so he was running back out to grab a fifty-pound bag of trout chow.

If it weren't for Red Bull and snuff, most deputies would've fallen asleep at the wheel. And the thing about working nights was that the mundane didn't stop just because a man needed rest. The grass still had to be mowed. The oil still had to be changed. Clothes folded. Supper cooked. The usual. All the chores that filled a life kept right on stacking up whether a man had the time or not. Make hay while the sun shines, folks had always said, and it seemed now more than ever that a good rain never found him.

At the stop sign, Ernie leaned forward against the steering wheel so that he could take a quick look at Caney Fork General Store and see who was stirring about. A little red Mazda pickup was parked at the pumps and Ernie immediately knew to whom it belonged. Tim McMahan had driven that truck since high school, an eighties-model hand-me-down from his grandfather that seemed as if it might run forever.

A couple cars passed on 107 and Ernie pulled out behind them.

As he swung into the filling station, Tim was topping off a pair of five-gallon gas cans, the red canisters sun-bleached pink on their tops from years of use. Ernie threw his truck in park, stepped out, and walked around the tailgate of Tim's pickup. As he came around the bumper, he tapped his hand on the sidewall of the bed a few times as if he were patting a horse.

"What you say, Ernie?" Tim said as he looked up. The smell of gasoline wavered around them.

"I thought that had to be you. Ain't but one truck like this still on the road."

"As much as they're wanting for a new one nowadays, I'm sure not in any hurry to buy one."

Ernie kicked the ground with the toe of his boot for a second, trying to find the right words. "Listen, I had a quick question," he finally said.

Tim picked the gas cans up from the ground and set them in the bed of his truck. "Oh, yeah? What's that?"

Ernie took a box of snuff from his back pocket and packed the tobacco to one side with a couple quick flicks of his wrist. He pinched out a dip and loaded it into the front of his mouth, then pushed the plug around to the side of his jaw with his tongue.

"So that fellow you arrested the other evening, the one down there at Harold's." He licked bits of tobacco from the tips of his fingers and shoved the can back into his pocket. "After we left that night I got to thinking more and more about that notebook and all them names, and so when I got off shift I ran back over to his vehicle and was going to take a closer look. But when I got to searching it wasn't in the car."

"Well, Ernie, I don't know what you're getting at."

"I don't know. I just know it wasn't there."

"No, I'm saying I don't have any idea what you're talking about." Tim pressed a button on the pump and took his receipt as the machine spit out a small slip of paper. "I don't remember any sort of notebook."

Ernie pulled his head back, baffled. "What are you talking about? Me and you stood right there in that parking lot and looked at it. Hell, I tossed it across the car to you."

Tim placed the receipt in his wallet and shoved the billfold into his breast pocket. He had his hand on the door of the truck like he was itching to leave. "I don't know what you want me to tell you."

"We searched that car together. We found that robe in the back, the revolver in the glove box, and that notebook on the seat."

"Yeah, I remember the gun. I remember that robe folded up in the back. But I don't know anything about a notebook and we ought to just leave it at that." Tim McMahan started to open the door of his truck. "Now, I've got to get—"

Ernie cut him off midsentence, stepped forward, and grabbed ahold of his arm. "You ain't going to take off like that and leave me standing here like a fool, like I've lost my goddamn mind. You know good and well what I'm talking about."

Tim jerked his arm away and his face turned sour. "Get your hands off me, Ernie. This ain't fucking high school. I've told you all I've got to say, so just leave it at that."

A midsized SUV had pulled up to the pumps beside them and the woman who'd stepped out studied them both nosily as they cussed each other back and forth. It wasn't the time or the place for any sort of knock-down, drag-out, but Ernie was roiling inside. If there was one thing he couldn't stand, it was a liar, and for somebody like that, somebody he'd known all his life, to look him square in the eyes and lie to his face, that was about enough to turn him inside out.

Ernie glanced at the woman and half smiled, tried to compose himself so as not to make a scene. "All right then, Tim. I'll let you get on."

Tim McMahan slid into his truck and when he slammed the door Ernie took one more step forward and leaned down to speak straight into the cab.

"I've just got one more thing to tell you, and this is all I've got to say." Ernie turned and spit a line of tobacco across the concrete like venom. "If you're going to crawl in somebody's pocket you better be damn well certain it's deep."

"Get the fuck off my truck, Ernie." Tim cranked the engine and Ernie stepped back as he dropped the pickup into gear.

9

Removed. That was the word that the girl had spelled. And to anyone who didn't know the history, that word raised questions. That was the beauty of it, a word that demanded an answer. Of course, Vess knew well what had been removed from that hallowed ground.

She lived a mile down the road tucked in a cove along the river. After the sheriff explained what her granddaughter had done, she drove to campus to see the work for herself. Standing there at the site of the original church, Vess remembered an old photograph of the building, which had been gone decades by the time she was born. There was nothing spectacular or ornate about it, just a whitewashed clapboard building with a single window and shake roof, an almost cookie-cutter shape about it. She closed her eyes and imagined that building beside her. Suddenly that place and the smell of that opened ground spun her mind awash with memories.

Homecomings were usually when the stories were told. Someone would bring up Will Rogers, who'd worked as the foreman of the reburying crew. Rogers had been born in East LaPorte and grew up in Monteith Gap. He was one of fifteen Black men from Cullowhee who'd volunteered and served during World War I.

They told stories of the people, and those stories inevitably brought about the details those people had passed down. Faces drawn back to skeletons, hands drawn back to bones. Caskets, clothes, everything at different stages of decomposition. Someone would always mention the hair, the way it had continued to grow in the grave. Vess couldn't imagine what that must have been like to witness. For her, the details were just parts of broken stories and still she'd carried them all her life like thorns.

There was a part of her that was proud of what her granddaughter had done, but there was also worry and fear. The periphery had always been the safer place, but here the girl stood front and center, and that was a dangerous spot to be.

That next morning a reporter drove up from Asheville to talk with Toya about the work. Vess offered to cook them breakfast, but both declined, and so she stood idly by the stove while her granddaughter was being interviewed. She called the work *Verb Choice* and said it was that single word on the plaque that had set the wheels in motion.

"'Moved,'" Toya said. "That's what it says. 'Moved.' And that insinuates a choice, that there was a willingness to have done that. But they didn't *move*. They were *re*-moved. That's how that plaque should read. That's what happened. They were forced to dig up their dead and carry them off that mountain. That's what this piece is about."

They sat at a small, square Formica table, Toya with her back to her grandmother and the reporter straight across from her. Toya had her hair down, and the braids were split evenly in the back and draped over both shoulders so that they hung across her chest like a stole. There was a plate of biscuits wrapped in a checkered cloth in the center of the table, but neither had touched them. The reporter hadn't even taken a sip of her coffee.

"So tell me a little bit about how you came into art." The reporter looked to be in her late twenties, early thirties, a White woman with sandy blond hair and black-framed glasses. Her foundation was darker than her complexion and only ran to her jawline so that her face was almost orange compared to her neck. She wore a pleated pair of navy slacks and a horizontally striped shirt that loosely followed her figure. "I know you said you're finishing up an MFA and that you came this summer to work on your thesis project, but how did you get started? Were you always interested in art?"

"I started as a painter, and I mean early on, as a teenager and all through high school, that's all I wanted to do. When I got to college I took this ceramics class and I got my hands dirty and something changed. I think maybe it was just that idea of tangible form, you know? With painting you're trying to create that, but with pottery and sculpture you can physically touch it. You can literally wrap your hands around it. So that was the next shift, was into sculpture, and really I think things just continued to get bigger. What I was trying to do, what I wanted the work to do.

"I remember being introduced to this artist, Mel Chin, and this installation piece called *See-Saw*. He buried these giant hydraulics underground so that when people stepped onto a piece of land—I mean, it just looked like grass, like any other spot in the park—but when they stood there their collective weight would make the ground sink, and in turn another piece of ground would lift on the other side of the park, maybe sixty feet, a hundred feet away."

Vess watched the reporter's face contort as she tried to make sense of what her granddaughter was saying. Vess found it hard to follow as well, but she was still in absolute awe. She'd never heard her granddaughter speak so passionately and eloquently about what she was doing. Then again she'd never really asked, at least not in any sort of deeper, meaningful way.

"I know, I know, it's hard to imagine." Toya laughed. "You'll have to look that up and see it to really get a picture. Mel Chin. *See-Saw*. But what that piece did was introduce me to this style of art where you're putting the work in public spaces for the sole purpose of having the public actively engage with it."

"So is that what you were trying to do with this piece?"

"I mean, yeah, in a lot of ways. I wanted to put something in a very public space so that it had to be confronted. The viewer had no choice but to engage with it. That's what made the whole medium interesting to me—the digging, the ground. It was the idea of unearthing something. The idea of exposure, of refusing to let something remain buried beneath the surface. The big difference, I think, is that Mel Chin's work was fun. His work was about play, and what I'm trying to do isn't like that at all.

"What I'm trying to do has this sort of graffiti element. I mean, when most people think of graffiti they imagine people tagging bridges, spray-painting train cars. But graffiti, philosophically, is this sort of idea of putting art directly in places where it isn't allowed to exist. Like, I don't think you can commission graffiti. You can commission a graffiti artist to paint a mural on a wall, sure, but that's not the same, right? That doesn't carry the same effect."

"That's really interesting, and, yeah, I see what you're saying." The reporter paused. "So I guess one of the questions this raises is the idea of permanence, of a piece of art lasting. So, with that other piece that you were describing, that Mel—"

"Mel Chin."

"Right. With that piece I assume that was something that remained there for a longer period of time. I guess what I'm trying to say is that with a piece like yours, or with something like graffiti, it doesn't last. Someone spray-paints city hall and the next week it's gone. It's not like a painting, like the *Mona Lisa* or something, where you can go see it years and years after it was finished."

"I was reading about these researchers recently who were trying to look at the paint pigments used in the *Mona Lisa* and how the colors have changed over the course of time," Toya said. "What I'm saying is that really even with something like that, something as iconic as the *Mona Lisa*, what was originally created, what it looked like right then, was temporary. Nothing is static. Everything is constantly changing.

"There's this artist I love named Andy Goldsworthy. He creates these beautiful found-object pieces out in the woods. He goes out into a landscape and he gathers up materials and creates a piece of art. But sometimes he might do this on a seashore or something where he'll build this sculpture out of driftwood, and then the tide inevitably comes in and the water washes it all away. It's this beautiful idea of impermanence, right? What he's doing is very Eastern thinking. And what I'm doing's not like that, but I think I have that same sort of comfortability with the work only existing as a physical piece for a very short period of time.

"I could paint a painting or make a sculpture with the same intent, trying to capture the same idea that I wanted to come across up there on that hill, and we could put that piece in a museum for people to visit, but what good does that do when the very people who need to see that work, who need to engage with that idea, never step foot inside? It does nothing, right? They're able to ignore it the same way they've been ignoring it.

"Instead, what I did was force the people who needed to encounter the idea to engage with the work. I left them no choice. They had to face it no matter how uncomfortable it made them. I guess what I'm trying to say, what I'm trying to get at with all of this, is what lasts is the impact. The impact that work makes on the world, that's more important than the work itself. That's more important than the work lasting in any sort of physical sense. It's art as an instrument of social change."

If Vess had been asked to describe the way she felt right then, standing there in the kitchen listening to her granddaughter speak, she would've said it felt something like falling in love—the butterflies in the stomach, the swimmy-headedness. She felt warm all over, but outside of that she couldn't really feel her body at all, as if she were just sort of floating there. She was swooning with pride. All of those feelings became too much right then. It was more than she could handle. She almost felt like crying.

"I'll be out in the garden," Vess said as she walked over to the table. She put her hand on Toya's shoulder and the girl reached back and covered her grandmother's hand with her own. Vess leaned down and kissed Toya on the crown of her head.

"We shouldn't be that much longer," the reporter said.

"Take your time. Just let me know if you need anything."

Outside, the chickens scratched and pecked the patch grass yard and the old woman looked up into the silver limbs of a white oak, where a hawk had been spending a lot of time. The bird wasn't there at the moment and she was relieved. She'd always kept chickens and for a long time she'd raised meat rabbits. Hawks were hell on both. In the old days, her husband, Lonnie, used to shoot them, owls too, but Vess didn't have the heart. He'd been gone a long time, but she still kept his shotgun—an old J. Stevens double barrel—loaded in the corner of the den behind his chair, though it'd been ages since she'd shouldered it.

Ever since Toya was little, Vess had worked hard to instill bits and pieces of this place and this culture into her granddaughter. Her daughter, Dayna, had always been too big for Cullowhee, and after she left she'd never looked back. There was nothing wrong with that. She and Lon didn't blame her or resent her for leaving. They were proud of their daughter and what she'd become. But that didn't stop the heartache of watching the place and culture they came from and loved slip through their fingers like flour.

There was a life here. There'd always been life here. Vess came from country stock, from mountain people who dug ramps and killed branch lettuce, people who picked Indian peaches and wrapped apples in newspaper to keep under their beds through winter. She remembered how one time when she was little they hadn't had enough money for seed potatoes and her daddy had begged a man named Dills for peelings, how he'd raised a whole mound from nothing like some loaves-and-fishes miracle. She remembered how he'd kept a ham hanging in the sugar shack, the way her mother would go out and cut pieces to stretch across three or four meals.

No one did that anymore. Most folks had never even heard of a sugar shack, much less smelled the way that ham had filled the air like perfume. Few people even kept gardens, or at least not gardens of any size. If they planted anything it was more of a hobby. It was three-dollar Bonnie plants from Lowe's, not seed and onion sets saved from the year before. People spent more to raise a basket full of crookneck squash than what it would've cost to buy it at the farmer's market, and that just wasn't the same thing at all. The ways were all but lost, and that broke Vess's heart. But the interest Toya'd shown in where she came from, who she came from, that meant something. That meant that it wouldn't be forgotten, at least not in the girl's lifetime. Having her there that summer, it had felt like putting up food, like storing something away that would sustain them.

The forecast called for a late-afternoon thunderstorm and the garden needed the rain. The bush beans were tall enough now that a heavy downpour would beat them into the ground, so Vess was in a rush to stake them up. A cinder-block shed sat against the wood line in the side yard. The stakes were bound together in the back corner and she gathered them along with a mallet.

She was nearly finished driving the stakes into the ground when Toya and the reporter came down the steps into the yard. Her granddaughter walked the woman to her car and after a minute or two Toya came back around the side of the house. She had on a lilac purple pleated skirt that ended against her shins. She was barefooted and wore a black tank top that showed a narrow strip of her stomach just above the waist.

Vess was humming a song as her granddaughter came through the yard. The old woman had a beautiful voice caught somewhere between tenor and alto, an effortless and natural vibrato resonating from somewhere deep inside.

"What song is that?"

"Oh, you wouldn't know it." Vess hammered the last stake into the earth and set the mallet in the dirt. "Hand me that string."

Toya walked over to the corner of the garden and picked up a spool of jute twine from the ground. She came back and handed it to her grandmother. "That's Nina Simone, isn't it?"

Vess laughed and pushed her glasses back above the bridge of her nose. "What do you know about Nina Simone?"

"Mama used to sing that song all the time."

Vess smiled. She hadn't expected that from her daughter, but it made her happy to hear. When Dayna was little, Vess had sung that song to her hundreds of times. They had grown apart since Lon passed, so it was nice to hear there were things that refused to leave her. "You know she grew up in these mountains."

"Who?"

"Nina Simone."

"No, she didn't."

"Yeahhhh." Vess dragged that word out threefold and chuckled. "Polk County. Nina was a mountain girl like me. You listen and you can hear it."

Vess pulled the tag end of the twine from the center of the spool and drew out a length between her hands. The stakes had screws preset and she tied the twine onto a screw at the end of the row of beans. Out of nowhere she heard the short piano run take off and dial back. She looked up from where she knelt in the garden and her granddaughter was staring down at her phone. There was the slow four-note drop from low to lower, the quicker four-note echo as the two pieces came together to play out courses of eight, and that was when the voice came.

"Ain't got no . . . ," Nina began to sing, and as the first words hit the air Vess closed her eyes and let them dwell in the center of her chest. Her granddaughter swayed with the music, dancing mostly with her shoulders at first, a slow twist of her hips with her head down so that her braids swept back and forth in front of her.

The beginning of the song was a lamentation and it had always struck Vess the same way, with an infinite sort of sadness. But what she'd always loved about that song was the promise of what would come, the hope in the way that it ended.

She continued to work her way through the garden while the piano carried that voice, the voice carrying Vess slowly from stake to stake tying the twine so that when she was finished the row of beans was lined on all sides and supported. The music began to build as she cinched the final knot. Vess cut the twine with a jack-knife she kept in the pocket of her duster as Nina set to pounding the keys and the song took its turn.

When the music broke loose, Toya was bouncing with her hands stretched up toward the sun, and it looked as if God Almighty had placed her in spotlight. Her whole body suddenly seemed electric, every inch of her in motion as she snapped her fingers in time, her face aglow as it rocked in a slow figure eight. The girl started to spin and her skirt spiraled out around her like the petals of a violet and Vess stood up and began to clap with the music and sing. There were tears in her eyes and she was laughing, and that happiness filled her until there was no more room inside her body to contain what she felt. It had been a long time since she'd touched that sort of magic, since she'd held it in her hands like a bird. For a few short moments the world dissolved into pure beauty. Joy quite simply overcame her.

10

The door to the sheriff's office stood open and Coggins sat with his elbows on the desk, his hands together in front of his face. His head was tilted down and the glare from the overhead light reflected off a pair of cheap readers so that from where Ernie stood he could not see Coggins's eyes. He looked as if he might've been praying.

The sheriff reached and flipped the page on a sheaf of papers in front of him, then laced his fingers back together. When Ernie saw this he rapped on the door lightly with one knuckle and Coggins looked up from what he was reading.

"Ernie Allison." He pulled the glasses from his face and folded the temples closed against his chest. He set the readers on the desk and sipped a cup of coffee. "What you roaming around here for on your day off? You not got nothing better to do?"

"Had something I needed to talk with you about if you got a minute."

"Of course." Coggins placed his hands on the top of his head and leaned far back in his chair so that his body was at a forty-five-degree angle and his chin rested against his chest. "Come in and take you a seat."

As Ernie walked into the office, he turned to close the door.

"Leave that open if you don't mind," Coggins said. "Keeps the air moving."

There was no one around this time of day outside the office staff and brass, but what he'd come to discuss demanded privacy. Ernie hesitated and thought to say something, but the sheriff prodded him on.

"Have a seat," Coggins said.

Ernie came in and took one of two chairs that faced the desk.

A turkey was mounted on the wall beside the door and it seemed oddly large and out of place in such a confined space. The bird's wings were spread and angled as if it were frozen in flight. No matter which way a man turned, the mount hovered in his peripheral vision so that it always felt as if someone was peering over his shoulder. Ernie glanced back, then scooted forward to the edge of his seat with his hands rested on his knees. All morning he'd been wrestling with how to say what he needed to say.

"What in the world's got you so antsy?" Coggins asked. "Something going on I need to know about? Your mama and daddy all right?"

"Yeah, they're fine."

"Ain't got some gal knocked up, have you?"

"No."

"Then I hope this ain't about a raise, Ernie, because I don't set the pay scale. That's county budget and Lord knows—"

"No, no, Sheriff," Ernie said, cutting him off. "It's not that."

"Well, what is it?" Coggins hadn't moved. He was still leaned back with his hands on top of his head like he was about to be placed under arrest. "For fuck's sake, son, you look like you're about to confess to murder." The sheriff laughed and lurched forward all at once. He took another swig of coffee and folded his arms across his chest.

There was no use beating around the bush, and so Ernie came right out with it. He told the sheriff how the shift had been slow that night, how it had been all he could do to keep his eyes open, so that when the call at Harold's came in he ran back up for the Sylva PD mainly to keep from dozing off. He told him about the man from Mississippi, the robe they'd found, and the notebook. Ernie listed the names that stood out on the pages and let fly how he'd gone back to get pictures. He explained how the notebook was missing that next morning, how everything else was just how they'd left it, and how Tim McMahan had lied to his face when he asked him about it later. When he was finished he felt relieved, but that reprieve was short-lived.

Coggins didn't rush to speak, and the longer the silence drew out, the more unsettled Ernie became. The sheriff braced his elbows on the desk. He squinted and stared off at the wall as if carefully considering what he was about to say.

"You're lucky I don't suspend you right now."

Ernie shrunk in his chair.

"What were you thinking going back there? Even if there *was* something in that car. There's chain of custody and then there's whatever the fuck that is. Criminal trespass. That's what it is. You weren't even on duty, and what, you thought you'd just pop open the door on some fellow's rig and go rummaging through his belongings? What the hell were you thinking?"

"Sheriff, I know I didn't go about it the right way, but you heard the names. Those are important people in this county. Are you telling me you wouldn't have been curious to know who else was on that list?"

"I bet I can tell you who the vast majority of them were. You think it's some revelation Slade Ashe is a certified son of a bitch? Anybody in this county been here longer than a summer could've told you that. Same goes for Holt Pressley and half them other folks you listed off. Snakes den together, son. That's nothing new."

"But what I'm telling you, Sheriff, is that these were names at every level of local government, past and present. The town board, the county commission, the chief of police, building inspections, tax office, you name it. We're talking every permit, every contract, every tax dollar in this county potentially running through those hands."

"You're making some pretty big assumptions off a couple names in a notebook."

"It wasn't just a couple names, Sheriff. And it wasn't just *any* names."

Coggins shook his head and chuckled.

"Look into it, Sheriff. That's all I'm asking. That's all I want you to do. Because if what I'm telling you is right, this could—"

"And what do you want me to do exactly? You want me to go ripping these people's lives apart off some conspiracy theory you cooked up after seeing their names in a notebook that may or may not even exist? Is that what you're wanting me to do?"

Ernie knew how crazy it sounded but deep down he knew he was onto something and he could not let it go.

"Look, I know how it sounds. And I know the way I went about it wasn't how it should've been done. But we're talking about the Klan, Sheriff. It wasn't some roster for a softball team. It was a contact list for the Ku Klux Klan. And the names that were on that list are people who've operated at every level of local government in this county for years. If that doesn't raise any red flags, then I don't know what does. All I'm saying is look into it. Call one of your buddies at the SBI and have them look into it. That's all I'm—"

"For fuck's sake, Lovedahl! Are you just gonna stand there all day or are you going to tell me what you want?"

Ernie whipped around in his chair, and when he did he caught another deputy standing in the open doorway. Nick Lovedahl was one of the last people on earth he'd have wanted behind him right then. Ernie immediately wondered how much he'd heard, but he couldn't take a word of it back. All he could do was assume Lovedahl'd heard everything.

"I'm sorry, sir. I just didn't want to interrupt."

"Well, you've already done that, so what is it?"

"I've got these reports you asked for."

The sheriff waited with his hand out for Lovedahl to bring the paperwork to him. Lovedahl peered down as he came past. "Ernie."

Ernie nodded to acknowledge him but didn't speak.

"Is that it?" Coggins held his readers up to his eyes and glanced at the reports.

"Yes, sir. That's all."

"Well, all right then." Coggins brushed his hand toward the door. "Scoot."

When they were alone again there was an awkward spell of silence that stretched between them and finally the sheriff was the one to break it. Coggins leaned to one side and propped his head up on his fist with this elbow anchored to the desk. He still had his glasses in the other hand and he put the angled tip of one of the temples into the corner of his mouth before he spoke. "All right, Ernie, I'll look into it."

Ernie ran his hands down the thighs of his shorts to dry the sweat from his palms.

"But if you ever go rummaging around in somebody's car again without a warrant, I'll take that badge and slap the cuffs on you myself. You got me?"

"Understood."

11

The roads were wet and the reflections of streetlamps made pearls against the pavement, a necklace strung from one end of town to the other. Most of the traffic dwindled about midnight, but a few cars passed and their tires hissed across the wetted streets. She'd always loved the smell of summer rain on blacktop. Having grown up in the city, she could close her eyes and that smell transported her home.

The past few months had been hard, being away from friends, from the places she'd known all her life. She was told there was a fairly large Black student body at the university, but not over the summer. She spent time with her grandmother, and on a few occasions they'd gone to see cousins and aunts, relatives she barely knew. It struck her how she code-switched between them all, how easily she shifted the way she spoke depending on the audience. She talked one way when she traveled home to Atlanta, another accent altogether when she was alone with her grandmother, and yet there was another still with the group she was with this night. It wasn't inauthentic or disingenuous, but something she'd picked up naturally, out of necessity even. And yet it was dizzying to jump around like that, almost like spending time in another country.

The group that had helped Toya dig the graves was made up of local graduate students, mostly people, like her, who were finishing up MFAs, but also a few friends of friends who'd volunteered last-minute when others backed out or didn't show. A ceramicist named Brad Roberts was the one who'd pulled them together. Toya had met Brad that summer when she'd approached the art department to see about using studio space to work on her thesis project. He'd found her a spot and they'd made quick friends. Over the past two months, he was the single constant outside of her grandmother, the one person beyond family that she was around every day.

Potters usually fell into three groups. There were the mudders, who loved to get their hands dirty, and that had always been Toya when she was throwing clay. Then there were the pyros, who were all about the firing process—soda firing, pit firing, sawdust, raku. But Brad fell into the third lot. He was a chemist. He was obsessed with glazes and learning how different chemicals reacted to heat.

That night they gathered at a local brewery for beers, and though Toya had never been a big drinker, she thought she owed it to them to go out and have a good time. She stuck to house-made ginger ale while the others downed IPAs, their conversations growing louder as the night progressed, and by the end she was almost drunk from conversation. A songwriter played an acoustic set until midnight, and then before anyone knew, it was two a.m. and last call and the cohort broke apart to head home—some together, some bumming rides, a few stumbling back to places close.

In a public lot across the street, a stray cat slept curled in the dry under her SUV. She drove a beat-up silver Pathfinder and on this night there was an aluminum ladder tied to the luggage rack on top with a length of yellow rope. The cat bolted when she hit the unlock button on her key fob.

"You sure this thing will get you home?" Brad asked. Over the past few weeks her SUV had given her fits. There was a loud knock in the engine and sometimes the motor wouldn't turn over at all, so Brad had been giving her rides.

Toya kicked the front tire and smiled. "I mean, I could lie to you, White Boy, but it's probably fifty-fifty whether she even cranks."

Brad laughed. He always blushed when she called him that and she found it cute. She meant it as a term of endearment and he knew, him being the sole person she'd allowed to get close. He had shoulder-length hair and was broad shouldered, his muscles toned from working clay, his skin tanned from days spent outside. His sharp-angled face was clean-shaven, and though he wasn't her type, she couldn't help but find him attractive.

He walked to the side of her SUV and shook the ladder as if to ensure it was secured. "You cleaning gutters?"

"Yeah, I'm cleaning gutters."

He eyed her skeptically and laughed. "Well, all right," he said, pausing a few steps in front of her like he was waiting for something he knew she would not give him.

"All right, White Boy. I'll see you tomorrow."

Brad slapped his hand against the hood and turned to walk away. He belted over his shoulder, "That's racist," singing those words as if he were performing an opera.

Toya laughed and shook her head, waiting by the front bumper until he was far enough up the street that he could not see her. He was headed the opposite direction from where she was going.

Sylva really was a beautiful town, especially at night. Outside of the influx of traffic and people, nothing had really changed since she was a girl. Picture small-town America, that two-story painted brick downtown, but nestle that image into a valley where a ridgeline rolls a rippled lip around you. Make Main Street a shotgun-straight lane with a hilltop courthouse on one end, a beautiful neoclassical building overlooking everything below. That was Sylva, and that courthouse was the image printed on postcards and T-shirts and signs. If you looked closely, even in the depictions, you could see the statue at the front—a dark silhouette splitting the building in two like a fissure that ran from foundation to center.

There was something about that summer, about the place she'd reached as an artist that had changed her. All of the books she'd read, the things she'd studied and learned over the past six years, had been carefully stacked like the makings of a campfire, and over the past two months the work became the match. She'd felt that fire at the table with the sheriff, any filter or hesitation burning away. And still she fully understood that there was a very thin line between fearless and foolish.

Toya parked in the lot at the side of the building. She carried the can of paint first, and as she unloaded the ladder she was careful not to make any noise. There were houses close, and people slept with windows open in summer to soak up the cool of the night. If she'd had it her way she'd have taken a jackhammer to the flag that was carved in granite on the base of the statue, but there was something to be said for the subtlety of how it had to be done. She braced the ladder against the forearms of the figured copper, then climbed until she was even with the soldier's hands.

Toya leaned against the rungs and hugged her arms around the back side of the ladder, then used a small flathead screwdriver to work the lid off the quart of paint. She'd chosen a color called "Gloss Banner Red," which was as bright a shade as a field poppy. As she began to pour the paint over the statue's hands, the blood ran down the length of the rifle and puddled at the soldier's boots, spilled over the edge as long fingers that dripped from the top of the granite pedestal to the ground.

The idea and image were simple, but what she feared might get lost was that it wasn't just the blood on the hands of the Confederacy, nor the blood of bondage that had drawn out for nearly 250 years before the Confederacy even existed. It was the legacy, the open wound that continued to bleed 145 years after the fact.

It was the lynching of Jesse Washington, a seventeen-year-old who was dragged behind a car, castrated, his fingers and ears cut off, burned alive, and photographed, with the pictures sold as postcards. It was Emmett Till at fourteen, beaten and mutilated, shot in the face, and sunk in the Tallahatchie River.

It was Emmett's mother demanding the open casket.

It was Eliza Woods kidnapped from the county jail, stripped naked, and hanged in a courthouse yard just like where Toya stood right then, Eliza's body ripped apart by bullets. It was the 130 other women murdered by lynch mobs from 1880 to 1930. As Malcolm had said, "The most neglected person in America is the Black woman."

Jump forward and it was Eleanor Bumpurs. It was seven-year-old Aiyana Stanley-Jones the spring of Toya's freshman year in high school. It was James Craig Anderson that next summer, beaten and run over with a truck in Jackson, Mississippi. It was Eric Garner, Michael Brown, Tamir Rice, Rekia Boyd, Kayla Moore, Margaret Mitchell, Eric Harris, Freddie Gray. It was names upon names upon names, all of which conjured faces, faces that flashed through her mind at the mere mentioning of them as if some painful curse had been cast upon her. Here it was the summer of 2019, and little had changed.

Toya looked down to where the paint dripped and pooled beneath her. The blood was still running and it seemed as if it might flow forever, and it was that continuum, the realization of just how endless it seemed, that was too much to handle right then. She knew this world could not hold.

12

A Carolina wren flittered onto the porch and hopped along the weathered planks until it was almost at the old woman's shoe. The bird tilted its head and studied her with a black bead eye, its back a russet brown, its breast as gold as an autumn poplar. Like she had all morning, Vess Jones held completely still while the bird gathered nest materials from the mess of strings piled between her feet. She'd spent the better part of the day working up a run of greasy cut-shorts she planned to can later in the week.

When the wren flew she followed the bird with her eyes to where it disappeared into a cord of firewood stacked by the shed. Right at that moment a vehicle came tearing into the driveway, the gravel loud and slipping as the tires slid to a stop. The door slammed, and before Vess could even push out of the rocking chair to see who was coming, the sheriff stormed around the side of the house, mad as a hornet.

"Where is she?" he growled. He had a way of talking when he

was angry that sounded like he had a mouth full of marbles, his face an ember as he stomped up the steps onto the porch.

"Who, John?"

"That granddaughter of yours. Now, where is she?"

"She's inside. But what in the world has got you so upset?"

"That statue's been there a hundred years. A hundred years and ain't nothing like this ever happened. She shows up for the summer and thinks she's got the right to change that."

"Change what? What are you talking about? What statue?"

"The statue at the courthouse, Vess. The statue that's stood there all our lives."

The screen door opened and Toya stepped onto the porch. She had on the same loose-fitting basketball shorts and tank top she always slept in, and she held a coffee mug with both hands in front of her face, blowing steam from the surface.

"Have you absolutely lost your mind?" the sheriff squawked. "There ain't a one of them commissioners going to cut you a bit of slack on this. Word gets out what you did and half of Jackson County will be down there at their offices and they'll have their heads if they don't follow through with charges. You understand? I can't get you out of this. I don't want to get you—"

"I'm not looking for anyone to cut me any slack, Sheriff. As a matter of fact, I don't think I've ever asked you for anything."

"You've got a lot of gall talking to me like that after the way I've treated you. I did all of that out of respect for the woman sitting there. I did all of that—"

"All of what? You did all of what, exactly?"

The sheriff clenched his teeth and stepped forward with his fists balled at his sides, and as he did Vess jumped out of the rocking chair and wedged herself between them.

"John, you're not fixing to come on my porch and step toward my granddaughter like that! You hear me?" Vess had her eyes locked on him, but Coggins was glaring over her shoulder at the girl. "You better pull yourself together! I don't care what she's done, you're not doing that!"

Vess could feel the anger pressing in from both sides but she stood between it like a wall.

"The two of you need to settle down, and we'll go in this house and talk like people with some sense. But you're not going to stand out here barking at one another like a couple squirrels. I'm not putting up with it. I'm too old to listen to that nonsense."

Vess Jones was normally soft-spoken but her word had always been gospel. She stood there with her chin up and took a slow, deep breath through her nose, exhaled, and did this again and again as if breathing the tension out of the air. Slowly the heat died back, and after a long spell, she eased her granddaughter out of the way with the back of her hand and opened the screen door to go inside.

13

The sheriff slid his cup of coffee onto the Formica table and tilted the chair onto its back legs so that he was leaned at a steep angle with his hands rested on his gut. The girl sat across from him and Vess was propped against the countertop in front of the sink, where sunlight through the window made a sort of halo around her.

"Look," Coggins said. "The thing is, that statue means an awful lot to a whole bunch of people in this county—"

"And that's the problem." Toya cut him off before he could finish what he had to say, and it ate him up the way she did this time and time again. He found her snide and arrogant, but he swallowed those feelings down. "You've got people idolizing slave owners. You've got people revering a time when people who looked like me were in chains. A hundred and fifty years after the fact, you've got people still flying a flag that only ever stood for one thing, and worse yet you've got that flag carved in stone overlooking your town. What's that supposed to mean to somebody like me who walks up those steps and stands there? How's that supposed to make me feel?"

"I don't know how it makes you feel, but as far as what it means—"

"I'll tell you what it means. It means get the fuck out. And I'm sorry to say it like that, Maw Maw. I'm sorry to use that word in your house." The girl turned to her grandmother, then scooted back in her chair and crossed her arms. She was wild-eyed and trembling with anger. "That's exactly what that flag means to me."

"But for a lot of people, that's not what that flag means at all. Me included. That's not what that statue stands for. Most of the people who were in these mountains never owned slaves."

"So where exactly do you think my family came from, Sheriff?"

Coggins didn't have an answer.

"Start of the war there's forty-six slaveholders and two hundred twenty-six enslaved people right here in Jackson County. After Emancipation, their names are listed on the census as farm laborers. Later some folks came from South Carolina and Georgia, but by the turn of the century you've got four hundred Black people living in this county. You've got a higher demographic at that point in history than you do now. So don't tell me they weren't here. Where do you think they came from?"

"I don't know. I—"

"And you want to sit there saying that's not what that flag stood for. Alexander Stephens said, 'Its foundations are laid, its cornerstone rests, upon the great truth that the Negro is not equal to the White man; that slavery, subordination to the superior race, is his natural and normal condition.' That's what he said. Said it was 'based upon this great physical, philosophical, and moral truth.' And you want to tell me that's not what it stood for. It's the same revisionist bullshit that's been passed down generation after generation, fed to us and fed to us, and I'm still supposed to eat it up like cake."

The more she talked, the more he felt as if he were going to explode. Coggins buried his face in his hands. "That's not what the flag means to me," he grumbled. "That's not what—"

"Then tell me what it means. Tell me what that flag means to you, Sheriff."

"You haven't let me finish a sentence since we sat down at this table. You haven't let me finish a thought." Coggins looked up wanly. "I don't think you have any interest in hearing what I think about anything, and the only reason I've bit my tongue as long as I have is out of respect for that woman at the sink.

"Now, there's a whole lot of truth to what you said, and you probably know more about it than I do," he continued. "You're smart, Miss Gardner. Same as your mama. And I bet you've read more books than I've ever opened. You can sit there and quote out of them books and you can spout that off, but there's one thing you don't know the first thing about. You don't know anything about what it's like to live here, to have grown up here. You've never lived here a day in your life, and I've never spent a day outside of it. Only two people in this room can say that. So why don't you ask your grandmother what it was like? Ask her how she was treated."

"John, I'm not going to do that," Vess chimed in immediately, and as she said it he felt choked. He believed at the very least she wouldn't stand there and let him be interrupted and chided like a child. "This here, this is between the two of you. It's between that badge you're wearing and whatever brought you over here to my house. Me and you go back a long ways, John, a long, long ways. But that girl sitting there is my flesh and blood, and if anybody in this world ought to know what that means it's you."

Having it put like that, Coggins understood, but it didn't take the sting out. Vess Jones knew him better than anyone. In his mind, she knew there wasn't a racist bone in his body. If anyone could attest to that it would be her. But he also understood why she couldn't say it. He knew what blood meant.

"'The great truth that the Negro is not equal to the White man,'" Toya quoted again. "That's what the man said. And that's the reason nothing can change what that statue stands for. 'Its foundations are laid, its cornerstone rests, upon.' That's what he said. Even the context of how those statues wound up where they did. It was just a Jim Crow reminder of who was still in charge, who'd always be running the show. So honestly, you're absolutely right. It doesn't matter to me what that flag or that statue means to you, Sheriff. I don't want to hear it because I've heard it before. I've heard it until I'm sick and tired of hearing it. The truth is, it can only ever mean one thing. One thing. And to stand there defending it is an act of White supremacy. That in itself is an act of racism."

"So now you're saying I'm a racist. That's what you're saying." The sheriff guffawed and ground his teeth. His fists were clenched and inside he was a furnace. "Just because I don't agree with you, that makes me a racist?"

"I honestly don't know you well enough to say one way or another what you are."

"Then ask that woman standing there. I've known your grandmother all my life. Your grandfather was one of the best friends I ever had, and if he were here to tell it I'd say he'd tell you the same thing. So, you're right. You don't know me. But that woman standing there does and that ought to mean something."

He turned and looked at Vess again, but she sank back into the counter as if she weren't in the room at all. That gesture reiterated that she had nothing to say, and the fact that her position was left unclear buried itself in him like a knife. The anger he felt toward the girl and what she'd said roiled into something more painful then, and he no longer knew what to think.

"Again, I don't know you, Sheriff, but what I do know is that there are a whole lot of people, even well-intentioned people, who are more bothered by the word *racist* than they are racism. There's a whole lot of people who care more about being called a racist than they care about addressing the institution."

"So that's it? It's that simple to you."

"What I know is that racism wears a whole lot of faces."

"What's that supposed to mean?"

"It means that this country was founded upon and perpetuated by White supremacy. It means this . . ." The young woman paused as if she were really trying to choose her words carefully. She stared at the table and laid her hands flat against the surface. As she started to speak, her hands stirred as if drawing a picture.

"The tree with the deepest roots in this country is a tree of White supremacy. And the thing is, you don't have to be the one who planted that tree or even the one who kept it watered or trimmed the branches to be someone who directly benefits from the shade it provides. There's a whole lot of people sitting comfortably under that tree, and some of them recognize where they're sitting and just won't do anything about it because they like where they're sitting, and then there are some of them who won't even acknowledge that the tree's there at all. Maybe they don't acknowledge it because they can't see it, or maybe they just don't want to see it, but in the end none of that matters because they're all benefiting from the same thing."

"And so what do you want to happen? What do you want to do?"

"I want to hand them an axe." Her voice shuddered as she said this. The young woman lifted her eyes and glared straight at him with a look that pierced like bullets.

Coggins didn't fully understand what she meant, or rather the magnitude of the statement did not fully reach him right then, but the intensity of what she'd said shook him just the same. The words she'd spoken felt powerful, and it took him a minute to gather his thoughts.

After a long pause, the sheriff dialed back to the only thing he could ever hold with any certainty.

"Well, the thing is, Miss Gardner, in this county, I'm the law." He leaned forward and rested his elbows on the table. "That's the axe I carry. And at the end of the day, it doesn't matter what you think about me or what she thinks or even what I think about myself. None of that matters. What I want, what I think's right and wrong, is irrelevant. It ain't got a thing to do with nothing. The minute I put this badge on there's just the law."

The sheriff reached for his coffee and took a sip, but the cup had gone cold and he no longer wanted to be there. He stood from the table and nodded at Vess as if to say he would be leaving, but she stared blankly at the floor and did not lift her eyes.

"Go on and get dressed so we can get going."

14

The front-page photograph was a close-up of the soldier's hands, blood from knuckle to heel and dripping down the rifle barrel he held as if he were wringing out a wetted rag. The headline read simply, "Sylva Sam Caught Red Handed." Before the story even ran, word got around and a group of overall-clad good old boys formed a guard to sleep on the courthouse steps.

By the second day, the county had built a fence around the statue and now Sylva Sam was fenced off like a dog. A chasm opened across the county overnight and split the mountain in two. Come Saturday there'd be a protest at the statue, a counterprotest at their throats. The line in the sand was drawn and both sides were champing at the bit.

Lucky for the sheriff, most of that headache fell on town police, but it was still county land, and from what Ernie'd heard, Coggins's phone was ringing off the hook. Ernie slid the newspaper into the center of the break room table and took his first bite of a Honey Bun he'd snagged for breakfast from the vending machine. He had to be in court most of the day for a felony drug case—a couple construction workers from Georgia shooting up at a pull-off beside the highway a month or so back. Usually folks pled to whatever deal the DA offered, but the driver in this case had lawyered up and made a shit day for everyone involved.

Three deputies walked into the break room, the one leading the pack a royal pain in the ass. Everything out of Nick Lovedahl's mouth was spewed at eighty decibels, as if he believed the whole fucking world was hard of hearing. People like him were the last thing a sheriff should have ever pinned a badge to, and yet for some reason or another this line of work had always seemed to draw those types like a magnet. Type A, for certified asshole.

"Better watch what we say in here, boys." Lovedahl smirked, one corner of his mouth rising to meet a squinted eye. "That fellow sitting there liable to turn you in." He looked back over each shoulder at the other deputies and chuckled. Neither of the other men spoke. One of them, a young deputy named Fowler, dropped his eyes to the floor.

"Why don't you quit pissing down your leg and say whatever it is you got to say?" Ernie had already caught wind that Lovedahl was smearing his name around the office, spreading rumors about what he'd heard outside Coggins's door that afternoon. Sooner or later things were going to come to a head.

"The thin blue line, Allison. To some of us that means something." Lovedahl strutted over to the table and balled his hands into fists. He pressed his knuckles into the tabletop and leaned out over them. "What I've got to say is that this thing here's supposed to be a brotherhood. But then you go throwing people's names around like none of that matters."

Ernie looked down at his uniform and the badge pinned to his chest. "You know, Nick, the difference is I care a whole lot more about what that badge stands for than I ever will some asshole who puts it on of a morning just so he can play God for a few hours out of the day."

"What the fuck's that supposed to mean?"

"It means I wouldn't be surprised if you had one of them robes hanging in your fucking closet, friend. Wouldn't surprise me one bit."

"Is that right?"

"Sure is." Ernie filled his mouth with Honey Bun and chewed with a wide smile.

"At least I ain't some nigger lover turns his back on his own. At least I ain't—" Right then the Honey Bun slammed into the side of Lovedahl's head.

Ernie had swung like he was pieing some clown at a carnival booth, and the lick knocked Lovedahl for a loop. When he got his feet under him, Lovedahl bounded around the table and crow-hopped for a haymaker, but Ernie was already barreling forward and speared him straight across the room. That big block head of Lovedahl's went crashing through the front of the snack machine like a wrecking ball, and that fast they were on the floor, Ernie on top with Lovedahl writhing beneath him.

Lovedahl went toward his belt for his Taser and Ernie locked both hands around his wrist to stop him from clearing the holster. With his hands tied up, he head-butted hard into Lovedahl's nose and the blood let loose like a popped balloon. One of the other deputies hooked his arms under Ernie's and pulled him off, and when Ernie got turned he could see it was Fowler who had ahold of him. The other deputy rushed in to fill the space between them, but Lovedahl didn't make it to his feet. He rolled onto his side and held his nose pinched in his hand.

"What the fuck is going on in here?" As soon as they heard his voice everyone in the room went silent and still like a group of schoolkids. The sheriff filled the doorway, having heard the commotion from down the hall. "What the hell happened to the Debbie cakes? That's the third machine you idiots busted this year."

Ernie was breathing hard through his nose and there was spit running from the corners of his mouth. He wiped his lips with the back of his hand. "Ask him." He motioned to where Lovedahl lay on the floor.

"God almighty, Lovedahl, you bleeding all over the damned place. Somebody go get him a paper towel. No, better yet, you take your ass down to the bathroom and get cleaned up. Jesus Christ!" he squawked. "You get that stopped and I want the two of you in my office, you understand me?"

"Yes, sir," Lovedahl whined with his nose pinched between his fingers.

"I said, you understand me?"

Ernie looked up and Sheriff Coggins's stare was boring a hole through him. "Yes, sir," he said, knowing for sure he'd punched his own ticket and would be handing in his gun and badge by the end of the day.

"Now, you two." The sheriff turned his attention to the other deputies. "One of you get a mop and one of you get a broom."

"They didn't have anything to do with it, Sheriff."

"Mr. Allison, did I ask you whether or not they had anything to do with it?"

"No, sir."

"Then I suggest you shut your mouth and do like I said. I've got too much on my plate to be babysitting a bunch of goddamn knuckleheads." The sheriff turned and stormed down the hall, his footsteps clopping against the tile.

Lovedahl wallowed to his knees and pushed himself up with one hand so that he could keep the other held to his nose. The fist at his face was covered with blood. Bright red beads dripped from his chin onto the front of his uniform. He looked at Ernie and his eyes were glass. Ernie couldn't tell whether it was from how he'd been hit or if he was crying, and really it didn't matter. Deep down he just hoped that nose was broken.

15

There'd been a time Coggins's father kept fifty to sixty head of Black Angus on their place, though even then that was more than the land could hold. Of the acreage they owned, about eighty was workable pasture, mostly long strips that ran vertical down the slope so that from far above it must've looked like fingers wrapping over the ridge and running down toward the bottoms.

Realistically, forty head was about as much as they could feed without supplementing hay year-round. Nowadays Coggins had the herd down to fifteen or so, mainly to keep the pastures worked. A year without cattle and the locust trees, stickseed, and greenbrier would've made a thicket of the place. That's how quickly things would turn once he was gone.

There were four calves born that summer and one was just as redheaded as a groundhog. Coggins sold whatever heifers he made up with calves each year and it was usually just enough money to keep the taxes paid. More than anything, he enjoyed the work. He enjoyed seeing the place just like it had always been and having one thing that could take his mind off whatever bullshit was happening at the office.

All evening a pair of calves had followed him up the fence line as he worked to get the barbed wire up in the gaps. The cows were bad to scratch their sides along the fencing so that keeping the posts up and the lines strung was like rolling Sisyphus's stone. A week before, one of the neighbors had caught an old heifer halfway to the four-lane, headed for town he supposed.

Down the cove he heard a truck coming up the road and could see the cloud of dust boiling off the gravel long before the pickup came into view. In just a second, a tan Toyota with a dog box in the back rattled sideways through a washboard curve and Coggins waved his arm to flag down whoever was driving. The truck slid to a stop and the dust whirled up around them so that Coggins had to cover his eyes and wait for the cloud to clear.

The truck door slammed, and when the sheriff looked a man named Rupert Bates was coming around the front bumper.

"Ain't mean to dust you, Sheriff. Figured you'd be up at the house."

"No," Coggins said. "Mending fence."

"Don't keep this four-cylinder hammer down I wouldn't make it up your drive."

"You not got four-wheel drive?" Coggins knew he did and meant the question more as, *Put your truck in four-wheel and you won't fuck up my gravel.*

"Yeah, it does. It does." A pair of Plott hounds shoved their noses through the slats of the dog box to sniff the air.

"What brings you up this way?" Coggins went back to tightening a strand of barbed wire with a come-along.

"Me and you got something we need to talk about."

"We do?" All day he'd been fielding phone calls from people

across the county tore up over the statue and he figured this was more of the same.

"I want to know just what you mean cutting that girl loose after what she done."

Coggins ratcheted once more on the come-along and stood tall. Rupert Bates was leaned with his back against the front fender with arms crossed at his chest. He was darkly tanned from outdoor work and wore a thick pair of glasses that tinted with the light.

"Now, look, Sheriff. I know you and that girl's grandmama go back. I know you and Lon used to hunt together some and was good friends, and well, that's all fine and dandy, but there's got to be consequences for what that girl done. You can't just cut her loose on account of you being close to her family."

"So what exactly you want me to do? Tell me that, Roop."

"The law's the law, Sheriff—"

"And the girl posted bail." Coggins cut him off, and the way he said it made the statement come out like end punctuation.

For a second or two, Rupert Bates didn't speak. He shuffled around with his eyes on the ground. Finally he mumbled and stuttered, "Well, well, that's not what I heard."

"Well, if I'm being honest, Rupert, I don't give a rat's ass what you heard. That's what happened. The girl was arrested. I made the arrest. Bail was set by a judge and she made it. Now, you tell me just what in the fuck I'm supposed to do about that?"

Rupert Bates didn't answer.

"I did everything required of that badge. I can't just go holding people in jail on account of you wanting me to. That's not how it works. You know that well as I do."

"Here's what I know, Sheriff. Folks ain't happy. Matter of fact, people madder than hell, and most every one of them thinks you let her off."

"And I ain't happy with what she did either. Matter of fact, I probably feel the same way about it as you do. But to be frank I don't give a shit what you or anybody else *thinks* happened. The girl made bail. End of story."

"You ought to care, Sheriff. You ought to care a whole lot. Who you think it was kept you in office all these years? Who you think kept that badge pinned to your chest?"

"In case you ain't heard, Rupert, I'm retiring. So like I said, I don't give one shit what you or anybody else thinks happened. I'm done politicking. I'm done keeping my mouth shut and bending over with my pants down and letting all of you sons of bitches powder my ass. I'm tired. You hear me? I'm tired. And I'm done with it. So if you don't mind I'd appreciate it if you'd climb on back in that truck and go the fuck on home. Sun be setting here before long and I've got work to do."

Coggins was growing angry and it showed, but Rupert Bates wasn't just some blowhard easily backed down.

"Here's what I know, Sheriff. You might should have kept that girl locked up for her own good. You ever think of that? Probably safer in there right now than just out wandering around."

"What's that supposed to mean?"

"It means people madder than hell, just like I told you. And it means if you ain't willing to do something about it, there's plenty of people who are. That's what it means."

Coggins stepped through the gap in the fence and dropped down the small bank into the road. There were only a few feet between them now and if anything more was going to happen that proximity would ensure that it happened now. "Like I said, Rupert, get the fuck on back in your truck and go on home. I've got work I've got to get done and I'm about sick of listening to you."

Rupert squinted behind those tinted glasses and his brow lowered. He unfolded his arms and stood up straight with his chest out. His chin was jutted out like something was just eating at him, like he was dying to say something or swing, but in a moment he just turned and walked around the front of his pickup and climbed behind the wheel.

The truck spun gravel until the tires caught, and the Plott hounds bayed loudly from the dog box. Coggins stepped into the crest of the drive and watched Rupert Bates tear the road apart in reverse until he found a tractor trail cutting into the pasture to turn around. There was a ringing in Coggins's ears and he stood there with his fists balled up until the truck disappeared.

16

Cawthorn had left more than a dozen messages over the past three days. Finally some sweet-talking woman from Slade Ashe's office called to tell him Mr. Ashe had no interest discussing Willy Dean's proposal and to consider the matter closed.

Slade Ashe kept a small real estate office right in the heart of town. Soon as Willy Dean busted through the front door he saw Ashe stand up from behind his desk in his office. A small waiting area with sofas and chairs and a bar-top workstation for the receptionist was all that stood between them. The receptionist's face turned hunted, but Ashe quickly shuffled out of his office and patted her on the shoulder.

"Why don't you take lunch, Cindy?" Ashe smiled as she looked up at him for reassurance. "I'm going to sit down with Mr. Cawthorn and discuss a piece of property he was interested in."

"Okay, Mr. Ashe." The middle-aged woman wore her hair big

and her dress tight. Her skin was tanning-bed sun-kissed, and from where Cawthorn stood he could smell her perfume.

"And if you don't mind, give Donnie a call on your way out. Let him know to swing by the office when he gets a chance."

She gathered her keys and purse and took another look at Cawthorn standing there sweaty and out of breath in his dark leather jacket. "You sure you're okay?"

Willy Dean felt the sweat running down his face and he wasn't sure if the question was intended for him.

"Perfectly fine," Ashe said. "Just give Donnie a call when you get a chance."

She came across the office with her hips swaying and her high heels clicking loudly against the floor. Ashe followed, and when she'd passed through the door he latched the dead bolt behind her.

"Mr. Cawthorn," he said as he turned and held an arm out as if to usher Willy Dean toward the back. "Why don't we step into my office?"

"You too busy to answer my phone calls?"

Slade Ashe spoke over his shoulder as he headed for his office. "If I'm being perfectly honest, yes. Yes, I am."

Willy Dean trailed along like some whiny cur pup.

"Close the door behind you," Ashe said. He shuffled around a wide desk cluttered with stacks of paper and a small black laptop and dropped into a seat in front of a large window that looked over the back side of town.

Cawthorn pulled the door shut and surveyed the two chairs in front of the desk but did not take a seat.

"People from all over this county are coming this Saturday and they shouldn't have to guard that statue alone. We ought to be right there beside them. We ought to be there making a showing."

Slade Ashe laughed. He dropped his face into his hand so that his eyes were covered and massaged his temples with his thumb and middle finger. Finally he looked up and spoke. "For what, Mr. Caw-thorn? What exactly will that accomplish?"

The question seemed rhetorical, the answer so obvious Willy Dean wouldn't breathe it to air.

"Mr. Cawthorn, if you want to march around yelling and scream-ing, waving goddamn tiki torches, then I suggest you climb in that fucked-up car of yours and drive on up to Virginia. But so long as you stay here in this county, you're going to keep your mouth shut and stay in that motel until we get word that you're good to go home. That's it. That's all I've got to say on the matter."

"A bunch of cowards in this place. Nothing but a bunch of fuck-ing cowards."

"No, son, I'm no coward. But I am a man with priorities. And it's like I told you on the porch that evening: the days of parad-ing around in the streets like a bunch of roughneck animals are behind us. We traded our robes for business suits. That's what the world sees."

"And just how in the fuck is anyone supposed to know we're still here?"

"Exactly."

"So you just sit back and don't say a word while they tear down everything our grandfathers fought and died to preserve?"

"I sit back and don't say a word while the adversaries keep them-selves busy with things that mean little anymore. But as for what my forefathers fought to preserve, it's the same thing I'm build-ing upon."

"What the fuck's that supposed to mean?"

"It means this, Mr. Cawthorn. It means that in this county the largest demographic shift of the last twenty years has been Latino. It means that whether I like it or not, the people I stand beside at the grocery store are getting more and more brown. It means that the minute those people start voting, the political landscape gets a whole lot more complicated than just drawing district maps to keep the bubble around that university strangled out and meaningless.

"So while everyone else is crowded around that statue yelling back and forth at each other like a bunch of children, I'll be behind this desk doing the work, because that's the real battleground. That's where the war is fought and won. On the small scale, it's town boards, the county commission, law enforcement, and every one of those things stands to make me money. But on the larger scale, it's Congress. It's the White House. And that's what you're too stupid or shortsighted to see."

Cawthorn grew angrier each second. "All of this, it used to mean something, and now these people tiptoe around with their tails between their legs like they're ashamed of who they are and where they come from."

"Let me remind you, Mr. Cawthorn, that statue was built to honor my family, not yours. So of course it bothers me. Bothers me a great deal. But at the end of the day that statue's nothing more than a chunk of granite and copper sitting in front of a library. That statue matters a lot less than the end goal. Holding on to history's not nearly as important as where we're headed. Pride matters less than power."

"We don't hold on to history and before long we won't have a leg to stand on."

"You think I don't know where we come from, son? You think I don't understand how we were founded? What I'm telling you is that the goal then was the same as it is now. It was about government. It was about controlling elections and maintaining power. It was about the big picture, and that's what all you dumb-shit rednecks who'd rather throw on costumes and parade around town have never been able to see or never been able to keep your eyes focused on for any length of time. You're like a goddamn bear dog running after a coon. They want to tear down that statue, fine. Tear it down. Now, get the fuck out of my office."

Slade Ashe stood up from his desk, and the second he did Cawthorn stormed forward shrieking, "You grubby little son of a bitch! I'll mash your damned brains out!"

When he reached the desk he pounded his fists against the stacks of paper, then lunged across and took hold of Ashe's lapels. Right then the door behind him slapped open and he turned just in time to catch a hard-swung hook square in the center of his forehead. The blow struck him like a baseball bat and he stumbled a few steps across the office. He tried to come up too fast and his mind went briefly white. Cawthorn collapsed to one knee, and before he could get his wits or feet beneath him, the man who'd hit him had him bear-hugged so tight the breath was squeezed from his lungs.

Slade Ashe knelt on the floor in front of him and unfolded a buck knife with a long clip blade that gleamed like a mirror in the light. He pressed the knife's edge flush against Willy Dean's throat and whispered, "The sharp end only makes up one part of the spear, boy. But make no mistake, it's there."

Cawthorn turned his shoulders, trying to get loose, but every movement inched him closer to slitting his own throat. Trying to turn his head to see the man who held him would've proven an act of suicide, so he fell limp and stared deep into Slade Ashe's eyes.

Ashe leaned in close until they were cheek to cheek. He whispered into Cawthorn's ear. "What we do requires anonymity. And there are two people who've pulled that curtain back over the past few weeks, two people who've threatened to pull the mask off who we are." He was breathing heavily and his words were hissed through clenched teeth. "Now, count your lucky stars you're the one I can't do anything about."

Slade Ashe pulled away, closed the knife, and stood.

Willy Dean felt a drop of blood run cold the length of his neck.

17

The night before the protest, the sheriff drove to see Vess Jones. He didn't know exactly what he was looking for or even what he would say, just that things seemed to be coming apart and she'd always had a way of holding them together.

Nine o'clock and the sun was down, but what light was left cast the sky a sapphire blue as if shone through the glass of a gemstone. Lightning bugs held against the wood line where blackberry and greenbrier gnarled a hard edge. In between the cars passing on the road, the thump of tires crossing the bridge, Coggins could hear the river, and that's what kept Vess on the porch most evenings this time of year, the sound of water coursing over stone the way it had forever.

She was sitting there just like she had those nights he and Lonnie came home with stringers of fiddler cats caught where the river emptied into Fontana. Just like then, she was humming a song.

"If you're looking for Toya she's up at the school," Vess said as Coggins came onto the steps.

The window light threw a low glow about the porch and he could see that she was barefooted in her housedress. A book rested on her lap and she still had a finger stuck into the pages to mark her place.

"No, I come to see you, if that's all right. Thought we could sit a spell."

"You're always welcome here, Sheriff."

Coggins grabbed ahold of one of the porch stanchions and groaned as he took a seat on the steps. "Why you got to calling me Sheriff all of a sudden?" There was a chair open beside her, but the steps were where he'd always sat. "All these years I've just been John and now all of a sudden I'm Sheriff."

"Well, that's what you been doing here lately, ain't it? Sheriffing."

"Vess, I didn't have a choice. You know that as well as I do."

"I do," she said. She pushed the chair back at a steep angle and let it fall forward. "A man has a job to do, he's got to do it. Ain't nothing personal."

"Then why are you acting so cold all of a sudden?"

"John, I'm not acting any sort of way. I was just sitting here on my porch reading my Bible. Got to watching those lightning bugs down there by the woods when it got too dark to see. That's all I've been doing. Same thing I do most every night. So why don't you tell me what it is that brought you over here?"

"I don't know," Coggins said. "I guess I just wanted to talk."

"About what?"

"The way everything's come apart. I don't remember a time it's ever been like this. Other places, sure, but not here."

Coggins paused, but Vess didn't speak.

"I just, I don't know what in the world's got into all these people."

"Same thing's always been in them, I reckon."

"What do you mean?"

Vess took the Bible off her lap and set it onto a small table beside her. She bent down and swatted a mosquito that had lit on her ankle.

"I remember one time when Dayna was little, I come home from running some sort of errand and there was a shoebox sitting in there on the counter. Now, she was always getting into something mischievous, so I hollered for her and she never come. I went outside and whistled loud as I could and ain't nothing come running but that mangy feist dog Lon used to keep, stayed under this porch all the time." Vess rocked a few times in her chair. "Well, my curiosity got the better of me and I went over there and I opened that shoebox and there was a snake. I'm telling you, John, I liked to keeled over right there. You know me, I can't stand a snake, and there one is staring me right in the eyes. I slapped that lid closed and almost took that door off as I come out the house."

Coggins chuckled and tilted his head back against the porch railing. He pinched a toothpick out of his shirt pocket and slid it into the corner of his mouth.

"You see what I'm saying, John?"

"No, Vess, not exactly."

"That snake was inside that box whether I opened it or not. There was a snake sitting right there on my kitchen counter."

It took Coggins a minute or two to unpack what she meant, but when he finally understood he found that truth hard to admit. "You really think it's always been like that?"

Her face was brooding, but she didn't answer.

"I mean, me and you, we ain't all that far apart in age. Seven, eight years. We went to the same school. Played on the same ballfields. You came over to my house and I came over to yours. Your church came to my church and ours came to yours. And in all them years I don't remember but a handful of times there was anything ever said out of line. I remember us cutting up and I remember us fishing. I remember us playing softball. I remember the music, the singing, the food, I remember all of that, all of us laughing, but I don't recall a time it ever felt the way it feels right now. It just feels like this place is being torn in two."

"We don't got to talk about this, John. I know where your heart is. I do. And we can just leave it at that."

"But why, Vess? Why can't we talk about it?"

Vess laughed and reached her left hand out toward the side table. She rubbed her palm nervously back and forth over the cover of her Bible. "You always been stubborn, ain't you?" He looked up and she was looking down at him, but when their eyes met she turned her attention back out to the yard. "All these years me and you've talked about everything under the sun, but we've never talked about this, have we? There's probably a good reason for that. So I guess I just don't know why we've got to now."

"Because things ain't always been like this, Vess, at least not that I can see. And like you said, we've talked about everything under the sun."

"I just don't know why I've got to be the one to explain things to you, John. Why does that fall on me?"

"Vess, I don't mean it like that. I don't mean it like some burden. I'm asking you as a friend, a close friend, and because I genuinely want to hear what you've got to say."

"Yeah, but you might not want to hear once you've heard it. That's the thing."

"But maybe I need to. You ever thought about that?"

She sat there for a good five minutes staring off at that place along the woods. The cars passed, and between those sounds the river whispered endless and steady. Coggins was beginning to think he'd upset her. He knew how uncomfortable it was to talk about things like this, but he also believed their relationship was close enough that she'd speak her mind. After a long spell, she tapped a four count with the tips of her fingers against the arm of the chair.

"You remember the other day we were sitting in the kitchen and Toya said something about the way racism wears a lot of faces. You remember?"

"Yes, ma'am, I do."

"Now, I know how you took that, John, and I know it hurt you when she said it. I could see it on your face. But the thing is, there's a whole lot of truth to what she said."

"How so?"

"People like to think racism looks a certain way, that it's a 'Whites Only' sign in a restaurant window or a cross burning in somebody's yard, but it don't have to look like that. It can be a whole lot more subtle than that. It can light every once in a while like them lightning bugs out there, just real subtle, so that if you wasn't paying attention you probably wouldn't even see it."

"I still don't see it, Vess."

"I don't know what to tell you, John." There was a glass of tea sitting on the side table next to her Bible and she took a sip from it, then rocked a few times back and forth from her toes to her heels. "It's the way Lon had to wait outside in the truck till somebody's husband got home before he could go inside the house and fix the heat pump or the sink or whatever it was they'd called him over to fix. Ain't no telling how many times he missed supper because some woman didn't want him in the house with her by herself, or maybe she did and it was the husband ain't want him in there with her. It's the things that go unsaid. Quiet things. But you live it and you know what it looks like. You notice it everywhere you look and it's enough to drive you crazy if you stare at it too long, so instead you make a joke out of it. You laugh about it. Lonnie'd get so tired of it he wouldn't even want to go over to them folks' houses, but we needed the money and I'd tell him I didn't blame them husbands one bit. I'd tell him it was on account of how handsome he was, that them women just couldn't keep their hands to themselves, and he'd just laugh. But we both knew good and well what it was. It's little things."

"But how do you know that's how they meant it?"

"Because it wasn't one time. Wasn't even a couple times. It was every day. You experience it long enough and it don't take a scarecrow's brains to figure out what somebody's saying, whether they put words to it or not. Don't even really matter how they meant it. Probably didn't think about it. Probably wasn't even intentional, because that's how it is. It's the same thing as when y'all would come to our church, it was always, 'Y'all sure do cook good,' 'Y'all sure can sing,' and I know there wasn't a one of you meant anything bad by that. I know that, John. But you can't hear how those words sound in my ears. It's the subtle things. Just lights up real low and dim to where if you ain't watching, you can't see it."

Coggins didn't know what to say, and for a long time the two of them just sat there quiet on the porch while the night bugs filled the woods with sound.

"Niggerskull Road," Vess said all of a sudden, and hearing that word from her mouth struck him like a clap of thunder. "All our lives that's what that road was named."

Coggins knew the place and he knew the story. The way the old-timers explained it, two escaped slaves had run north out of South Carolina and somehow fought their way through briar fields and laurel hells out of the flatland and into the mountains. A winter storm blew in, night fell, and as temperatures bottomed, they climbed inside the cavern of a hollowed-out tree and clutched tight to one another for every speck of heat their bodies could kindle. They froze just the same, so that months or years down the road all that was found was two skeletons braided together like vine.

That was the official name of the state road until the early nineties. Once upon a time there had even been a Niggerskull 4-H club. A professor at the university petitioned the change so that the road was eventually renamed Cedar Valley, but of course that didn't stop local folks from calling the place what they'd always called it. Sometimes he'd still catch that name come across the scanner as older volunteer firemen spouted off directions to a wreck or fire in the area, but hearing her say it right then caught him sideways.

"When they went to changing the name of that road I was standing at the farm supply getting a sack of scratch for the chickens, and this woman I've known all my life tells me she don't know why in the world they needed to change that name, that there wasn't nothing racist about it, that that was just what they found up there. That's what she told me. And let me tell you right now, it took every ounce of faith in my heart not to snatch that woman up by her hair and drag her ass all over that store.

"Even after, wasn't twenty years ago the state went to changing the name of that whole cove, Niggerskull Mountain, Niggerskull Creek. They were changing those names all over the state, and you know what our congressman said—a state congressman, now, born and raised right there in Sylva—you know what he told the paper? Said he hadn't heard anybody was offended by it, that it was just what it'd always been. Now, he might have talked to some folks and they may very well have told him that, but do you think he ever come asked me? That's a man stood in our sanctuary when he needed a vote, but you think he come and ask us whether or not that word meant anything?"

"I don't know what to say," Coggins said, and that was the truth. He'd come with empty hands and now they were full, and he didn't know what to do with what he was holding. What she'd handed him was heavy and he had no place to sit it down.

Vess pushed up in the chair and stood. "There's things like that word and things go unsaid and a whole lot of things fall between. That's all I'm saying, John." Her bare feet slid along the porch planks and she stopped with her hand on the screen door. "I'll be back in a minute," she said. "Got something I've been meaning to give you."

Coggins sat out there in the dark with the night sounds around him and chewed his toothpick. There were a whole lot of things rolling about his mind right then and he couldn't pin a one of them down. He didn't know how to feel anymore.

The porch light flicked on and he squinted until his eyes had time to adjust. When she came back onto the porch the moths were already batting around the light, and she closed the screen fast to keep from letting them inside.

"Tell me who these young men are," Vess said as she walked over. She had a photograph held out in her hand, and as Coggins took it from her she snickered.

Lonnie Jones had driven a brown Chevy LUV pickup, and him and Coggins were sitting on the tailgate together with a deer stretched between them. "They Lord almighty."

He remembered that day in detail. It was a big-bodied forked-horn Lonnie shot way off in a hole on the back side of Chink Knob. He'd called Coggins for help and it had taken them all day to drag it out. By the time they got the deer back to the truck they'd worn the hair off one side. In the photograph, Lonnie was holding up the buck's head by its antlers, and the deer's tongue hung from its mouth. Coggins had his eyes crossed and his tongue hanging out, and Lonnie was laughing with a great big smile Coggins could still hear echoing through the back of his mind.

"You ever seen that picture before?"

"I don't think I have. Got a pile of pictures of us turkey hunting, but I don't think I ever saw this one before."

"Well, you keep that. I must've had doubles printed. Got another one just like it in the house."

Coggins couldn't turn away from the photograph. He missed Lonnie something fierce and he knew that was a feeling that must've eaten at Vess every minute of every day. There came a time when all the folks you knew and loved started passing away and it was almost a curse to survive them.

"Now, this here is what I wanted to give you."

He looked up, and she was holding a small scratch box turkey caller Lonnie had made from a slab of rainbow poplar, a narrow piece of slate that had served as the striker rubber-banded to the top of the call. Coggins had never been able to run a scratch box, but there was no telling how many longbeards Lonnie'd struck or finished with it through the years. He placed the picture in his lap and took the call from her hands.

"Vess, I can't take that."

"Sure you can. What in the world I'm going to do with it? That call ain't doing nothing but sitting in a box with a whole bunch of other things I don't have any business keeping. You the only man I ever knew as eat up with them birds as Lonnie was. You take it. He'd want you to have it. Matter of fact, he'd want you to use it."

"Yeah, so he could get a good laugh."

"Maybe." Vess smiled.

The two of them sat there together for a while longer swapping stories about the man they'd both loved, and as the minutes passed the weight slowly lifted, so that when it came time to leave Coggins no longer felt the way he had an hour before. Of course, nothing had really changed. His mind had simply found a new place to light. There was still the world coming down, and in the morning he would see its reckoning.

The shoebox was still on the counter. The snake was still curled inside.

18

There was no one in the building that night except her. Most of the time Brad stuck around and worked in his own studio while she was there, but he was busy with other things. He'd swung by earlier to unlock the doors and let her in, but after that Toya was alone. She didn't mind. In fact, she preferred it, the silence and emptiness channeling her focus to a singular point.

It wasn't that she didn't enjoy being around people. Sometimes she even relished the give-and-take idea flow between herself and other creatives. But when it came time to do the work, the presence of anyone else had always been a distraction. Her creativity necessitated that she remain completely inside herself, and that was part of what had made the work that summer so difficult. What she was doing required the help of others, and that was new country for her as an artist. Collaboration required trust, and it was hard to put that sort of faith in someone with a project this intimate and personal.

She'd come to the mountains to trace the roots of where and whom she'd come from. For months leading up, she'd purged her mind of any preconceptions, any biases she'd held, so that she could step into that space blindly and without hang-up. When she'd arrived from Atlanta she'd had no idea what the search might look like or where it would take her. All she'd really hoped was that whatever she discovered might serve as inspiration for art, for her thesis, that the journey itself might become an origin story.

The idea finally came one night while she was in the university library. She was digging through microfiche of old newspapers for anything at all about the church when she stumbled onto a black-and-white photograph of her great-grandmother. It wasn't that she'd never seen the woman before. There were a dozen or more pictures scattered through family albums. But this particular photograph was different. It was as if she were looking into still water and seeing her own reflection.

The woman's name was Tawni, though everyone had called her Bird. In the picture she stood by the river struggling to hold up a fish that ran the length of her leg. The fish was all light and shadow, deep grays and bright whites in heavy contrast, though enough detail remained to make out the armored scales down its sides. The caption read simply, "Bird Clawson catches first sturgeon ever recorded in Tuckaseigee." The article explained how she'd caught the fish on a small piece of cut chub meant for redhorse. She was beaming in the photograph, a smile stretching wide across her dark face, her eyes squinted and lit, and it was that expression that had struck the girl.

The second she saw it she scrolled through photos on her phone looking for a selfie she'd taken that spring in Atlanta with one of her girlfriends after a Tobe Nwigwe show. Holding the two photos side by side, she was taken aback. The likeness was uncanny. Anyone who didn't know better might have sworn it was the same person. In that moment she was taken aback by the power of blood.

Everything she'd spent the summer searching for, the answers of where and whom she'd come from, was a living, breathing thing beating inside her chest.

The second that thought solidified, the concept of the work consumed her. She gathered all the photos she could find of Bird and studied the expressions on the woman's face. The first molds she made herself while staring in a mirror with plastic wrap pulled over her braids and Vaseline on her skin to keep the plaster strips from sticking. It was hard enough to do the work alone, but holding the expression throughout that process proved impossible. After a handful of failed attempts, she knew she would have to ask for help.

Brad was a godsend. He immediately recognized what they could do to make it work. They made molds with alginate, the same material dentists used to make molds of teeth, and though it took some trial and error, they slowly dialed the process in. Toya would sit back in the chair while Brad worked the material onto her face. She imitated the expressions captured in the photographs and soon there were molds mimicking every picture. When she cast them in plaster and held them in her hands she began to see not only herself and Bird but the faces of her mother and grandmother, expressions that had traveled down through four generations of women.

Music played on a small Bluetooth speaker behind her. Dust coated her arms like chalk. She was busy smoothing out one of the plaster casts with a sanding pad. The album playing was one Brad had turned her on to, by a band from Asheville called the Honeycutters. All summer they'd swapped music, the conversation having grown out of a shared love of David Bowie and Sam Cooke, the Velvet Underground and Outkast. She gave him Add-2. He gave her the Chocolate Drops.

Out of the corner of her eye she saw her phone light up with a text message and knew without looking it was Brad. All night he'd been hounding her about the protest. Toya didn't want to go but he'd been adamant that she be there. The screen went briefly dark, then lit up again. When she looked, there were thirteen text messages from him and she knew she could only put him off so long.

What she wished she could explain was that thin line between fearless and foolish, that tightrope she'd walked all summer. For her that line was as deep and dangerous as a canyon, but for Brad it didn't even exist. There was no mistaking on which side her going to the protest would fall.

Toya looked around the room she'd used as a studio that summer. When she'd approached the art department about a space to work in, they'd brushed her off, and it was Brad who'd found her the space and set it all up. Though it wasn't much bigger than a closet, it was all she'd needed.

The walls were covered with photographs of Bird, her grandmother, and her mother. There were other photographs of people and places she did not know but had discovered as she thumbed her way through the archives trying to gain an understanding of a community that was all but gone. Standing there, she was surrounded by history. She was surrounded by all the things that were buried somewhere inside her. What she was doing here had become something spiritual. She'd turned that room into a sanctuary.

Right then her eyes settled on the picture of Bird, that giant smile and that monstrous fish. She set the sanding pad onto the table and ran her hands across the cast of her face, the curves now smooth and soft as skin.

In the end, there was only the work, and that was what no one else seemed to understand. The work was the one thing, the only thing, she owed anyone.

19

Ernie's house had belonged to his grandparents. It wasn't much, just a two-bed, one-bath farmhouse with good bones on a block foundation. His punishment for breaking Nick Lovedahl's nose was a two-week suspension without pay, which would've hurt a lot worse if the home weren't paid for. As it stood, though, the time off was a blessing.

With the way work had been over the past few months, Ernie was burned out and needed a break. He was looking forward to catching up on chores, to napping, and to feeding the fish in the backyard stream. He was looking forward to hunting chanterelles, black trumpets, and boletes, to time in the woods scouting deer for fall. Lovedahl, on the other hand, had been fired as soon as the sheriff learned what he'd said, and how quickly Coggins had made that decision was one more reason Ernie respected the man he worked for.

The dishes in the sink had been soaking since supper and Ernie went into the kitchen to knock them out before the water got cold. When he was finished, he dried his hands and grabbed a beer from the refrigerator, then returned to the den to wait on the ten o'clock news. He was eager to see if they'd mention the protests. Rumors were stirring that people were coming from all over western North Carolina, and regardless of whether that was true, he was certain the whole thing would turn into a shit show.

A window across the den looked onto the front yard, where white oaks cut the moonlight and cast the house in shadow. The porch light wasn't on, so the windowpane was dark aside from a dim reflection of the room where he sat in a worn-out recliner. Out past the white oaks, the driveway bordered a cattle pasture the neighbor'd left vacant all summer for hay. He was watching the television, but in his peripheral vision he saw a pair of headlights sweep into the field. When he looked, the lights flicked off.

There weren't many places along this road to pull over and it was common for people to use his driveway to turn around. This vehicle, though, had appeared to park. Ernie crossed the room to peer out but it was too dark to see past the trees. He opened the door and stepped onto the porch. He was barefooted and the concrete slab was cold against his feet. He wore a tattered T-shirt and a pair of canvas carpenter's pants, the bottom hems tucking under his heels as he made his way out to the trees.

A man named Knotty Luker owned the surrounding pasture, and Ernie's first thought was that he'd probably come to take care of something late. Usually Knotty left his truck running and the headlights on so that he could see to work the lock loose from the gate. Typically, he could hear Knotty's diesel chugging loudly from the house, but there was no sound right then aside from crickets and peepers.

From the oaks, he could make out the silhouette of a long sedan parked crossways at the end of the drive. The car was a few hundred yards out, and in such low light he could not discern anything more than its shape. The hood didn't appear to be up and no one seemed to be milling around, but he figured it could be someone having car trouble.

To avoid the gravel, he slipped along the fence line through grass trimmed short to the ground, dew wetting the cuffs of his pants. As he got closer, he could make out the tops of someone's shoulders and the outline of their head. They appeared to be peeping over the roof of the car, and for one brief moment it seemed like they might've had binoculars held up to their eyes. Slinking along that edge, he was certain they couldn't spot him, so when the distance had been cut in half he walked in the open, for he did not wish to surprise them.

He yelled hello, and just as soon as that word echoed down the driveway the person came around the back of the car. It was still too dark to make out anything other than shadows but he watched as they climbed behind the wheel and the engine squealed to life. The headlights brushed through the hayfield and the tires spun briefly in the gravel and just like that, they were gone. Ernie stood puzzled, wondering if it had been someone looking at the house or if his eyes had deceived him.

All he'd really seen was an outline, and he couldn't be certain whether they were facing his direction or looking away. It was probably just some drunk who'd stopped to take a leak, he told himself, and if not that, then something equally benign. Walking back to the house, he wrote the whole thing off.

20

By three a.m., Coggins knew there was no chance of rest. He'd gone to the couch around midnight to keep from waking his wife, and for the past three hours he'd been scrolling through Facebook on his cell phone, reading comments on news stories despite the fact that he knew better.

His bare feet made a sticky sound against the linoleum as he walked into the kitchen and opened the cabinet for coffee. He waited at the table while the pot percolated and stared dumbly at a bowl of fruit—apples, tangerines, and a few bananas gathered in an enameled tin bowl that had belonged to his mother.

"You coming back to bed?"

Looking over his shoulder, he saw his wife peering in from the threshold. Her eyes were half closed and she yawned while she waited for him to answer. She had one hand resting on the wall, her gray hair tied into a softball-sized bun at the back of her head. A fuzzy pink robe was pulled tight and cinched at the waist.

"No, Evie," he said. "I don't think I am." Her name was Evelyn but he'd always called her that, ever since he was sliding notes into her locker their freshman year of high school.

Evie shuffled across the kitchen in a pair of worn-out slippers and took a coffee mug down from a hook on the side of the cabinets. Pouring a cup from the pot, she brought it over to the table and slid it in front of him. She traced her hand across the side of his face before taking a seat and scooting her chair close.

"What is it, John?" She looked worried. "What's got you so worked up?"

"A lot of things," he said. There was so much going on and so much that had happened he hadn't had time to process it, let alone make sense of the emotions he was sorting through. "I went and saw Vess."

"Aww," Evie said. "And how's she doing with all this?"

"You know Vess. She don't get shook up about much."

Evie had her head cocked to the side and resting on the tips of her fingers, her elbow anchored against the tabletop. Her blue eyes had seemed to change as she'd gotten older, almost a steel gray now, just a shade darker than her hair. Coggins looked at her deeply, and like always the mere sight of her made the hairs stand up on his arms.

"You know, we got to talking about different things, and I asked her if she'd ever experienced much racism growing up here, living here all her life. In all them years of riding around with Lon I don't think me and him ever talked about something like that. I don't know that it ever even crossed my mind to ask. Guess I just thought if he'd wanted to tell me something he would have."

"And what did she say?"

Coggins had the picture Vess had given him on the table, he and Lonnie sitting on the back of that truck with the deer between them. He took a sip of coffee and pushed the photograph in front of Evie.

"Lord." She smiled and chuckled. "Where in the world did you find that?"

"Vess give it to me," he said. "Give me Lon's old scratch box too."

"That's special, John."

Coggins had a whole lot of things he wanted to say but he didn't know how to say them. Truthfully they were subjects he'd never broached, things he'd never had to discuss and perhaps even avoided because it was just easier that way.

"The other day we were sitting there in her kitchen, me and Vess and that granddaughter of hers, and we were talking about that statue and what it meant. I kept trying to explain to that girl that it wasn't like how she took it, that it was more complicated than that, and she just kept talking over me and wouldn't let me finish what I had to say, and I'm telling you, Evie, I got so eat up I felt like I was about to catch on fire."

"What was it, you think?"

"I don't know."

"I mean, what was it that got you riled up like that?"

"Yeah, I know what you're asking, but I don't know what to tell you."

"Was it because it was coming from a woman?"

"Of course not, Evie. You know me better than that."

"You think it was because she's Black?"

"Jesus, Evie! Why would you even ask me that? That's two times in the past few days somebody's painted me out to be some racist—"

"Now, that's not what I said, John. And you know that's not how I meant it. You know that. But it's worth asking if it helps you get to the bottom of this. That's my job, to ask hard questions, things you might not ask yourself. And I'm asking because you've very rarely been one to just fly off the handle. When it does happen it's major, but it's rare. So for her to have pushed your buttons the way she did, it had to have been something. Was it her age? Was it just because you don't know her? What?"

He couldn't see it, of course, but it was all of those things. The problem was, the titles that went along with recognizing and admitting something like that, those titles tended to make people so defensive they went blind. "I don't know. Maybe. Maybe on account of she's only twenty-four years old. I mean, what does she know about it?"

"You can't let something like that get to you, John. These kids, they don't think about things the way we do. They didn't grow up like we did or like Vess or Lon."

"It's not that simple." What he was trying to say was getting lost. What he really wanted to know but couldn't find the words to ask was something bigger. He wanted to know whether or not his feelings about something like that statue even mattered if the end result was someone else's suffering. He couldn't put his finger on what it was that had made him so angry. Sure, it was her cutting him off and his not being able to say what he wanted to say, and sure, it was likely on account of how young she was and the fact she knew it all, but afterward he'd just felt confused. It was the questions what she'd said had raised in his own mind, and how uneasy those questions made him.

"What were you trying to tell her, John? I mean, what was it you wanted to say?"

"I don't know, Evie." He shook his head. "I don't know. And the more I sit and think about it, I don't know what it would've mattered."

"But it doesn't have to matter to anybody else, John. Not right now. Right now it's me and you talking. It's me and you. So if it made you that mad that you couldn't say it, so mad that you didn't have the chance to explain, then explain it to me now. Obviously it mattered, or at least it mattered to you right then, so what was it?"

"It's like I told you. It was that she kept saying that flag and that statue, that those things could only mean one thing, and it don't. It just don't."

"So what do they mean?"

"They mean all sorts of things, Evie. I mean, I used to ride around in that old step-side with that flag on my front bumper. Hell, Lonnie rode around in that truck with me for years and never once said a thing about it. Didn't think twice about climbing in."

"Did you ever ask him whether it bothered him?"

"No," he said. "Of course not, and why would I? There wasn't nothing he wouldn't have said to me. He knew he could've said anything in the world and at the end of the day I'd have loved him just the same. So if it bothered him he'd have said it. He'd have said something. I believe that." Coggins fixed his eyes on the photograph, then looked up at his wife. "But you think about somebody like H. K. Edgerton, how every year he used to drive over here from Asheville and put on that gray uniform and march through town waving a Confederate flag. That man was Black as the ace of spades. He was the head of the NAACP, for Christ's sake. So how in the world could it be that simple? How in the world could it just mean the one thing?"

"So again, John, what does it mean? What does that flag mean to you?"

"I don't know. I don't know what to tell you." Trying to put words to it left his mind spinning doughnuts until finally the tires blew out from under him. "It's about heritage," he said. "It's about being proud of who and where you come from. I think about that statue and I think about that photograph of its dedication and how my great-great-grandfather is standing there with his chest stuck out and his eyes hollowed from what he'd seen and done, and I'm not saying that war didn't have nothing to do with slavery because it most surely did. It did. But it couldn't have been just that. It couldn't have been. Because that man in that picture was barely clearing enough from farming to keep food in his stomach, and he done that beating his own hands to pulp. So what was he fighting for? Why did he load up and go?"

"I don't know, John."

"And I don't know either, but I know I'm proud to come from men like that. I'm proud to come from folks been tied to this place and these mountains and this county for that long. You know, I think about why I had that flag on my truck to begin with and for the most part it didn't have nothing to do with that war. It had to do with being proud to be born and raised here."

She sat there for a while staring at her lap and tugging at the tag ends of the cincture that held her robe to one side of her legs. "I remember one time I was up there in the waiting room at the dentist, and you know how he always had all them Civil War paintings hung all over the walls." Evie grinned as she told the story. "Well, I was looking at one that morning and it had the dates of the Confederacy, and for whatever reason it struck me that we was in high school that long, John. I'd never thought about it until right then. We were in high school about the same amount of time that flag really meant something. And it got me wondering why a hundred years later people are still so caught up on it, and so there's a part of me thinks you're right. I think it's more complicated than just that war. I think that flag come to mean all sorts of things."

"Well, here's what she told me. Here's what she said, Evie. To defend that flag is 'an act of White supremacy.' That's what the girl said."

"And for a whole lot of folks, she's probably right. Surely that's what it means to a whole lot of people. There's folks flying that flag ain't ever stepped foot in the South, so what in the world are they doing that for? What in the world's it mean to them?"

"I don't know," he said. "But the thing I just keep thinking is if it means that to some people, or if that girl walks up to that statue and it means that to her, or say some little kid is riding down I-40 with their family on vacation and sees that flag flying on the side of the highway and it means that one thing, what difference does it make what it means to me? If that's the lot I'm cast with for putting that flag on the front of that truck, what's it matter?"

Coggins knew he couldn't explain what he meant, or rather how deeply it forced him to question things he'd always held as truth, and that was no fault of his wife's and really no fault of his own. How could he explain something to her that he couldn't even settle in his own mind? Suddenly there were all of these thoughts and feelings tumbling around inside of him that he'd never considered and never felt until then, and maybe that was the crux of what that girl had been saying, maybe that's what she meant by forcing someone to confront an idea. All he knew was that the whole thing made him uncomfortable. And *that* more than anything was what had set him on fire. It was the discomfort.

"You want me to get you another cup of coffee?"

"No," he said. "I think I'll just sit here awhile."

"Well, I'm going back to bed." Evie took his hand and ran her thumb across the tops of his knuckles. "You're a good man, John Coggins. Don't lose sight of that. You think too much, but you're a good man with a good heart."

21

The morning of the protests Vess Jones was crisping livermush in a cast iron skillet on the stove when her granddaughter wandered into the kitchen. She'd fried cube steak for dinner the night before and saved the cornmeal in a bowl that she now whisked into batter for hoecakes. The chickens were laying a dozen eggs a day and at that rate she couldn't even give them away.

Vess shoveled a spatula under each rectangle of livermush and flipped them onto a paper towel to cool. She poured circles of batter into the pan and cooked the hoecakes golden, and after that the eggs took no time at all.

"Better get some breakfast," she said.

Toya came to the stove and made her plate, and when she finished Vess gathered what was left for herself. They sat at the table and took their time. For once the girl didn't seem to be in any sort of hurry.

Vess picked up her cup of coffee and held it with both hands in front of her face, the mug warm against her palms. "You going downtown this afternoon?"

"I guess," Toya said. She picked up a piece of livermush with her fingers and tapped one corner against her plate, then lifted it to her mouth to take a bite.

Vess ran her hands against her thighs nervously. She took a moment before she spoke. "You really think that's a good idea?"

Toya looked up. "Do you not want me to go?" she asked.

Vess didn't know how to answer.

"If you don't want me to, just tell me."

"I can't do that," Vess said. "You're full grown. You can make those decisions for yourself. But I will say this. It's one thing to kick a hornet's nest and another altogether to stand there once it's done."

Toya pulled her braids to one side so that they ran over her right shoulder and down her chest. She drew them through her hands like grapevine. "You don't think I should've done it, do you? You think I should've left that statue alone."

"No, now I'm not saying that. I'm not saying that at all." Vess knew her intent was getting lost. She also knew that what she was trying to drive home was something that had been pounded into that girl's head from the moment she was old enough to listen. Still, she felt the need to come right out and say it once more. "You asked what I want and the only thing I want is for you to be safe. That's all. So what I want you to ask yourself is how many people look like you or me you think you're going to see down there today if you go?"

"I know, Maw Maw." Toya nodded. "I know. And I've thought about that. As a matter of fact, that's all I've thought about for three days."

"Honey, I know your mother raised you with some sense, and I'd like to think I've done the same." Vess had her head tilted to the side and she hoped that her granddaughter was taking every word to heart. "So what is it makes you think you need to go down there?"

Toya groaned and rocked her head back and forth as if thinking long and hard about her reasons. "Brad really wants me to be there. And I've sat with it and I've thought about what you're saying, and it's just, a part of me feels like I owe it to him."

Vess stared toward the window over the sink. She worked the tips of her fingers through the curls of her hair and scratched her scalp. "So who is this Brad you've been spending so much time with?"

"Just a grad student there at the school."

"Is that all?" Vess cut her eyes at Toya with a smirk like she wasn't buying.

"No, Maw Maw, it's not like that." Toya smiled and shook her head. "I've got too much going on to get bogged down with some boy."

"Bogged down." Vess slapped the table and cackled. "Girl, that's your mama made all over."

"And look at all she's done." Toya raised her eyebrows and cut her eyes across the table. "She's already made partner at her firm."

"I'm not arguing, child. I promise. It's just I don't want to see you let your life get away from you's all I'm saying. It's good to be driven, but there's a lot more to living than working it all away. That's all I'm saying."

Toya clicked the tines of her fork against her front teeth nervously. "Maw Maw, why is it the two of you always butted heads?"

"Your mama's just always been headstrong," she said. "She was like that as a little girl." Vess broke the yolk on an over-easy egg that sat in the middle of her plate. She cut a bite of livermush with the side of her fork and ran the meat through the yellow like it was sauce. The yolks from her hens were so much richer than anything she could've bought from a store, and she closed her eyes to savor that flavor on her tongue.

"You know I didn't have your mama till I was almost thirty. Wasn't that we hadn't wanted kids. We'd tried and tried and it just never took. Stubborn, I guess, so in the end stubborn's what we got." Vess laughed. "I remember one morning your mama got restless in church and started acting up. I smacked that leg and she just kept right on. After that Lon took her outside and he whooped her good. He told me later he said he looked at her and asked if she was ready to behave and your mama stared right up at him and shook her head no. He whooped her again and asked her that same thing and she shook her head no. Your granddaddy never was much of a disciplinarian but he said he whooped her until his heart broke and your mama just stood there and took it. She probably wasn't five or six years old. That's how she's always been."

"And you think I take after her?" The two of them chuckled at each other for a minute before Toya spoke again. "I think I take after my daddy."

"Well, that laugh of yours came from your daddy, there's no doubt about that. Your daddy always had a laugh made you feel about like sunshine." Vess placed her hands flat on the table and stroked them over the surface like she might've been feeling a yard of fabric. "But the rest of what you got, now, that come from one place. All of that you've got flying around inside of your head, all of that dreaming, that burn-the-world-down kind of heart you've got pounding inside of your chest, that's your mama's doing. Can't nobody take credit for that but her."

"And where did she get it?"

"I've been trying to figure that out since the day I had her. I don't have the slightest idea, sweet girl, but it sure wasn't me."

They ate their breakfast, and when Toya got up to pour herself a glass of orange juice from the refrigerator she carried the pot of coffee to the table and topped off her grandmother's cup. Toya had on a pair of tight-fitting blue jeans rolled up at the bottoms to just below her knees. A black tank top was dark against her chestnut skin.

"You've got so much of your mother in you it's scary," Vess said. "And there's a whole lot of good in that, a whole, whole lot. But part of the reason we were always butting heads was that she thought I should've been more outspoken and it just wasn't in me. She thought me keeping my mouth shut and going about my business was submissive. What she never could understand was that it wasn't submission. It was survival. Things were different when she was growing up. They're even more different for you now. Especially outside of this place. But for me, it was always head up, eyes forward, one foot in front of the other. That's how you walked through this world. That's how you made it through the day. You understand what I'm telling you?"

"Kind of."

Vess thought about the conversation she'd had with Coggins the night before. There were so many things she hadn't mentioned. Things hadn't always been as pleasant and accepting as he wanted to remember, and the truth was he couldn't have understood if he'd wanted to. They'd grown up in the exact same county, but in another way they hadn't grown up in the same place at all.

She remembered things like catching a stringer of yellow perch on Bear Lake with Lon one Saturday by the docks and how the game warden who checked them for licenses had called the fish nigger preachers, something he said proudly just to watch the way their faces fell. She remembered how she physically felt her spirit draw back inside her at that exact moment, how she swallowed that feeling in silence the same way she did every time she heard someone mention Nigger Town or Nigger Hill, the places Black communities had held for generations. Those were things Coggins couldn't have known, feelings he could have never hoped to understand. There were two separate worlds and she'd only ever known the one. And despite all of that, or rather in spite of that, she wouldn't have traded that life for anything.

"In the end," Vess said, "my happiness was my defiance. My joy was my act of dissent." Vess folded her hands and rested her chin on the tops of her knuckles. "And that's the difference between us, sweet girl, for the good and for the bad. That's what your mother never has been able to accept. And that's okay. She doesn't have to and neither do you. Each one of us has to live our own truth."

Vess stood and walked out of the kitchen. There was an old treadle Singer sewing machine in the hall and she opened one of the drawers to grab something she'd been saving. That morning finally felt like the right time. When she came into the kitchen Toya had cleaned the table and was washing their dishes at the sink. Vess came up behind her and opened the clasp on a thread-thin sterling necklace. She put the chain around her granddaughter's neck and Toya pressed her fingers against the pendant as it came to rest at her heart.

The girl turned and held the charm out to try to get a better look. It was a small square turned on end so that it hung in the shape of a diamond. The outer edge was rolled silver tarnished a dull gray. A small piece of smoothed and rounded glass had been fitted over something deep black with grains like wood.

"What is this, Maw Maw?"

"It belonged to your great-great-grandfather," Vess said. "When he joined the army and left for the war, your great-great-grandmother, my grandmama, had this made for him so that he'd always have a piece of her with him. Did you know we sent fifteen men from Cullowhee to fight in World War I? I ever told you that?"

"I don't think so."

"Well, your great-great-grandfather was one of them, and what you're wearing around your neck is a lock of my grandmother's hair."

Toya looked up and tears rose in the corners of her eyes. "I can't take this, Maw Maw."

"Of course you can, sweet girl." Vess reached out and pressed her knuckle to the corners of Toya's eyes to keep her granddaughter's tears from falling. "You're going to take it and you're going to wear it around your neck and you won't ever forget where you come from. Long as you've got that, you've got everything."

Toya leaned in and kissed her grandmother on the lips. She wrapped her arms around Vess's neck and for a long time they stood there swaying back and forth as if they were dancing. It had been a long time since she'd felt her heart that full, and even as the moment passed she recognized that it was something she might never feel again.

22

The first of them gathered around the statue at daylight. They were mostly older men in overalls with trucker caps propped high on their heads advertising tire shops and heavy equipment. They passed around a thermos of coffee and chewed tobacco and laughed about people and things that Cawthorn knew nothing about.

The Daughters of the Confederacy showed up midmorning with biscuits and apple butter and more coffee, and Cawthorn helped himself to the refreshments, though they eyed him like he was some vagrant milling around a soup kitchen. A few men marched up dressed in heavy gray uniforms and sweat-stained kepi hats, and though the sun was still an hour or more from overhead, the air was humid and they sweated as if they'd just finished mowing their yards.

The weather had the dog pecker gnats swarming, and one middle-aged man with dark hair and a volunteer fire T-shirt cussed them as he wiped one from his eye with the back of his knuckle.

"I'll tell you how to get rid of them," Cawthorn said.

"How's that?"

"Cut you a hole in the back of your britches." He laughed, but everyone else crumpled their faces in disgust.

"There's women here," one man said, and Willy Dean almost told him what they could do but quickly thought better of it. He was doing his best to fit in and align himself with everyone around him, to blend in as one of their own.

The fence the county had built around the statue was a small squared-off section of panels, and the people crowded around, their conversations and voices growing ever louder. There were maybe a hundred or so now. A few folks waved flags, and in a few hours a couple county officials and politicians were set to speak and campaign. Everything so far seemed peaceful, and that was part of why Cawthorn wished the Knights had come, because that would've changed the air of things. Their presence alone would've filled that space with fire.

Tensions kindled mildly midafternoon when the counterprotestors started to gather at the base of the stairs leading up to the courthouse and statue, but a police presence had already filled the gap between them. People shouted a few things back and forth, and those around the statue groaned as the group below started to chant, "Black lives matter." One mid-thirties man who was standing by the statue with his fingers linked through the wires of the fence screamed back, "All lives matter!" and Cawthorn immediately hollered, "White lives matter!" and the people around him went briefly silent.

Suddenly he felt out of place. It wasn't just Slade Ashe who was a coward. This whole damn town was soft. Here they were gathered together like a cup full of gasoline and no one had even considered striking a match.

Willy Dean walked up the stairs and strolled around the side of the old courthouse. He found a hedge of boxwoods to dip into to relieve himself from all the coffee he'd drunk over the course of the morning. His head was pounding. All that caffeine had him more on edge than usual, his hands jittery and an almost sick feeling eating at the pit of his stomach.

As he came around the back of the building, a car was pulling out of the parking lot and the driver flicked a cigarette out the window. Some punk kid on a skateboard wheeled over out of the shadows. He picked up the butt and took a few quick drags to keep it lit. As the boy lifted the cigarette to his lips, he caught Cawthorn staring at him, but there was no shame on his face, just a sort of fuck-you look that Willy Dean found perfect for the plan he was piecing together.

Everything Slade Ashe had told him was fresh in his mind. He could still feel the edge of that knife flush against his throat and knew he had to walk the straight and narrow for now. In time, Ashe would get what was coming to him, but at the moment Willy Dean had to keep his nose clean. Nevertheless, what was happening in front of the courthouse, or the lack thereof, was a travesty.

He thought about the men standing there with those flags. There was so much potential for things to be bigger than this. Without somebody spurring the horse, they'd all just climb into their cars at the end of the day and head back to their houses for bologna sandwiches and tater chips. They'd doze off in their recliners half-watching reruns of *All in the Family*, snickering at jokes that slipped through the cracks between wake and dream until they were snoring and fast asleep, the events of the day almost forgotten. These people were treating this thing like a Bible study.

Willy Dean marched across the parking lot toward the kid. "You keep picking up smokes like that you'll wind up with a cold sore big as that mountain."

"Fuck you!"

Cawthorn laughed and kept right on coming. The closer he got, the more timid the boy became. His shoulders slumped and he looked as if he thought Willy Dean was going to scold him or hit him, but as Cawthorn got close he pulled a soft pack of Cheyenne Reds from the pocket of his jeans and shook a cigarette free.

"Here," he said. "Take one."

The boy studied him for a split second, then flipped the hair out of his face before slipping two cigarettes out of the pack. Willy Dean took one for himself, struck a lighter, and set the tobacco to flame. He blew a whistle of smoke into the air above them, then offered a light to the kid.

Cawthorn rested his arms over the back of someone's tailgate. "Crazy what's happening out there, ain't it?"

"I guess," the kid said, disinterested and only halfway paying attention.

"I tell you what would be a sight, be funny as hell."

"What's that?"

"Naw, you wouldn't do it. I can just look at you and tell you're a pussy."

"Fuck you, old man."

"Ain't got it in you."

"What?"

Cawthorn guffawed under his breath and looked the boy square. "I'd bet this pack of smokes and a twenty-dollar bill you wouldn't have the balls to do what I'm thinking."

The kid stepped closer and looked into the bed of the pickup truck where Cawthorn leaned. There was a dented shovel and a red brick lying on the rubber mat across the bed. "Mister, for twenty dollars and them cigarettes I'll throw this fucking brick through this truck's window."

Willy Dean crowed loudly and flung his cigarette on the pavement like he was slamming a winning hand onto a poker table. "You won't have to do nothing like that," he said. He stared up at the sun and felt it warm against his pockmarked face. Things were about to get a lot more interesting. This kid was a struck match.

23

There was a palpable anger that dizzied the air like heat haze. But if it had not been for that, for that feeling floating around like everything was about to ignite, the whole thing might've seemed comical. People peered through the cyclone fence at the statue as if they were visiting some caged animal at a zoo. It was silly. It was honest-to-God silly.

The paint from earlier in the week was gone except for a few tiny specks that held in the smallest nooks and crannies of the copper. Toya'd used latex paint for a reason, and most of it had peeled right off when county maintenance got there that afternoon. That's what she'd wanted, an easy cleanup after people saw and the pictures were taken.

The judge had set bond dead center of the bail schedule, $6,250, and rather than call a bondsman she'd paid the sum in full. Brad Roberts raised the money in half a day. He threw up a Go-FundMe that went viral on social media and she was back at her grandmother's house by dinner. He stood beside her now with a BLACK LIVES MATTER sign held over his head.

Town police had sectioned the two groups off, those defending the statue standing guard at the top of the steps, the counterprotest there by the fountain at the edge of Main Street. Officers held positions at intervals between the two groups, and so far everything had remained peaceful aside from a few words volleyed back and forth between them.

Midafternoon, a group of politicians used the opportunity at the statue as a chance to campaign. They wired up a portable amplifier and microphone to speak. First, a county commissioner spouted off the heritage-not-hate cliché that everyone had come to expect, the whole group nothing more than head nods, uh-huhs, and amens. After that some slimeball who announced he'd be running for sheriff skipped the niceties altogether and cut straight to the meat. He was sick of political correctness. He was sick of cancel culture. He was sick of history being rewritten and the liberal left brainwashing their kids in schools. He was sick of the war on White men and history, and he'd be damned if some woke bitch from Atlanta was going to come in and erase this county's history. And as the people cheered his face grew red and his voice became riled and furious until he was spitting into the microphone and spewing things that even managed to make that crowd cringe. He was nearly out of breath when a stubby bald man in a suit that swallowed him shuffled forward and cut the mic, and the man stomped up the steps and disappeared over the top of the hill, less embarrassed than just so goddamn mad he could've punched a wall. There was some sort of short-lived, sorry-for-that-folks apology and then the show was back up and running, the whole crowd cheering again, with four or five waving Confederate flags against an overcast sky.

Sheriff Coggins stood at the top of the first tier of stairs. There were three sets between the fountain and the statue, and Toya didn't know whether the spot he'd chosen signified something, whether perhaps it was some subtle sort of statement about on which side he stood, or if he'd simply picked that place as it gave him the best position. She knew what he'd said in her grandmother's kitchen and she'd witnessed his anger. But if all of those things that stood between them could've fallen away, if they could've gotten past that, past the tension and passion and emotion they both felt in that moment, she believed there was something else to him. There had to be. For her grandfather to have spent so much time with that man, there quite simply had to be.

Toya glanced around at all the people who'd come out to protest what that statue stood for, and she was struck by how much of a shift had taken place in the past few years. Aside from the ones who'd helped her dig those graves, aside from Brad, she didn't know a single person there, and yet there were nearly a hundred White men and women gathered at the foot of those steps with signs in their hands and smiles on their faces. They thanked her for what she'd done. They wrapped their arms around her and told her to let them know if they could help with anything at all, and for a split second that love had filled her with hope.

But just as quick as that feeling found her, it was replaced by the recognition that she was the only Black person there. The thing about it was, she was surrounded by good intention, but at the end of the day none of those people carried the same risks. The potential for real consequence was something they did not have to bear. Toya Gardner carried that burden alone. She knew this. She'd known it going in, and now she couldn't help but wonder whether she'd made a tremendous mistake.

Right then all of the people and all of the noise and all of that energy became a collective weight that pressed in around her, that tightened around her chest like a corset until she found it hard to breathe. There was an electricity about the air, a feeling as if a wire had been drawn too taut and would snap. She could smell it. She could smell the bodies around her, smell the smoke of the lit fuse. She took a few steps away from the crowd to find space to breathe.

Glancing up the hill, she caught a man at the top of the stairs glowering with a look that made her shrink inside herself. He was tall and wiry with a long neck and small head. He wore blue jeans and a black leather jacket that seemed odd in such heat. Greasy hair lapped at his shoulders but was trimmed short up top, and as if by some predatory instinct he seemed to recognize that she'd noticed him, that she saw him staring down at her, and a smile crept over his face. At that exact moment, a loud commotion broke out behind him.

Off to the right, some teenage kid had grabbed ahold of one of the battle flags. He had his fists balled in the fabric and was trying to rip it away while the man who'd carried it clutched tightly to the pole to which it was fastened. For a few seconds there was a tug-of-war and then the fabric ripped free, and when it did both sides lost footing. The man who'd carried the flag fell on the landing, while the kid who'd snatched it stumbled backward, tripped, and rolled down the hill. The grade was steep and his body gathered momentum, then his feet caught and sent him toppling end over end, that red flag lashing about the air like licks of flame.

In that instant, the group by the statue turned mob. Off the hill they poured like ants from a mound. Toya looked for the sheriff, and he was barreling ahead of the wave. All of the officers scrambled to contain them, but the police were outnumbered ten to one and were easily brushed aside. The crowd was running down the stairs and the people around her seemed to be readying themselves for what would soon converge. They coiled tighter around her, everyone holding their ground. And in those final moments she could not have run if she'd tried.

She glanced back toward the statue, and the man who'd been

watching her stood alone at the top of the stairs. He had a crazed light in his eyes, and as the crowd neared he appeared to be laughing. Once again he seemed to recognize the moment their eyes met, and his face warped then into something more sinister. He started down the steps at a casual pace, the ones before him teeming headlong and fast. He held her gaze until that final moment when the bodies melded together and the crowd closed around her like a fist. Just like that, they were upon her.

24

In the dog days the trout moved to the heads of the deepest holes and held to the bottom like cold stones to escape the summer's heat. There were still the slight shifts as fish repositioned in the current, the delicate fold of fins holding them steady, but to the untrained eye the stream might've seemed empty. Ernie knew better as he slung a Dixie cup full of trout chow sidearm over the creek. The pellets rippled a crescent shape against the surface and suddenly the water was boiling with fish. Like always, the mere sight of them seemed some miracle that filled him with an immense joy.

According to the five o'clock news, things had turned cowboy outside the old courthouse. There were twenty-three arrests but somehow no one had been seriously injured except one man who'd split his head open on the sidewalk when he fell. All in all, the officers were lucky. With that many people and tempers that high, the situation could have escalated beyond anything they could've controlled. Ernie was just thankful he hadn't had to fool with it.

When the trout stopped rising, Ernie walked back to the tool shed and tossed the empty cup into a metal trash can where he stored the food he fed them. He latched down the lid to keep the coons and wharf rats out and headed across the yard toward his spring box at the edge of the woods. The spring he used for water had spit five gallons a minute for three generations, never missing a beat even in drought. The problem with spring boxes, though, was they required constant maintenance. Heavy rains had a habit of pushing sediment into the box and clogging the intake.

There'd been downpours all summer, and just like he'd expected, the overflow was spilling into the creek. He lifted the lid off the spring box and a dusky salamander about as long as his finger was resting on the rim. The spring lizard shot into the water and swam to the bottom as Ernie reached in and wrapped his hand around the outlet pipe. He ran his grip up and down the pipe, feeling the pin-holes that filtered the water against his palm, and after a few passes he shook his hand dry and fit the lid back onto the box.

Out of nowhere a sharp crack split the back of his head, something striking him like a widow-maker out of a pine top, and in the brief moment before full black he had just enough awareness to realize something had hit him. There was a minute or so of semi-consciousness. He could feel something cold against the left side of his face. He could hear muffled echoes that could have just as easily been water as voices. None of this lasted long. Maybe a few seconds. Then dark.

When he came to, he was in the trunk of a car, the hatch open and the sunlight a piercing white above him. There was a gag in his mouth, cloth of some sort, for he could breathe through it if he tried and he could feel the texture of the fabric dry against his tongue. His arms were bound at his back and his ankles were fastened together. He bit down on the gag and blinked groggily but the light above was blinding.

Over the drone of cicadas, Ernie heard footsteps on gravel, then two silhouettes hovered there like cutouts at a shooting range. He tried to squirm out of the trunk but just as soon as he moved, one of the figures leaned in and got his hands balled in the front of his T-shirt. The man pressed down on Ernie's chest, pinning him there to the floor of the trunk, and the other figure, a shorter figure, came forward. In the sunlight Ernie caught a quick glimpse of a needle. He screamed against the gag as the syringe found his arm and a warm sensation bloomed through his body. He took one great gulp of air like some fish tossed on a bank, and as the shadows backed away, the curtain fell.

The lights were blinding bright when the world came back, but night had long since fallen. Ernie was on his side beneath a giant cross. He rolled onto his shoulder so as to look straight up to where the structure stretched some sixty feet above him. The cross was lined with fluorescent streetlights. Cyclone fence made a square around the base of the cross, and the top of the fence was strung with barbed wire. There were balsams nearby lit from the glow. He was on top of a mountain, and as he looked straight overhead there was only darkness above him.

Though it took him a while to realize, he was at Mount Lyn Lowry, the site of a memorial built by a couple who'd lost a teenage daughter to leukemia back in the sixties. Locals had always called it the Balsam Cross, and on a clear night that landmark could be seen from thirty miles away. For more than fifty years anyone driving that stretch of highway from Haywood to Jackson had seen those lights shining on the top of that mountain like a beacon.

Ernie's wrists were still bound behind him and his ankles were lashed together tightly, but the gag had been removed from his mouth. He could taste blood, but he was thankful to catch his breath and to be outside. Rolling about, he managed to get to his knees. At the foot of that cross he looked like some altar-call sinner kneeling at the front of a church. Whatever drug they'd used to subdue him had left him in a fog.

Right then twelve men appeared out of the wood line. They all wore robes that hung to the ground with tall pointed hoods hiding their faces. They came forward and Ernie shouted for them to take off their masks and show themselves, but none would utter a word. They approached in unison and in silence, their steps in perfect time like some death-knell drum line, and when they were close he could see chains and batons and tire irons held in their hands.

When the first blow came, he fell onto his side. He pulled his legs into his chest but his body opened out like an accordion as something heavy cracked his ribs. The pain came through him like a jolt of electricity and his eyes fired open, and for a second he stared at a pair of leather cowboy boots with wide squares as if they might have been made from the hide of a serpent. The foot drew back, and when the toe came forward it caught him just under his left eyebrow. That was the last thing he saw.

Without one word spoken, they beat him until there was nothing left.

25

A man named Curtis Darnell was the one who found the body. It was off a bank at the head of Dicks Creek. Earlier that spring, Curtis had seen a snake inside his house, and so all summer he'd been sleeping in the cab of his truck.

Some nights a chill would catch him and he'd crank the engine to keep warm, but the thing about it was, the floorboard was rusted out and the exhaust manifold leaked, so that on those mornings he sometimes woke up woozy and sick to his stomach and had to walk two miles of fresh air before he'd ever get his feet put back beneath him. That was what he said, anyhow, what he was doing when he found the body.

"First I seen it, I thought I was looking at a little bear cub been hit in the road," Curtis said. Even his brother said he was crazy as jizz on a light pole. "Way them legs tucked in under that log, I couldn't see the blue jeans till I got down in there."

The body was about thirty or forty feet down the bank and had settled on a lip of flat ground not much bigger than a sofa. What was strange was the way it had been covered. There were leaves kicked up over parts of the body, but then there were little round bits of moss that had been cut and patchworked together, most of the back and torso having been hidden in that way.

Leah Green had never seen anything like it. She'd made detective two months before and this was the first homicide she'd ever worked. For a long time she stood there on the edge of the road and stared down on the body, trying to soak up every detail. Off to the left there was a wash stripped to slick mud where Curtis Darnell, and later the deputy who'd first been called to the scene, had slid down the bank to get to the body. According to Curtis, there'd been no other tracks before him.

Leading down were a few places where the leaves were roughed like turkey scratch. They were spread farther apart than what anyone would expect as single lengths of stride, but as Leah knelt on one knee and tilted her head at an angle, she could see the right, left, right progression of footsteps. After those final steps the subject had fallen and skidded the last little bit, coming to rest against a log. What those details meant, though, was that this person hadn't been tossed off the bank postmortem. The feet wouldn't have come down that way, one after the other. This person was alive when they left the road and those were the last steps taken, or rather the last prayer for footing on a grade too steep to provide.

She stared, puzzled by the way those pieces of moss were placed so methodically, as if each chunk had been set as careful as cobble. That was the one thing that really threw her for a loop.

"You know what done that, don't you?" Curtis Darnell said as if he were somehow reading her mind. He stood there on the roadbed smoking a cigarette with one hand, his other hand resting on the small of his back so that his left arm bent like a folded wing. He squinted as if waiting for her to answer, but when she didn't he took a drag from his cigarette and blew a cloud of smoke straight above his head. "Bobcat. That's what put all that moss like that."

Leah stood up and pulled her hair back over her shoulders. She wore a navy business suit with a beige blouse, and it was just her luck that those were the clothes she'd thrown on that morning, only to be called to a scene like this. There was no way she could make it down the bank wearing slick-bottomed flats. Until a couple days ago she'd kept a pair of hiking boots in the trunk, but she'd taken them out over the weekend to do yard work and forgotten to put them back. Her only choice now was to go barefooted.

"I don't know if they trying to cover up the smell or they just trying to camouflage it so don't nothing else find it." Curtis walked over and stood beside her. He was tapping his foot against the gravel like he was keeping time with some song that played only for him. "All I know's that's what done that. Ain't nothing else on this mountain cover up the dead the way that's done. They odd creatures, bobcats," he said.

Off to the right, a tangle of grapevine spiraled up the hill toward the road, then climbed a dead-stand locust with shelf lichen covering the trunk from root to bough. Leah walked over and slipped off her shoes. She took off her jacket, folded it neatly, and set it on top of the shoes to try to keep the dust and dirt from ruining the fabric. Her blouse was sleeveless and her fair-skinned arms caught a chill as she tied up honey-blond hair into a doubled-over ponytail at the back of her head.

"You want a hand?" Curtis mashed his cigarette out on the gravel under his boot.

"No, you just stay put." Leah grabbed the grapevine and tugged a few times to test its strength. "We'll talk some more in a few minutes," she said. When she was confident the vine would support her weight, she pressed her heels into the soft ground and started down the bank as if rappelling with a length of rope.

"Shit, there you go," Curtis hollered. He doubled over and slapped his knee, completely enthralled by what was happening before him. "You tough, ain't you? That girl's mountain," he hollered, but Leah bit her tongue and went on.

She wished to God he'd shut up and go to his house. Truth was, the only thing out of the ordinary about what she was doing right then was those goddamn outfits the sheriff insisted his detectives wear. She was more cut out for briar britches and logging boots than prom dresses and church clothes.

When she was even with the body, she got situated and let go of the vine, but there was still enough angle to require her left leg to stay bent in order for her right to stretch straight and anchor her. Getting over to the body was less a matter of walking than just trying to stay upright, and she made her way slowly, grabbing ferns to steady her and studying the ground before each step so as not to disrupt the subtlest piece of evidence.

Now that she was close, she could see things more clearly, the legs bent and angled under the log as if sliding into a base on a ballfield, the blue jeans stained and slick with clay. One arm was tucked under the body and the other was stretched out straight. That outstretched arm was the only thing completely uncovered by leaves or debris, slender and dark brown, a hand clutching a fistful of dirt. The head lay on its side but there were leaves strewn over the top so that she could not make out a face, just leaves and black braids of hair.

"Norris," Leah hollered up the bank. "Norris!"

"Yeah," a voice answered from the road. She looked up, and the deputy who'd been called to the scene stood at the crest looking down on her and the body like a buzzard.

"Tell Sam to get his camera gear together and get down here. I don't want to touch anything until we get some pictures."

The deputy turned and disappeared from view, and Leah

glanced over to where Curtis Darnell stood near the grapevines she'd used to come down. He had both hands on the small of his back and he was rocking forward and back, toe to heel, toe to heel, with a curious and entertained look about his face.

"Curtis, why don't you go on back down to your house and I'll be there in a bit. We're going to be up here awhile."

"All the same to you, I think I'll stay right here. I ain't got nothing I got to get done. Nothing else on my plate at all. This here's better than TV."

"Curtis, I said get on back down to your house, now. This ain't something for you to stand around and gawk at." Leah said this as if she were disciplining a dog, and in a second he wandered off down the road toward home.

She turned to the body and watched the flies and yellowjackets bicker for places to light. Even without moving the leaves away, she knew who lay beneath them. A month ago she wouldn't have had a clue, but over the past few weeks that face had been all over newspapers and Live at Fives until anyone in the county could've made that ID from where she stood. Toya Gardner had been shot multiple times center mass.

For years Leah'd busted her ass, taken every shit detail thrown her way, because this was the job she wanted. All her career, this was the promotion she'd chased. Now, for the first time since she'd made detective, doubt crept in, a feeling that took hold like a cancer. Standing there, her legs trembled. She didn't know if she was up to the task. The ground was damp and cold underfoot and a shiver came through her. Goose bumps rose on her arms. She flexed her biceps and held them that way to try to warm up, but it was no use, and so she stood there shaking just the same, unable to tell whether that feeling was temperature or fear.

In a few minutes she was going to have to call the sheriff, and she didn't know how on earth she was going to tell him who they'd found. And if that weren't hard enough, by the end of the day, she'd have to notify the family. There was no amount of training that could prepare someone to deliver that kind of news. How could you soften the swing of a wrecking ball? There was no way to lessen the blow.

26

Pacing around the hospital waiting room, Coggins felt outside himself, like he was stumbling drunk through a dream. He hadn't slept more than an hour in two days. Not long after sunrise that morning a photographer had swung into a pull-off along the Blue Ridge Parkway to take a leak and found one of Coggins's deputies lying there in the parking lot beaten to within an inch of his life.

Ernie Allison had been dumped beneath a sign for the Confederate Veterans Memorial Forest, a 125-acre tract of land that had been planted with 125,000 balsam and spruce spaced at six-foot intervals to memorialize the number of soldiers North Carolina provided to the Confederacy during the Civil War. The forest was a jaunt from Jackson County, located at the southern end of neighboring Haywood near a craggy top known as Devil's Courthouse. That's where the photographer had been that morning, up on that rock face shooting the sunrise.

Medics had found Allison's department ID in his wallet and

realized he was a deputy, and that was why they'd called Coggins first. Allison wasn't married, didn't have any kids, but his mother and father were still alive and he had a brother drove a dump truck for an outfit in Tuckasegee. Coggins had known the whole family for as far back as he could remember, the boy's mother having been a schoolteacher at Smoky Mountain, his father a mechanic at the county maintenance shed. He'd already called them and they were on their way from Johns Creek, but it would be at least an hour before they made it to the hospital in Asheville.

There were three other people in the waiting room, a Hispanic mother who didn't speak English with two young boys, the kids restless and wrestling on the waxed tile floor. Coggins passed them and the woman averted her eyes as he glanced down, then walked to the wall and pressed his forehead against the painted cinder block. He let the coldness of the wall wake him up, stretched his eyes wide and blinked a few times to try to collect himself, but he was dog-tired and drained.

When he turned, a doctor was standing there in a white smock with a clipboard held in one hand at his side. He was a young, pale-faced man with thick black hair and round glasses, and he had this curious way of twitching his nose every few seconds as if he were about to sneeze.

"I'm Dr. Hoffman." He held out his hand but Coggins was so far back in his own mind that he just clambered around awkwardly. "I wanted to come give you an update."

"Okay."

"We've got him stabilized, but we're going to keep him under, probably for at least a few days, until we think we've got a better handle on everything. Right now being awake would do more harm than good."

"Okay," Coggins said. "So what about injuries?"

"Got a pen and paper?" the doctor joked, but Coggins just

stared at him blankly. "I'm sorry, but it's a long list." He looked at his clipboard. "Both wrists are fractured. He's got fractures in two lower ribs on his right side and those are pressing against his liver, but luckily there doesn't seem to be any organ damage there aside from some heavy bruising. He's got two ribs fractured on the other side, compressed vertebrae."

He spoke quickly and Coggins had a hard time following. There was so much information and he was so exhausted that all of it washed together into a garble of words he knew he wouldn't remember.

"There's a lot of damage to the face. Fractured orbital on his left side, a couple pretty bad cuts to the back of his head, but just a lot of swelling and bruising. There's some swelling and bruising on the brain as well, and that's something we're really concerned about. We've got to stay ahead of that.

"But his breathing is good. Heart rate, blood pressure, all of that is stabilized right now, and part of that is why we'll keep him under, so that we can control those things. I don't want to say we're out of the woods, but he's pretty lucky. Most of these injuries are skeletal and muscular, not anything life-threatening. That's not to say something couldn't change, and, like I said, we've got to keep a close eye on that brain swelling, but other than that things look pretty good."

"Can I see him?"

"Yeah, I think that will be fine. Just give me a minute and I'll take you back."

The doctor crossed the room and disappeared through a pair of double doors that swung like saloon doors in a western as they closed. Coggins leaned back and let the wall hold him upright. He angled his head so the crown of his skull came to rest against the block and stared up into the overhead lights until their brightness was all that existed. His mind was thoughtless and empty. His body was numb and his ears were ringing. Only when the doctor spoke his name did he break out of that trance. Coggins knew the man had spoken to him, but he hadn't caught what he'd said.

"What was that?"

"I asked if you're all right."

"Yeah, yeah, I'm fine," Coggins stuttered. He blinked his eyes and readjusted to the room. "Just tired's all."

"Are you sure? I'd be more than happy to sit down and take a look."

Coggins waved him off and followed the doctor down a hall, their footsteps echoing loud but lost amid the beeps and alarms and respirators droning a steady madness from glassed-off rooms where people lay still and dying. Every room they passed, he looked in and tried to soak up the details, but there was too much to absorb. The place was unnerving.

When they reached a room at the end of the hall, the ward opened up into a small reception area where nurses raced past to put out fires. The blinds were closed on the windows of the room but the door was open, and Coggins could see Ernie Allison lying there with tubes and lines running all over his body like a muss of fishing line.

"You can go in," Dr. Hoffman said, but Coggins didn't move. He stood there at the threshold, the room dimly lit and the ward a heavenly white light behind him so that it cast his shadow long across the floor. "You need anything, just talk to one of the nurses. All right? If it's not something they can help you with, they'll know where to find me."

When he finally stepped into the room, Coggins hovered at the bedside and studied the bruises and cuts on Allison's face. Allison looked like he'd had his head sent through a rock crusher. His left eye was swollen big as a plum with a dark cut through the purple marking the slit of his eyelid. There was a gash across his forehead that had been stitched closed and gauzed, but the bandage had lost its hold on one side and hung down over his right eyebrow. His entire face was surreal, nearly unrecognizable.

In this line of work, a man saw all sorts of things, and eventually he came to believe he'd seen it all. But if he'd been at it as long as Coggins, he'd come to know that there was no border, no grand finale, no ending or limit to the wicked of this world. There was always a darker darkness still.

As he stood there, his phone rang in his pocket. When he checked, it was Leah Green, a fireball deputy he'd made detective a few months before. As a deputy, she'd been instrumental in one of the biggest drug busts to ever happen in western North Carolina, and it was that role that had led to her promotion.

Before he could answer, someone shouted his name from down the hall. When he turned he realized it was Ernie Allison's mother, Clara, racing as fast as she could with her arms stretched before her. Sheriff Coggins stepped out of the room and braced himself. It would take every bit of strength he had to catch her.

27

Toya's body was taken to a state medical examiner in Asheville. Because this was a high-profile case, she'd likely be held a week or more for autopsy. Her mother drove straight from Atlanta as soon as Detective Green made the call, but she arrived too late to visit that night. Neither Vess nor her daughter slept. They curled together on the couch as if trying to keep each other warm.

Detective Green pulled up as daylight broke that next morning and drove them to the city. Vess didn't fully believe that any of this was real until they were standing there. Toya's body lay on a cold steel gurney with a white sheet draped up to the top of her chest. Bright fluorescents beamed against the white tile floor and reflected off the steel surfaces of cabinets so that standing in that room, Vess felt caught within some dreamlike glow. Vess's arms were wrapped around her daughter, her right arm around her waist, her left hand resting on Dayna's stomach. The light shone brightly on Toya's face, and her braids were pulled to her left shoulder.

The tears swept over them in waves, and while Vess paced the room, Dayna stood by her daughter and kept stroking her thumb down the side of Toya's face, following from her forehead along the curve of her jaw. Vess approached once and placed her hand on Toya's shoulder, but it was more than she could stomach. It felt so unnatural for all of that heat to be gone from her body. It felt as if she were holding her hand to a flame and feeling no warmth at all. She had to take a seat in the corner of the room to keep from falling over. The room was cold as an ice chest.

For nearly four hours they stayed, until the medical examiner told the detective they would have to leave. Dayna fought tooth and nail, but they finally convinced her that what came next was something she would want no part of, and at that moment a cold and stoic emptiness fell over her. On the ride back to Jackson County, Vess placed her hand on her daughter's leg. Dayna stared through the window with a pair of wide sunglasses shielding her eyes and she did not speak. She gazed at the mountains, at the way they rose and fell and rolled in one continuous and unending line as if she might've been crossing a body of water.

When they pulled onto the road that led to Vess's house, Vess could see a string of vehicles hugging the ditch just past her driveway. She and Dayna were in the backseat of Detective Green's car and Vess leaned toward the middle to get a better view through the windshield. There were vans with small satellites attached to the roofs, the logos of local news stations painted brightly on their sides. She couldn't believe they had come here, and as they pulled into the driveway Detective Green turned to them and said simply, "Just stay in the car and I'll take care of this."

"It's fine," Dayna said, and those words took Vess by surprise. That was the first thing her daughter had said in nearly two hours.

When they stepped out of the car there was an eerie and uncomfortable silence, dead air that felt heavy to wade through. Vess wrapped her arm around her daughter's waist and Detective Green stayed a few steps behind them as they made their way around the side of the house toward the back porch. A young female reporter finally spoke up, just a three-word question that stopped them all in their tracks. "Is it her?" she asked. And when no one answered, the rest of the chorus chimed in and the scene erupted into a chaotic chatter as if a group of starlings had descended upon them.

Vess quickened her steps, and when she reached the door she tried to wrangle her keys from her purse, her hands trembling, and as she slid the key into the lock she dropped the set to the porch. She felt panicked then and the tears welled up in her eyes. Suddenly her daughter's hand pressed gently into the small of her back and Dayna leaned down to pick up the keys. When she stood, she turned toward the crowd in the yard.

"You don't have to say anything to them," Detective Green said, but Dayna didn't so much as cut her eyes in the woman's direction.

She wore a dark black sleeveless dress and a pair of flats with straps that crisscrossed to just above her ankles. Her hair was cut short with a mid fade that surrendered at the tops of her ears. There was an unmistakable power and confidence in the way she walked, something defining and characteristic but that Vess found hard to imagine she could summon in that moment. When she reached them Dayna took her sunglasses from her face, folded them together, and held them at her chest, one finger pecking at one of the lenses, as she seemed to search for words. Her hands dropped to her sides when she found them.

"I'm not going to answer your questions," she said. Her eyes were turned to the ground. "I'm not going to make any sort of formal statement. But I'm going to tell you one thing." Dayna raised her eyes and stared them down as a whole.

"Look at where you're standing. You are standing here in my mother's yard uninvited. We didn't ask you to be here. We do not want you here." She paused. "I'm sure there are still plenty of folks you can lead around by the reins, but I can promise you one thing: I am not the one. I am not going to put up with it. Not now. Not tomorrow. Not ever. Now, if you have one speck of humanity or decency, then you will get back in those vans and you will leave this place."

The people before her looked as if they'd been gutted. They stood with mouths agape and their postures slumped as she turned and left them there.

When they were inside, Dayna walked to the kitchen sink and filled her hands with water. She splashed it against her face, did this again, each time stretching her eyes and taking as deep a breath as her chest could hold. Her hands gripped the edge of the countertop tightly and she looked as if she were about to collapse. That was the moment she broke. Her body crumpled and she melted to the floor. Her legs tossed and she leaned with her back against the cabinet, the water still running in the sink above her, and she let out a guttural cry that felt as if the house would cave in around them.

Vess rushed forward and dropped to her knees. She pulled her daughter to her chest and the two of them shook as a single body. Detective Green was by the door and she came beside them, kneeling down and placing her hand on Dayna's shoulder. Dayna's eyes snapped open when she felt her.

"I don't need you here in this house," she said through clenched teeth. "I need you out there tracking down whoever did this to my daughter." And as she muttered that sentence, the word *daughter* broke apart into a million pieces.

Detective Green left the house, and as the door eased closed and the sound of the screen door creaked behind it, Dayna rose to her feet and stormed off to what had once been her bedroom. She locked herself inside and Vess knew there was no point in chasing her.

Right then her daughter needed time and space, and those were perhaps the only two things Vess Jones could provide.

On the back porch, Vess found Detective Green standing in the yard staring off at the wood line. Above her shreds of clouds stacked together along the horizon and built into something bigger. A hard rain was going to fall. Vess came off the porch and when she reached the detective she stood beside her and turned her eyes to the mountains.

"I know I asked you this yesterday, Mrs. Jones, but is there anything at all you think might be helpful? Anyone you can think of I should talk to?"

"Like I told you, the only person Toya had any connection with here was a boy named Brad that she met up there at the school. I never met him. Just saw him a time or two when he came by to pick her up and give her a ride. Her car had been on the fritz. Think she'd blown a head gasket. But he come by a couple times and give her a ride different places. She climbed in the car with him and that's the last time I ever saw her."

Remembering that detail, the way her granddaughter had looked, how she'd pressed the charm Vess had given her that morning against her chest with the tips of her fingers, she felt that image settle onto her heart like a yoke.

"How did she know Brad?"

"She didn't," Vess said. "Or I mean, not until this summer. She went up there to the school to see about using some studio space while she was here. I think he helped her with that and they just sort of hit it off."

"Was there anything more to their relationship?"

"I don't think so. I think he might've liked her, but Toya, Toya didn't have time to fool with no boys." Vess paused. "There was this one afternoon, though, when the two of them seemed to be arguing in his car."

"You have any idea what about?"

"Not a clue," Vess said. "They were leaving. I never thought to ask anything about it and she never brought it up."

"Did he put his hands on her?"

"No. No, I don't mean it like that. I just mean they looked like they were bickering back and forth. But like I said, I was inside just looking through the window, so it could've been anything."

"Do you remember when that was?"

"Sometime last week, but I couldn't say for sure."

Vess stared blankly at Toya's broken-down SUV in the driveway. The whole summer rolled around in her mind and she tried to think if there was anything else she could put her finger on that might be of any help at all. Recalling the way her granddaughter had looked through the windshield that afternoon as the car backed out of the drive, she remembered something she'd wanted to ask a few hours before. "Was Toya wearing a necklace when you found her?"

"No, ma'am. I don't think so," Detective Green said.

"I'd given her an old necklace that belonged to my grandmother, something she gave me when I was about Toya's age. I gave it to her Saturday morning, Saturday morning—" She repeated the phrase but couldn't finish her thought. Instead, the last memory she held of her granddaughter got the better of her. She thought about how warm she'd been in her arms, the way Toya's braids had felt against her fingers as she'd traced them from the crown of her head down the length of her back.

"What kind of necklace was it, Mrs. Jones?"

"It was just an old silver chain with a diamond-shaped pendant about this big." Vess held up her fingers to indicate the size of the charm. "Was sterling silver, the back of it was, but it wasn't worth nothing. Not any money anyways. Can't imagine somebody taking it. There was a small piece of glass fitted into that silver setting and it laid overtop a lock of hair. My grandmother had given it to my grandfather when he left for the war."

"She wasn't wearing a necklace that I can remember, but if we find it I'll be sure to get it back." Detective Green felt around in her pocket and checked the time on her cell phone. "Before I forget, I've got something out in the car I'd like to give you."

Vess followed Detective Green back to the car and she leaned through the open window to grab something she'd left in the console. She held a small device out between them that looked like an old Walkman the kids had carried back in the eighties. "What's that?" Vess asked.

"It's a recorder," Detective Green said. "And I want you to keep that in there by the phone. Anyone calls with information, you could turn your phone on speaker and record the conversation, and if not you can just repeat it all back right after while it's fresh in your mind. Anything at all comes to you that you think might be helpful, anything, like the way you remembered that necklace, just hit record. No matter how little or unimportant you might think it is, you just hit those two buttons right there and it'll record everything you want to say. I put in a brand-new tape. Brand-new batteries."

Vess looked down at the recorder and the row of buttons. She was horrible with technology and didn't know whether or not she'd be able to make it work. "Those two buttons?"

"Yes, ma'am. Those two right there."

"Would it be okay if I just wrote it down?"

"Of course it would. Whatever's easiest for you. I just want to make it easy." Detective Green climbed into her car and started the engine. "In the meantime, if there's anything you need, you call me," she said. "You've got my number. Day or night, Mrs. Jones. Anything."

"There's one thing I would like to ask if that's all right."

"Name it," Detective Green said.

"You think you could ride me out to where you found her? I'd just like to . . ." She stopped, unsure how to explain exactly what she meant. "I'd just like to see it for myself is all." Vess wasn't entirely sure what she expected to find there, but she was certain she needed to see that place, that she needed to physically stand there.

"Of course I can, Mrs. Jones."

28

Standing in the curve of that road felt like déjà vu. That's what Vess Jones said when Leah took her to the place they'd found the body. Seventy-five years in that county, there were few places she hadn't stood at one time or another, so in that way of course it did. Leah asked if there was anything more, whether she could pinpoint any detail that might've made that spot significant, but the old woman just stood there on the gravel road and stared off with a disoriented look about her face. In the end, she said nothing else at all.

Bradley Roberts was easy enough to track down. The department head at the university had nothing bad to say, just that he mostly taught introductory art classes to freshmen and stayed at the kiln. He volunteered to open and close studio spaces at night, a responsibility no one else wanted, and overall he just didn't seem to have much of a life outside of school.

He agreed to meet Leah Green at the sheriff's office that afternoon and was already waiting in the interrogation room when she returned from lunch. Leah was nervous. This was the first interview she'd ever conducted on a murder investigation.

As a suspect, Brad Roberts checked all the right boxes. Vess had watched her granddaughter climb into his car that afternoon. She even remembered their having an argument. He was the last person seen with the girl when she was alive. Less than 9 percent of women were killed by strangers. It was almost always a crime of passion. Unrequited love was about as strong a motivation as a person could have, Leah thought, which was to say that the man who sat on the other side of that door might have very well been the one to have killed her.

He didn't look at all how she'd expected. For some reason, she'd thought he'd be smaller and less good-looking. Instead, throwing clay had toned the muscles in his arms. Brad Roberts was thick through the shoulders and wore a white undershirt that was stretched about the neck, the front spattered with specks of glaze. Raised veins traveled from his forearms up the fronts of his biceps. His hands were flat on the table, and when she came into the room he tossed a head of shoulder-length hair away from his face to look at her. Leah showed no expression and they just stared at each other blankly as she walked to the table and took a seat beside him.

The room was all block and carpet, both being similar shades of gray, the walls just slightly darker than the floor. It was a space purposefully devoid of color, put together to desensitize suspects over a period of time. You didn't want to give them things to look at or focus their attention on. You wanted them to stay inside themselves.

"Thank you for coming down, Mr. Roberts. I'm Detective Green." She slid a manila file folder onto the table in front of her and held out her hand. His grip was strong but he made no attempt to overpower her. "So you know why I've asked you to come down today?"

"I do," he said. "To help with the investigation."

"So you understand what happened to Toya?"

"Just what's been said on the news." Brad made a fist of his right hand and fit it inside his left to crack his knuckles. He had piercing green eyes and a face shaved clean to the hard lines of his jaw. "To be honest with you, none of this seems real."

"Let's start with how the two of you met," Leah said.

"We met earlier this summer. She emailed the department head—"

"Susan?" Leah interrupted. She wanted to make it clear that she'd already spoken with people who knew him.

"Yeah, Susan Blaylock, the department head. But Toya had emailed her about possibly using some studio space while she was here this summer and Susan copied me in to see if I thought we could accommodate her. The department's just sort of shoveled all the studio responsibility onto my plate. Think it's a headache for most of them, but I get a kick out of it. I like seeing what the kids are working on. I like being surrounded by that process. So I met with Toya at the Tea House down in Sylva and we talked. She told me what she was up to and I really dug what she was trying to do. We didn't have anything big to offer really, but there was a small space a graduate student had been using who'd just graduated in the spring. They'd emptied the place out and no one was going to be using it until this fall, so we set her up in there to work."

"Her grandmother said you'd been spending a good bit of time together. That you'd been giving her rides."

"Yeah, her SUV was shot. Not that my car's much better." He took a deep breath and swelled his cheeks as he exhaled with his eyes spread wide. "But, yeah, I gave her a ride when I could. Mostly just back and forth to the school. She was bad to want to walk home late at night by herself."

"And the two of you rode together to the courthouse the afternoon of the protest?"

"Yeah, I picked her up at her house—"

"What time?"

"I don't know." Brad squinted and looked overhead toward the ceiling as if trying to remember. "One. Maybe one thirty. Everything was supposed to get started around two, I think."

"Did you pick anyone else up on the way?"

"No, it was just the two of us."

"What did you talk about?"

"Nothing really. She just kept changing the station on the radio and laughing about how nothing came in up here."

"And did you give her a ride home afterward?"

"No," Brad said. "When the fighting broke out I looked around and she was gone. The cops started putting people in handcuffs and we got the hell out of there. I figured she'd caught a ride with someone else."

"Who else would've given her a ride?"

"I thought maybe one of the people we were with. There were a handful of us who'd helped her dig the graves up there at the school."

"But none of those other people remember seeing her?"

"No," Brad said. "And I've spoken with all of them. Most of us actually met up for a beer at the taproom in Dillsboro, and nobody remembered seeing her. I called her a dozen times and it just kept going straight to voicemail. Tried texting."

"And can you give me a list of the names of those other people, maybe their phone numbers?"

"Absolutely," he said.

"And what about after that?"

"I ran by my apartment and grabbed a quick bite to eat and then I went to the school. I was at the studio until about midnight, same as always."

"Was anyone there with you? Or are there any sort of records of that?"

"Yeah," he said. "I mean, we keep sign-in sheets. I can't remember if there was anybody who came in to work that night or not. I was throwing clay. But there're sign-in sheets. And I'm sure the housekeeper will remember me being there. A lot of times it's just me and her."

It was good that he had an alibi that could be fact-checked, but there was still the issue of motive. "Toya's grandmother thought that maybe you'd had a thing for Toya, and that maybe she hadn't felt the same way you did. Is there any truth to that?"

"I mean, yeah." Brad chuckled. "She was gorgeous and she was smart and she was funny and talented. Of course I liked her. How could you not?" Brad ran the tips of his fingers across the knuckles of his opposite hand, making a low and irritating washboard sound. "I asked her out, I don't know, maybe a week or two into the summer."

"And what did she say?"

"She slugged me in the arm like I was her brother or something." Brad grinned and dropped his head. "Always called me 'White Boy.'"

"How did that make you feel? I mean that you liked her that much and that she didn't feel the same, that it was just sort of a joke to her?"

"What are you asking exactly?"

"I'm asking how it made you feel."

"Are you asking if it made me angry? You think I'd have done something like this because she didn't want to hook up?"

"Look, this isn't personal, Mr. Roberts. We're following every lead we have and we're asking these same types of questions of everyone we talk to."

"Well, no. It didn't make me angry. Not at all. After that we were friends and I knew that's all it was ever going to be and that was plenty. It was an honor just to be around somebody like that."

"What do you mean *like that*?"

"That talented. Somebody who thought about things the way she did."

"Do you own a gun, Mr. Roberts?"

"No," he said, seeming almost irritated by the question. "Of course not. I've never even shot one."

"Where'd you grow up?"

"I went to high school in Hendo."

"And you've never fired a gun in your whole life?"

"Look, my parents moved here from Seattle. My dad teaches poetry at UNCA. My mom owns a fucking health food store and teaches yoga. I didn't exactly grow up with NRA stickers on the back glass of our minivan. We were a Local Food, Jerry-Bear family. I was raised by a couple hippies who were forty years late on the whole back-to-the-land movement."

"Her grandmother mentioned something about an argument."

Brad's face twisted. "I'm not sure what she's talking about." He tapped his fingers against the table. "Did Toya mention something to her?"

"It was more something she remembered seeing one afternoon when the two of you were in the car."

For a second he seemed to be racking his brain for what she might've meant, then his expression eased and he nodded. "Okay, yeah. She probably saw us that Friday, the afternoon before the protests, but we weren't really fighting. Wasn't anything really."

"What was it exactly? What were the two of you arguing about?"

"I wouldn't even say we were arguing. It was just that she didn't want to go the protest and I thought she ought to be there."

"And why did you think that?"

"Because she was the reason people were going. It was her work that brought those people out, and if the county gets off its ass and finally does something about that statue, it'll be her work that made that happen. Eventually she caved. Called the morning of and told me she was going to go, that it was because of me." Brad's eyes got wide. "Jesus," he said. "If I had it to do over, I don't know that I'd tell her to go."

"And why's that?"

"What do you mean why? It was those people who did that to her."

"What makes you think that, Mr. Roberts?"

"Because who else would've done something like that? Who the fuck else would've had that much hate in their heart to do something like that?"

The heaviest card she held was still in her hand. Leah placed her palm on the folder on the table. She wanted to show him a couple photographs from the crime scene just to judge his reaction. She knew it was a bulldog move that could go either way. His response might show the chink in his armor, might open up something vulnerable. But if he had nothing to do with what had happened, she would be forcing him into something traumatic. Pictures like the ones in that folder had a way of sticking with you, of bubbling back to the surface the rest of your life. She knew that firsthand.

"I'd like to show you a couple photographs," she said.

"Of what?"

"Of Toya. I'd like to show you a couple pictures so that you know what happened to her. Would that be all right?"

"No." Brad looked disgusted and shook his head. He brushed his hair back behind his ears. A sickle-shaped strand fell back across his forehead. "If it's all the same, I don't want to see a picture of what happened to her."

"Why?"

"What do you mean why? Because I don't want to see something like that." He shifted in his seat and folded his arms across his chest. "I don't want to see what happened to her. It's morose. Why would anybody want to see that? I'd rather remember her just the way she was. Goofy and laughing. Always singing. That's how she was, even on the ride downtown, and that's the way I'd prefer to remember her."

Leah couldn't help but feel that what he was saying was sincere. Of course, someone capable of killing would likely be capable of bearing the lie, at least for a spell, until the weight gnawed them in two. Still, he had an alibi, and it wasn't just some I-went-home-and-played-video-games bullshit. There were leads she could follow to fact-check. He had names and numbers. He had people he'd been with and documents placing him somewhere else at the time.

"Do you think we could get those sign-in sheets from the school?"

"Absolutely," he said. "We can ride over there right now." Brad kept staring at the folder on the table and Leah moved it to her lap.

"Let's do that," she said. Leah stood from the table and walked to the door. She held the door open for him to pass so that she could follow him down the hall, but when he reached the threshold he stopped and spoke.

"Would you like to see it?"

"What's that?" She thought she must've missed part of what he'd said, because she wasn't certain what he was referring to.

"Would you like to see it?" he repeated.

"See what?"

"What Toya was working on all summer. Do you want to see? I don't know that there'd be anything helpful in there, but—"

"Yeah," Leah said as she shut off the lights and pulled the door closed behind them. "Absolutely."

29

The walls were crowded with photographs. The studio where Toya had spent the summer working might've been eight by twelve, and not even the ceiling had been left uncovered, so that standing there, the images were too much to take in at once.

Leah focused on the left-hand wall. There were mostly black-and-white photographs of buildings and large groups of people. A few of the places she recognized. There was the old River View Baptist Church with its oddly shaped veneer and steeple, the tops of windows triangular panes that matched the shape of the soffit vents at the eaves. The building still stood off North River Road and most folks nowadays didn't even know that it had ever been a church, just a dilapidated shell surrendered to time and kudzu.

There were photos of other churches as well, Liberty and Zion and one she couldn't recognize, for it had burned down in the early eighties when she was still too young to remember. There were groups of people cooking and laughing, couples standing beside cars, families lined up together with low brows and stoic expressions, a crowd of more than a hundred gathered along a creek for a baptism.

When she turned to the right-side wall there were a dozen or so photographs, all of the same woman. They were printed different sizes and collaged together so that one ran straight into the next, some overlapping. In one photograph the woman smiled. In another she was resigned. The full range of human emotion was captured within the series, the laughing, the crying, the depth of things. The wall straight ahead had a window at its center that lit the darkened room with a disorienting light. Around the window the same photographs of the woman were repeated, but here they were cropped in tight so that only the smile or only the eyes filled the entire frame. A small desk made an elbow with a longer table that stretched the length of that wall.

The table was covered with blocks of something that looked like chunks of soapstone or chalk, each about the size and shape of a football split lengthways so that they sat there like flipped boats. Leah walked over to the table and when she looked down, the girl's face was there in a block of plaster, a series of expressions captured like death masks. Seeing Toya's face took her by surprise.

"What is this?" Leah asked.

"This is what Toya'd been working on. This was going to be her thesis."

"But what is it?" she asked again.

Brad brushed past Leah and picked one of the casts up from the table. He ran his hand along the outside as if he were tracing the rim of a bowl.

"All of these photographs come from Jackson County," he said. "And the series here on this wall, this is her great-grandmother. Mrs. Jones's mother. Bird. What she was trying to do was capture these expressions. There are ten in all and she worked all summer trying to get these molds right. We had the process pretty much dialed in by the end. She hadn't talked to her grandmother about it yet, but the plan was to do the same thing with her mother and grandmother so there'd be this series of three generations, four generations if you include the photos, of the same bloodline and the same expressions."

Leah was having a hard time following what he tried to explain. It was so conceptual, and her brain had never worked like that. She was tactile. She was numbers and facts. "So what was she going to do with them?"

"Well, that's the thing." Brad set the cast back on the table and stared out the window with an odd smile on his face. "Early in college, she was a ceramicist like me, and so I'd been trying to convince her that she didn't need to do anything else, that she could glaze these like they were, or maybe work them onto vessels and kind of follow out that whole mountain tradition of face jugs, have a whole series lined out." He chuckled. "She thought that was the dumbest thing she'd ever heard. She actually told me that. 'That's dumb, White Boy.' So I just shut up and listened." He laughed.

"So what was her plan?"

"She was going to cast them in bronze. She was going to make this massive sculpture and cast it all in bronze. Had this crazy idea of repurposing an old monument. Getting a town to take down a statue like Sylva Sam and melt it down and recast it as something new."

"And you really think she could've done that?"

"Absolutely. I mean it might not have been the statue here but she'd have found somebody willing to buy into what she was doing. She had a way of thinking and talking. You just couldn't say no to the girl." He searched around the table and found a large sketchpad where Toya'd drawn out what she had planned. "I mean she was tracing the ancestry of where she came from and who she came from, but it was bigger than that. She was tracing the lineage of emotion, like something as subtle and essential as a smile."

Leah leaned against the table and studied the molds carefully. She followed each up to the wall and matched the expressions to the photographs that had inspired them. When they came together and the image slowly developed, she was awestruck by how beautiful and powerful an idea it was. Tracing the tips of her fingers across one of the casts, Leah closed her eyes and focused entirely on the ridges of her nose and cheekbones and lips. She found it hard to breathe right then.

"You see now why I didn't want to look at your pictures." When he spoke, it shattered that short-lived trance that had fallen over her. Brad reached onto the table and picked up one of the plaster casts.

Toya's eyes were squinted and raised into crescents by her cheeks, her smile spread wide in an expression that seemed to somehow carry sound.

"She was beautiful." His voice cracked as he said it, and when he looked at Leah there were tears in his eyes. "All I know is that she was beautiful. And when I say that I mean it in the deepest sense of the word. There are very few people ever born with a mind like that."

30

On the other side of Moody Bridge a road cut off to the right to follow the river back toward Caney Fork. Purple martins swept the air above the water, and along a seam of current midstream Coggins thought he saw a trout rise to feed. This stretch had always fished well, though it was too hot right then for a man to do much of anything.

Tim McMahan lived on a pretty piece of property just above the road with a modular home on a painted block foundation. There were no shade trees and the sun beat down on his freckled back as he poured a quart of motor oil into the little red Mazda he'd driven forever. When he was done, he wiped his hands on a grease-stained rag and shook a couple belts to make sure they were tight. He didn't hear Coggins pull up or see him come across the yard.

"Is it burning oil?" McMahan flinched as Coggins spoke. The sheriff stepped up to the open engine compartment and peered in.

The tiny four-cylinder looked like it might've come off a lawn mower or go-kart.

"No . . . no, it's not burning oil," McMahan stuttered. He had his hair trimmed high and tight, a thinning carrot top on its last leg. "There something I can help you with, Sheriff?"

"I guess you heard what happened to Ernie Allison."

"No, sir. Can't say that I have." McMahan unhooked the prop rod and let the hood down gently. When there were two or three inches to go, he dropped the hood and let the weight slap it closed. He turned then and rested against the front of the truck so that he was facing the sheriff while they spoke. "Wait, do you mean what happened between him and Nick Lovedahl? I did hear—"

"No, that's not what I'm talking about."

"Then, no, sir. I don't know what you mean."

Coggins found it hard to believe he hadn't seen the story on one of the local stations or heard it from someone around town. The whole county was abuzz with what had happened to Ernie and Toya. "Two mornings ago a fellow on the parkway found Ernie beaten within an inch of his life."

"What are you talking about?"

"Guy pulls into a parking lot to take a leak and finds Ernie laying there with his brains stomped out. You not got a TV in that house? You not watch the news?"

"I've been out of town, Sheriff. Had a couple days off and took the kids up Hazel Creek to camp and fish a little bit before school started. Just got home this morning."

Coggins glanced at the front door, where three or four fishing rods were leaned against the railing. A tackle box sat on the porch.

"Is he okay?"

"They don't really know," Coggins said. "They've got him stable. But there's some swelling on the brain."

"Shit, Sheriff. I had no idea."

"Well, that's what brings me over here."

"I'm sorry?" McMahan phrased this as a question.

"Ernie told me you and him had a little bit of a row the other week at the gas station. I was thinking you might be able to tell me what that was about."

"You want to go in the house and get out of this heat?" McMahan wiped the sweat from his forehead. His shoulders were red and sunburned. "Think the wife's got some tea in the fridge."

"This won't take long," Coggins said. "Just wondered if you could tell me what the two of you were arguing about."

"Wasn't nothing, really. He'd helped out on an arrest. Guess he just didn't like the way it was handled. Thought we should've done things differently. That's all."

"That's not exactly how he put it." Coggins was feeling him out. "The way Ernie told me, the two of you'd found something in that car."

The color left McMahan's face. "I don't know what you're talking about, Sheriff."

"I think you do. I think you know exactly what I'm talking about. And the thing is, where Ernie wound up makes me think those two things might be connected. Matter of fact, I'd about lay a bet that where he wound up had something to do with that notebook y'all found in that car, the one that just up and disappeared."

"What do you mean where he wound up?"

"He was found at the Confederate Veterans Memorial Forest. That doesn't seem like some accident. That seems like a message, don't you think? So what I'm saying is I believe he'd spilled the beans on some folks that didn't like having their names thrown around."

The gravity of what the sheriff was saying came down on McMahan like a felled tree. His face went slack and he looked scared to death. The door on the house opened and a little boy about four or five years old poked his head onto the porch.

"Mama said to tell you lunch is ready," the child said to his father, but he was staring right at Coggins. The sheriff smiled and the boy dropped his head and covered his grin with his hand.

"Tell her I'll be there in just a minute."

The boy ducked back into the house and the door slammed closed. Cicadas were wailing from the trees along the river. There was no air stirring at all.

Tim McMahan walked over to the porch and grabbed a T-shirt and ball cap that were hung on the landing newel of the front steps. He slipped into the shirt and ran his hand across the top of his head to clear the sweat before placing the cap.

McMahan had taken a seat on the steps and the sheriff inched closer so that he was standing directly over him when he spoke. "You know, it's like that old saying goes. Evil triumphs when good men do nothing, or something along them lines." Coggins shoved his right hand into his pants pocket and jingled his keys. "Now, I'm not here because I think you had something to do with what happened to Ernie. I'm here to find out why you lied about that notebook and those names. You've got a chance to do what's right. And all I want to know is what you found and who told you to cover it up."

McMahan stared vacantly into the yard as he started to speak. He never once looked at the sheriff while he explained what had gone on that night, how they'd gotten a call about a drunk-and-disorderly outside Harold's and how when he arrived he found the stranger asleep in the car. He told Coggins about what they'd found during the search, about the robe and the notebook and the gun.

And as Tim McMahan confirmed everything Ernie'd told him that day in the office, the sheriff's mind wheeled to those names he'd shared.

"I got off that next morning and about midday I got a call from my lieutenant wanting me to come back down to the station. Didn't say what it was about and there'd been rumors floating around about layoffs, and so I was afraid it had something to do with that. But when I got down there he told me the man I'd arrested the night before had been released and that the charges had been dropped. Didn't say why and at first I thought I'd done something wrong, but he said he'd read through my report and just wanted me to know it was nothing I'd done.

"Now, I hadn't put anything in the report about what we found in the car except for the gun since the rest of it wasn't taken into evidence, but I did mention it to another officer at shift change and I guess that had gotten back to my lieutenant. He told me not to mention it again. Said from that point forward, it hadn't happened."

"And that didn't seem odd to you?"

"Of course it did. I kept thinking about the chief's name and phone number being on that list, but what was I going to say? Like it or not, that's who I work for. And that was my commanding officer telling me to forget it."

Coggins didn't answer.

"Look, Sheriff, I knew something was off, but I got two little ones running around that house and another on the way this fall. This is about the only line of work there is anymore with good benefits, at least the only one I'm cut out for. Maybe I could get on with the county or go work shit hours at the paper mill, but I like what I do. I enjoy the work and I enjoy helping people."

"Did he happen to mention who'd told him to call you in?"

"What do you mean?"

"I mean I'm assuming this order came down the chain of command, so when your lieutenant told you this, did he happen to mention why?"

"No," McMahan said. He dug a can of Copenhagen out of his pocket and packed the box but didn't take a dip. "I assumed it had to do with Holt. I mean, the chief's name was the one we'd seen. Pretty obvious why he'd want to keep that under wraps."

"Can you think of anything else, something he might've said or any other names that might've stuck out that night?"

"No, sir." McMahan shook his head. He opened the tin of tobacco and pinched a wad of long-cut between his fingers. "You don't really think the chief could've been involved with what happened to Ernie?"

"I don't have a clue, son," Coggins said. "But until Ernie wakes up we don't have much to go on. So like I told you, I don't think him laying where they found him was any sort of coincidence."

McMahan loaded his lip with tobacco and pushed it to the side of his jaw with his tongue. He stared off at the river as if in deep contemplation.

"You think of anything else, you give me a call, all right?"

"I will, Sheriff." McMahan rose and held out his hand but Coggins had already turned for his truck. "Sheriff," he called when Coggins was halfway across the yard.

The sheriff stopped.

"If you ever have an opening, I sure would like the chance to work for you."

Something about his having the gall to say that right then hit Coggins the wrong way. The sheriff marched back across the yard so that what he said next would not be taken in jest.

"You know, I'm usually pretty good about reading folks, Tim, but I've been wrong a time or two. I've made some mistakes and took some chances on folks I probably shouldn't have," Coggins said. "But you give a man enough time and he'll almost always show you who he is. Sometimes it'll surprise you."

McMahan had a dumb expression as he tried to decipher what the sheriff meant, but Coggins wanted there to be no confusion.

"Thing is, Tim, you've already shown me who you are." Coggins stared him down until McMahan averted his eyes. "I wouldn't be expecting no phone call. That's what I'm saying."

31

Nearly two hundred people gathered downtown for the candlelight vigil. Everyone from Zion, her close friends, and a dozen or so other familiar faces she recognized from Liberty Baptist had come, but most of the crowd was comprised of people Vess did not know. Some were dressed in dark clothes, as if attending a wake, others looking as if they'd just come from work or home or simply broken away from whatever lives they led to be here. There were solemn looks on their faces and they stood there in silence as if waiting for direction.

They were gathered where the protest had taken place. Five chairs faced the crowd and a podium and microphone were set off to the left. The sheriff sat on one end with an empty seat beside him. He'd been with the family all day, and though he was not the type to show emotion, he'd seemed on the verge of tears from the moment he walked in her house. Coggins was dressed in a dark suit with a white shirt and red tie. He was hunched forward with his elbows on his knees, blank-faced as he stared straight off toward the other end of town with eyes bloodshot and tired. Vess sat with her daughter on one side and her best friend, Lula Shepherd, on the other. The reverend was at the podium, nearly finished now with his address.

He was a young minister in his mid-forties named Carson Tillman. His hair was rippled into waves and it shone like black water in the streetlights. His beard was trimmed close and lined up with hard edges, everything cut straight and sharp as if he'd just stepped out of the barber's chair. Carson carried a slight grin at all times, the wheels constantly turning in his dark eyes. Most days he wore a pair of slacks, a white dress shirt, and a checked wool vest, but rarely a tie. He kept his collar loose and on Sunday mornings he sang with one of the most beautiful voices Vess had ever heard.

She felt a hand touch her own and without turning she knew it was Lula. Lula Shepherd wore a teal skirt that hit her just below the knee with a dark green jacket and a hat that matched the skirt. A heavy gold necklace hung low to mid-chest and stood bright against her black blouse.

Lula'd been sitting beside Vess for years, every Sunday at church, across the table as her partner in spades when both of their husbands were still alive and they'd gather to play cards on Friday and Saturday nights. Vess turned and looked at her best friend and it struck her how old she looked—the wrinkles, the slight slump in her shoulders as her posture fell, the tissue-paper skin of her hands. They were only three months apart in age and it hit Vess then how old she must've looked as well.

Nowadays, Vess and Lula made up one-third of the congregation at church most Sundays. Once there'd been nearly a hundred people filling the pews, but they were lucky if six to ten showed anymore. For the most part, the children had moved away, some by choice, others priced out by rural gentrification and a lack of job opportunities. Regardless of how they'd left, Vess and Lula represented the last of a generation, that generation the last of this community. When they were gone, that would be that, a way of life and a people blinking out like a meteor.

When the reverend finished speaking, he took his seat between the sheriff and Dayna. He rolled the papers he carried into a small bat, leaned back, and crossed his legs. Dayna stood and slowly approached the podium. They'd told her she didn't have to speak, that she didn't have to come if she didn't want to, but she'd been insistent that if people were gathering in her child's name, then she would be there.

Most times she wore dark clothes, pantsuits and drab pencil skirts. She'd said you didn't want to pull attention in the courtroom, that you wanted the evidence and argument to stand for themselves. But this evening she wore a sleeveless tangerine blouse and a pair of high-waisted slacks that fit tight at the hips, flowed loose over her legs, and cinched down into cuffs at her ankles. The pants were a light, oat-colored hemp fabric that seemed to float as she walked. This was an outfit Toya had put together, and it showed. Dayna was bright as a Turk's-cap lily standing there before the crowd.

"While I sat and listened to Reverend Tillman I didn't know exactly what I was going to say or if I was going to say anything at all, and the truth is I still don't know what to say. But one thing I'm touched by is the fact that so many of you, probably most of you, didn't know my daughter at all. And yet here you are. You are here, and that is a testament to who she was. That's a testament to her and the power she had over others. You could not stand beside that girl, you could not be in the same room and breathe the same air, and not feel her presence. Toya carried that kind of energy all her life. She was a fire, and to be around her was to feel that heat in your bones.

"So what I've decided I want to do tonight is to tell you about her so that you might leave this place having gotten to know her a little better." Dayna placed her palms on the top of the podium. She looked up into the sky for a moment before she continued. The sun was nearly down, so that the horizon along the ridgeline was rim-lit white and transitioned to blue, then darker, the first stars just beginning to pierce the night above them. They stood in the glow of streetlamps that had just flicked on and buzzed as the bulbs warmed inside their rippled glass globes.

"Everyone's heard or asked this question before, I'm sure," she said. "You ask a child what they want to be when they grow up and you're liable to hear anything. I had a little boy tell me one time he wanted to be a stripper." A few in the crowd got tickled and Dayna briefly smiled. "But soon as Toya could talk, she wanted to be an artist. That's what she said. And the difference between her and most kids is that she became exactly that. It was as if she knew from the very beginning what she was sent here to do, like it was a calling . . ."

Her words trailed off as a large dually Dodge diesel with tinted windows came roaring up the road from Dillsboro. A pair of flags rattled and whipped behind it, one secured to each side of the tailgate. The truck was revving its engine loudly, so that Dayna was forced to hold off. She stared down at the podium and slowly rocked from side to side, biting her lip and waiting for the moment to pass. Vess struggled to read what was written on one of the flags as the truck slowed behind a line of traffic caught at a light.

It was an American flag with a cross centered between two assault rifles, the words GOD, GUNS, TRUMP written along the top and bottom. On the other side, the stars and bars fell limp. The traffic light turned and the driver floored it to cast a cloud of black smoke into the air and over the crowd. In a moment, the truck was gone and the crowd lumbered and whispered for a few seconds before falling quiet. Vess wasn't sure her daughter would say anything else, but in a moment Dayna picked up where she'd left off as if nothing had happened at all.

"I remember the day I had her and the doctor laid her in my arms for the very first time. He looked at me and said, 'There's something special about this child,' and at the time I figured that was something he told every mother whose baby he delivered, but the more time's gone on, the more I don't think that's what it was at all. I think he meant it. I think he felt the very same thing every one of you standing here tonight felt. She was special. She was a fire and you couldn't help but want to stand close—"

All of a sudden the diesel was upon them again. The driver had circled the block. There was no red light now but the truck stopped beside the crowd and revved its engine until the air popped and cracked like firecrackers, each time bellowing smoke from a basketball-sized tailpipe as the turbo crescendoed and whined. The crowd covered their faces with their hands. They shielded their eyes and ducked their noses inside their shirts so as not to breathe or be blinded by the exhaust.

The sheriff pushed up to his feet and stormed forward, but Vess did not see this, for her mind was blank and humming. The old woman slipped off her shoes. She took her earrings from her ears and set them on the ground and folded the chair she'd been sitting in so that she could carry it with her. She glanced down at Lula Shepherd, who sat with her legs crossed and her hands folded in her lap, an expression on her face as if she could see the future.

When Vess passed the sheriff, he tried to grab ahold of her shoulder but she yanked away, dismissing him the same as everyone else around her, and that fast there were people between them so that all he could do was scream after her. Vess never heard a word, and as she came upon the truck the engine thundered and she reared back and swung with all of her might into the side glass, and when the chair struck it was like watching a stick of dynamite. The window exploded and the glass shattered and fell like sand. Right then the only sound was the ringing in her ears.

She looked into the cab, where two teenage boys cowered slack-jawed, both scared shitless and silent. All of a sudden it hit her, what she'd done, her mind having been utterly empty until then. Her shoulders slumped and the chair clanked against the blacktop when it fell. The driver couldn't have been more than sixteen, and as they watched each other his face turned ghostly white and he looked as if he might cry. Vess was so worked up she couldn't breathe.

"Jesus, Vess." The sheriff placed his hand on her arm, and the second he touched her she nearly fainted.

The crowd started to shift and move and chatter behind her, the diesel still rattling at idle, and all of it became too much right then, so that her legs could no longer hold her. Vess tripped a few steps backward, and when she reached the curb she collapsed with her legs folded beneath her, the world awash and blurred. It had been ages since she'd felt that sort of rage.

32

The road snaked across broken pasture, small fields of broomstraw and hay threaded together by tractor trails cut through big timber. Through the years the place had proven all but impossible for both farmers and the cattle they kept. The Cogginses had lived here in the Savannah community of Jackson County for six generations where Cowee surrendered a sliver of its grade to laurel hells and rock bluffs.

Joe-pye and goldenrod bowed along the ditch line, the weeds swaying briefly as Leah's car shot past and the dust swirled up in her wake. The town had taken a couple days to deliver the body cam footage from the protests. To be honest, it wasn't much help. The nice thing was that the cameras were linked, so that as soon as one officer's started recording, every officer on scene went live. The problem, though, was that the place had been too crowded, too close quarters and chaotic, to make sense of much. What *was* captured was Coggins coming down the stairs at the last second ahead of the crowd.

A camera on a nearby bank building captured the rest of the story. It was angled back up the street so that it looked right at the fountain, where the fight had broken out. Sheriff Coggins stood between both groups, and the moment the mob poured off that hillside he took off ahead of them like he was running from an avalanche. When he reached the bottom of the stairs, he fought through bodies and disappeared among them, and then the two crowds melded together into one pulsing swarm that was impossible to pick apart. But as the protestors thrashed, the sheriff emerged with Toya Gardner thrown over one shoulder. He carried her away from the riot to safety, and when they were clear, he let her down and the two disappeared left of frame up Keener Street.

Leah played the segment of video a dozen times—zooming in, slowing it down, panning out. The details were unmistakable. Later, when she played the footage from the *Sylva Herald* webcam down the street, Coggins's pickup appeared, and as it passed she could make out someone in the passenger seat beside him. The angle of the footage made it difficult to say with any certainty, but it looked like she was with him. Coggins was the last known person to be with Toya Gardner while she was alive.

The sheriff lived in a long one-story brick rancher that ran across a shelf on a hill. The driveway came around the front of the home, as there was no room behind, the pitch as steep as a mule's face. A short set of steps came off the front porch, and as Leah pulled past she saw Coggins's wife beating the dust from a rug with a broom. There was a small barn around the other side of the house with a gravel lot in front, and this is where she parked.

Coggins's wife, Evelyn, had on a pair of Key overalls with the legs rolled halfway up her shins. She was barefooted and wore a T-shirt beneath with sleeves that cut hard angles just below her shoulders. Her arms were tanned the color of cork.

"Goodness gracious. Is that Leah Green?" She had a smile as big as Memphis. "Let's go in the house," she said. "There's been yellowjackets swarming all day. This time of year it's like they lose their minds."

In the kitchen she made them a pot of coffee and they played catch-up, neither having seen the other in a great length of time. They swapped gossip about people they knew. She told Leah how Jerry Watson had been caught cheating on his wife, and Leah told her how Watson's wife had been caught stealing meat at the Ingles. She'd shoved a whole chuck roast under her dress and tried to keep it clamped between her thighs. The manager said she'd waddled down the aisle like a penguin.

They both laughed and sipped their coffee. Coggins was nowhere around.

"Other night he come home after all that mess at the hospital with Ernie and he'd bought a bottle of scotch." Evelyn paused and stared at Leah with a look of concern. "Leah, he hasn't drank a drop in almost thirty years."

"There's a lot on his plate right now, Mrs. Coggins."

"I know there is. And seems like there's more of it every day. I guess you heard what went on last night, heard about Vess breaking the glass out of that boy's truck."

"I was there." Leah almost laughed as she remembered the look on that kid's face when he stepped out of the truck. "You ask me, he got what he had coming."

"I don't disagree, but all I know's John was up half the night trying to talk that boy's father down from pressing charges. Finally got him to agree to just let her pay for the damages and call it square."

"Hell, I bet his daddy bought him that truck." Leah couldn't have cared less about that kid or his father, but she did understand the stress the sheriff was under.

"And now he's got Reverend Tillman stirring things up."

Leah wasn't sure what Evelyn was talking about. "I haven't heard anything about that."

"He's planning a march downtown. Trying to get media coverage. And I mean, I know his heart's in the right place, but I don't understand why anybody would want to make this thing any bigger than it already is. What good is that going to do? Just one more thing for John to have to worry about."

All of this was news to Leah and she wanted to know more, but right then didn't feel like the time to press for details. Instead, she tried to steer the conversation elsewhere. "Look on the bright side, Mrs. Coggins. Won't be long before he retires and the two of you can do whatever you want. He won't have to deal with any of it anymore. Be somebody else's problem."

"Drive each other crazy's what we're likely to do." She wrapped her hands around her coffee mug and watched something through the window over the sink. "When we first got married and he was running patrol, he was bad to drink. He always handled it fine, but as soon as he come through that door he expected me to have him one poured and waiting." She took a sip of coffee and continued. "When he made up his mind he wanted to make a run at sheriff, he put it down and ain't touched it since. Best thing ever happened to him."

"Probably just all the stress right now," Leah said. "Probably just falling back on old habits because he don't know how else to cope."

"I think it's the not sleeping. He'll go days not sleeping," she said. "Other night when he got to drinking was the first time I've seen him sleep hard in I don't know when. Was like watching a bear." She laughed, and the screen door slammed at the front of the house. "Speaking of . . ."

Coggins stopped at the entryway into the kitchen. He looked surprised to find Leah sitting there. "Green. What brings you up this way?"

"Had something I wanted to talk with you about."

"Well, all right," he said. "Just give me a minute to get out of these clothes."

When Coggins came back into the kitchen he'd changed out of the khakis and polo and into a pair of briar pants with protective chaps sewn onto the legs. A ratty T-shirt hung loosely from him and a ball cap was pulled down so that the bill shaded his eyes.

"In all my years of knowing you, Sheriff, I don't think I've ever once seen you with a hat on."

"You get to be my age and them doctors start cutting on you like a science experiment, you start doing all sorts of things you didn't do before. You start doing whatever the hell they tell you to do."

"Skin cancer," Evelyn whispered, as if Leah might not have caught the gist.

"Come on," Coggins said, motioning with his hand for Leah to follow him. "Let's me and you take a ride."

In the barn, they climbed into a dusty side-by-side with knobby tires and a giant suspension. Coggins hefted a couple bags of feed into the bed of the vehicle and the shocks bounced as the weight came down. He went back to his truck and returned with a Lil' Oscar cooler, from which he took two cans of Busch and offered her one across the bench seat. She shook her head and he sucked that first one down as if he'd just spent forty years walking the desert with Moses. Coggins crumpled the can and tossed it into the back. He popped the top on the other and set two more onto the seat between them.

When they took off, the air blowing in from the open sides felt good in the heat and Leah gripped tight to one of the rails so as not to tumble out as he swerved through the switchbacks. The engine was loud and she was nearly yelling to speak.

"Why didn't you tell me you gave Toya a ride from the protests?"

The sheriff glanced over but quickly turned his focus back to the road. His beer was situated between his legs and he took a long swallow before answering. "I did tell you, Leah."

"No, Sheriff, I'm pretty sure I'd remember that. I've been chasing my tail trying to figure out where she went that afternoon. No one had any idea. Finally the town got back to me with the body cam footage. I wound up pulling the footage from the cameras downtown and saw you get her out of there."

"Yeah, I gave her a ride, but I'm sure I told you. I'm sure of it." Coggins looked addled. The side-by-side spun briefly sideways as he came around a bend faster than she was comfortable going. "Shit, I don't know anymore. Half the time I can't remember what I had for breakfast or if I even ate at all. If I didn't, I'm sorry. I guess things might've just got jumbled around in my head."

"There's been a lot on you, sir."

"Yeah, but that's a shit excuse, Leah, and you know it. There's always been a lot on me and I've always carried it just fine. Getting old, I guess. Losing my edge. Hard to admit, but that's the goddamn truth of it." He seemed demoralized by the way his mind had failed him. "I thought sure as the world I'd told you. But between being over at the hospital and running around trying to check on Vess, I guess I just got spread thin. I don't know. I don't know what to say."

There was a pained expression on his face that she found hard to bear. In all those years of working for him, she'd never seen any sign of weakness. "So where did y'all go when you left town? Did you take her back to her grandmother's?"

"No, she wanted me to drop her off there at the school. Said she wanted to go back up there where she'd dug those graves, where the old church used to be, said she'd walk home from there. I dropped her off and headed back to the office for the shit show." He paused for a second. "She ever make it back to Vess's?"

"No. Not according to her grandmother anyways."

"Shit, I should've known better than to let her walk. I should've took her on home. But she'd been walking that stretch of road all summer. Didn't even cross my mind, really. Should have, but like I said, I'm losing that edge." Coggins shifted his weight on the seat. "I'd say whoever it was, though, likely picked her up between the college and that house." The back window of the side-by-side was propped open and when he finished that second beer he tossed the empty can into the bed through the opening. "Hell, that could have been anybody."

He was right about that. Tempers were high and there wasn't a soul in the county who wouldn't have recognized her walking down the side of that road. Leah'd lived here all her life and she couldn't remember having ever seen the place as torn up and on edge as it had been in the days building up to the protests. Lately her mind kept telling her what had happened to Ernie Allison was somehow connected to the death of Toya Gardner. He'd been found at the Confederate Veterans Memorial Forest. She'd been killed over that statue.

"You think what happened to Ernie had something to do with what he told you?"

Coggins gripped the steering wheel casually in his right hand and clung to the roof of the vehicle with his left. "Hold on," he said, and before Leah could get a solid grip he'd turned sharp and dropped down through a ditch.

The side-by-side bucked hard and the tires whirled briefly in the muddy bottom before catching and pulling them up a steep hill along a narrow trail. The path was crowded with brush and briars, all of it slapping and lashing at the sides of the vehicle as they drove so that Leah had to lean into him to keep from being whipped with thorns.

"How do you know what Ernie talked to me about?"

"Come on, Sheriff. The whole office knows. Lovedahl told anybody'd listen. Figured that had something to do with them getting into that fight, that and what he said." Leah found it hard to believe he was unaware of the rumor mill. "But you can't tell me there's not a connection between all of that and where they found him laying. There's just no way that's a coincidence."

They were at the top of the ridge now in a stand of red oak and poplar. The trail had opened up as it came to a gate. The woods were clean and the shaded ground was laced knee-high with bracken. Coggins stepped out of the side-by-side and unlatched a chain from the gate. He came back and drove through, hopped out, and shut the gate behind them. He cracked open his third beer before they went any farther. They were at the top of a pasture and a string of cattle were trotting up the slope to meet them.

"He's a real son of a bitch, ain't he?" Coggins said as they took off again.

"What's that?" Leah hadn't caught exactly what he'd said over the engine noise.

"That Lovedahl. Said he's a real son of a bitch, ain't he?" He finished his beers fast, and as the alcohol found him his mood seemed to lighten.

Leah chuckled and looked back at the cows chasing behind them. "Yeah," she said. "He sure is."

Soon they were pulled up to a pair of long troughs and Coggins cut the engine. Outside, he hefted one of the bags of feed onto his shoulder. When he was next to the trough, he cut the corner off the bag with a sodbuster from his pocket and emptied the cattle cube into the crib. The cattle were all around them now, and the biggest pushed and shoved to the front of the line to feed.

"I guess what I keep thinking, Sheriff, is that these two cases, all of this might be tied together. What happened to Ernie and what happened to Toya. If Ernie was right about what he told you, then I'd bet dollars to doughnuts we're looking for the same people."

"That's a mighty big jump, Detective."

"Come on, Sheriff. You know where he was found. And you know good and well that had something to do with what he told you. If we're talking about the Klan, you telling me those folks wouldn't have been the kind to have killed Toya Gardner?"

"I'm saying there's nothing to make those connections right now but a hunch." Coggins reached into the bed and grabbed the second bag. He fought his way through the cattle and emptied the grain into the trough. "Ideas are great, Leah, but at the end of the day ideas aren't evidence."

"All I'm saying is we could be working together on this."

"That's not my job, Detective. Work your case," he said. "Work your case, and if those two trails wind up running together, then I'll be there when it does. But right now you need to follow the evidence. Look at them . . ." Coggins pointed down the hill to where two calves were chasing each other through the field. The calves stopped and watched as if to judge the amusement of their audience.

Leah stepped out of the side-by-side and the shoes she wore sank into the hoof-trod mud. One of the calves was cinnamon colored and the other was black as night with a white spot of swirled hair square in the center of his forehead. The reddish-brown calf marched up the hill and Leah took a step closer, the calf rearing back when she did. The calf took a few steps closer, stopped, a few steps more. It was a matter of trust.

"I tell you somebody you ought to talk to."

"Oh, yeah? Who's that?" The calf was nearly to her.

"Rupert Bates," the sheriff said. "Wasn't two days before all this happened he stood right down there in my road and told me I should've kept Toya locked up for her own protection. Said it wasn't safe for her to just be out wandering around."

33

The church glowed like a candle in the falling blue of dusk. Inside, the pews were filled, the remainder of the sanctuary standing room only. More were gathered on the steps and in the yard. The windows had been opened to move the air and so that those outside might catch the words being spoken.

It had been a long time since Vess had seen the church like this, filled with people and voices, heat and pressure. They were packed into that place like gunpowder.

Over the past few decades, the congregation had dwindled down to its elders as younger generations walked away, some leaving the mountains, others just leaving the church. She did not recognize most of the faces around her, but on this night the room felt like it had before. People fanned themselves with folded bulletins and the shift of those who stood sent a steady creaking through the floor. The building was nearly a hundred years old and she was not sure the joists would hold.

For the last hour, Reverend Tillman had delivered a sermon about love and loss, grief and triumph. He spoke of passivity and he spoke of action. He wore a pair of pleated black slacks and a tight black shirt that stretched against his thick chest and shoulders. Sweat beaded against his forehead and glistened in the light like crystals.

Vess was on the pew where she always sat, Lula Shepherd on one side, her daughter, Dayna, on the other. Dayna's eyes were hidden behind sunglasses. Her head was down and her lap was filled with shreds of Kleenex, her tearing the tissues from the moment they'd sat down as if she were stringing beans. Vess placed her hand on her daughter's knee and could feel the tension wringing her body to stone. She took a deep breath and turned her eyes back to Tillman.

He'd charged the community to march each Sunday from the steps of the old courthouse to the doors of the Justice Center until Toya's killer was found.

"There are people all around us who'd prefer that Toya's murder just fall behind that ridge and fade like the sun into darkness," he preached. "There are people driving past right now who'd prefer her name never be spoken again. And that's why we're gathered here tonight, because that's the work that lies before us."

Tillman turned his back to the congregation and gripped tightly to a waist-high railing that separated the altar and pulpit. He was hunched forward with all of his weight seeming to bear down on that place. His back was still turned when he spoke and what he said next came out in a low rumble.

"I will carve her name into the cliff face before I let that happen." A few people in the pews echoed with amen. Tillman stood tall then and raised his eyes toward the ceiling. "I will scream that child's name from the top of this mountain until it rings in every ear the entire world over." More joined then with amen, their echoes seeming to drive him forward, and he turned back to the room.

"That's the work that lies before us. That's the road that leads us out," Tillman proclaimed. "We must not allow Toya's name to be ushered into silence. We must not allow our suffering to be brushed aside as if this is our lot to bear.

"As King said that day on the steps of the Lincoln Memorial, we dream of a day when 'every valley shall be exalted, and every hill and mountain shall be made low, the rough places will be made plain, and the crooked places will be made straight; and the glory of the Lord shall be revealed and all flesh shall see it together.'

"But make no mistake, it was also 'written in the book of the words of Isaiah the prophet, "The voice of one crying in the wilderness, 'Make ready the way of the Lord, Make His path straight.'"'

"We cannot afford to sit passively and wait, because nothing will be made for us. He will lead us out, but He will not carry us on His back. King knew this. I know this. And deep down every soul in this room knows the same. We must work. We must walk. We must make His path straight."

34

Rupert Bates had run a motor grader for the state for thirty years. Like most men who'd lived in the mountains all their life, he was never meant for idle, so that when he retired it lasted all of a week and a half. A local grading and excavating outfit approached him and begged him for help. He agreed so long as he could set his own hours and take his pay off the books. To watch him work was to witness a thing near artistry.

The morning Leah went to find him he was grading a system of gravel roads in a midlevel gated community halfway between Canada and Rosman. She sat in her unmarked patrol car eating a bear claw and drinking coffee while he tilted the blade effortlessly to crown the road. The machine was loud and she rolled up her windows to cut the noise as it approached. When the grader neared, she stepped out and waved for him to stop, something he did not seem to want to do.

Rupert hit the kill switch and the engine rattled down into

silence. He opened the door and leaned out from his perch with an agitated look, like, *Get on with it.*

"Are you Rupert Bates?"

"I am."

"I'm Detective Green with the Jackson County Sheriff's Office." His face bent as she said it. "Was wondering if I could talk with you for a second or two."

Rupert double-checked his controls to make sure the grader was stationary. He climbed down off the machine and eyed her quizzically. He was a fairly short man with thick arms and heavy shoulders, a beer belly that stretched his bright red T-shirt like the skin of a beefsteak tomato. He wore faded blue jeans and logging boots, suspenders that hugged the outsides of his gut and ran tight to his shoulders.

"What exactly can I do for you, Miss Green?" He pulled a braid of tobacco out of the breast pocket of his T-shirt and bit a chunk off between his teeth as if he might've been chewing a candy bar. Leah hadn't seen anybody chew braid since she was a girl and old men gathered around ice chests in rockers outside filling stations.

"You're pretty good on that machine," she said. It was a lame attempt to soften him up.

"You sit in that saddle long as I have, you get to where you can about run it off feel." There was a worn-out and sweat-stained ball cap propped on his head like a pancake. He pulled the hat off by the bill and wiped the sweat from the top of his head with his biceps.

"Pretty amazing to watch."

"I just pretend I'm floating through the curves at the Daytonee 500." He horse-laughed with tobacco stuck in his teeth and spit into the dust at his boots. "Now, you telling me you drove all the way out here to compliment my grading?"

"No, sir."

"So why don't you get on with what you're wanting. I hate to be short, but there's a lot of road in here."

"I wanted to talk with you about Toya Gardner."

"Who?"

"Toya Gardner," Leah repeated. "The young woman that was found earlier this week up Dicks Creek."

"Now, what in the world would I know about that?"

"I was told you made some statements recently about her safety. I was told that you said it would've been better if she'd remained in custody so that nothing would happen to her."

"Oh, for crying out loud!" Rupert took his hat off and slapped his leg with it. He turned his eyes up toward a bluebird sky and cussed under his breath. "Coggins send you up here? That son of a bitch has lost his rabid-ass mind!"

"The sheriff said you came by his house a few days before all of this happened."

"Yeah, I went by there."

"And do you remember saying she would have been safer in custody?"

"Of course I do."

"So what exactly did you mean by that, Mr. Bates?"

"I meant it exactly how it sounds, and damned if I wasn't right as rain." The chaw in his cheek garbled his words. "Don't take a fortune teller to know she was running ninety mile an hour down a dead-end road. Half the county hated that girl."

"Did you hate her?"

"Damn right."

"Mr. Bates, do you have anyone who can vouch for where you were last Saturday?"

"My wife."

"And do you remember where you were?"

"Down there by that statue all day. Luckily we left before the nonsense. Wife was getting hungry. She got bad sugar and gets loopy if she ain't ate by about four. So we went on and got supper, come home, went to church that next morning. It was our week to keep nursery."

Leah had a small notepad out and she was jotting down the details.

"Look, I ain't hate that girl because she was Black . . ."

Leah stopped writing and looked up.

"If that's what you're thinking you can get it on out of your mind."

"So what was your reason, Mr. Bates?"

"I hated that girl because she come here and tried to tear down something ain't have a thing in the world to do with her. She ain't grow up here. That statue's not honoring any of her kin. That's why I hated her, and it ain't just that girl. There's plenty of folks White as your teeth trying to do the same thing she was, and I hate every last one of them too. Everybody wanting to make that war out like the only thing it had to do with was slavery. My family ain't own slaves."

Leah didn't want to fall into some argument over history, but she knew where he was headed before he finished. She'd heard the same story again and again all her life. Everyone who'd grown up with family that tied back to that time and place had heard it. She was kin to three of the 164 soldiers from Jackson County who'd served in the Confederate Army. "How do you know that, Mr. Bates?"

Her question caught him off guard. "What do you mean how do I know? Look around you. These mountains look like plantation country to you? My granddaddy built his first house off a crop of tobacco. Dirt floors. Tarpaper. That's how I know. On account of where I come from and what I've been told all my life. And on account of as long as I've been breathing air there's been folks coming down here trying to gobble up everything we got like it's theirs for the taking. That's what that war was about and ain't nothing changed."

"All I'm saying, Mr. Bates, is that I was told the same things all my life. And when my father passed I got into researching our family and putting the pieces together and there it was: Benjamin Green owned one slave, black female, age seventy."

"And what the fuck's that got to do with me, huh? What the fuck's that got to do with that war or that statue or anything at all?"

"I'm just saying what we're told all our lives might not be everything there is to know. Sometimes there are things we've been told all our lives that are flat wrong."

"Well, we'll just have to agree to disagree."

"I don't know what that means."

"It means I'm done arguing about this. That road out there's not getting any shorter us standing here talking and it damn sure ain't going to get up and grade itself."

"Is there any way I can speak with your wife?"

"You found me out here, I'd say you'll find our house just fine." Rupert reached into his cheek and pulled out his chew. He chucked the wad of tobacco off into the woods and climbed back into the cab of his machine.

35

Curtis Darnell sat on the tailgate of his truck with his feet swinging under him like a child. He was eating Vienna sausages, stabbing them out of the can with the sheepsfoot blade of a stockman folding knife and mashing them onto soda crackers.

There were three crackers lined up and ready down his thigh, and he zigzagged a squirt of neon-green relish onto each of them from a small condiment packet he'd likely swiped from a gas station hot dog stand. When he was finished, he stacked them together and shoved them all in his mouth at once. With his cheeks stuffed, he licked his fingers and spoke, shards of crackers flying from his lips like birdshot.

"It's like I told you before, you sleep in that truck of a night with the engine running and you liable to wake up dead." He swallowed down everything in his mouth and it looked like an egg sliding down his throat. "But that's just a risk I have to take, see? I be damned if I'm laying in that house with a snake in the wall. I can't stand a snake. I'd just as soon huff gas as sleep with a snake."

Leah didn't want to be there listening to him rattle on about God knew what. Something about Curtis Darnell made her skin crawl, but right then she didn't have much to go on and she hadn't made it back to his house the day they found Toya Gardner's body to question him.

"So if you're sleeping in your truck, then you'd likely see anybody that comes up this road, wouldn't you?"

"See all sorts of people. A whole lot of Mexicans lately. Don't know what in the world they're doing up there. Then there's the drunks and the dopers, always been that. Every pull-off up through there littered with beer boxes and needle tops."

"You remember seeing anyone that night?"

"What night?"

"The night before you found the girl, Curtis. Do you remember seeing anyone come up the road?"

"No," he said. "No. Can't say that I do." He was fixing another row of crackers down the length of his jeans, stirring the last of the Viennas up inside the tin with his knife. "You want one of these crackers, girlie, you better speak up."

"I'm fine, Curtis. I've already eaten lunch."

"Might be a can of Hormel chili in the glove box, but that's about all I've got to offer. Done eat all the fruit cocktails they give me. Commodities," he said. When the crackers were loaded up and ready he shoved his mouth full again and stared at the mountain with a dumbstruck wonder as if he were watching fireworks. After a long spell, he spoke. "You know, come to think of it, I do remember a vehicle coming up the road that night. I was having a dream I was at the movies, at the Ritz, that movie theater used to be downtown. Used to call that place the Ratz, was always a bunch of wharf rats running all over the floor during the picture, but there was a truck come up the road there making a racket and that's what woke me up out of that dream."

"That's good, Curtis. Real good. Do you remember anything else about it?"

"Good how?" he said. "I told you the damned thing woke me up out of that dream I was having. I was on a date with that black-headed woman off *Designing Women*, except she was young. Looked like she was in high school. Delta Burke. That was her name, see? Not on the show but in real life. Delta Burke. And we were watching *Convoy* and she'd bought me a big old bag of popcorn with butter dripping all over it. Stirred it up in there with her fingers. I'm here to tell you her hands was just a-shining."

"What color was it?" Leah was about to lose her mind. Trying to keep Curtis Darnell in a straight line was like talking to someone from another planet. She just kept waiting for the antennae to come poking up out of the top of his head.

"What do you mean what color? Same color as any popcorn, I guess."

"The truck, Curtis. Do you remember what color it was? What make or model?"

"You about to give me a headache," he said. "Slate-gray Ford, one of them new bodies. Crew cab. Come through, woke me up, and it had done got cold as a bald-assed rat. Couldn't get back to sleep, me just a-shivering. I had to crank the truck up to get warm and that's how it all come together, see? That's why I had to go walk of a morning. Like I told you, see?"

"That's good, Curtis. That's a lot of help." Leah didn't know how much more conversation she could take. She was almost drunk from listening to him, but what he'd given her was more than she'd expected. "Do you remember what time it was?"

"Not really."

"Did you see the truck come out?"

"You get this sucker here cranked up and running"—he slapped the tailgate with an open hand—"this baby's louder than an airplane. I'm telling you, you ain't hearing a ding-diddly-ding-dang thing."

Leah pulled a small notepad out of the back pocket of her pleated navy slacks and jotted down the vehicle description.

"And speaking of airplanes, now, that next day after y'all was up there this strange-looking old bird come wandering down the road there asking if he could borrow some water. Big, tall, lanky fellow. Had a neck drawn out like a splitting stump."

"I'm not sure I'm following you, Curtis. What's that got to do with what we're talking about? What's that even got to do with airplanes?"

"Well, you ain't let me finish. So this fellow comes walking down that road there, sweat just a-pouring off him, and I was sitting out here just like I am now, eating my lunch. Always eat my lunch right about this time. Got to stay on a regimen, see. Got to eat right about this time every day on account of my bowels. But so he comes up and asks if he can get some water. Just so happened I'd just opened me up a cold drink. Hadn't even took a swig yet. So I held it out there and told him to get him a swallow and he told me it wasn't for him, that it was for his car. Said his car'd overheated about a mile up the road and he needed some water for his radiator.

"So I asked him if he had a bottle or something and he said he didn't, and I asked him how in the world he figured he was going to carry that water up the mountain and he said he ain't know, and I said in your hands? I said that, he said he guessed he'd be needing a bottle too, and I told him I figured he was right. See, now we were getting somewhere. You got to use your head about things, see? But we start digging around looking for that bottle and he gets to asking me all sorts of questions about that girl and the law being up there and what they found and who I'd talked to and what I'd told 'em. Real odd fellow. You know what I mean? You ever been around somebody just gives you the willies?"

"I have," she said.

"Now, I want you to know I looked high and low every place I knew to look back in that junk heap of mine and I couldn't come up with a bottle to save Francis. Found a bucket had a hole in it, just like the song, squirrel done gnawed it all up. Finally we just filled up a pair of old rubber boots I had from when I was doing septic work. That's what I used to do, is clean septic tanks back before I got on the disability.

"Anyhow, we pile in this truck and head up there and he's holding them boots trying to keep the water from sloshing out and the whole time he's asking me about that girl and about what y'all'd found. Told him I ain't rightly know and the whole time he just keeps hounding me, kind of like what you're a-doing. But we get up there and he had this station wagon long as a battleship. That's what he was driving. Parked right on up around that bend there from where I found her. So we get that water poured in the radiator and I get my boots back from him and he fired that buggy up just as loud as an airplane. Left him with it. Ain't seen hide nor hair of him since."

"Did you happen to get his name?"

"No. No, can't say that I did." Curtis sucked at one of his back teeth and fished around the inside of his mouth with his tongue. "Creepy fellow, though. You know what I mean? Kind of fellow makes your skin crawl."

Curtis cracked the top on a can of orange soda and lapped it back till the fizz all but drowned him. He was still sitting there coughing on the edge of his tailgate with his feet swinging under him when she left, and that was where he'd likely be when the spaceship came to get him.

36

Doctors kept Ernie Allison in a medically induced coma for a week. Three days in, the swelling on his brain hadn't worsened, but it hadn't gone down. They were on the cusp of removing a piece of skull to relieve pressure. Untreated, his brain could compress and push down onto his brain stem, a development that could prove fatal.

Luckily on the fourth day the swelling broke like a fever. When they brought him out of the coma, his parents were in the room. Ernie's mother stood at the foot of the bed with her hands cupped over her mouth and nose. With no idea where he was or how he'd gotten there, Ernie clawed and kicked wildly, snarling as he tried to fight his way up from the bed. His mother, Clara, screamed for help, and as his father rose out of his chair a team of nurses rushed into the room to pin Ernie down so that he wouldn't hurt himself. For a long time he lay there with his eyes jutting around the room, gasping for air as if he'd resurfaced from deep water.

Over the next twenty-four hours he asked a lot of questions, and the answers made little sense. He asked how long he'd been out and they told him. He asked where he'd been found, who'd found him, how he'd gotten here, and they answered those questions as well. When the questions turned to him, to what he remembered, Ernie was at a loss. "Nothing," he said. "I don't remember nothing."

A few days later, Sheriff Coggins tiptoed into the room, and when he saw Ernie a wide smile spread across his face. "Your mama said they ain't fed you anything in here but mush." There was a doggy bag in his hand. "Figured I'd sneak you a little something in from the Coffee Shop this morning."

Coggins set the bag on the tray by the bed and patted the top of Ernie's hand.

"Now, I told June I was bringing breakfast over here and she assured me this was what you always ordered. Hash, two eggs, grits, and toast. I run blue lights all the way from Sylva to keep this warm, so you better get at it." The sheriff chuckled and patted him on the hand again, harder this second time, as if testing the water.

Ernie swung the bedside tray over his lap and dug into the bag. He shoveled hash onto a triangle of toast, scooped it through the grits like he was dipping a chip, and filled his mouth to the brim. "You tell June thank you, Sheriff. I swear they woke me up I was starved to death. I bet I could eat—"

"You keep eating like that you're going to choke to death, what's going to happen." Coggins pulled up a chair.

For the next few minutes they caught up on news from the doctor. Ernie was healing up faster than expected. He was still in a lot of pain and he'd lost some of his sight in his left eye, but they were hopeful it wasn't permanent. With any luck, the doctors believed, he could go home by the weekend and stay at the house under family care. He was looking forward to that.

When Ernie finished eating, the sheriff took the empty box and bag over to a trash bin by the door. As he came back to where he'd been sitting, he cut straight to business.

"So, Ernie, I know they've told you where that fellow found you, and your mama said they've hounded you to death, but I needed to come here and ask myself. Do you remember anything at all about that night?"

"There's bits and pieces starting to come back, but it's not much, Sheriff. I don't remember much at all." Ernie took a sip from a glass of water, then set the cup back on his tray and pushed the tray to the side of the bed.

"Okay, then tell me what you do remember."

"I just remember being outside my house. I'd just got done feeding the fish. We'd had that big rain a few days before and I went over to check the spring box. Something hit me in the back of the head and I went out cold. I don't remember anything after that."

"Well, the doctor said there was a drug in your system called xylazine. Evidently that's something vets use to knock out animals, horses mostly. You remember anything at all about how that might have wound up in your system?"

"No, Sheriff, I sure don't." Ernie's mind was getting muddled again. No one else had shared that detail with him. "I don't know what you're talking about."

"It's okay, Ernie. There's no need to get worked up over it. It's just some questions I wanted to ask. Thought maybe talking it out might help you remember's all."

The sheriff stayed a while longer and continued to pry, but Ernie had nothing to tell him. Deep down he knew there was something there, but there was just no finding it within that great big empty. As he struggled to recall any detail at all, the confusion morphed into frustration, that frustration growing into anger.

Coggins seemed to recognize how much stress he was causing, and so after a while he left Ernie be. The sheriff told him he'd be back in a few days to check in, to call if he needed anything. Ernie told the sheriff he was sorry to hear about the girl, that he'd seen the story on the news and knew how close he was to the family.

Later that night Ernie started hurting bad. The physical therapist had worked with him most of the afternoon and he'd pushed himself too hard. The nurses were weaning him off morphine, but he was in so much pain right then they told him he likely needed the drug to stay ahead of it. He gave in and the nurse worked up the dose in the corner of the room, then came bedside to administer the needle into the line.

When Ernie saw that needle it was as if a levee broke and all the memories of that night came pouring into his mind at once. He remembered being inside the trunk of that car. He could see the two men, one holding him down, feel the sharp sting in his arm. He remembered waking up on top of that mountain and how the wind had been cold against him. All of that light stretching above him. All of that light eating away at the darkness.

Ernie could see that giant cross, and he knew exactly where he'd been. But right then his mind settled onto a detail that he couldn't make heads or tails of, just a still-frame image that made no sense at all. He knew that he was lying on his side and he knew that it was the last thing he'd seen. It was a pair of cowboy boots with a raised pattern of squares like net. The leather was almond brown and deeply oiled, but it was that pattern that set them apart. It looked like the hide off something otherworldly.

"Ernie, are you okay?" the nurse asked, her voice breaking his trance.

"Y-yeah," he stuttered, his hands trembling as all the blood left his face. "Yeah, I'm, I'm fine."

"You look like you're about to be sick. Are you sure?"

"I need my phone." He leaned to the side so that he could see around her and winced in pain from having moved too fast. When she stepped back he spotted his cell phone on the table. "I need my phone," he said again.

The nurse picked his cell phone up from the table and handed it to him. "Are you sure you're okay? You're white as a fish."

"I'm fine," he said. "I'm fine. I promise. But give me a minute, okay? I have to talk to the sheriff. I need to talk to the sheriff before I lose it all again."

37

In all the decades of seeing those lights burning at night on Jones Knob, Coggins had never once stood at the foot of the Balsam Cross. To see the lights from Sylva he knew the structure had to be massive, but standing there he was all the more impressed. The Mount Lyn Lowry cross rose six stories into a cloudless blue sky, heavy pipe bleached white as whalebone with streetlights attached every ten feet or so vertically, with two more on the crossbar, one mounted to each side.

He'd only been twelve or thirteen when the Lowry family flipped the switch for the first time. A church in Webster had organized a hike up to the ridge above one of the deacons' houses, something he remembered because this kid named Odie Nichols didn't shut up about it for a week at school. He also remembered that a year or so later the evangelist Billy Graham came to dedicate the cross, and he remembered that because his parents and grandparents had spoken so highly of the young preacher's mission. Graham was a saint in these mountains.

The mountaintop opened into a small meadow there at the cross. A long-distance view stretched off to the east and he stared out at mountains he did not know the names of, their finger ridges in shadow appearing as dark as scars. Most visitors hiked in from the Waterrock Knob trailhead off the parkway, but there was a gated road that led all the way up to the base of the cross, and surely that's what they'd used to get Ernie Allison's body to the top. The odds of anyone dragging an unconscious man five miles over that terrain were slim to none, and not only that, they'd have had to carry him out.

Both the cross and the Confederate Veterans Memorial Forest, where Ernie'd been dumped, were located in neighboring Haywood County, and Coggins suspected that had been done deliberately to try to keep the case out of his hands. Thing was, he didn't give a shit about jurisdiction. Jurisdiction was usually something used to pass the buck, to hand off cases you wanted no part of, a "That's not ours, it's yours," sort of excuse. But those lines wouldn't stop a man from getting answers if he wanted them.

That morning he'd met Haywood County sheriff Bruce Sellers at the Buttered Biscuit and eaten sausage gravy over eggs and a cathead biscuit while he shared everything Ernie'd told him the night before. When they'd finished breakfast they'd ridden out to the cross and met the property manager at the gate. Mount Lyn Lowry was technically private land that the family allowed hikers to visit, but the road was gated off and only a few people had keys to the lock.

Nearly a week and a half after the fact, any evidence that had been left on that mountaintop had been washed clean by summer rain and boot traffic. Still, Sellers had brought a forensics team up to scour the meadow for any traces, and Coggins had stayed there to oversee the effort while Sellers went back down to talk with the property manager. When Sellers came back up to the top, he walked over slow with his hands shoved in his pockets. He was tall and high shouldered, wore dark slacks ironed to a knife's edge. There was a constant sadness to him, like he'd seen too much or just couldn't stop from thinking. As he came over, Coggins could see the wheels turning.

"They find anything up here?"

"Not yet," Coggins said. "And doubt they will with as much rain as we've had."

"Been wet all summer."

"How about you? You find out anything?"

"Well, I found out a lot of things." Sellers still had his hands stuffed in his pockets. He shifted back and forth to widen his stance, as if he were stepping into a batter's box. "Found who's got keys, and that's a problem. Started off Emergency Management and the Forest Service and me, but if I had one I'd say I've got about as good a chance of finding it as I do the keys to that Chevelle I had in high school.

"The problem is he said some boy at the Forest Service made copies for somebody he bear hunted with, a cousin or something, so he could get a bear out, and that key led to another key led to another key." He took his left hand out of his pocket and ran his fingers from his forehead through his widow's peak. "Way it sounds, John, there ain't a bear hunter from here to Murphy couldn't get their hands on a key to that gate."

"Well, shit," Coggins said. He spit between his feet and kicked at the ground with the toe of his boot.

"So while I'm down there, though, sorting all this out, that old boy remembers they've got a game camera set up there in the woods aimed at the gate." Sellers smiled and shook his head.

"You'd have thought he'd said that soon as we pulled up. There any pictures?"

"Card was wiped clean the night of. Thing's hooked up to a little solar panel there for power and it wouldn't have been all that hard to spot if a man was looking, especially if he'd been up here a time or two. But there wasn't a picture taken up until that night. The next morning there's a doe with two little ones, spots all over them, couldn't have been more than a few days old, come walking right up that road. He said he hadn't checked the card since about May, so it was wiped just sure as the world, but depending on how they did it we might still be able to get to them pictures. I've got a boy there in the office that'll be able to find them if they're on there. A lot of times with these electronics things aren't swept clean quite as good as folks think."

They stayed there at the cross another hour or so but the forensics team never found a thing with any hope of tying Ernie Allison to that spot. Thing about it, there were only two crosses lit up like that anywhere close to Jackson or Haywood, and the other was down at Lake Junaluska in a parking lot and wasn't a quarter the size. If this was where Ernie said that he was that night there wasn't a doubt in Coggins's mind that they were in the right place. Proving it, on the other hand, was another thing altogether.

38

From sunup to sundown, Leah'd beat the pavement and knocked on every door from campus to the grandmother's house. No one had seen Toya Gardner walking the road that afternoon. It wasn't until she got home that night that she heard the news about Ernie. That break was one bright spot at the end of a day she'd just as soon have forgotten.

After listening to what he remembered, she drove to the top of a ridge where she could see the Balsam Cross glowing in the distance like a lighthouse, and for reasons she could not recognize at the time, she wept and prayed. While she sat there she imagined the details he'd told the sheriff, that giant cross burning so bright it was blinding, the men in robes and hoods standing over him like haunts. Those images melded with what she'd witnessed firsthand that morning, Toya Gardner shot and dumped like a poached deer. The world suddenly seemed as if it could not hold.

She remembered something her father had told her once about a friend of his named Silas Crane who lived off Wolf Mountain and could fix any gun ever made. Her father had mentioned in passing how Silas was approached once by the Klan to serve as their arms keeper. It was a tiny fragment of a story that had stuck in her memory because it was the only other time she'd ever heard mention of them in this place.

Whether the sheriff wanted to believe it or not, these two cases were connected. Now that they knew who was responsible for what happened to Ernie, she was certain the same would hold true for the girl.

Silas Crane lived above Tanasee Lake in a teardrop camper with blue tarps strung through the trees to keep the place in the dry. His house had burned down a decade or so before, and rather than rebuild, he'd dropped the insurance money into a 401(k) so that he could retire from the mill a few years early. A light rain had been falling since daylight and the clouds lay over the mountains like a quilt. She spotted him through the haze as she pulled up. He was sitting in a folding chair by his camper poking at the coals of a small fire with the end of a walking stick.

"I bet I haven't seen you since you were ten years old playing softball down at Mark Watson Park." Silas wasn't as old as he looked, maybe a few years older than the sheriff, but had been rode hard and put up wet. He had a disheveled beard and curly white hair that met his shoulders. "Me and Prelo Pressley rode down there to watch you after your daddy went on and on about how good you could hit. We bet on it and you went four for four with two doubles, and Prelo had to buy my beer for a week."

"I wish I could tell you I remember," Leah said, "but that's been a long time."

"I'd say." Silas smiled and opened a small cooler, where a six-pack rested on ice. It was only noon but he was retired and there was nothing else getting done in the rain. "Old Prelo bought my beer for a week." He ripped a can from the plastic yoke and cracked it open, rushed it to his lips to suck back the foam. "I bet it cost him two hundred dollars." He cackled and leaned to the side to rest the can on the ground. "I've slowed down right much since then, but I used to could've drunk the river dry."

"You, Prelo, and my daddy must've made for a wild bunch."

"Throw Raymond Mathis in and we was hell on wheels, the whole damned lot of us." Silas picked at his teeth with his finger. "Wonder we ain't wind up in prison. Think it was you and your mama saved your daddy. Probably Doris saved Ray. But it must've been the good Lord looked after Prelo and me. I bet we turned that old boy's hair white."

Leah was enjoying listening to Silas talk about men she knew, but she didn't want to let him stray too far. When folks here took to remembering, one memory sparked the next and the next until hours had passed and the day was shot. "So the reason I stopped by was because I remembered something Dad told me once."

"Lord, there ain't no telling." Silas took a drink of beer and watched the fog filter through the trees. The smoke from the camp-fire held in the shelter of the tarp, no air at all to move it. "I'd say there's about a ninety percent chance it was true."

"Well, I don't remember the details really. I just remember him mentioning that you were approached by the Klan to be their arms keeper."

Silas snorted and laughed and slouched down in his chair, rest-ing his beer on his chest so that he could easily tip it back to his lips. "Yeah, that's true," he said. "Fellow named Dumpy Rice asked me. Old Dumpy's dead now. Died, I don't know, five or six years back. But your daddy and them used to give me hell about that. Used to act like I was secretly in the Ku Klux Klan."

"So what happened?"

"I told Dumpy to eat shit. That's what happened. That's all that ever come of it, really." Silas finished his beer and poked the coals red and hot. He tossed his empty can into the fire and opened another. "See, I used to do a lot of gun trading back then, kind of like a second job, a lot of buying and selling and traveling around to gun shows. I had a Class Three license and that's what it all boiled down to. They wanted to get a dozen or so fully automatic weapons to set back in case shit ever hit the fan. But you don't just walk into a gun store and say, 'Hey, I'd like a machine gun.' There's a lot of paperwork, hoops to jump through. They were just wanting to use my license to cut through all that red tape."

Leah jumped forward to try to make the connection. "I'm sure you've probably heard everything that's going on. What happened to one of our deputies, Ernie Allison, and then about the murder of Toya Gardner."

"I have."

"So one thing we know is that Ernie was targeted by the Klan because he'd uncovered some names, and I can't help but think that if those are the people responsible for what happened to him, then they're likely the same ones responsible for what happened to her. And the thing is, until all of this happened it never even crossed my mind that anything like this even existed in this county. Up until a couple weeks ago, the only time I'd ever heard mention of the Klan was that story."

"I mean, they've always been around in some capacity or another." Silas pulled his beard through his fist. "Never was much of anything. Wasn't like some places you hear about where they're marching around town, showing up at parades. To hear them tell it back then it was like they were a social club. That's what they wanted me to believe, like it was all about history and Jesus, and all I kept wondering was if that was all it was, then why the fuck did they need an arms keeper?"

"Why do you think they approached you?"

"On account of that license," Silas said. "On account of the guns they were looking for wasn't the type of shit you just walk into a store and pluck off the shelf."

"Yeah, but why would they have thought you'd have been on board with everything else?"

"That's a damn good question, and that's why your daddy and the rest of them peckerheads give me so much shit about it through the years. They knew how far out of place it was to think I'd have ever been a part of something like that." He held his hands down by the flames. The coals were hot and the beer can he'd tossed into the fire crumbled away like burned-up paper. "You know, we'd all grown up together, Dumpy and me and a couple others. And back in high school I had rebel flags on my truck and drawn on my notebook. Guess they just remembered that and assumed we was like-minded. I don't know really.

"Here's the thing, though. I mean, I grew up knowing the family history and all, but for me it wasn't ever about that. For me it was just a rebel flag. That's all it ever was, a middle-finger sort of thing. I remember a few years back this kid got arrested for spray-painting an anarchy symbol on one of the buildings downtown. Had his picture in the paper. Had a big tall Mohawk and looked just dumb as cheese, but now, what do you think that kid knew about philosophy? Hell, I was driving through Sylva not a month ago and seen a teenage girl with her head shaved bald and a picture of Che Guevara on her T-shirt. What I'm trying to say is kids attach themselves to all sorts of shit they don't fully understand just because they think it looks cool or tough or whatever."

Leah's mind flashed back to the kid in the truck at the candle-light vigil.

"So maybe the difference is I grew up and started reading books and realizing half that shit I'd been told wasn't right to start with. Maybe that was the biggest difference between me and them." Silas watched the flames lick about the air in front of him. A breeze had picked up and was carrying the smoke off toward the wood line. "You can be proud of where you come from and not proud of everything that history entails. That's what so many of these people don't seem to be able to wrap their heads around."

She couldn't help but think about the conversation she'd had with Rupert Bates just a few days before. She wished that he was sitting across the fire right then to hear what Silas was saying, and she wondered if having it come from a man like him would've made a difference or if he'd have written it off just the same.

"Dumpy Rice flunked ninth-grade algebra twice. He was in summer school every summer of our lives and never did get a diploma. Hung it up in the tenth grade. Now, you think he ever sat down and cracked open a book after that?" Silas tilted his head back and drained half of his beer. "Them boys don't read books. Only history they know's whatever bullshit their daddy told them, and all he knows is whatever bullshit his daddy told him. They just use what they want and toss what they don't, same as these people on TV do with the Bible. It ain't never been about history, just like it ain't ever had a thing in the world to do with a man on a cross.

"This is what nobody will tell you, what nobody wants to admit. There was a right many folks in these mountains fought for the Union. So where's them folks' statue? Why ain't their kin dancing around in uniforms playing dress-up and slapping stickers on the backs of their pickup trucks? Why ain't they hung up on some little four-year window a hundred and fifty fucking years ago? Tell me that."

Leah wasn't sure what to say.

"Because it's all bullshit, that's why. Every goddamn bit of it. Lies and bullshit."

He seemed to be growing agitated and she felt as if she might've pushed him into thinking about things he'd rather not have discussed. No one wanted to talk about any of it. There was comfortability in the silence. They sat there for a while and neither said anything at all, and then she tried to wrap things up so that she could leave him be.

"I do appreciate you talking with me, Silas. Like I said, all of this started when Ernie Allison uncovered those names, which is to say we've got some people we're fairly certain are actively involved, but I guess I was hoping you might could fill in the gaps."

"I'm sorry," Silas said. "I just don't see how I'd be much help." He was still slumped in his chair and he poked at the fire with his stick. "That story you were asking about was almost thirty years ago. Nowadays I stay up here and drink up my Social Security and that's about it. Most them boys from back then are dead and gone and I ain't far behind them."

Leah was a bit disappointed but not at all surprised. She'd come up here on a whim and more just to try to wrap her head around some of the things running through her mind. She thanked him again and got ready to leave.

"I will say this. Like everything else up here, it's always been a matter of family. Grandfathers to fathers, fathers to sons. Everything gets passed down, just like houses and stories and all that other bullshit." Silas threw his empty can into the fire but did not reach for another. He moved the cooler out in front of him for a footrest and propped his boots up on it. "What I'm trying to say is if you was to give me a name I could probably make a pretty good guess as to whether they'd be affiliated with an outfit like that or not."

All of a sudden the rain came heavy and Leah turned to run for her car.

"People are what they've always been," he yelled through the downpour, and it wasn't until later, when she was alone, that the gravity of that statement would find her. "Tell that old buzzard you work for to come by and see me sometime."

39

The rain had not let up since morning. A few times through the day it fell heavy, but for the most part it came steady and continuous, the kind of rain that soaked a garden and set into the ground. Coggins walked out of the service station and paused where a sheet of water cascaded off the edge of the roof. He had a case of beer tucked under one arm and he covered the top of his head with his free hand as he hustled off for the pumps.

The pickup he drove matched the color of the clouds, and he opened the rear driver-side door to slide his beer behind the seat. There was a black step bar along the side of the truck that he placed one foot on to climb into the cab, and as he briefly rose he spotted a station wagon shoot past with tires hissing loud as a snake against the wetted pavement. The back glass was cracked and the wood paneling down the side was long faded and peeling. There was no doubt in his mind to whom it belonged.

He didn't catch up with the car until the last light out of town, and as the Caprice passed the high school, Coggins mashed the gas to tail him. There was no real reason to force a stop. There was nothing yet placing Cawthorn at the cross, nothing to indicate he'd had any involvement with what had happened to Ernie at all. He was the catalyst, but there was no evidence to suggest he was the cause. For now, the sheriff just had a few questions he wanted to ask.

The day was almost gone and the clouds and rain left the world in dark gray light. Up ahead on the right, a roadside merchant crouched beneath a giant umbrella peddling watermelons he'd brought to the mountains from Florida. Just before the stand, South River Road cut off to follow the Tuckaseigee back toward Webster, and that's where Cawthorn slowed and turned. The road was narrow, just a two-lane ribbon that hugged each bend of stream. Suddenly the station wagon took off, doubling its speed in a matter of seconds, and the sheriff knew instantly he'd been made. His truck was unmarked and he hadn't hit the blue lights that were hidden in the grille, but from the looks of things, Cawthorn must've spotted him just the same.

The road was too winding for a high-speed chase. He hit the lights and went in pursuit but he did not race to catch him. Rounding a bend, he caught sight of the vehicle for a split second as it nearly lost control in a curve, but through the next few hairpins there was no sign of the Caprice at all. When he finally spotted the station wagon it was just the taillights glowing red in the fog over the water at first, the car having dipped over the bank and crashed into the river.

Coggins whipped the truck to the shoulder and left the lights flashing as he exited the vehicle. Cawthorn had wrecked where a small island split the stream in two to form a narrow passage of runs against the bank closest to the road. Out in the river, the engine roared. The exhaust was boiling the water with smoke. The rear tires were spinning like waterwheels and every few seconds the tread would catch just enough traction on the cobble to heave the vehicle a few feet farther downstream.

Coggins slid down the bank and was knee-deep in cold water before he found footing. He waded out and slipped every few steps, his boots unable to grip the slicked stones. The water was soon up to his hips and he could tell the river was high from the day's rain. As he got closer he could hear Cawthorn yelling inside for help.

The car was facing downriver, so that when Coggins approached he was on the passenger side, and he knew the pressure against the door would keep it sealed like a coffin. Along the right side of his belt he kept a small collapsible baton in a leather sheath just in front of his service weapon. Coggins pulled out the baton and whipped it to full length with a flick of his wrist. He swung and the side glass shattered like a thin sheet of ice. Inside, Cawthorn wrestled frantically with his seat belt.

"It's stuck!" He was yelling as loud as he could to get his words out over the revving of the engine. The water was up to the seat and rising. "I can't get out!"

"Take your foot off the gas!" Coggins screamed.

"My foot ain't on the gas! The goddamn pedal's stuck! That's what happened! The goddamn pedal's stuck!"

The sheriff knew he would have to cut the seat belt free, but there was no way in hell he was handing Cawthorn the knife. He took the baton and ran it back and forth across the windowsill to clear the shards so as not to slice his stomach when he leaned inside. The knife was fastened to his pocket, and when it was free he flipped the blade open with his thumb and dove into the car. Right then the wagon lurched forward and threw Coggins against the back angle of the opened window, his feet kicking wildly outside as if he were already swimming.

When the vehicle stopped, he grabbed ahold of the seat belt and sliced it clean above the buckle, quickly sliced again below. Both sections fell limp against Cawthorn's lap and shoulder. The sheriff wriggled back out of the car like a tunnel rat and soon he was in the water. The front bumper of the vehicle was wedged now against a heavy deadfall and he knew the car could not go any farther, though they were in a deep hole and the river was nearly up to his chest.

William Dean Cawthorn was all knees and elbows trying to unfold himself from his ride. Coggins was already wading downstream to where he knew the water shallowed. Cawthorn followed, and when they stopped he stared straight above so that the rain beat against his face. He stood nearly a foot taller than the sheriff.

Cawthorn lowered his head with a wicked smile cutting his face. "I thought sure as shit I was dead!" He howled then with a wildness known only to beasts and vermin. Behind them, the car's engine still roared. "I thought sure as shit I was off to meet my maker, but you saved me! You saved me, Sheriff!"

Whether it was the adrenaline of the moment or the slow building up of everything, a sudden rage swept over Coggins right then. Out of nowhere his hands fired forward, his fingers clenching the neck of Cawthorn's shirt. They stood where the water hit him midthigh, and he had always been a bulldog, so it took very little for him in that river to sweep Cawthorn onto his side.

The sheriff climbed over him like he was stepping over a log and he held Cawthorn's head just above the surface. He scowled down at him when he spoke. "Were you at the cross that night with the rest of them?"

"What cross?" Willy Dean's face was smeared with confusion. "What are you talking about?"

"You lie to me and I'll drown you, boy. I swear I will." The rain came hard now and it pelted against his back, but he did not feel this, for his body was numb and his mind was empty. "Were you at that fucking cross?"

"I don't know what in the fuck you're talking about, Sheriff!"

"You're going to tell me the name of every cocksucker in this county wears a robe and hood or I'm going to hold you under this water till you're forced to breathe it."

"Fuck you!" Cawthorn screamed, and Coggins dunked him under the surface like a baptism, only he did not let him up. When he finally lifted him for air, Willy Dean was coughing and choking, his arms and legs driving like pistons but finding no place to land. "Get the fuck off me!" he squalled.

"Tell me their fucking names!" Coggins wailed.

Willy Dean said nothing, and this time Coggins held him under with no intention of ever letting him up again. As Cawthorn scrambled to get free, the sheriff caught movement on the bank, and when he looked there was a man hustling down the road. The fog flashed blue in the strobe from Coggins's truck and the man appeared in each course of light, closer and closer.

"I've got help coming, Sheriff!" the stranger yelled. He appeared as little more than a shadow.

In the distance Coggins could already hear the sirens echoing through the valley. At that moment it was like the world suddenly came back to him. He could feel the rain beating down on his shoulders, the river up to his thighs, that cold water soaking him to the bone. He took a step back and let Cawthorn clamber to his feet. Cawthorn's face was blank and terrified, white as the sheets he wore.

Soon the road was crowded with emergency personnel—patrol cars, ambulances, fire and rescue. They crawled up the bank one after the other and medics crowded around them to check for injuries. No one knew what had just gone on and they sat them together in the back of an ambulance to check their heart rates and breathing. There were no immediate reasons to transport them to the hospital, and so for the next hour they waited in that ambulance while medics circled back every few minutes to monitor their vitals and ensure that nothing had changed.

They were alone when Cawthorn finally broke the silence. The rain had stopped and the two of them were standing by the back bumper of the ambulance, all of those lights still flashing a dizzying madness around them.

"Whatever it was you asked out there, Sheriff, I don't know what you're talking about. I don't know nothing about a cross." He was wrapped in a towel they'd given him to keep warm, but his hair was still wet and it hung about his shoulders as if slicked with bear grease. "But as far as giving up names, my answer won't change. I'm a whole lot of things, Sheriff, but I've never been a snitch."

The sheriff wished Willy Dean would've just kept his mouth shut, because that voice of his made all of that rage well up again. Despite knowing better, the sheriff could not bite his tongue, and right then he didn't care who heard him.

"If it wasn't for that man on that bank I'd have held you in that river until your body went limp." Coggins turned so that they were facing each other square. His fists drew tight and bloodless at his sides, his entire body coiled and loaded. "I wish you'd just say some-thing, boy. Say one more foul word and I swear I'll knock your fucking teeth down the back of your greasy throat."

Willy Dean smirked, then ran his tongue against the roof of his mouth. His front four teeth dropped away and he flicked his tongue so that the partial rattled with a sound like beads clacking together. "Wouldn't be the first time, Sheriff."

Out in the river, the car was burning.

40

The church owned no parsonage. Instead, the reverend rented a white vinyl-sided house off Chipper Curve from a member of his congregation. The home had no gutters, and the heavy rain had left a knee-high stain of red clay around the house's perimeter.

Leah stepped onto the stoop and wiped the soles of her shoes on a welcome mat. The front door was open and she could hear him stirring inside through the torn mesh of a dull aluminum screen door.

"Reverend Tillman," she muttered, the screen door rattling against its frame as she tapped with one knuckle, trying not to startle him.

Appearing around a corner with a dishrag in his hands, he pushed the bridge of a pair of wire-rim glasses to the peak of his nose as he came to the door.

"Reverend Tillman, I'm Detective—"

"Yes, ma'am. I know who you are."

"I was wondering if you had a second."

Tillman eyed her skeptically, then opened the door with the back of his hand without speaking. He scanned the yard as if trying to see if anyone was with her or watching, but the only things behind her were passing cars and the steam from the paper plant rising to meet the clouds.

There were no lamps on inside, the rooms lit only by midmorning sun sifted through dusty windows. He led her into the kitchen and pulled a chair out from a small wooden table, finished drying his hands, and tossed the rag onto the counter.

"I was just washing some dishes," he said, sliding out a chair of his own so that he was directly across from her when he took his seat. "So what is it I can do for you?"

"I'll cut right to it," Leah said. Instead of talking to the sheriff about what Evelyn had mentioned, she'd decided to speak with the reverend directly. "I heard you're trying to get some broader media attention for the case."

"We are," he said. "I actually just got off the phone with Frank Stasio. He hosts 'The State of Things' for North Carolina Public Radio, but he was saying he could share the story with some colleagues at NPR. I'm still waiting to hear back from some folks. Got a lot of irons in the fire."

"I guess what I'm wanting to ask is what you're hoping this will accomplish?"

The reverend stretched his eyes wide as if aggravated or amused, she could not tell. "We want the same thing as you, Detective. We want the person responsible for Toya's murder found and brought to justice."

"Well, I can promise, we're doing everything we can. *I'm* doing everything I can." Leah took a deep breath. "I'm going to find who did this, Reverend. But in the meantime, I don't understand how this helps me do that."

Tillman placed his hands together as if he were about to pray and tapped his lips with the edges of his index fingers. He seemed to be searching for the right words.

"Here's the truth, Detective, and I seriously doubt this is something you can fully understand, but our lives tend to be worth a twenty-four-hour news cycle. That's if we're lucky. And in the case of most Black women, it's not even worth that. So you ask me why, that's why. Because otherwise Toya Gardner will be a name that burns off this mountain like fog. And the vast majority of folks would prefer it that way."

Leah sat there, unsure how to respond. She understood his intent, but that did not ease her concern.

After a minute or two, Tillman patted his palms against the walnut tabletop. "What are you so afraid of, Detective? What is it you're afraid will happen?"

Leah'd been staring off at the wall and her focus returned now. "I'm afraid it'll hinder the investigation."

"How?" Tillman shouted. He was visibly annoyed by her response.

"Reverend, over the last month I've watched this county split in two. Not once in my life have I seen people this on edge, and what I fear is that bringing folks in from the outside . . . Look, you know how this place is. You know how mountain people are. Strangers show up and start asking questions and these people are liable to shut down entirely. They're liable not to say another word."

"Detective, this place has always been split in two. That's not something just happened over the last month. That's not anything new. Now, maybe you don't see it because you don't have to. But I know the world I live in and I know what I am in that world. Every thought I have, every decision I make is governed by those facts. Even so much as letting you into this house, sitting at this table with you alone. There's not a second in my life I lose sight of that because that would be a mistake. For you it's a luxury not to see it, but for me it would be a grave mistake."

Leah had not come to argue and she tried to sit for a moment with what he was saying. Right then she found herself staring at her hands, nervously massaging her right thumb into her left palm like a mortar and pestle. When she looked up, Tillman was staring straight at her as if waiting for her to speak.

"Okay," she said. "But if that division's always existed, if it's always been this way, how do we bridge—"

"Whoa," Tillman interrupted, "let me stop you right there, Detective." The reverend shook his head and briefly chortled before his expression fell flat and stern. "Now's not the time for you to come and ask me how to bridge the gap."

Leah felt her cheeks flush, her face glowing red. She was taken aback, unable to understand how her question had offended him.

"Here's what I want you to ask yourself, and I want you to take this home with you. Live with it for a while before you try to answer."

Tillman's hands were balled together and pressed to his lips. His chin was down, eyes up with lines creasing his forehead. He moved his hands away from his mouth so that his words would not be muffled.

"Why did it take Toya's murder for you to come here and ask me about bridging the gap?" He paused. "Why did it take Toya Gardner losing her life for you to so much as *admit that the gap exists*?" He pounded the table to emphasize those words, and that sound and those questions made the house seem to shake around her.

"The truth, Detective, is that it shouldn't take a Black life for you to have some moment of insight, some moment of clarity. And yet time and time again, that is what this world requires," Tillman said. "So like I said, there are questions you need to ask yourself. And until you do, I don't have any use for bridges."

41

Cars lined both sides of the long gravel drive so that Leah had to park off the main road. She pulled through a ditch against a barbed-wire fence where field grass stood knee-high. Out in the pasture Angus cattle grazed and loafed like always.

Her mind was still churning from that morning's conversation with Tillman. Those questions had settled deep into her and she hoped Ernie Allison's homecoming party might offer some reprieve. When she approached the house she saw Ernie Allison's brother, Larry, lift the heavy lid of a giant smoker with both hands like he was opening the hood of a school bus. The smoke rolled out around him, and when the air cleared a whole hog was splayed flat on the top rack.

Larry traveled all over the southeast to barbecue competitions, lugging that smoker behind his pickup and sleeping in the cab to skate motel costs. There were at least fifteen chickens spatchcocked and sizzling on the bottom rack, all of the drippings from above crisping those birds to a deep golden brown. He mopped everything on the smoker with a thin vinegar sauce, tossed a dry rub like he was sowing seed, then lowered the lid back closed.

Ernie lived in a white clapboard house on a block foundation. Two massive white oaks out front kept most of the sun from ever reaching the house. A bed of moss covered the asphalt shingles and there was a tinge of green over the painted block. A couple folks Leah didn't recognize lounged in rocking chairs on a poured-slab porch. The front of the house was square and even, the door centered and a window off to each side. Lichen bloomed on the shutters like pale gray roses.

Everyone from Ernie's church, all his family and friends, and the entire Jackson County Sheriff's Department had shown up on Caney Fork to welcome him home. At least a hundred people were spread all over the property. Kids ran screaming and playing in the creek, the whole scene chaotic and loud. Leah came around the side of the house and almost ran face-first into Sheriff Coggins. He was twirling his truck keys on his finger.

"Heard you had a wild night, Sheriff," Leah teased, and slugged him in the shoulder. She'd heard about the car chase and the water rescue from a half dozen people. "You retire, you can get you a summer job playing lifeguard at the Sylva pool."

"I might just do that," he said with a stoic expression she found hard to read. Coggins shoved his keys in his pocket, and in the other hand he held a Dixie cup that he lifted to his mouth to search for one last drink. "I'm glad you come out, Detective. It's good to have everybody here supporting Ernie."

"Wouldn't have missed it," Leah said. She had more than one reason to be there. Just minutes after she left Tillman's, the initial autopsy report for Toya Gardner had arrived from the state and she desperately wanted the sheriff's take. "Hey, if you got a minute there's a couple things I wanted to run by you."

"I was just headed out. Came back to say goodbye right fast, but Evie's already waiting at the truck."

"The report came back from the state." She hoped that news might pique his curiosity but he appeared to be in a hurry to get gone.

"That's good," he said. "Fast turnaround for the state. A lot of times these things get held up forever."

"I'd love to sit down and talk it over if that's all right."

"Of course," Coggins said. He shoved his hands in his pockets and jingled his keys inside against his leg. "I should have a copy waiting for me on my desk. Come by tomorrow and we'll look it over. Just got to get Evie to the pharmacy before they close or she's going to have my hide."

Leah couldn't help but press him. Maybe it was that it was her first big case, or maybe it was just how much she respected his experience and opinion. "I had this odd hunch the other day and I went to talk with Silas Crane," she said. "He said for you to come by and see him."

"Oh, yeah. What made you go talk to Si?" Coggins was looking over her shoulder toward his truck.

"Just a story I remembered Dad telling one time," Leah said. "But there was something Silas said about how it's always been the same families. Made me think that if I took some still shots from the footage down there at the protest and let him look at who all was there, maybe he could piece together someone who might be active."

Coggins rattled the ice in his Dixie cup, took a cube into his mouth, and crunched it loudly. He tossed what was left out into the yard.

"What I'm saying is that if we can start building a list of anyone we know is active, that'll at least give us a starting place. That'll at least give us some people to question. But that's why I keep saying we need to be working together on this, Sheriff. These cases are connected. They've got to be."

"No, Miss Green, these two cases don't have to be connected at all." It struck her that he'd stripped her of her title right then. He'd almost always made it a point since her promotion to call her Detective. "It's like I told you. You're making a whole lot of leaps without having your eye on where it is you're going to land. There's some big differences between the case you're working and what happened to Ernie, and one is that the fellow sitting back there told me that the men who put him in the hospital were standing at a cross in white robes and hoods. That's not speculation. That's not a hunch. That's a fact."

His aggravation made her shrink inside herself. Once again, he'd quickly brushed her off and not even taken the time to consider what she was saying. Leah did her best not to take it personally, but between Coggins's reaction and her conversation with Tillman, her typical thick skin had been worn soft as suede. There was a lot going on and perhaps the sheriff just couldn't afford to spare any mental energy at all. Right then he seemed to recognize that he'd upset her and his face relaxed.

"Look, I know what you're wanting, Leah. I know. But I can't help you with that case. I just can't." He stared at her with a pleading look in his eyes. "I'm too close to it. I'm too close to Vess and the rest of that family. It was all I could do just to sit there with her and Dayna at that house the other day. Took everything I had."

Suddenly she understood why he'd been so standoffish. She remembered how worn out and empty he'd looked the night of the vigil.

"Like I said, though, you come by the office sometime tomorrow and we'll look over that report together. Okay?"

She nodded and dropped her eyes to the ground. Coggins squeezed Leah's shoulder and strolled off toward his truck.

This death had eaten her up and she hadn't known Toya Gardner at all, couldn't imagine what it must've been like to be that close. Digging into the details was unbearable with that sort of history. Coggins had dived headlong into Ernie's case, and she wondered if that was his way of coping, of keeping himself busy so he wouldn't have to deal with the loss. As he disappeared from view, she felt bad for hounding him.

Behind the house a small outbuilding made of brown-painted tin rested in direct sun, and there was a trail worn to bare dirt from the back steps of the house to the shed, then on to the stream. Off near the wood line a picnic table was tucked in the shade of a willow along the creek, and that's where Ernie sat with his mother beside him. The folks who'd been crowded around the table speaking to him headed off with empty plates in their hands and Leah figured now was as good a time as any to speak.

Ernie had a patch over his left eye and the side of his face was still yellowed with bruising. He wore braces on his lower back and wrists, a ball cap and a navy blue T-shirt with TUCKASEGEE TRADING COMPANY printed over the breast pocket. His movements were stiff and somewhat robotic.

"Leah Green, is that you?" Ernie's mother, Clara, stood and came over to hug her.

"How are you doing, Mrs. Allison?" Leah squeezed Clara and was overcome with the smell of perfume and bug spray. "I don't think I've seen you in a year."

"Last fall." Clara kept her hand on Leah's shoulder. "Mountain Heritage Day."

"That's right," Leah said. "I couldn't remember if it was there or out thrifting."

"Liable to find me anywhere there's a deal, hon. You get you something to eat?"

"Not yet, but I will."

"I'll get you a plate," she said. "I was just about to go grab another one of those deviled eggs Doreen Stroup brought."

"I'm okay," Leah said. "I'll fix me a plate here in a little while."

"Mama, grab me another one of these Busch Lights out of the cooler on your way back, would you?"

"How many is that, Ernie? You're not supposed to drink on those pills."

"And you're not supposed to be worrying about me no more." Ernie shook his head and smiled. "I'm twenty-eight years old."

"And stubborn as the day you was born," Clara mumbled over her shoulder as she shuffled off toward the house.

"Come sit over here beside me." Ernie brushed the bench off as if clearing her a spot. "Be nice to have a pretty woman to sit beside for a minute or two."

Leah was more than ten years his senior. He was an absolute doll baby, but she was too settled in and set in her ways to go breaking horses. She took a seat, leaned over, and kissed him on the cheek. "You saying your mama ain't a pretty woman?"

"She's going to drive me crazy before this is over with. Got a heart of gold and I wouldn't trade her for nothing, but I'm about ready for some alone time, some peace and quiet. I can't wipe my ass without her knocking on the bathroom door."

"How you feeling?"

"Oh, I'm all right. Stove up, but I'm getting better. How you like this eye patch?" He leaned in close and stretched his good eye wide until she laughed.

"It's very becoming."

"Yeah," he said. "I look about like a goddamned pirate."

"Well, if nothing else we'll get you a peg leg and set you out front down at the fish camp. You can make some side money on the weekends."

"You wasn't such a sight for sore eyes, I'd take offense to that."

Ernie polished off the last swig from a brown glass bottle on the table. He'd completely peeled off the label. "*Sore eye*," he joked.

There was something nice about sitting there with him. Ever since they'd found Toya Gardner's body she'd been absolutely sick with work, and for one split second her mind wandered off to someplace different.

"How's your case coming?" Ernie asked.

"Just got the initial report back from the state."

"Anything jump out at you?"

"Not exactly. I mean, she was shot three times in the chest, and one of those bullets passed through both hands, like she must've had her hands up trying to protect herself. I was hoping there'd be some DNA under her fingernails, something, but there wasn't. Just dirt from where she clawed at the ground where she fell."

"They know what kind of gun was used?"

"Thirty-Eight Special."

"So I guess they recovered bullets from the body?"

"They did," Leah said. She stared off into empty space as they spoke, the world seeming to go silent around her as her brain chewed over the details. "Two of the bullets shattered to bits, the jackets just completely separated altogether, but one was still in pretty good shape. Bullet held together and stopped against her spine."

"They think it's in good enough shape they could match it to the weapon?"

"That's the hope," she said. "But first we've got to have a weapon."

Ernie took the empty bottle of beer and spun it on the picnic table like they were at a high school party. When it finished spinning the bottle pointed back toward the house, and he stood it up and started toppling the neck back and forth between his fingers. After a long spell of the only sound being the tap of the glass against wood, he spoke.

"Now, this is an absolute shot in the dark, but I'll tell you one person I know with a .38 Special riding around in his glove box."

"Who's that?"

"That fellow we took in over at Harold's that night. Same fellow Coggins pulled out of the river yesterday. William Dean Cawthorn," he said. "Did you see the picture of them dragging that car out?"

"No, I didn't."

Ernie struggled to wrestle his phone from his pocket and scrolled until he found the picture and faced the screen her way so she could see. A tow truck had a line stretched out to midriver and was pulling the station wagon back to the bank.

"I'd say there's a whole lot of folks riding around with .38 Specials," she said. "Dad used to keep a .357 Mag under the driver's seat of his truck. A Ruger SP101. He shot .38 Specials out of it until the barrel burned out. I can't go rounding up every gun in this county. There's got to be some sort of connection between the person who owns it and the victim. So what is it?"

"I don't know," Ernie said. "I'm just running roads. You the big-shot detective."

"Yeah." Leah chuckled and buried her face in her hands. "Most times I think I'd be better off back on patrol."

"Okay. Here's your connection. Your victim was there at the protests, right?"

"She was."

"Well, so was William Dean Cawthorn."

"Now, how do you know that?"

"The sheriff told me. Said he seen him standing there just as sure as shit."

The lead was a stretch, but it wasn't completely harebrained, and even more so it fit into her theory that the two cases were connected, that what had happened to Toya tied back to the Klan.

Truth was she didn't have a thing else to go on. The only suspects so far were a nut job who'd turned over his house to a rat snake, a grumpy old cuss who'd been riding a grader too long, and a college kid who had no motive other than a summerlong crush. Instinct told her none of them were guilty, but nothing so far was panning out, and so nothing was out of the question.

"The sheriff doesn't seem to think these two cases are connected. He doesn't believe what happened to Toya Gardner has anything to do with the Klan."

"And what does your gut tell you?"

"My gut tells me it does."

"Then there you go," Ernie said.

They sat there for a while longer chewing the fat, and the conversation got back to things that took her mind away from the case and away from those questions Tillman had raised, even if just temporarily.

"One of these days you're going to have to let me take you dancing," Ernie said, slapping his fingers against the edge of the tabletop. "What do you say to that?"

Leah placed one hand on top of his, the top of his hand hidden under the wrist brace. "A woman like me'd break you in half." She stood and got ready to go.

"Perfect," Ernie shouted. "You talking to a man's already there."

She stood behind him and set her hands on his shoulders, leaned down, and kissed the top of his head. "Come to think of it, I do sort of have a thing for pirates."

Off in the distance a cloud cast a shadow shaped like a Plott hound against the mountain. With its nose down and tail straight, the dog worked a trail north to south over the ridge and gone. Two kids came tearing past and the little girl in front grabbed ahold of Leah, using her leg to spin around and gain a nose in a game of chase. Leah stopped for a split second to take it all in—the smell of barbecue cooking on the smoker, the screams of kids and parents, the mountains green and glowing.

This was how it had always been, a place that appeared perfect and charmed, the type of tight-knit community the rest of the world had long ago lost. Her mind could not reconcile the way things had always seemed with the events of the past few weeks. As if what had happened to Ernie weren't horrible enough, the murder of Toya Gardner marked an unraveling. Now she found herself trying to peer past the smiles and laughter, to place her finger on something she'd never believed was there. For all Leah knew, the wicked were right there among them.

42

A decade or so back, Coggins had stumbled across a pair of fully automatic Colt M1A1 Thompson submachine guns while taking inventory of the county armory. The weapons dated back to the Depression and he enlisted the help of Silas Crane to sell them. Silas tracked down a collector who bought them both, the rifles bringing in nearly thirty-five grand apiece. With the money, Coggins was able to outfit every deputy in the department with new body armor and rifles, something the county had refused to place in the budget. Silas wouldn't even take a commission on the sale.

When the sheriff pulled up to the camper on Wolf Mountain, he could see him hunched over and stirring inside through a heavy tan curtain that glowed yellow in the night. There was a screech owl whistling its quavered and lonesome song from the top of a tall hemlock that looked like the skeleton of a fish silhouetted against the sky. The sheriff waited there in his truck with the door open and listened to the owl for a minute, just staring off at nothing and knowing all too well that feeling.

He'd come to visit for a couple reasons, but mainly because he'd wanted an excuse to drink and couldn't at home on account of Evie. Deep down there were remnants of the alcoholic he'd been, embers that had lain under the ash for years without showing so much as smoke. His relapse had started with the girl, with not being able to wash her out of his mind on his own, and so that first night he'd opened the bottle and drunk himself into a dreamless sleep. The ember had lit a fire, and now that old part of him was burning.

The thing about an alcoholic's mind was that it was so goddamned logical. All day that part of his brain cooked up excuses so that even when he told himself to go one night without a drink there was always a better reason to have one. He'd gotten a lot of work finished. A couple drinks would help him sleep. It was Friday. One beer was nothing. Two beers, a six-pack. He told himself he wasn't buying the quart of liquor for himself. He told himself it was for Silas Crane as an overdue thank-you and because he hadn't been by to see him in forever. It was easy for men like Coggins to justify a drink.

He rapped on the camper door with one knuckle, and the latch was busted so that the door rattled with each knock. Silas opened the door and leaned way back as if surprised, a wide smile spreading across his face, when he saw him. He'd always worn his curly gray hair long, but he had it braided into a ponytail at each side, and with that gray and white beard he looked like Willie Nelson.

"They hell, Sheriff!" Silas held the door back with his hand. "Get in the house before somebody sees you and thinks I've turned state's witness."

The camper was small and cramped, and though neither was a tall man, they both stooped so as not to knock their heads against the ceiling. There was a small four-eye stove and oven, a counter and sink straight across from the door. A window unit was running wide open, the place as cold and dry as a meat locker.

"You want a beer?"

"I'd love one," Coggins said.

Silas grabbed a couple camo-can Busch Lights out of a mini fridge under the counter. He held one back toward Coggins while he was still bent over and facing away. When he stood, he worked quickly on the right side of the camper to fold and unfold parts from the wall so that in short order there was a small table and two places to sit, as if they might've been about to play a game of cards.

The quart jar was rolled up inside a brown paper poke. Coggins slid into the seat nearest the door and unwrapped the gift he'd brought.

"I don't think I ever thanked you properly for helping us with them Thompsons," Coggins said as he stood the jar on the table.

"Where'd you get that?" Silas's eyes lit up.

"Some of them Luker boys." Coggins laughed. "Stopped by on the way up."

The light inside was low and dim like a barroom. An old Alabama song played softly from a small radio on the windowsill by the bed. Silas took the jar and held it sideways in his hands. He shook the liquor up and watched it bead. When the bubbles were gone, he spun the cap free and held the jar to his nose. "I've always thought good liquor had a smell about like cherries."

"Well, go on," Coggins said, excited for him to taste it. "Take you a horn." He cracked open his beer and emptied half the can with his first swallow.

Silas sipped from the jar and smiled. "Birch," he said. "Hard to believe you'd remember a thing like that."

Coggins reached across for the jar and filled his mouth and swallowed. The liquor was smooth and the birch gave it a slight hint of root beer. "Of all the things ripe to remember, what a man likes to drink ranks right up there with how he likes his women and what denomination he attends."

"Best I recall, you were a scotch man, John."

"See?" Coggins said. "Some things you don't forget." He passed the jar back. "I remember you used to be bad to drink that Dr. Mc-Gillicuddy's when you couldn't get ahold of any white."

"Still am." Silas chuckled and reached behind a coffeemaker on the countertop for a small pint bottle that looked about like mouthwash. He took a sip of the moonshine and chased it down with beer. "Had to switch to Busch Light from Busch heavy. Doctor's orders. I ain't had good birch in ten or fifteen years."

"Ahh," Coggins groaned as if surprised. He spread his mustache across his lips to keep from wetting it while he drank.

"Can't find it anymore," Silas said. "Last time I went to get a quart of liquor, they had about twenty flavors. Peach pie, apple pie, pear, strawberry, blackberry, watermelon, goddamn pumpkin pie, and every bit of it taste about like Kool-Aid."

Coggins finished that first beer and stretched toward the fridge for another. "Probably marketing to all these sweet-tongue sons of bitches moving up here and buying these mountains out from under us."

"I'd say you right." Silas set the jar on the table and pushed it to the middle so that it was equidistant between them. "A couple years ago I went and seen them Luker boys, and Frank's daddy had put bear galls in a quart. Said that shit would turn your pecker hard as an axe handle. Well, I was dating this girl worked down there at Dugan's Pub in Brevard and I knew she was coming up here to see me later that night, so I took me a big pull off of that, and let me tell you, Sheriff, we done it right there in the floor."

Coggins was halfway through taking a swig from the jar, and as he listened he got tickled and the liquor went down the wrong pipe. He coughed and laughed and choked. "God almighty, Silas!" he squalled. "You about to kill me!"

"Well, it's the truth." Silas Crane sipped his beer and rolled his shoulder as if working a crick from his neck, then gazed across the camper with a shit-eating grin. "There we was right there on this floor, and I caught a cramp in the back of my leg and I seized up, and by God that old gal thought she'd turned me inside out."

"Stop!" Coggins hollered. He was still coughing and laughing and couldn't catch his breath. "You lucky you ain't throw your damned back out wallering around as old as you are."

For the next hour they sat there telling stories and talking about the way the county had changed. They drank the beer and 'shine like water, and the words flowed freely between them.

Silas told the sheriff how 281 had turned into some tourist-trap raceway for sports cars and motorcycles. Nowadays, he said, it was like living off the Tail of the Dragon in Swain County or the Rattler in Haywood and Madison. Every weekend car clubs and motorcycles with out-of-state tags came tearing through like hurricanes. Silas said he missed the quiet. He said he missed the old days when they could've drug a logging chain across the road and run them sons of bitches off with shotguns and splitting mauls.

They laughed about a story from thirty years ago when Archie Manring got stuck behind some dickhead on a bicycle coming off the big hill, him hauling a load of stone with the jake brake thumping like a jackhammer. When they finally hit the bottom, the bicyclist flipped Archie the finger and Archie blew that old boy's bike out from under him with a load of birdshot as he passed. "They'd law a man's ass for that nowadays," Coggins said, as if he weren't the man wearing the badge.

The empties stacked up around them and Silas brought up what had happened to the girl. As soon as Coggins heard Toya's name, his thoughts shifted to Vess. His head filled with images and memories, her rattled voice echoing from a few days before, and for once he was thankful Lon was gone. It was torture seeing her in that kind of pain, seeing Dayna emptied like a husk, and that weight was more than he could stand right then. He took a long drink and turned the conversation to Ernie because he did not wish to dwell on something so painful for more than an instant. Over the next few minutes he told Silas where they'd found Ernie lying that morning, about the coma, the hospital, and all the details Ernie'd recalled when he woke up.

"Well, as far as that cross goes, your guess is as good as mine." Silas shook his beer can by his ear to test how much was left, but he'd already drunk it dry. "But them fancy boots, Sheriff, you know good and well who that sounds like."

Coggins looked across the table, puzzled.

"There's only one man I've ever known made it a point to strut all over town in a real fancy pair of boots. Matter of fact, he used to keep them propped on the board of the county commission."

The second he said that, Coggins's mind spun off like the lid of that mason jar. He was surprised it hadn't come to him sooner. Not only did the sheriff know exactly whom Silas was talking about, it was one of the names Ernie'd mentioned that day in his office.

Silas leaned over from where he sat and opened the refrigerator. "Damned if we ain't drunk every beer I had," he griped, and slammed the fridge door before falling back into his seat.

Coggins stood up too fast and knocked his brains out against the ceiling. "I best be getting on down the road," he said. Right then he couldn't tell if it was hitting his head or the liquor, but he was dizzy and his legs felt like feathers beneath him. "I drink much more and I won't be fit to drive."

"Comes to that, Sheriff, we can always fold this table back up."
Silas slapped his hand on the tabletop and a string of bubbles fizzed
up through the shine. His eyes were low and red, and a troublemak-
ing smile crept across his face. "Presto change-o and you've got
yourself a bed."

43

There was something bugging the sheriff about the day they'd spent at the Balsam Cross searching for clues after Ernie's memory returned. A voice in the back of his head kept telling him they'd missed something. So that next morning after drinking with Silas Crane, he drove back to the scene with a headache splitting his skull like an apple.

There was only one road to the top of the mountain. Coggins drove slow by the houses, hoping he'd spot someone out in the yard he might ask a couple quick questions about anything they might've seen or heard that night. Unfortunately, it being the middle of a weekday, most honest folks were at work. There was a little brick rancher with white shutters and a covered porch set real close to the road, and as he passed he noticed a doorbell camera affixed to the front of the house.

When he knocked, a white-haired woman about his age or a fuzz younger with hair buzzed short answered the door. She had on a pair of loose-fitting pants that hung about like a dress and was barefooted with a barn coat pulled over her T-shirt. She eyed him from boots to mustache with an air of skepticism, like he might've been some Bible thumper or pest control salesman.

"Hello, ma'am, I'm Sheriff John Coggins from over in Jackson County and I was just up the road there and come by, seen this doorbell camera you had here." Coggins reached out and pecked the lens of the camera with the tip of his finger.

"Yeah, my daughter bought me that last Christmas. We kept having packages go missing off our porch. You can't leave nothing out anymore. People steal you blind. What line of work you said you were in, Sheriff?"

Coggins chuckled and she grinned at how he took the joke. The longer he looked at her, the more she resembled a toad. "You like that camera?"

"Ain't worth a shit," she said. "Way it's pointed out through there it takes pictures of everything comes up the road. My daughter had it all set up to where it would send me notifications on my phone and that thing would just ding, ding, ding all the ding-dong day, all damn night, about drove me crazy. Finally she come and visited some time back around Easter and we got it worked out to where it just emails them now. If I've got a package I'm expecting and it goes missing, I'll go back and look through them, but other than that they just all go to spam."

"Do you have a computer?"

"Have to. Small as the screens are on these things I can't half see who's calling without putting on my readers." She held up a cell phone he hadn't noticed she was holding.

"I'm sorry, ma'am. I don't even think I got your name."

"Myrtle Erb." The way she said it made the whole name sound like one word and it took Coggins a second to break it in half.

"I don't think I know anyone named Erb."

"You wouldn't," she said. "All my family was Florida crackers. I grew up in horse country. But I've been here long enough. Been here a long time."

"Well, Miss Erb, this is going to sound funny, but do you think we might take a look through some of those pictures from a couple of weeks ago? There's one night in particular I'd like to take a look at if you don't mind."

"You more than welcome, Sheriff. You drink coffee?"

"Like water," Coggins said.

44

Heavy dew flickered like a busted bottle broken over the church-yard, and it wet the pants legs and ankles of the men who'd gathered there. The women remained in the parking lot and on the short sidewalk leading up to the sanctuary doors so that the damp lawn would not stain the leather of their shoes. Their heels clopped like hooves as they rambled from one group to another, making their rounds to speak.

The original church had looked two-dimensional, like a cookie-cutter-shaped building thrown up as the backdrop of a play. It had been simple clapboard with a single window and a cedar-shake roof. The only similarities between that building and the one they stood outside now were the clapboards and the steeple, two doors at the base of the tower, a pyramid-shaped cap with a spire at its top. Mount Zion was white with a rust-colored asphalt-shingle roof and a row of tall windows down its side. The ground was uneven, so that the foundation tapered down from the back of the building to the steps leading up to the doors.

Vess Jones and Lula Shepherd stood like bookends at Dayna's sides. In the pines above them, a pair of crows cawed, and Vess wished she had a gun to shoot them from their perches. She glowered into the trees, and finally one of the birds seemed to notice and the two took off together, one following the other toward the ridge above that cast the cove in shadow.

By the time the state had finally released Toya Gardner's body, her mother had finished the arrangements. Tomorrow there would be a closed-casket service and interment in a mausoleum. But today the body was to be transported from Asheville to a funeral home in Atlanta, and that's why the people had come. The afternoon before, Reverend Tillman had led the first march through Sylva. They'd shut the roads down as nearly five hundred people attended, with news trucks traveling from as far away as Charlotte. This morning, though, it was just the congregation from Zion and a few members of Liberty Baptist in Sylva who'd gathered outside the church to organize themselves into a cavalcade. Within the hour they would climb into their cars and follow the girl home. They refused to let her make that passage alone.

A large truck eased up the road in front of the church and Vess immediately recognized it as the sheriff's. Coggins tapped his brakes as he tried to find a place to park. There was no room left in the lot, and so he wheeled into the grass where the quarter-acre cemetery butted up to the wood line. When Coggins stepped out she felt her daughter draw taut as a plait. The night before, Dayna had learned he'd given Toya a ride, and now she blamed him fully for what had happened.

Coggins walked up and nodded at Dayna, then turned his attention to Vess when he spoke. "I've made some calls and we've got blue lights to escort you through every county from Buncombe to the Georgia line."

"I appreciate that, John."

"Wish I could go with you, but I'm pretty tied up here."

"Doing what exactly?" Dayna snapped. "We don't need you here, Sheriff. There's no reason for you to be here. You've already done plenty."

Vess lowered her head. She was equally mad, but the difference between them was that Dayna's anger had stretched outward and found its place to light, whereas Vess's was aimed at herself. She just kept remembering what Toya had said that morning. "If you don't want me to go, just tell me," her granddaughter had said.

"I'm sorry, but I'm not sure what you mean." Coggins had his head tilted to the side while he waited for Dayna to explain.

"Why would you just drop Toya off like that? Just took her up there and left her to walk home."

"That's what she asked me to do."

"Dayna, if it wasn't for John there's no telling what would've happened down there at the courthouse. Don't forget he's who got her out of there."

"What might've happened? What are you talking about, Mama? What do you think we're doing here? Nothing could've happened there that's worse than this. He knew good and well what kind of danger she was in and he left her just to walk down that road by herself. That badge he's wearing, he's supposed to protect people in this county, not leave them to fend for themselves."

Vess looked at Coggins and she could see that what her daughter was saying was hurting him. He looked at Vess for a split second, then dropped his eyes to the ground, turned to Dayna as he looked up, and spoke.

"Your daughter was a grown woman," he said. "I did exactly

what she asked me to do. Now, I come here to see y'all off because I know how much pain and suffering y'all are going through right now—"

"You don't know shit about my suffering."

Coggins took a step back and Vess thought she saw tears in his eyes. "If you don't want me here, that's fine," he said. "I'll head on."

"Well, I don't, Sheriff. I don't want you here."

Coggins looked at her and nodded, then turned and started to leave.

"I want you to find who did this," Dayna yelled as he eased away. "That's what I want you to do!"

Coggins raised his hand as if to acknowledge he'd heard.

Reverend Tillman had been standing with the other men and now he jogged over to try to catch him, but Coggins did not turn. Everyone who was gathered there stood speechless and watched as the sheriff crossed the churchyard and climbed into his truck.

45

The Smokehouse was crowded, same as every other restaurant in town. There was always a rush at lunch and dinner, but during tourist season most places stayed packed open to close so that it was hard for working people to find a place to sit down and grab a quick bite to eat. Coggins sat alone in a booth by the kitchen and finished his plate of brisket. He'd eaten a double helping of collards and was sopping up the puddle of baked beans with a slice of Texas toast when the waitress came by to check on him.

"You doing all right, Sheriff?"

There was still food in his mouth as he answered. "Think I'm ready for a check."

"No dessert? We've got peach cobbler and banana pudding."

He scrubbed the corners of his mustache with a napkin, balled the napkin up in his fist, and tossed it onto his empty plate. Leaning back against the wooden booth, he patted his stomach like it was the head of a drum. "I couldn't fit another bite if I tried."

"What about a tea to go?"

"I'm good," he said. "But thank you."

The waitress pulled a notepad from a pocket in a black apron tied around her waist and slid the check onto the edge of the table. "I'll take that whenever you're ready."

She hurried off to field an order from a large party that had just pulled two tables together in the center of the room. Coggins looked at his tab, opened his billfold, and slid a twenty-dollar bill under the edge of his empty plate. He rattled the ice that was left in his glass and took the last sip of a half-and-half tea.

The front door slapped closed and three men walked into the dining room. A stubby fellow with a purple nose strutted into the restaurant like he was cock of the walk. His voice was boisterous and insufferable, and Coggins knew the sound without looking up. The sheriff leaned onto his hip and pushed his billfold back into his pocket. He stood as a waitress led the men to a table at the far corner of the room.

Slade Ashe had been born with Senate-floor dreams in a dirt-floor shack and was just snakey enough he might have slithered all the way to Washington had he ever found enough eggs to swallow. Instead, he worked backroom deals on the county commission, taking every bribe offered over the course of six terms. In the years since politics, he'd become a slumlord leeching off people who couldn't afford to feed their families. In a world that rewarded the selfish and the cutthroat, he'd managed to make himself a mint.

Coggins knew the two men with him as well. Donnie Franks played Mr. Fix-it for the foreclosures and short sales Slade'd scooped up when the market crashed. Now that Slade'd moved into renting out chipboard tool sheds as tiny homes, Donnie served more as henchman than handyman. Donnie Franks actually wasn't a bad guy, just dumber than a corncob and too long in the tooth for his own good.

The last man at the table had moved to the county from Florida a year before and immediately gotten to schmoozing with what went for movers and shakers in a place like this. Jesse Waldrop was retired law enforcement turned sheriff hopeful. He'd made his intention clear just as soon as Coggins announced his retirement, and Coggins had nearly decided to stick it out another term just to keep him from having a chance.

Coggins strode over to where they sat and stood at the head of the table. They all looked up at once and he smiled as he rubbed a circle around his stomach with his right hand. "Gentlemen, how are we?"

"Doing good, John. Doing good." Slade Ashe spoke for the group. "You leave anything for the rest of us?" He sniggered with a smart-assed smile, his elbows on the table and hands clasped together.

Donnie Franks was propped up in the corner with one arm stretched across the top of the booth. Waldrop looked away from Coggins, and from the slight shake of the back of his head Coggins could tell he was laughing.

"They's surely a chicken or two left back there somewhere. Your kind just unhinges that jaw and swallows them whole, don't they?"

"Looks like you've done emptied the coop." Slade turned in the booth, and when he did his boots showed from under the table. He unrolled his silverware, took his fork, and poked Coggins in the stomach. The whole table cackled, and for a split second Coggins thought about driving stakes. From where he stood he could've clobbered every one of their goddamned brains out.

"Them some fancy boots you got on. What kind of leather is that? That some sort of crocodile or something?"

"These?" Slade held his feet up and looked around the corner of the table so he could get a better look. The boots he wore were light brown with a heavy checkered pattern, the edges of each square raised. He turned his feet side to side. "You going to have to pick up a second job you want a pair of these. These here are arapaima."

"What the hell's that?"

"A fish, John." Slade said it matter-of-factly, as if the sheriff were an idiot for asking. "They catch them down there on the Amazon, see. Fish about as long as them tables drawn together over there." Slade motioned toward the center of the room. "Like I said, though, these here a little pricey for a man of your stature."

"Probably ain't a whole lot of boots like that floating around. I'd say a man be hard-pressed to find another pair in Jackson County."

"I'd say you're right." Slade Ashe slid his feet back under the table and clasped his hands together like he'd been sitting when Coggins walked up. He leaned over his elbows and set his mouth against his thumbs so that when he spoke his words were inside his hands. "But just what the hell's got you so fixed on these boots of mine?"

"Just not every day a man sees a pair of boots like that, that's all. Whereabouts you find something like that?"

"Gatlinburg. Little store there on the main drag. Bought this pair last fall. Took the wife to Dollywood for her birthday. But like I said, John, you'd need to take out a second mortgage on that junk heap of yours to get into a pair of boots like these."

Everyone at the table hooted and cackled, and Coggins smiled wide until they all went quiet with anxious looks about their faces.

"No, I don't think I'll go hunting me down no fish boots any time soon, but I do appreciate it." He leaned to one side and rolled his knuckles against the tabletop as if to signal he'd be going. "Oh, I almost forgot. You still driving that old Dodge with the service body, Donnie?"

"Yeah, what about it?"

"Been looking for one about like that's all, if you was ever of a mind to sell it."

"No, I don't believe I'll be looking to sell it no time soon."

"What about the service body?"

"No, I don't believe I will."

"That's all right," Coggins said. "All the same I might come by and take a look at it. Come off an old DOT truck, didn't it?"

"It did."

"How'd you manage to fit a Ford bed on a Dodge chassis?"

"A little redneck ingenuity." Donnie thought that sounded witty, and he ran his eyes around the table to see if anyone was laughing with him, but they weren't.

"Well, like I said, I'd love to take a closer look. Might know where I can find me another service body like that. I've got an old Dodge about like yours, just an old farm truck, but I bet it's about the same model."

"Welcome anytime, Sheriff."

"Thank you." Coggins started toward the door.

The only one who hadn't said a word while he stood there spoke up then. "Love to have your endorsement next fall."

Coggins stopped in his tracks, spun, and squared up to the table. He'd heard all the things Waldrop had said behind his back, heard what he'd said up there by the statue that afternoon, and it ate him up that there was anyone in this county who'd listen to a word of it. In a place like this, a man's name was all there was, a legacy if he was lucky, and Coggins had devoted his entire career to building his.

"Son, I wouldn't sell some Dade County sunburnt son of a bitch like you breathing air in a glass jug," he said.

The man smirked and shook his head. Coggins stood there for a moment, but no one else had a word to add. As he walked through the door, he raised his hand as if to wave goodbye to anyone in the dining room he might've known, a habit he kept so as to never high-hat anyone.

Those idiots at the table had just shown him their hands, and now it was just a matter of figuring out how to play his own. If Slade Ashe had been the one stomping Ernie's head into the ground, then Franks was most likely the one holding him down. The difference between them was that Slade Ashe wouldn't leave a trail. He'd slither under a brush pile on his belly, coil up in the shadows, and lie low, tongue flicking, till the dust settled. Donnie, on the other hand, was just dumb enough to slip up. All Coggins needed was to put his foot to his throat.

46

They'd reached the part of summer when thunderstorms bubbled up every afternoon. Clouds dark as wetted slate built over the ridgeline and the air smelled of rain. Straight overhead the sky was still relatively clear and there was always the chance it would stay that way. The mountains had a strange way of breaking up storms. Sometimes a front might settle over a holler and empty itself completely before breaking apart into heat lightning and starlight. There was seldom any way to tell.

In the back of a cove off Greens Creek, Donnie Franks was running a wood splitter in front of his home. There was a mix of red oak and cherry bucked but not busted, and he was feeding those logs into the machine, quartering them into firewood one piece at a time. He wore a pair of Liberty overalls with no shirt, dark hair on his arms and chest, his back covered just as thick as he turned and grabbed another section of log. He was a short brute with wrists big around as axles and a neck that barely tapered from his ears to his shoulders.

Coggins angled his pickup beside the mound of firewood and stepped out just as Donnie tossed a few more pieces into the pile. "How we doing this afternoon, Mr. Franks?" The sheriff reached down and picked up a bucked section of oak that had rolled near his feet and handed it to Donnie, who pitched it onto the machine without a word. "Seems too early to be putting up wood."

"A man don't stay after it, the year will flat get away from him." The wood splitter sputtered and smoked as the wedge drove through the red oak and the halves fell off to each side. Donnie Franks picked the split sections up and fed one piece into the cradle, then the other. "Blink your eyes and it's winter."

"You selling much firewood?"

"A half cord here and there. All I can fit in that truck since I put that service body on it. Sold my other truck and this one ain't got much of a bed." Donnie motioned toward the pickup pulled lengthways against the front of his double-wide. They were both speaking loudly to avoid being drowned out by the machine. "Took a load over to Mrs. Neely's about two weeks ago. Say she's probably about due for another way she burns through it. Old woman still heating water on a woodstove. Still cooks that a way."

"Sounds like my grandmama. She ran that old cast iron woodstove till the day she died. Prettiest stove I've ever seen," Coggins said. "Turquoise enamel, looked like an old Chevrolet or something. They just don't make anything like that anymore."

Donnie Franks hit the kill switch on the wood splitter and the engine rattled into silence. "Same as this thing here," he said. "Dad bought this when I was in middle school. Buddy, we thought we was in high cotton not having to swing that go-devil no more. I've run the piss out of it ever since. Couldn't buy a new one now for what they're asking and wouldn't want one if I could."

Coggins bent over and grabbed one of the split pieces and pitched it onto the pile. He knelt when he grabbed the next, staying crouched as he turned the wood in his hands to look it over. "Funny how that splitter leaves that line like that." There was a triangular impression driven straight through the length of the wood, darkened and smooth, as if it were almost burned from the friction.

"Every piece," Donnie said. "Been like that long as I can remember." He continued to talk as he flung pieces of wood over his head without looking at where they were landing. "All these old splitters leave something like that, every one a little different. You show me a piece of firewood and most times I can tell you whose machine it come off. The Hoopers' looks one way. Messers' another. Don't know what it is, but I tell you it's about like fingerprints."

Coggins flipped the piece he held onto the mound of firewood and looked then at the truck by the house. "What year's that Dodge of yours, Donnie? 'Seventy-four? 'Seventy-five?"

"That's a 'seventy-six," he said. "Wasn't a whole lot of difference." The truck had been painted red at one point in time, but through the years the sun had beat it down into a flat and faded pink. The service body he'd attached to the back was an oddly bright contrast, its paint still shiny and yellow as a finch.

"Mine's a 'seventy-five," Coggins said. "Dad's old farm truck. That one a V8?"

"Yeah, a four forty with the Dynatrac."

"I think that one of Dad's is a three sixty," he said. "But I don't really know. We might as well be talking about growing flowers."

"They were all good trucks," Donnie said. He was checking the oil on the wood splitter and wiped the dipstick against the bib of his overalls.

"Well, like I told you the other day, I've got a line on a service body just like that. Come off a DOT truck down there in Cashiers. Fellow named Lewis Medford got one up under his porch with a tarp pulled over it. Told me it was mine if I wanted it, but I just didn't know how I'd get a Ford bed put on a Dodge."

"Like I told you, Sheriff. Redneck ingenuity." Donnie Franks smiled like a mule eating briars as he leaned down into the pile of firewood and hugged eight or so pieces to his chest. He started off toward a covering of framed timbers roofed with old tin that sat at the edge of the woods. Cords of firewood were stacked neatly beneath it to season. As he crossed the yard, he hollered back over his shoulder, "Go take a look if you want."

Beside the rear driver's-side tire, Coggins crouched on his hands and knees to make it look like he knew what he was doing, but the truth was he didn't give a flying shit how that halfwit had fixed the bed to the frame. Coggins didn't own a Dodge. Like all people of any account, his father had been a Chevrolet man.

The photographs captured by that old woman's doorbell camera the night Ernie wound up at the cross weren't the clearest pictures ever taken, but they'd captured a string of vehicles making their way up the mountain a half hour past midnight. A few hours later, that same procession came down Greenspire Drive, three trucks and two sedans, with one sticking out like a pair of arapaima boots.

From the looks of it, Donnie Franks had used a cutting torch to salvage parts off an old tractor or trackhoe, cutting the heavy steel into lengths that he'd bubblegum-welded across the existing frame to meet the mounts of the new bed. There was no telling what the ass end of that truck weighed with all of that metal, but it likely wouldn't make eight miles to the gallon. Coggins was wriggling out from under the truck on his back when Donnie threw his foot up on the rear bumper. The soles of his logging boots were breaking apart into layers so that they looked like a hand of tobacco.

"What you think?"

"I like that, Donnie. Some real clean welds. You do that yourself?"

"Not the prettiest you'll ever see, but one thing's for sure." He balled up his fist and pounded hard against one of the cabinets on the side of the service body. "It'll hold."

Coggins backed away from the truck and whistled like he was surely impressed. "You care if I get a couple pictures right fast? I got a fellow down in Sylva, hell of a welder, owes me a favor."

Thunder echoed against the mountains and rattled the window-panes of the double-wide. "Lay with it," Donnie said. "I need to get this wood put in the dry. Looks like this storm's going to be on top of us directly."

Coggins took his phone from his pocket and snapped a few quick pictures right as the bottom fell out of the sky. The rain came and he hustled back to his truck, but by the time he hit the cab his clothes were drenched clean through. Through the windshield wipers and the rain, he watched Donnie shake the water off of himself like a dog in the shelter of the tin roof.

47

The first thing Leah noticed when she pulled up to the house was a king snake hanging from a noose in a dogwood tree. The snake was nearly six feet long and twisted in the breeze like some dollar-store whirligig.

Curtis Darnell was at the side of the house checking frames in a bee box. Honeybees swarmed around him and crawled up his bare arms. He had on a ratty T-shirt and black dress slacks, and there was a football helmet on his head. The bees rammed into the helmet and bounced off as he slipped the frame back into the box and sealed the hive.

"What you wearing that helmet for, Curtis?" Leah asked as he came across the yard to where she'd parked.

"Them bees never been bad to sting, but they'll ram into your head like they've been fired out of a slingshot. Get in your hair, and now that's when they'll sting you. You see that?" Curtis smiled at the snake. He took off the helmet and she could see that one of his

front teeth was split in half on a diagonal. "I'll be sleeping inside
now." He laughed. "I finally got my house back."

"What happened to your tooth?"

"Damned old black gum," he said. "Fellow down the road told
me he give me as much of it as I want for firewood. You'd have an
easier time splitting the moon in two. Go-devil jumped up and hit
me right in the mouth."

"You all right?"

"Oh, I'm fine." He rolled his top lip back so that his teeth showed
and pushed the tip of his tongue through the gap. "Got me an ap-
pointment made up there at the free dental clinic next Tuesday.
They said they'll fix me right up."

"Sounds to me like you should've been wearing that helmet then."

"You ain't telling me nothing."

When he walked over to the tree where the black snake hung,
she saw that the serpent ran longer than he was tall. Blowflies buzzed
and lit, and Leah could smell the rot from where she stood.

"Tell you how I did it," he said. "Now, it's like I told you, I'm
scared to death of snakes. Can't stand a snake. And of a night you
couldn't have paid me a million dollars to stay in that house. But
during the day, see, it didn't bother me as much because I could see
good. So I was sitting in there yesterday watching my soaps. There
was a hole in the wall and that's where I'd seen that snake the first
time, so I'd tied me this little slipknot on a piece of fishing string and
I had that loop pushed back in that hole like a foot snare. My daddy
used to catch rabbits like that in the summertime when they was
holding to the fencerows.

"But anyhow, I had that slipknot pushed back in that hole and
the other end run out to the spool, and I had that spool on a pencil
and that pencil shoved down between the cushions on the couch. So
I'm sitting there watching *Days of Our Lives*—that Hope Williams
Brady, I've always loved that Hope Williams Brady. She's a cop like

you. Hair's darker but got eyes about like yours. But so I'm sitting there watching *Days of Our Lives* and drinking a soda dope, and the line off that spool starts running. I look down and that line's just a-getting it. So I jumped up and I got ahold of that string and drug that snake out of that wall and mashed his head flat with a broom handle, I mean mashed him till his brains was coming out his ears." Curtis clapped his hands together and danced a jig with a giant smile spread across his face. He crowed loud as a rooster. "I got my house back. You believe that? I got my house back."

"That's good, Curtis. I'm happy for you," Leah said. She'd learned when talking to him that it was best to let him go, that his mind shorted out if you interrupted or didn't let him finish his thought. The more Leah was around Curtis, the more she came to have a strange affection for him. He was crazy as a bedbug, sure, but there was also something oddly sweet about him. "Listen, I've got that picture here I told you about."

"All right," he said.

Leah went back to her car and got a folder she'd brought from the office. She'd printed the photos large so that he'd have an easier time seeing them and called to explain before she'd come. On the trunk, she pulled out a photo of William Dean Cawthorn's car being towed from the river. Patrol units were positioned on both sides of the wrecker, a long cable off the boom running out to where it was lassoed around the station wagon's front axle.

Curtis walked over and peeked over her shoulder. "Yeah, that's the car all right. Looks like the USS *Jacob Jones* floating out there on that water, don't it? Just like I told you. Stretched out like a battleship."

"So that's definitely the vehicle you saw the man driving that morning?"

"Didn't see him driving. Saw him dump two boots' worth of water down that radiator, though."

Leah moved to the second photo, a mugshot taken of Cawthorn the night of his arrest outside of Harold's.

"That's him," Curtis said. "Sure as the world. You can't forget a face like that. Tell me that man there don't make your skin crawl."

Leah's heart pounded in her chest. She could place Cawthorn at the scene and she knew the gun he'd had was the caliber used in the killing. Cawthorn had the means, the motive, the opportunity. For the first time since she'd stood over Toya's body, she felt like she had an answer.

Curtis Darnell reached around her and flipped back to the first photo. The two of them stood staring at the picture of Cawthorn's car.

"And that truck, now, it was just like that one there except it ain't have all them lights and stickers and whatnot. Ain't have none of that on it," he said.

Leah only half listened to what he said now, her mind already someplace else, already slapping cuffs on that man from Mississippi. "Thank you, Curtis," she said. "I could just about hug your neck."

"Well, now that I've got that snake out of my house, you welcome to visit most anytime." Curtis smiled with that fang of a tooth sharp as a dagger front and center. "Give me a holler and I'll fix us supper."

All she needed to hang him was the gun. A ballistic match to the bullet they'd found in the body, and that would be it.

William Dean Cawthorn was staying in a run-down motel where the train tracks followed Scotts Creek through town. The single-story strip of rooms should've been condemned and torn down, but an ex–county commissioner had scooped it up for pennies when the recession hit. Weekly rates kept the clientele consistent—migrant workers bedding down short-term as they followed contracts hand-to-mouth, junkies and riffraff holed up with doors locked and the curtains drawn.

Leah found him sitting outside his room watching the world go by. A pair of patrol cars had followed her from the office, two young deputies full of piss and vinegar in case he decided to run.

"William Cawthorn?" she asked as she walked up, already knowing it was him.

He stood and smeared his hands down the front of his shirt as if he had something on them and was afraid she might ask to shake hands. "Normally I'd want to know who's asking, but a woman with a frame like you, honey, I don't give a shit who sent you." He seemed oblivious to the other officers, who stood by the trunks of their cars while he slicked his slimy fingers through the sides of his hair and offered a yellow-toothed smile. His eyes were an unnerving blue, his face sun-beaten as dried leather, and he struck her as one of the ugliest men she'd ever seen.

"I'm Detective Green," Leah said. "Jackson County Sheriff's Office."

"Should've known." He plopped back down in his chair and stared off at the steady stream of traffic driving by. "You people really do know how to make a man feel welcome. Ain't been here a month and I think I've met every badge-wearing son of a bitch in this country. What you here to do, beat my head in with a stick?"

"You are Mr. Cawthorn, correct?"

"Willy Dean, Dean, Coonie, Coonass. I go by all sorts of names. Don't make a shit really. Shotgun Willie sits around in his underwear."

"What?"

"Biting on a bullet and pulling out all of his hair."

"I don't know what you're talking about, but if you're William

Dean Cawthorn I need to have a word." Leah was curt, already getting sick of his mouth.

"Calm down, girl. It's just a song. I'm just singing a song."

"Well, I didn't come for karaoke, so how about giving me your undivided attention."

He sat there and chewed at a thumbnail, waiting on her to continue.

"I was told by another deputy that the night you were arrested down at Harold's they found a firearm in your car. Is that correct?"

"They did. And thankfully they gave it back when they cut me loose. Look around you, darling. You think I want to spend a night in some dump like this without a pistol under my pillow?"

"Do you still have that weapon now?"

"Of course I do, but what's this about? I got my concealed carry just like I told them that night. And they dropped all them charges you talking about, so what exactly are you asking?" Cawthorn had now seemed to notice the two deputies and he kept his eyes on them as if trying to weigh his options.

"Do you have that weapon on your person right now?"

"On my person? On my person, what the fuck does that even mean? Why don't you people just talk like normal goddamned human beings, huh? Why don't y'all try that for once in your life?"

"Sir, where is that weapon right now?"

"In there on the nightstand. Why?"

"What caliber is the weapon?"

"Thirty-Eight Special. Like the band, honey. But what in the fuck's got you so curious about that gun? What in the world you hounding me for?"

"Mr. Cawthorn, I've got a warrant here to search your motel room, and assuming the gun's the caliber you've said, I also have a warrant here for your arrest."

"Arrest! Just wait one damned minute, now. I need to see that warrant. And you still ain't said what you're here for."

The two deputies stood at Leah's sides now like bouncers.

"Sir, I'm going to need you to stand up," one of them said.

"Just what the fuck for? You ain't answered one question I've asked."

The deputy reached down and grabbed ahold of his wrist.

"Oh, for fuck's sake." Cawthorn didn't fight and as he stood up he shook his head, seeming to already know what was coming. "What in the hell have I done now?"

The deputy pulled his other arm behind his back and Leah waited until the cuffs were locked to his wrists to answer. "Mr. Cawthorn, you're being placed under arrest for the murder of Toya Gardner. You have the right to—"

"Murder! Murder!" he squawked. "Just what the fuck are you talking about? The murder of who?"

"Toya Gardner," Leah said as the arresting officer began to read him his rights.

"Are you fucking kidding me?" he screamed. "There ain't a thing in the world tying me to that girl and here you come wanting to rake me through the coals. What, you can't find who done it, so now you'll just pin it on a stranger?"

"So you *do* know who we're talking about?"

"Of course I do. What's that sign right there say?" He nodded toward the motel sign by the road, and as Leah read the words he said them aloud. "Free cable."

"What are you saying?"

"I'm saying I get damn near two hundred channels in that room and it ain't all titty flicks and talk shows. That girl you're talking about been on the television every damned night for weeks. Of course I know who she is. Everybody in these mountains knows that porch monkey's face. And if you ask me, I think she got what she had coming. You ask me—"

Leah interrupted him midsentence, afraid if she let him say one more word she was liable to sweep his legs out from under him and crack his skull against the pavement. "Mr. Cawthorn, just answer the questions you're asked. I don't need the fucking commentary."

"No, I'm the one talking now, Detective. What, you think just because of that robe y'all found in my car that I must've been the one dumped that girl off in the woods? You think I'm the only one around here believes she got what she deserved? There's people all over this country feel like I do, people driving past right there behind you think the same thing, use the same words I do."

Leah was boiling inside but she was doing everything in her power to keep some sort of composure. The thing that was really eating her alive right then was that she knew what he was saying was right, that there were people all around her who felt just like him. And the hardest part of it all was that she hadn't really thought about any of it until these past few weeks. Sure, it wasn't like she'd never heard those words before. Growing up, she'd bitten her tongue like everybody else, having been too scared to speak up when someone cracked a joke. But the truth was none of that affected her daily life, and so she'd learned to just glance past it, she'd learned to just keep her distance. It was a luxury for her not to see it. That's what Tillman had said, and he was right. He was absolutely right. That on-off switch, that ability to walk through the world with blinders, was a resource of the privileged, and she knew this now.

There were people she'd known all her life whose names were written in that notebook. And then there were people whose surely were not, but who'd stood at that statue beside them just the same. There were people like Rupert Bates, who'd spewed the same sort of bullshit Cawthorn was screaming right then minus only the sheer vitriol. She'd seen the way people at the coffee shop looked at Toya's picture in the paper. She'd heard them mumble under their breath thoughts they wouldn't share aloud. The world was surely split in two, but discerning who stood on what side was not black and white. It was gray, and gray was the scarier color because so often you couldn't pin it down. You couldn't put your finger on it and say, "That's him. That's the one." How could she know what anyone truly believed if they wouldn't come out and say it? How could she know what anyone was truly capable of? People like Cawthorn were the easy ones. But it was the ones we thought we knew, those were the ones who broke our hearts.

Leah signaled toward the patrol cars and the deputies led Cawthorn away. As she entered the motel room, he was still howling like some animal caught in a trap. The deputies shoved him into the back of the car and slammed the door and she could still hear him screaming at the top of his lungs. The room was small and muggy and the air smelled like mop water. On the nightstand lay the gun he'd used to do it.

48

After the detective notified them of the arrest, Vess and Dayna held each other most of the night. Neither spoke, and at times Vess wondered what her daughter was thinking, though she did not ask, for she was afraid any words at all would only serve to drive the knife back in.

They were still too close to everything for the news to come as any relief. They weren't even a week out from the wake. Vess hoped that in time this moment would mark a turning point in her daughter's grief. She hoped that having an answer would eventually be a stepping stone for moving forward. But right then they were huddled together in that small, fragile space and there was barely enough room to sit.

Hours passed before either moved. They were bunched at one end of a black leather sofa in the living room of Dayna's town house. The television was on but muted, Vess having cut the sound when the call came. Dayna had her head rested against her mother's chest, and Vess alternated between tracing her fingers across her daughter's hair and leaving her lips and nose pressed against her scalp, breathing in that smell as if she were still a newborn baby.

When the tears had finally waned and the quiet had settled around them, Dayna crossed the room to the kitchen. It was an open floor plan and Vess watched as she dug around in the refrigerator for a bottle of Pinot Grigio and poured them each a glass. Aside from the muscadine wine Lon made and the occasional sip of brandy on nights they played cards, Vess had never been one to drink. Her daughter handed her the flute and she took a sip. The wine bit at her tongue.

There was something nice about how cold the wine was in her mouth, the flavor some subtle cross between green apple and pear. For the next few minutes they sat there and sipped their drinks, both staring blankly at a room that felt less confining than infinite. It was as if they were trapped within a void, and it was Dayna who finally spoke, her words drawing the world back to that tiny space between them.

"You know, I've thought a lot about that night of the vigil and what I was going to say."

Vess turned and looked at her daughter. "Oh, yeah?"

"I remember one night I was studying for the bar and Toya toddled out into the living room with marker all over her face and she had a smile . . ." Her words tapered off and her eyes glassed over. She paused until she'd fought the tears back. "I was working full-time trying to finish up law school. I was already at the end of my rope, and I remember I just started crying." Dayna took a sip of wine. "I remember she took me by the finger and led me into her bedroom, and let me tell you there wasn't a thing in reach she hadn't colored—the walls, the dresser, the bed, all of it."

Vess chuckled, remembering similar stories of her own. "So what did you do?"

"I think most kids would've known they'd done something wrong, but Toya looked up at me just glowing, and the thing was, she was so proud that I couldn't even be mad. I couldn't bring myself to clean it up. Because it was beautiful. If you pulled back your focus and took it all in, if you just soaked it all up at once like a gulp of air, it was like music. And I just fell down on the floor and wept."

Vess held the cold glass of wine against the inside of her wrist and closed her eyes while her daughter spoke.

"I was sitting there crying and Toya came over and wrapped her arms around my neck and told me everything was going to be all right, that it was okay, and I want you to know that I believed her. I was the adult and she was the child, but *I believed her.*"

Dayna was sitting with her legs crisscrossed beneath her. Vess reached across the couch and rested her hand on her daughter's knee.

"I think all those people that night were expecting me to tell them how this world was robbed, and it was. It absolutely was, Mama. But I couldn't stand there, and I most certainly can't sit here, lamenting what she might've been. Because that would dismiss and ignore what she'd already become."

Vess groaned as the statement hit her.

"That girl had already made a greater impact on this world at twenty-four years old than most of us can hope to achieve in our lifetimes. I mean, look at us, Mama. We're sitting here in the footprint she left."

49

The lights were on at the house, but Leah hadn't called to ask if he was home or if he minded her stopping by. When she came around the side of the house Ernie was there at the picnic table staring off where the nightglow slipped away to darkness. It was as if he hadn't moved from that spot since the cookout.

Leah whistled so as not to startle him.

Ernie looked up and smiled. "Damned if it ain't the best kind of company," he said. "A pretty woman with an arm full of beer."

Leah didn't speak but lifted the can she was drinking into the air while she cradled a case of Bud Light under one arm as if toting a newborn calf.

"What'd you bring me?"

The beer hadn't been in the gas station coolers long enough to get cold. "If you can drink it this warm you got more trouble than that eye patch."

Ernie laughed and flipped the lid back on an Igloo cooler

guarded between his feet. He still wore the back brace and bent stiffly, but the braces were off of his wrists. He shook the ice off a can and tossed it to her as she set the box on the tabletop. When she took a sip it was so cold it hurt her teeth.

"God almighty, Ernie! How'd you get this beer that cold?"

"Ice-cream salt." Ernie tapped his temple with one finger as if to say it wasn't all mashed potatoes floating between his ears.

Leah took a seat across from him and he held his beer out over the table until she clinked hers against his. He finished what was left and crumpled the can in his fist, chucked the empty into the yard like he might've discarded the core of an apple. "So what brings you over here aside from happy hour?"

"We made an arrest."

"You serious?"

"Hell yeah, I'm serious. William Dean Cawthorn," she said. "Got a witness places him at the scene and then we found the revolver sitting right out in the open in his motel room. Thirty-Eight Special, just like you said. Same caliber pulled from Toya Gardner's body."

Ernie looked shocked, and she couldn't tell whether he was surprised or in disbelief.

"You not going to congratulate me?" His face had turned sour and she found it hard to read him. "What's the matter with you?"

"How'd he act when y'all took him in? Did he try to run?"

"No, he didn't run."

"And the gun was just sitting there?"

"By the bed."

Ernie didn't say anything, but Leah knew what he was thinking.

"What? So now you don't think it was him?"

"No, I'm not saying that."

"Then what are you saying?"

"I'm saying if I'd killed somebody, I don't think I'd have kept the gun. And I damn sure wouldn't have just had it sitting in there by the bed."

"Well, Cawthorn's about as bright as a Folgers tub full of night-crawlers."

"Yeah, maybe," he said, and took a long swig of beer.

"Jesus, Ernie! I thought surely you'd be the one person as happy as I am."

"Don't take it like that. I am," he said. "I am happy for you."

They sat there for a while with only the noise of a late-summer night whirring around them. She wondered if there was any weight to what he was saying. She remembered hearing how Cawthorn had run the night they found him drunk and asleep in his car. If he'd tried to take off then, why on earth had he not tried to get away when they showed up, and him guilty of murder?

"Look, I'm sorry," Ernie finally said. "I didn't mean nothing by it."

"No, don't be. It's good to question everything," Leah said. "And you're right. It's odd he didn't bolt. Doesn't make sense."

"Yeah, but you've got the gun. And like you said, you've got someone who can place him at the scene. That gun matches and it's all over."

The idea that any of this could ever be over took her mind to what had been keeping her up at night. It was one of the reasons she'd wanted to come here and see him. "There's something else I wanted to talk to you about."

"Okay." He sloshed another beer out of the cooler and popped the tab, waiting for her to speak. Leah tilted her head back and drank until the can was dry, and when she finished Ernie immediately reached into the cooler to hand her another.

"About a week ago I went over and saw Reverend Tillman, the

minister there at Mount Zion. I had a couple things I wanted to ask him," Leah said. "Anyways, we're sitting there in his kitchen and I mentioned how I'd never seen this community so divided. I mean, until this case and what happened to you, I just hadn't. But he said that maybe the reason I hadn't ever seen it was because I hadn't had to."

Leah cracked her knuckles and looked off at the woods. "I was thinking about that the other night, and I started remembering different things. I remembered how when my grandmother was in the nursing home with Alzheimer's she had this real sweet Black nurse named Erica. My grandmother called her every name under the sun and Erica would just smile like it didn't faze her. Now, I loved my grandmama to death. I loved her more than I've ever loved anybody, and never once in my whole life do I remember her speaking poorly of anyone before that. But when her mind went back, it was like all the sugar'd been licked off the candy, you know?"

"I do," Ernie said.

"The thing that eats me up is that when I think about my grandmother, when I remember her, I don't think about the things she said to that woman. It's like I choose to forget the ugly part," Leah said. "I look back on that and the whole time it was happening I never said a word. Not once. That nurse just smiled and kept on doing her job and I never said a fucking word."

"That's not surprising, Leah."

"But why? I mean, as soon as she said it, I can remember it felt like I was trying to swallow a mouthful of gravel. I think back on all that and it's like I chose to overlook what she was saying, and maybe that's the thing that tears me up the most. I chose to do that."

Ernie stared at her like he was trying to read her mind. "You heard why I hit Lovedahl, didn't you?"

"Sure."

"So you think that's the first time I'd ever heard somebody say that word?" He paused for a split second. "I've heard folks say shit like that all my life and most times I was just like you, just kept my mouth shut and hoped the moment would pass."

"Then what was different this time?"

"I don't know. I guess there comes a moment you start realizing that keeping your mouth shut's the same thing as nodding your head." Ernie took a long swig of beer with his chin up and his eyes closed. He smiled and set his can on the table, rotated it slowly in a circle between his hands. "You know, it's always torn me up how everywhere else in this country people want to act like the South's got some sort of monopoly on racism. Like it only exists one place. But I've got news for you, that shit's as American as Bud Light and baseball games."

Leah traced her finger around the letters of the label on the case of beer she'd brought. "Tillman asked me something else." She flicked the tab of her opened can nervously with the tip of her finger and let the reverberation cease before she continued. "Why did it take Toya Gardner being murdered for us to sit here and have this conversation? I mean, if it's like what you're saying, if it's like that, and me and you can both see it for what it is, why does it take Toya being murdered for us to talk about it?"

"I think we're just real good at pretending," Ernie said, then finished his beer. "I think we've got a really bad habit of believing if we don't talk about it, it'll just go away." He balled the empty can up in his fist and chucked it out into the yard with the others. "But what the fuck do I know?"

Leah sat with that answer and it melded with everything Tillman had said. You don't see it because you don't have to. You don't talk about it, and the reason's the same. Then something happens like Toya Gardner being found and you've got no choice, though deep down, even then, you wrestle with that desire to close your eyes and plug your ears and let the moment pass. You hold your breath. A minute goes by. The room goes quiet. You forget. You have no reason to relive or remember, and that is the fortune of your hand.

There were just the sounds of the night bugs and the creek then, the locusts and crickets bickering a chorus that had seemed a dull background until there were no more words to be said. It was the first time in either's life they'd had an open conversation about such things, and maybe that was what rendered them speechless. They sat there and drank their beers until the cooler was empty, each having raised questions the other lacked the confidence or surety to answer.

50

Back in the early fifties there'd been a sheriff named Griff Middleton who was shot to death while on a manhunt in Little Canada. In the wake of his murder, Griff's wife took the reins and served the remainder of her husband's term. After that, the badge fell on a man named Frank Allen. Allen carried a no-bullshit approach to the law, even arresting his own brother once, which might not have sat well at family reunions but built him a reputation in the community he served.

The plan Coggins cooked up stemmed from a dream he'd had about one of Allen's cases that had been featured in an old issue of *Front Page Detective*, a TV series and magazine that detailed crime stories of the time. A husband and wife had been killed in Little Canada, the man shot and the woman beaten to death with a stick. Allen solved the case by matching the weapon used to kill her to the tree that the limb had come off in the murderers' backyard.

When Coggins was a kid his mother had had a copy of that

magazine, and he remembered the picture of Frank Allen standing there in his suit and tie, a fedora tilted on his head. He had the stick in his right hand and the shotgun in his left with his index finger extended to point at a small detail in the wood, a clue he'd used to pull the case together. Coggins had been dreaming about that black-and-white image when he snapped awake out of breath. His heart was pounding and he immediately knew what he had to do.

"You really think this is going to work?" Sheriff Bruce Sellers asked. He sat in the passenger seat of Coggins's pickup outside Donnie Franks's double-wide. "I mean, don't get me wrong, I think you're right. Matter of fact, there's no doubt in my mind. But you know how something like this plays out in a courtroom. I doubt I could even get an arrest warrant with what you've got. What's a lawyer supposed to do with a picture of a truck riding down the road? It's circumstantial at best."

"This boy here couldn't spell *circumstantial*," Coggins said. "You let me do the talking and you just play up what we've got. I'm going to hold my foot on his throat, and you're going to offer him air."

"John, the two of us go knocking on that old boy's door and the jig's up. This thing's just as liable to turn sideways as it is to play out like what you're thinking."

"You're going to stay out here in the truck until I text you." Coggins turned off the engine but left the keys hanging in the ignition. "Right now Donnie don't have a clue what's going on. He still thinks I'm nagging him about that truck."

"And what if the second you go pulling the wool back off his eyes he decides he don't want to play ball? You back a man into a corner like that and what's he supposed to do? You back a dog in a corner and you liable to get eat up."

"It won't play out like that," Coggins assured him. "I've known this boy all his life. Only reason he's caught up in this mess to begin with is because he's let other people do the thinking for him. He was the same way in middle school, high school, twenties, thirties, all his miserable life. Someone else would set the nail and they'd make him swing the hammer. For once I'm going to let him do the thinking for himself."

"You ain't back out here in twenty minutes I'm coming in to get you."

"I wouldn't sit out here eyeing your wristwatch." Coggins opened the door and stepped into the yard. With his hands on the roof of the cab, he glanced back in with a sarcastic smile. "Things go like you're expecting, you're going to hear gunshots."

When he slammed the truck door, Coggins reached into the bed and grabbed a piece of firewood. As he approached the front steps, he was carrying that piece of split red oak in one hand with a laptop cradled by his side. He knocked on the front door and Donnie Franks hollered from inside the house to come in.

The kitchen and dining area were straight across from the entrance with windows that looked onto the backyard. Donnie was at the counter spooning something out of a mason jar onto a slice of white bread. He wore a pair of duck-brown carpenter's pants with the back pocket ripped out on the right side. He was barefooted and shirtless, though the hair on his body made him look fully clothed. His head was shaved to the skin, and from where Coggins stood it looked like an egg resting in a bird's nest.

"What brings you back over this way, Sheriff? I've done told you I ain't selling that truck." Donnie mashed a piece of bread on top of his sandwich until the whole thing was flat against the counter. "You want something to eat?"

"What you making?"

"Meat sandwich," Donnie said. "Groundhog Mama canned."

"Y'all get him recently?"

"No, last winter. You don't want to shoot groundhogs this time of year. They're grass gutted," he said.

"You care if I sit down?"

"Course not. Take you a seat over there at the table." Donnie nodded toward a small dining area to the right. "I'm going to get me something cool to drink. You thirsty?"

"No, Donnie. I'm fine."

The place was immaculately clean, and Coggins found that surprising considering Donnie was unmarried and showed few signs of order with regard to any other aspect of his life.

There was an ovular dining room table with a blond-stained cherry top, the frame and legs an off-white with four chairs painted the same. Coggins took a seat against the wall so that he was squared up with Donnie. The sheriff stared out of the bay windows to his right onto the backyard for what seemed a long time, searching for words, but it was Donnie who finally spoke.

"If it's not that truck, what exactly is it brought you way out here, Sheriff?"

Coggins slid the laptop onto the table in front of him. He had the piece of firewood laid across his lap. "Why don't you come take a seat, Donnie? I've got a few things me and you need to talk about."

There was a visible shift in Donnie Franks's demeanor. His body coiled into a knot, and a grave expression dropped over his face that made everything Sellers had said just a few minutes before hit home. Coggins watched Donnie's eyes, and it was like staring at a rabbit in a brush pile.

"Donnie, you've got a look come over you just now that's making me a little bit nervous," Coggins said.

Donnie Franks didn't say a word. He just held there, jaw clenched and unblinking.

"Son, you need to listen to me now. I don't know what's rattling around inside that head of yours, but I can assure you of one thing, and that's that there's no way out through that door I come in or that one behind you." Coggins dipped his head toward the back door, just a few short strides from where Donnie stood. Coggins had his left hand flat on the table, but his right was hidden, and he moved it back from the piece of firewood to the service weapon that was holstered to his belt. "There's only one way now, Donnie, and it's sitting right here at this table."

As he walked over to the table and took a seat, Donnie wore the look of a panicked child. He set his head in his hands and rubbed circles against his temples with the tips of his fingers.

"From the look on your face, Donnie, I think you know good and well why I'm sitting here, don't you?"

He still didn't speak. He just hovered there with a dumbstruck look, staring at the center of the table, his mouth hung open like a trout's.

"I've got a couple things to show you, and we're going to have us a long talk about where we go from here. In the next few minutes, you're going to have some hard choices to make, and those choices are going to determine whether or not you ever spend another night in this house or you ride out the rest of your life down east someplace in a prison. You understand?" It was like talking to a block of granite.

As plainly as he could possibly lay the details out, Coggins explained everything they had to go on. There was the place where Ernie'd been found, there was the detail Ernie recalled about those boots, and there was the Balsam Cross.

"And wouldn't you know, we make it to the gate going up to that cross and there's a game camera with the memory card wiped clean," Coggins said. "But what you boys didn't realize was that there was another camera on down that road at a house taking pictures of every car that drove by." Coggins folded open the laptop and double-clicked a group of images. He turned the screen so that Donnie could get a good look at what he was showing him. "Now, whose truck does that look like to you, Donnie? You could cut my eyeballs out of my head and I could still spot your truck at the junkyard."

Pulling the firewood from his lap, Coggins set the piece of red oak in the center of the table. The day after that dream about Frank Allen, he'd waited for Donnie to head off to work, and when he was gone Coggins came up to the house and took a piece out of the dry. The sheriff angled the piece of red oak so that the mark left by the splitter was facing Donnie's direction.

"Now, you and I both know that piece of wood right there come off your splitter. That line right there, that dark spot running from one end to the other, you told me that yourself, said it was about like a fingerprint. Well, I found that piece of firewood sitting right in the middle of the parking lot where Ernie's body was found. You believe that? Talk about shit luck, son. I mean, you must've hit a pothole or something and that piece of wood just fell out of the bed of your truck.

"But what that does, Donnie, that puts you in both places. And if you're there at the Balsam Cross, then what are the odds those boots Ernie remembers kicking his face in are the same boots I seen Slade Ashe wearing the other day at the Smokehouse? I'd say those are pretty good odds, friend, and the thing is, Slade had motive.

"Now, what you need to remember is that the other thing Slade's got is money. He can buy a team of lawyers that'll work day and night to keep him out of prison. But do you think he's going to extend that luxury to you just because you work for him? Or you think that team of lawyers might try to convince folks he didn't play near as big a role in what happened that night as you did? Jump forward and we've got a jury looking at a wore-out old man, used to be a county commissioner, ain't got a scratch on his record but politicking, and there you sit, built like you are, with a rap sheet stretched out like a week's laundry. Who you think they're going to believe, Donnie? And so the question you need to be asking yourself is, are you prepared to spend the rest of your life in prison for a man that's going to hang you out to dry?"

When the rains came heavy and the creeks climbed up, Coggins remembered how his grandmother would tell him as a kid that it wasn't the rise he had to keep an eye on. If the creek dropped suddenly, that's when they needed to head for higher ground. A tree falls or a bank slides off and debris stacks up, but no matter how it happened, the flooding would dam behind it. Below, the creek might fall to river rock, but when that hitch finally broke loose there'd come a wall of water that'd knock a house off its foundation. That's how it came when Donnie Franks fell apart.

By the time Sellers came into the house, Donnie was unglued. Coggins stayed hard after him, and just as scripted, Sellers convinced him that with full cooperation he could get him a deal with the district attorney to where he wouldn't spend much time behind bars. Of course it was all bullshit, but that didn't matter. They just needed to convince him to turn state's witness, to spill his guts. Whatever it took to lead that horse to water, that's what they were going to do.

As it turned out, Donnie and Slade had been the ones at Ernie's house. Slade'd borrowed an eighties-model Mercury Cougar from a paisley-faced drunk who slept off his days in a mildewed single-wide Slade rented on the back side of Dillsboro. He'd promised him a month's rent to take the car for the night, and by the way that old man reacted, they'd have thought he'd hit the lottery. Donnie was the one who knocked Ernie unconscious there at the house, and once they had him tied up and in the trunk, they hid the car in a pull-off along the parkway until dark. That's when the others joined them.

Coggins knew every name mentioned, and most came as a

surprise. There was a general contractor who built luxury homes at the south end of the county, a fellow who owned a hardware store off the four-lane. There was another fellow had a grading business and a local veterinarian who served all the family farms. They were all just workaday good old boys born and raised right there who'd have never been suspected of anything in the world. There was also one of his former deputies. Nick Lovedahl had played a part that night at the cross, and hearing that name ate Coggins up, because he'd pinned a badge to his chest. The only high-profile name aside from Slade Ashe was Holt Pressley, the chief of police, and that was the name they'd been waiting to hear. From what Ernie'd told him about the list, and the conversation he'd had with Tim McMahan that day at Tim's house, Coggins had known Pressley was involved all along. But up until right then there'd been no way to tie him to any of it.

When Coggins asked about William Dean Cawthorn, Donnie Franks got really perplexed. Turned out the fellow from Mississippi hadn't had anything to do with what happened. From the time he'd shown up in town, Slade Ashe had done everything in his power to keep Cawthorn at a distance. He'd come to the mountains to lie low while things cooled off back home, he having burned someone's house to the ground.

Everything was on the table now. When they stood up, it was in unison, and Sellers sidled up behind Donnie Franks and took his right arm by the wrist. At that moment it was like the latch had been left open on the gate and the bull in the stall went wild. Donnie Franks rammed his head straight into Sellers's chest and laid him flat on his back. The blow knocked the wind out of Sellers and he was heaving for air when Coggins unholstered his weapon.

Donnie Franks shot down the hall, and Coggins heard the door to the bedroom slam shut. He knew then that they were in over their heads. Kneeling beside Sellers, he placed his hand on his chest to check his breathing. Sellers finally rolled around for a moment on the floor, then crawled to his feet. Coggins stood and took a step forward so that he was right at the edge of the hall with his back against the wall, peeking over his left shoulder toward the bedroom door. Sellers stayed low and hustled to the kitchen to use the bar top for cover.

"Goddamn it, John! I told you this was a bad idea!"

Coggins looked across the dining room. Sellers was hunkered behind the divide with his hands and gun resting on the bar top and ready. "Why in the hell'd you try to put him in cuffs? Where was that in the game plan?" Behind him Coggins heard the door open and he glanced over his shoulder to find Donnie Franks peeking through a small gap in the doorway, his head down on a shotgun.

"I'm not going to prison, Sheriff."

"I don't see any way around that, Donnie."

"I thought you said you were going to help me."

"I did and we are. But all that flies out the window the minute you go losing your head. Nothing's changed from a minute ago, Donnie. Everything we told you still stands. You help us put them boys behind bars and I'll do everything in my power to make sure you're treated fair. You understand me? You've got my word on that, Donnie. You know I'm a man of my word."

"I'm not going to prison, Sheriff."

"I've got eyes on him, John."

Coggins was still focused on the doorway, and he flinched as Donnie swung the barrel toward the kitchen. The sheriff's heart sank and he flicked his eyes to Sellers, who'd shifted to the far end of the bar to find a better angle. "Don't do anything crazy, Sellers. We're all just talking. We're all just talking, Donnie."

51

Dispatch called for all units to respond, and deputies from all over the county poured on scene. Leah heard all the commotion playing out over the radio, but she did not check en route. At that moment she was in no condition to help anyone. News had just come in that the gun was not a match. William Dean Cawthorn was a free man.

Everything that was taking place at Donnie Franks's had switched to a private channel to keep eavesdroppers with basic scanners from tuning in to what was happening. Leah pulled into the parking lot at Caney Fork General Store and switched over to the encrypted line so that she could listen to the deputies on scene. One of the deputies inside the house relayed details to those holding the perimeter. The sheriff had called Donnie Franks's mother to the scene and they were all three in his bedroom with her, trying to talk him off the ledge. There was silence on the radio for a few minutes, and then out of nowhere the news came through all at once.

"Deputies, stand down. The suspect's in custody and we'll be coming out the front."

When she pulled up to the house, her headlights swept from one end to the other and she saw his shadow pass behind a thin white curtain drawn closed across the window. The front porch light was on and moths batted around the glow. Ernie Allison opened the door before she had a chance to knock, and the second she saw him she felt like she would crumble. He was shirtless and barefoot, wearing nothing but a pair of jeans and his back brace, and he held the screen door back with his arm.

"What's wrong?" he asked.

"The—the gun," she stammered. "The gun didn't match." Leah looked up at him as if he might have some sort of answer or wisdom that could hold the world together.

"Fuck, Leah. I don't know what to say."

She fell forward and buried her face in his chest, and he wrapped his arms around her. For those next few minutes, Ernie was all that kept her standing.

52

Flowers and photographs and artwork crowded the wall where Toya had been interred. The gifts grew daily and the cemetery sexton had already spoken with Dayna about the mess. He tiptoed around and tried to break the ice gently, said she'd need to start taking some of the items home or else they'd have to be thrown away.

Vess knelt and ran her fingers over a roughly finished clay sculpture that came up to her knees. There was a picture tucked under the base of the sculpture, a Polaroid of Toya and a girl about the same age wearing goofy expressions in a brightly lit studio with clay smeared on their faces. Toya had been so loved, and it showed. Everyone who knew her came to honor and remember her. To stand there surrounded by all the gifts and remembrances was like kneeling at an altar. "Can we just leave it for a month?" Dayna had asked, and timidly, the sexton had agreed.

They came here every evening after Dayna got off of work. The law office had begged her to take some time, but she had been right back at her desk the Monday after the service. Vess knew what her daughter was doing, and she knew she could only stay underwater for so long, that sooner or later she would have to come up for air or she would drown. But how could she tell her that without adding weight to her shoulders?

Grieving was an individual process, and the only constant was time. A person had to learn to swallow the second in order to survive the minute, the hour, the day. There was no right or wrong way and there was no assurance that you would ever heal. There was only time and learning how to manage it, because a loss like this was a life sentence, and right then everything was still so fresh and fragile. Dayna could feel the weight, but she had yet to learn its true measure.

For the past week, Dayna would swing by the town house around seven o'clock and scoop Vess up on the way. They'd stop by a florist and grab a fresh bouquet of flowers. They'd fight traffic to the cemetery, usually not saying much of anything on the ride. Dayna would replace the oldest flowers with the new, a bright garden of daisies and toad lilies and asters and sunflowers blooming against the wall.

Sometimes while they stood there, Dayna would mutter things under her breath. Sometimes she closed her eyes and prayed. Sometimes she wailed and screamed and pounded her fists against the stone. And sometimes she just stood there, dumbstruck. But every night Vess would feel the air slowly ease around them. Her daughter seemed to take this time like slipping into a bath, and only afterward was there room enough for words.

"Are you hungry?" Dayna asked as she pulled her seat belt over her shoulder and started the car.

"I could eat," Vess said. She thought about the squash and zucchini and tomatoes and corn and cucumbers and beans that had been coming in heavy at home when she'd left. She hoped Lula was making use of the garden.

"Are you in the mood for anything in particular?"

"We've got the rest of that chicken in the fridge," Vess said. "I could pick what's left off the bone and whip us up a pot of dumplings."

"You don't need to do that, Mama."

"I don't mind," Vess said. "That's what I'm here for."

"Let's just stop somewhere and grab a bite."

The ride was all car horns, flashing lights, and sirens, and Vess gripped tight to the seat and door as her daughter weaved back and forth across six lanes of traffic. The landscape was flat, so that the lights and concrete seemed to stretch on forever and ever against the horizon, and that endlessness made the old woman uneasy. The way the mountains surrounded her back home had always felt comforting, like she was being held in the palm of God's hand. At home, you could place yourself. Getting your bearings was as simple as climbing a ridge and finding Double Top. But here everything was wrung tight and stretched thin, a place pulled taut as a banjo string.

"You remember that story I used to read when you was little?" Vess asked.

"Which one, Mama?"

Vess glanced at her daughter and the streetlights swept by, lighting her face in bits and pieces. "That Aesop fable," she said. "The one about the mice."

"'The Town Mouse and the Country Mouse.'" Dayna smiled. "What made you think about that?"

"I feel like that mouse," Vess said.

Dayna laughed as if her mother were telling a joke, but Vess meant what she'd said. She was worn out and ready to go home, and now there was something she carried that only stood to add more weight and more time. Earlier that afternoon Vess had gotten a call from Detective Green. She'd heard the news that the gun wasn't a match and that they'd cut the suspect loose. Vess wasn't sure how Dayna would take it, and so all day she'd kept it to herself. She made small talk to keep her daughter's mind from being left to its own wandering, but inside she was coming apart.

"Last night I woke up in the middle of the night and I thought I heard a bird singing," she said. "I looked at the clock and it was two in the morning. I went out on the stoop and sure enough, there was a bird chirping away under one of them streetlights like he was sitting in the sunshine."

"They do that, Mama."

"And that don't bother you?"

"Why would it bother me?"

"What kind of bird sits out there chirping all night?"

"Never really thought about it. I guess you get used to it."

"I wouldn't," Vess said.

They stopped at a red light, and when it turned green they made it a block and a half before another light caught them. Vess gazed out the window at where a crowd of people had gathered around the ice chest outside a corner store. The stragglers and loafers laughed and cut up, arguing loudly as they took drinks from bottles in brown paper bags and hyped the tobacco and cancer paper from Black & Milds they passed around to share.

"You ever miss it?" Vess asked.

"What's that?"

"I mean, you think you'll ever move back home?" The land where Vess lived had been in Lonnie's family for four generations, and she wondered what would come of it when she was gone.

"I've thought about it," Dayna said. "Thought maybe when I got older I might like to move back, but to be honest, it just doesn't feel the same anymore. Everybody's left. And besides, this is home now. I made my home here."

The buildings along the streets slowly shifted into something nicer and newer and the lights were brighter, and Vess recognized that transition as a sign they were entering Buckhead, where Dayna lived, on the outskirts of the city.

"You ever miss the dark?" she asked.

"What do you mean?"

"I mean all these lights. Everything's so bright. It hurts my eyes. And it's loud. You ever miss the dark? You ever miss just sitting in the quiet?"

"You just get used to it, Mama." Dayna glanced at her as if trying to unravel where all of these questions were coming from.

Vess tried to hold it together, but she didn't know how on earth she would tell her daughter what had happened and she was terrified that Dayna would fall to pieces when she did. No matter what, she knew that she could not leave her.

She missed the mountains and her porch and the chickens. She missed the stars and the dew on the grass. She missed the way the dirt felt hot on the soles of her feet those sun-stroked afternoons when the tomato vines wilted as if they would not survive the night. She missed the rain and the way it growled against the roof. She missed the card games and the laugher and Lonnie. But most of all she missed the girl.

Right then her mouth was too dry to swallow any of those feelings down. There was a tissue wadded up in her hand and she squeezed it as tight as she could until it felt like a buckeye in her fist. Tears stung her eyes, and she looked out the side glass so that her daughter would not see them fall. There were times when her strength forsook her. Like a child, she just wanted to go home.

53

The jailers found Slade Ashe hanging by his bedsheets in his cell the morning after the arrest. Deputies swore he looked like a gigged frog the way his legs were stretched out stiff, his stubby arms dangling from his chest. Holt Pressley, on the other hand, had a smirk that couldn't be wiped off with striking paper, and unlike the rest of the group, he lawyered up first chance he got.

Leah was less surprised by the big names than she was by everyone else involved. Ashe and Pressley were both crooked as sourwood and that was no deep secret. She wasn't even all that surprised to have found out Nick Lovedahl was there. But the other men were people she'd known all her life, people she'd grown up with and gone to school with, folks she would've never expected.

The case put the cherry on top of Sheriff Coggins's career, and while Leah was surely happy for him and Ernie, none of that felt as good as she might've expected. Toya Gardner was in the tomb and she was no closer to solving her murder than she'd been that morning she knelt by her body.

She drove up to the house first and found Evelyn Coggins out on the porch with a camp stove running two canners at once. She was putting up quarts of purple hull beans, but the sheriff wasn't around. The weights rattled on top of the canners while she spoke, said he'd been out in a back pasture most of the afternoon shooting clays and that he was drinking pretty heavy.

When Leah found him, he was standing over a tractor tire that lay on its side with a clay thrower bolted to the sidewall. Coggins leaned down to cock the arm of the thrower, and as he did he stumbled a bit to get his footing. He had an old nickel steel Model 12 cradled in one arm and slid a fresh clay onto the machine. Leah'd left her car down at the house and walked the pastures following the reports of his gunshots to find him. He turned then and looked at her with a giant smile on his face. "Best cover your ears, girl," were the first words he said.

Leah shoved her fingers into her ears just as Coggins yanked the release on the clay thrower. The target launched out over the field and he was quick to stance, the shotgun shouldered fluidly, his head fully down on the gun as he swung the barrel and fired. The pellets caught up to the target and the clay exploded into little more than a puff of smoke. He racked the bolt back and the empty yellow hull flipped into the field grass. He cycled the action two more times to ensure that the gun was cleared and then turned back to where she stood.

"Heading to South Carolina this weekend for a dove shoot," Coggins said. "Fellow's got sixty-four acres of pasture all planted in standing corn and sunflowers."

"That ought to be a good time," Leah said. She was lingering by the back tire of the side-by-side. The tailgate was down and there was an open box of clays in the bed, a couple boxes more of high brass number sevens. She had her eyes on an open fifth of Aberlour that was almost empty.

When Coggins reached the back of the side-by-side he grabbed the bottle and took a long slug.

"Evie said you been out here drinking all day."

"And I'd say I deserve a drink. I'd say I deserve ten. Hell, get yourself a horn if you want. We ought to be out celebrating."

His words were slightly slurred, but she could tell he was far from gone. "Just please tell me you ain't drink all that today."

"Like I said, it's a celebration." He placed his hand under his shirt and used the fabric to wipe down the barrel and receiver of the shotgun, then walked around the vehicle and set the Model 12 on the seat. "If you ain't going to have a drink with me, then what is it brings you out here?" Coggins came back around and took a seat on the tailgate.

"I just wanted to talk about the Toya Gardner case, sir. I've hit a wall, and to be quite honest, I don't know what the next move is. I thought we had him. I'd have bet my house Cawthorn was our man." For a second she stumbled to find the right words, and when she couldn't she finally just blurted out exactly what she was thinking. "Look, I don't know if you want to bring somebody else in on this or not, but what I'm telling you is that I'm sitting here with dick, Sheriff. I don't know how else to say it. I don't have a goddamn thing."

The sheriff shook his head and chuckled.

"I'm sorry, Sheriff, but I just don't know how to—"

"No, no, now, you don't need to go apologizing to me. Ain't a person in our office don't talk rough as a cob, and I might be the worst of them. To be perfectly honest, I like it. Shaves the bullshit off a conversation, you know? I never have been one for dancing around."

"Me either, sir."

"That's why I've always admired you, Leah. A lot of folks would say you take after your daddy, but if we're being honest, you and me both know it's your mama. She was a pistol if there ever was one. I'd say she's the one you take after."

Both of her parents had passed years earlier and it was hard to hear him bring them up. No matter who she ran into, her parents were always the first thing they mentioned when they spoke to her. That's just the way things had always been. All it took was a name for someone to place who you were and where you'd come from. In these mountains, that was all that ever mattered.

"You know, most people believe a case goes cold because the tips and leads quit coming in, and, yeah, I mean, sure, that's part of it. That's always part of it." Coggins reached for the bottle and took another sip of scotch. "In the beginning you've got all of this information pouring in and it's pulling you in all of these different directions and any one of those leads might be the one that breaks the case wide open. That whole idea of the first forty-eight hours after a homicide being the most critical, that's not bullshit, Leah. That's not bullshit at all. But in the long term it's a lot more like deer hunting. Working homicide is like tracking a deer."

"What do you mean?"

"Let's say you're sitting there and a deer comes out and you shoot, but that deer don't fall, that deer takes off running, and you watch where he goes until he's plumb out of sight. If you're inexperienced, it's easy enough right then to forget where that deer was standing when you shot in the first place. But even if you are experienced, you get down and you're there on the ground and maybe you find blood and maybe it's good blood and you're following it and you can see right where that deer went, and all of a sudden the blood just dries up. Or maybe you don't find any blood at all. You know he's hit but there's nothing there, and so you just start wandering around looking. You go right to the last place you saw him when he run. Either way, before long you're all kinds of turned around and you can't even get back to where you lost the trail. A lot of times you're standing in the middle of nowhere and can't find your way back to where you started."

"I'm not sure I understand."

"What I'm saying is that it's easy to get turned around. It's really easy to get pulled so far away from where it all started that you can't make heads or tails of where you're standing anymore."

"And so what do you do?"

"You go back to the last place you had blood. You get down on your hands and knees if you have to, but you're looking for that next speck, because you know that deer was right there. That's the one place you're sure of."

"And what if you never had blood to begin with?"

"Then you go back to where that deer was standing when you shot. That's your last point of contact. That's the last piece of concrete evidence you can put your fingers on, so you go back there." Coggins drained what little was left of the bottle. He turned then with a crooked smile and bloodshot eyes. "And you know what? Nine times out of ten if that deer's hit good, if it's fatal, he's laying dead within a hundred yards of that spot. Nine times out of ten, that's where you'll find him."

Leah wasn't sure what to make of what he was saying. He was drunk, and the more she watched him and listened, the more worried she became. She'd known John Coggins a very long time, and in all those years she'd never once seen him unglued. Though he was in good spirits at that moment, she could tell it was a cover. Deep down his good time was nothing more than a show.

"Reverend Tillman is upping the pressure again," Leah said. "The other morning I walked into the office and I had sixteen messages, and probably two dozen other emails of FOIA requests."

"Why don't you let me worry about the reporters? You just work the case." Coggins grabbed the bottle by its neck and rotated his wrist to make a slow circle and watch the last drop roll around the bottom. "What you say we load up one more shell and I huck this thing off at that mountain? I bet my ass you can't hit it."

"What you say I drive us back up to the house?"

Whether he'd admit it or not, the past month had done him in. But what Leah couldn't figure out was whether it was just the things that had happened to Ernie and Toya Gardner or if this was forty years of wearing a badge and bearing that burden and seeing the worst the world had to offer finally coming home to roost. Was this what the end of that road would look like? Was this what was in store for them all?

54

Dayna had spoken with venom the night before, every word razor sharp and slicing her mother to the bone. The thing about it was, she had every right to scream, every right to be filled with rage. But that didn't make taking the brunt any easier.

They hadn't spoken a word the entire meal tonight at dinner. Dayna had brought home takeout, a vegetable plate from Cracker Barrel for Vess and sushi for herself. She'd opened a bottle of white wine when they sat down, and now she poured a third glass after placing her chopsticks into the empty takeout container.

"You want a glass of wine, Mama?" Dayna offered the bottle, but Vess waved it off. "Is the food good at least?"

"It is," she said.

Dayna took a sip of wine, set the glass on the table, and rubbed her eyes with the heels of her hands. When she opened her eyes, she stared at a clear glass centerpiece filled with pine cones and a tall candle that smelled like milk and honey. "I want to apologize for last night," she said.

"It's fine."

"No, I'm serious, Mama. I want you to know that I'm sorry. I didn't have any right to talk to you the way I did last night. All you're doing is trying to help and I know that. I shouldn't have lashed out. I shouldn't have talked to you that way. Okay?"

"It's fine, Dayna. I promise." Vess finished off the last few bites of fried okra and for a few minutes they were silent again.

"The other day I got a card in the mail from an old friend and there was something they'd written in it that struck a chord with me. They said the depth of your grief reveals the depth of your love for your child, and I can't help but think that's right." Dayna waited a second to continue. "There're times I'm walking and it's like the way Daddy's back used to go out. I mean, there I am and I'm fine, and then it's like somebody snapped their fingers and I just crumble. Out of nowhere."

Dayna's voice cracked and she stopped herself from going on. She finished what was left of the wine in her glass, then emptied the rest of the bottle into it. When she'd collected herself she said simply, "I miss her. That's it. I just miss her." And Vess understood.

She'd felt the same when Lonnie passed, and in a lot of ways she felt those same things now. But she also knew what Dayna was experiencing was a type of grief that she could not fully comprehend.

"I'm just mad," Dayna said. "I just want to hit something, Mama. Somebody. I just want to take this glass in my hand and smash it against that fucking wall. And I know none of that will do a bit of good. None of that will change anything, but that's how I feel. That's what that was last night, and I'm sorry. I'm sorry you were the place it landed."

"You don't need to keep apologizing, Dayna. I know." Everything that had happened over the past few days, that rapid unraveling, was exactly why Vess had not wanted to share the news of Cawthorn's release.

"You know, before they arrested that man, I just kept telling myself that when they found him, maybe then there'd be some sort of closure, that maybe that's when I could start to move on. But then they made that arrest and nothing changed. I might've let on like it did, but nothing changed." She took a sip of wine and gazed toward a pair of French doors that opened onto a small back deck. "I don't think I realized it until they cut him loose, but the truth is it was stupid to ever believe there'd be any sort of closure. It was stupid because there's not going to be any getting past this. There's never going to be an end, is there, Mama? This is just the way it is now."

Vess watched as her daughter's eyes once again filled with tears, and she didn't know what to say. She knew the answer. She knew the truth of it. But that answer was no remedy.

There was nothing she could say or do to make anything better, and it killed her as a mother to feel that sort of helplessness for her child, to see her staring down a tunnel that had no other side. Right then she just didn't want her to feel alone.

"There's something I want to tell you," she said. She balled her napkin up in her hand and stared straight into the light above them. "A part of me has been scared to say this, and I think it's because saying it aloud meant admitting it to myself, and I don't think I was ready for that, but you need to hear it because you need to understand you're not alone. All of that rage you feel burning inside of you, I feel it in my bones, sweet girl. I feel it coursing through my body like a fire. But the difference is that yours is aimed outward and mine is aimed in. It's burning me up inside."

"I don't understand."

Vess took a deep breath and tried to summon the courage to say what she needed to say.

"That last morning I spent with Toya she told me that if I didn't want her to go, all I had to do was say it. She told me that if I didn't want her to go, she wouldn't." Vess looked up and when her eyes met her daughter's she could not hold back any longer. "Dayna, I didn't tell her not to go." Vess wept and for the first time she made no attempt to hide it. "I didn't tell her not to go," she repeated, this time barely able to get the words out of her mouth.

Dayna reached across the table with both arms and took her mother's hands. Vess was too scared to look up. She couldn't breathe.

They were both crying now, each all the other had left to hold.

"Mama, you don't think I feel that same thing?" Dayna said when the tears finally surrendered enough for words. "The last long conversation I ever had with Toya was at this table the night before she come to stay with you this summer. She asked me what I thought and deep down I felt that very same thing you must have felt. I felt it in the center of my chest and I swallowed that feeling down and I smiled and told her to follow her heart. That's what I said.

"But here's what you're forgetting. From the time I could talk you showed me what this world was, from the time you believed I could put two and two together. And I can assure you that I raised my child the same. All her life I held her in front of a glass door and showed her what was waiting outside. I made her look in the glass and see herself. I made sure she understood the difference between what she saw and what that world would see when she stepped out that door alone. So don't get it in your head for one second that Toya didn't understand that. She knew it just as clearly as you or me. She knew it because of you and me. So don't you dare blame yourself for what happened, Mama. And don't you get it in your head for one second that I'm mad at you. I'm not mad at you, and I'm not mad at myself. I'm mad at this world for what it is."

Vess knew what Dayna said was true, and yet knowing didn't make it any easier. Whether it was fair or not, they were the protectors, and as the elder, Vess believed she sat squarely at the head of the table. She couldn't help thinking that in some way or another she had failed, and now all she could hope was that her daughter might somehow be okay. Dayna let go of her mother's hands then and leaned back in her chair.

"I don't know if you'll remember this or not, but it was about a month or so after Daddy died and I'd come home to see you and you told me you just wished everybody would leave you alone. You told me that you wished they'd stop coming by and checking in and bringing you dinner and mowing your grass and picking up groceries. You said you knew their hearts were in the right place, but that all you wanted was for them to leave you be. All you really wanted was to be by yourself. You remember that?"

"I do."

"And do you remember what else you said?"

"I do." For Vess it was like a day had not passed. "Those chores were the only chance I had to stop from thinking, to get outside my own head. That was the only time I didn't have to focus on what I'd lost, the only time I had to catch my breath. They thought they were doing me a favor being there and doing all of those things. But really they were doing more harm than good. I didn't need any of that right then. I needed space."

Dayna held her wineglass up to her lips with her hands cradled around the outside. She didn't drink. They watched one another, and in her daughter's eyes Vess came to realize what she was trying to say.

"I understand," she said, and in a way she was relieved because deep down she needed that same thing herself. There was only so much that either could do for the other. Some healing had to be done alone.

Dayna took a sip of wine then and there was a look of satisfaction that eased the tension in her face.

55

Robertson dormitory was boring and brick, just a monotone mono-lith plopped on the top of a hill. It was late afternoon and headed toward evening, the sun already behind the pines and falling fast for the ridge. Leah'd been thinking nonstop about the sheriff's advice, about getting turned around and losing track of where you were standing. Aside from where they'd found Toya Gardner's body, this was the end of the trail.

The chatter of heat bugs rose and fell from the treetops, a con-stant droning that made the world seem as if it might consist solely of sound. She walked into the courtyard and stood where the graves had been filled, the mounds still red with clay, as no seed so far had taken. The white river stones had been placed back so that the word Toya had spelled remained.

"Said they had to fill them in on account of liability."

The woman's voice caught Leah by surprise, and when she

turned she spotted one of the housekeepers tying a quick knot in the top of a trash bag from a bin by the sidewalk.

"Said they was afraid one of these kids would fall in and break their neck." She chuckled to herself and left the bag of trash sitting by the bin as she walked across the courtyard to where Leah stood. She wore a pair of jeans that were stained at the knees and a tan scrub top like a nurse might've worn. The woman smelled of chemicals and cigarettes. She pulled a pack from her pocket and lit one with her eyes creased to shield them from smoke. "Glad they put the rocks back, though."

"Me too," Leah said. She looked at the stones and read the word silently.

"A real shame, what happened to that girl." The housekeeper crossed her right foot over her left so that she was standing on one leg with the toe of her opposite foot tapping the ground. She was jittery. She folded her arms and took a drag, flicked her hand to knock the ash from the end of her cigarette. "What she was doing was important, I think. She was a sweet girl. Bright as church glass."

"Did you know her?"

"Not really, but yeah." The woman smiled but shyly threw her hand over her mouth to hide her teeth. "My name's Catherine, but everybody calls me Mimi."

Leah grinned. "Thought for sure you were going to say Cat."

"Yeah," she said. "That'd make more sense, wouldn't it?"

Leah held out her hand. "Well, it's nice to meet you, Mimi. My name's Leah."

"What's your last name?"

"Green," she said.

The woman switched her cigarette to her opposite hand so that she could shake. "Call me that on account of cartoons," she said. "Road Runner. When I was little I used to zoom around all over the place hollering *meep meep* just like that cartoon. Somehow or another that became Mimi and just sort of stuck. Everybody called me that all my life. Say you a Green?"

"Yes, ma'am."

"Known a bunch of Greens through the years."

"There's a lot of us around," Leah said. "How'd you know Toya?"

"Well, like I said, I didn't know-her know her. I always start up here with these two." She turned toward the brick buildings behind them and at their side. "But by the end of the night I'm down the hill at the Fine and Performing Arts building. That's the three buildings I keep. And that one down there usually takes me most the night. It's a real bear," she said. "But she used to be there working on different things all hours and I'd run into her on occasion. In the bathroom. Coming and going from the studio room. Always spoke to me. She was always nice as she could be."

"So I take it you know Brad Roberts as well."

The woman's face turned to a question mark. "I do."

"I'm sorry," Leah said. "I should've mentioned I'm with the Jackson County Sheriff's Office. I'm a detective."

"You working this case here?"

"Yes, ma'am. I am."

"And you think Brad could've had something to do with what happened?"

"No." Leah shook her head. She was slightly taller than the housekeeper and she widened her stance until they were eye to eye. "Not really."

"Shooo," she exclaimed, brushing the back of her hand against her forehead as if relieved. She chuckled nervously and took a long drag from her smoke. Her voice was coarse and gravelly. "Had me worried there," she said. "Some of these kids around here can be real assholes—pardon my French, but they can. Entitled. But Brad's always been good to me. Couldn't imagine he'd have been involved with something like that."

Leah nodded but didn't speak.

"So you have any suspects? I mean, I know that's a little bit nosy, but like I said, it's just a shame what happened to that girl."

"If I'm being honest, we're kind of at a dead end." Leah looked into the trees above them. A small downy woodpecker tapped at the shaggy trunk of a white oak. Off in the distance she could hear squirrels cutting the hickories and she knew fall was coming. "Guess that's what I'm doing out here. Trying to think of where to go."

"Oh, yeah? Why's that? I mean why here?"

"Because this is the last place I can put her alive."

The woman was almost finished with her cigarette but she fished out another from the pack and lit her second with the end of her first. She pinched the spent one between her fingers until the cherry fell to the ground, then slipped the butt into her pocket. "What exactly do you mean by 'put her'?"

"Well, what we know is that after the protest in Sylva that Saturday, Toya took a ride with the sheriff and they came here. He dropped her off and that's the last spot we can place her. Right here. It's about a mile walk to her grandmother's house. She'd walked that road a lot. But somewhere between here and there she just up and vanished."

"Well, I remember them standing out here that afternoon like you're saying, but when that girl left from here she climbed back in the truck."

"What's that?"

"If you talking about that Saturday before y'all found her, she was standing out here with the sheriff just like you're saying, but when she left, she left with him."

"How do you know that?" Leah's mind was suddenly dizzy.

"Like I told you, I got three buildings I clean. These two here and that one down the hill. And I always clean this one first." She tilted her head straight back to indicate the building where they stood. "That afternoon I was right in there sweeping up. They'd had some sort of luncheon for the RAs coming in. Made a fucking mess, excuse my French, but I saw the two of them out here just like you're saying, just as clear as day."

"Where were you exactly?"

The woman turned and pointed to a window not fifty feet from where they stood. The path was straight and unobstructed. She dangled her cigarette between her lips so that it jumped about as she spoke, lifted one foot, and scratched her ankle. "They were jawing back and forth about something, but I couldn't hear them. I just figured it had something to do with this here." The housekeeper pointed at the graves. "Didn't think nothing of it other than that, really. And like I said, they walked right back over to his truck, she climbed in with him, and they was gone."

"And you're absolutely sure it was the sheriff you saw with her?"

"Of course I am, honey." She mashed her cigarette out onto the ground and stuck the filter in the pocket of her jeans. "I've known John all my life," she said. "Me and him went to school together."

The housekeeper turned and walked back toward the sidewalk. She grabbed the bag of trash as she passed and soon enough she was gone. Leah stood there shaking. Her mind was turning in a thousand directions trying to make it make sense, but there were only more questions, no place logical to light. She stared at the ground and her face felt afire. Right there at her feet was another drop of blood.

56

Mount Zion wasn't much more than a sanctuary, a white clapboard building with a short set of stairs that entered into the back corner of the room. Inside, most of the light came from a succession of tall windows running along the walls every five or six feet, but it was night out now and where she sat was nearly full dark.

The pews were simple thin slats of stained oak, high-backed and uncomfortable, the same as they'd been all Vess's life. There were throw pillows strewn about some of the pews and she was sitting by a window in the front row where a small wall heater was fastened near the floor. This was where Vess sat every Sunday and it was mostly because Lula Shepherd stayed cold. Soon as fall set in she'd hound Tillman about how she shivered through service and he'd try to hold off on heating as long as he could on account of the electric bill. She'd threaten to pay everything herself if he didn't crank it up, and in the end, Lula tended to get her way.

Vess had only been home a day. She closed her eyes and took a deep breath. Any room that sat this still turned stale and dusty, but here that smell had always served as a promise—the doors open in spring, the scent of redbud and dogwood filling the air at Easter; strong perfumes and colognes fusing, the most stifling determined by where you sat and who you sat beside; the traces of wooden pews and wax burning down on the candles in winter. Those were the smells that staleness and stillness built into, so that even in their absence the place nourished her, because she knew it would come again.

She rested her hand on a hymnal and stared at an angle toward the railing and kneeler where she'd prayed so many times. Her eyes had long adjusted to what little light filled the room and there was a single firefly traveling the place like a ghost, an odd thing as the season was at its end. Being a trustee, Vess had kept keys to the church for years. She'd started coming here alone some nights after Lonnie died. There was something about being inside her own house during that time that she couldn't stomach, and so this had become her place of solace.

Houses were vessels of the lives lived in them. In the case of Vess Jones, hers had been filled with love and laughter and dancing and song and food and fighting and sadness and grieving and all of those threads that make up who and what we become. Once Lonnie was gone it felt like that place became suffocating. She'd bury her face in his clothes, wash her body with his soap, close her eyes and believe for one split second he was still there. Vess would find something as simple as one of his hairs on the shoulder of his coat and it would break her. It had taken months to stop crying, more than a year before she ever found any sort of new routine, and now those same feelings were here again.

Toya's clothes were still hanging in the closet. Her lotion and face wash and moisturizers were still there by the bathroom sink. Her SUV was broken down in the driveway. Every day in that house was a reminder of what Vess had lost. It was the quiet, the absolute quiet, the absence of what had beat inside that house like a heart, that haunted her. The silence was simply unbearable.

The sanctuary door squeaked open behind her and Vess was in such a trance that the noise barely entered her mind. She put her arm on the back of the pew and turned to glance over her shoulder. The open door made a bright rectangle of blue and she couldn't make out the silhouette that stood there dark as a shadow.

"Mrs. Jones?"

The moment she spoke, Vess knew the voice. "Yes," she said.

"I hope I didn't startle you."

"No, darling, I'm just sitting here."

Detective Green shut the door and came up the aisle, her footsteps clopping loudly inside that small and silent space.

"I heard you were back, so I went by your house, but I didn't see your car. I was passing by here on my way home and spotted it in the parking lot."

"Yeah, I couldn't sit in that house. Just feels empty." Vess looked around and chuckled, because she realized how silly it must've sounded given where she was sitting. "There's been too much happened inside these walls for it to ever feel that way. It's like somehow or another this building holds it forever."

"No, I know what you mean," Leah said as she took a seat on the pew behind her. "My mother went first, but after Dad passed I couldn't even go in their house to start packing anything up for close to a year. I couldn't stand being in there."

Vess reached back with her hand and patted around until she felt Detective Green's leg. She left her hand on Leah's knee for a second. It felt good to not be alone.

"A couple of your chickens were still wandering around the yard. Couldn't get back in the fence."

"Oh, they'll put themselves up," Vess said. "Fly out, they can fly back in. I get home and I'll shut the door on the coop. They're good about going to bed."

"Who's been taking care of them while you've been gone?"

"Lula Shepherd," Vess said. "But between you and me, I'm not so sure she did much but shut them up of an evening and let them out of a morning. That woman is scared to death of chickens. You'd think you was asking her to pick up a copperhead."

"Listen, I don't want to keep you, but I just had something I wanted to ask."

"What's that?"

"Did the sheriff ever mention giving Toya a ride that afternoon?"

"Of course," Vess said. "You know that. John gave her a ride back up there to the school once everything went crazy in town."

"No, I mean after that. I mean did he ever mention where he might've taken her once they left the school?"

"What do you mean? He didn't give her a ride anywhere else. He took her up there to the school and she walked home."

"Were you at the house all afternoon?"

"I mean, yeah, all afternoon." Vess thought for a second. "I ran down to the grocery for something. I can't even remember what it was I needed now, but I couldn't have been gone more than thirty minutes. Was the middle of the day, best I recall. Matter of fact, I know it was. Maybe one, two o'clock. I was going to get one of those rotisseries to keep from having to cook."

"Okay," Leah said.

"John never told me that." Vess was baffled. "Why in the world wouldn't he have said that? Said he gave her a ride to the school's all."

"There was a lot going on. He was so tied up with everything happening with Ernie Allison that morning that some of the details probably just got jumbled up in his mind. He was at the hospital all day that day. I couldn't even get him to pick up his phone until late. There was a lot on his plate that week."

Vess wasn't sure what to say. She couldn't wrap her head around any way he could screw up the details like that, any reason he'd have told her he dropped her off at the school if that wasn't what happened.

"I'm going to talk to him first thing in the morning and I'll let you know what he says." The detective put her hands on the back of the pew in front of her and stood up. "I'm sure it's nothing. I'll come by sometime tomorrow afternoon or evening. For now, though, I'll leave you be."

"No, I need to be getting on," Vess said. "I'll follow you out and lock up."

They walked together to the back of the sanctuary, and when Leah opened the door the firefly passed over them and floated into the night. Vess watched that yellow orb blink and rise until it was high in the pines and gone.

57

As Leah steered through the last bend before Coggins's house came into view, a barred owl swept low in front of her car. She tapped the brakes and the owl rose nearly vertical to its perch. On the hill above, the yellow glow of window light broke the darkness and the last few gravel switchbacks leading up to the house shone blue as water from moon and sky.

When she pulled up, her headlights brushed the porch before angling out toward the wood line and she caught a glimpse of Sheriff Coggins standing there on his front steps. He still wore his khaki cargos and dark polo tucked in from his day at the office, but he was barefooted, with his right hand shoved into his pocket, his left gripping a jelly jar at his side. The Cogginses kept their cars parked in the barn at the side of the house, but Leah stopped when she reached the porch. She rolled down the window and he took a sip from his drink.

"What in the world brings you up here this time of a night?"

"Had a couple more things I needed to ask right quick."

"And you couldn't have called?" He leaned back on his heels and looked off toward the mountains.

As Leah stepped out of the car, Coggins took a seat on the steps. She leaned against the front fender to face him. Off in the distance the owl screamed and the two of them turned in unison toward the sound.

Leah'd thought about holding off until morning and having this conversation in his office, but it was useless to go home and lose sleep over something simple. And that's what this had to be. Simple.

Coggins rattled the ice in his glass before polishing off the rest of his drink. "So what is it got you so worked up it couldn't wait till morning?"

Leah wasted no time mincing words. "I wanted you to go through that Saturday one more time, when you gave Toya a ride from the protests."

"It's like I told you before. She wanted me to take her up there to the school and so that's where I took her."

"And what about after?"

"What do you mean after? That was it. I gave her a ride to the school."

"Whereabouts did you take her?"

"What are you asking, Leah?"

"I'm asking where on campus."

"You know that already. I took her up there by that dorm where she'd dug the graves. That's where she asked me to take her."

"And after that?"

"Jesus, this is like a game of who's on first."

"I know that wasn't where you left her because someone saw her get back in your truck. They saw the two of you drive off from there. So where did you go? Where did you take her after that?"

The sheriff's face fell blank for a moment, and he searched for one last taste of whiskey in his glass but found none. "I don't know who you've been talking to, Leah, but they're mistaken. I dropped her off on campus just like I said."

"What were the two of you arguing about?"

"What are you talking about?"

"The same person who saw her get back in your truck said the two of you were arguing outside in the courtyard. What was it about?"

He slid the jelly jar onto the step where he sat, and when he let go he accidentally knocked it over with the back of his hand. The glass rolled off the edge and toppled down the last stair into the yard. He stared at the spot where it settled but made no attempt to reach it. For a few seconds there was silence, even the night bugs having ceased their chatter.

"We *were* arguing out there in the courtyard. That's true. I was telling her it wasn't safe for her to walk home, that there were people all over this county wanted to see Xs on her eyes, and she was standing there cussing me like a dog. Finally I got her talked into letting me take her home."

"And so you took her to her grandmother's?" Leah instantly regretted how she'd phrased the question. She wished she'd simply asked where he took her.

Again, he took a long time to speak. He stared blankly through her and she could tell the screws were turning. "No," he finally said. "No, I tried, but she got out when I come to the stop sign on the back side of campus. There where the Hardee's used to be."

There was something about his answer that didn't sit right, but if what he was saying was true, then, technically, he *had* dropped her off on campus.

"Should've followed her on home, I guess, but if I'm being frank, I'd had my fill for the day. Said to hell with her. She wants to walk so bad, let her walk."

Leah wasn't sure what to add. She couldn't tell whether he was lying or if things had just gotten turned around in his head. On top of the fact that she'd known him nearly all her life and wholly believed there was no way he could be capable of something like that, Coggins didn't have motive. And that was the biggest thing. He just didn't have any reason to have killed her. As that fact settled into her mind, she felt the burden budge. "Thank you, Sheriff," she said.

"Don't worry about it. That's my fault," Coggins said. "I probably just wasn't speaking real clear's all." He pushed himself up from the stairs and leaned down to grab his whiskey glass as Leah climbed back into her car.

When she cranked the engine, her headlights shone on the vehicles parked in the barn. From that angle, she could see the back driver's-side quarter panel of his pickup, the slate-gray bed and the strobe replacements in his taillights. He drove a Ford F-150 Super-Crew, a new body with a blacked-out grille and heavily tinted windows, and right then it hit her, what Curtis Darnell had remembered about that night up Dicks Creek, how a truck just like the one Coggins drove had woken him out of that dream. Not only that, Curtis Darnell had pointed at that truck in the photo of Cawthorn's car. "It was just like that one there except it ain't have all them lights and stickers," he'd said. Coggins's truck was unmarked.

The way his face had fallen for that split second, the way he'd paused as if realizing she'd stumbled onto something she was never meant to know. Her thoughts ricocheted between those two places and she stared vacuously through the windshield with her hands clenched tight on the steering wheel and shift lever. A sharp rap beside her nearly ripped her heart out of her chest, and as she turned she found Coggins hunched by the window, having struck the glass with his knuckle.

Leah fumbled for the button and the window came down. "I tell you what," he said. "You come by the office around lunchtime tomorrow and we'll go grab us a bite and we'll ride over to see Vess."

Leah stared at him, and it felt like there was nothing left between them, just an empty void right then, as if she were looking at a painting. A sick feeling settled into her stomach and left her light-headed. She remembered how he'd always carried a small revolver in an ankle holster as a backup gun when he worked patrol. Everyone in the department knew the story, how Coggins's grandfather had been a deputy and how that was the service weapon he'd carried, a nickel steel snub-nose Colt Fitz Special. There were two stories he told every single person who ever stepped foot in his office: one was about the turkey mounted on the wall, and the other was about that revolver.

"There something else you wanted to say?" Coggins broke the silence. "You got a real odd look on your face all of a sudden. You feeling all right?"

"What caliber was that revolver you used to carry? The one that belonged to your grandfather."

"That was a Colt .38 Special," he said. "But what's got you thinking about that?"

Something passed between them then that sent a chill through her body. "You still carry that gun?"

"Sure don't," he said. "Don't even have it anymore. Sold it a few years back when Evie needed a root canal."

Leah knew they had good insurance and that they weren't hurting for money. Even if they were, there was no way he'd part with that gun. "You remember who you sold it to?"

"You know, it's been so long I don't recall."

"Pawnshop? Gun store?"

"Private sale." Coggins grabbed ahold of the door where the window'd gone down. He gripped so hard the tops of his knuckles turned white as milk glass. "You know, Leah, that's an odd thing to ask me. A line of questions like that, you got something you want to say, why don't you just come right out with it? Me and you've always shot straight, ain't no sense beating around the bush now."

"I think I'll be getting on, Sheriff." Leah dropped the gear lever into reverse and waited for him to let go of the car so she could go.

"We on for lunch tomorrow?"

"I'll let you know," she said. "Think I've got to be in Cashiers most the day looking into that larceny case."

"Well, just let me know," he said.

Coggins slapped his hands hard on the door and took a step back so that she could leave. Leah curved out into the yard, and as she dropped the gearshift into drive, she glanced back one last time where his silhouette cast a long, dark shadow in the house light.

58

That night took on a heavy chill, and it was the first sign of what was to come. Before long the trees would catch fire and the roads would fill with leaf lookers, and then fall would give way to winter and render the landscape to pen and ink. Coggins had already slipped into his boots, but his barn coat hung in the bedroom closet.

Evelyn sat in bed with three pillows stacked behind her to hold her upright. Her readers were perched on the tip of her nose and she was tapping the end of a pencil against her bottom lip. "Here's one you might know. 'Squirrel's nest.' Four letters. Ends in -ey."

Coggins heard the question but his mind was someplace else. He flicked on the light in the closet and shoved a row of shirts and pants on hangers down the rod. He found his barn coat, a faded Trebark-pattern Cabela's jacket he'd worn for twenty-five years, and he slipped his arms into it and yanked the sides of the open front to situate it over his shoulders.

"Four letters, ends in -ey. That's assuming 'Monday, Monday' is right for the Mamas and the Papas. That one was twelve letters and started with an M. That had to be it. 'Monday, Monday.'"

"Drey," Coggins said.

"What's that?" Evelyn looked up from her crossword with a stumped look. He couldn't tell whether it was the answer he'd given her or the fact he was putting on his coat. He'd never been much help with crosswords.

"D-R-E-Y. A squirrel's nest is a drey."

"Where in the world are you headed this time of night?"

"I got to run down to the office."

"Can't it wait till tomorrow? It's almost eleven o'clock, John."

"No, I better get to it," he said.

"John, you can't keep running like this. For a month now you haven't stopped long enough to take a breath. There's no telling what that's doing to your blood pressure. Remember what the doctor told you? Said you needed to ease up. He said you had to start getting some rest or that job was going to kill you. That long talk we had, that's when you decided this was going to be it, that you'd finish out this term and retire. But look at you. You're running more now than ever. On top of that, you've got to drinking again, and not a beer on a Saturday, but drinking. Drinking like you used to. And I know you've got a lot you're dealing with, but you're going to kill yourself."

Coggins put two fingers against the side of his neck as if to check his pulse. "Still ticking," he said.

"It's not the ticking's going to kill you. It's the stopping."

"About like the old Tin Man, ain't I?" He walked over to her side of the bed, placed his hand on the side of her face, leaned down, and kissed her forehead. Her hair smelled sweet as flowers. "Oil can," he squeaked through creased lips. Evelyn took the crossword she held with both hands and whacked him hard on the shoulder.

Out in the barn, tube lights flickered overhead and buzzed until they caught, and he walked through that white light to a row of red Craftsman tool cabinets that lined one wall. A small tin lunch bucket with rusted clasps rested on one of the shelves, and he picked it up by its stiff leather strap, something his grandfather had fastened for a handle when the original metal rusted in two. Soon as he opened the lid, the smell of Hoppe's No. 9 overcame him. He reached in where a thin cotton handkerchief stained with oil and fouling held the revolver.

A photograph was fitted inside the lid of the lunch bucket, a faded color Polaroid of Coggins and his grandfather sometime in the eighties with a limit of rainbows stretched on a stringer between them. He shut the lid quickly so as not to have to face it.

John Henry Fitzgerald had been a gunsmith for Colt around the time of the First World War. He'd made a name doing custom work on stock Colt revolvers, shaving down and fine-tuning them for concealed carry. The Fitz Special that had belonged to Coggins's grandfather started life on a nickel steel Police Positive frame with the barrel shortened to two inches. The hammer spur was bobbed, the butt rounded, and the entire gun dehorned of hard edges to take all the hitches out of pocket carry. What made the gun odd looking to anyone who'd never seen or held one, though, was that the front of the trigger guard was cut away to provide more finger room in the event that the shooter wore gloves.

Coggins took the gun from the handkerchief and held it flat against his palm as if he were holding a fish. He'd wasted every second of the last month trying to convince himself that eventually things would settle in and get back to normal, that all the monsters holding him hostage, keeping him up until he crashed from exhaustion and woke from nightmares, that all of that would stop. He'd held out hope that one day, like a snap of the fingers, all of that would just up and disappear. But the reality now set in that he could never go back to the world that had been before.

A man could bury all sorts of things in the ground, but in the end they almost always outlived him. There was about an hour's drive ahead to reach the dam at Fontana. That was where the water was deepest.

59

By suppertime that next day Vess was too beat to cook. Instead, she collapsed into her husband's recliner and ate a can of tuna on saltines while she watched old cowboy shows. Through a large picture window she saw headlights sweep across the backyard and knew someone had pulled into the driveway. The television blared a spaghetti western called *A Fistful of Dollars* and she dialed back the volume, expecting Detective Green had come by to share whatever news she'd heard from the sheriff. When Vess opened the door she was surprised to find the man himself.

"Evening, Vess," Coggins said. "Hope I didn't catch you at a bad time." He peered around her as if to check whether she was alone.

"Trying to fight going to bed," she said. "That's all I'm doing. Been cleaning this house all day. Think I've finally wore myself out."

"Gets easier and easier, don't it?" He shifted nervously and kept looking past her into the house. "You mind if I come in for a minute?"

"Of course not, John. Come on in." Vess stepped aside with her arm stretched to hold the screen door open. "You want some coffee or a glass of water?"

"No, I'm good, Vess. Thank you." The sheriff followed her through the kitchen and into the den.

When Vess reached the recliner where she'd been sitting, she took the remote control from the arm of the chair and muted the television completely. "Take you a seat over there if you want." She gestured toward a plaid sofa that ran beside a half moon of cobble laid and stacked as the hearth for a potbelly woodstove.

Vess leaned back in the recliner and fixed her eyes on the mantel above the Fisher stove. A row of family photos tapered toward the center, where a wind-up clock she and Lonnie had received as a wedding gift still kept good time. It was a quarter till nine, but this far past the solstice the night was full dark outside. There was a large painting over the mantel, a picture of a tobacco barn caving into a yellowed field, the sky cloudless and blue.

"I wanted to come by here and apologize." Coggins plopped in the middle of the couch, and the worn-out springs surrendered to his weight so that it appeared as if he were sitting in a hole.

"What for, John?"

"What Dayna said that morning outside the church has really been eating at me. I just shouldn't have let her walk home on her own."

Vess found it a bit strange that he would come by and bring this up. She wondered if he'd spoken with Leah, but she didn't ask or push it further. "That's not your fault, John. You couldn't have known what was going to happen."

"Way everybody was riled up over that statue, I should have, Vess. And that's what I wanted to say."

For a minute or so, they both sat there without saying anything, each staring off at someplace entirely their own, their minds churning thoughts they could not speak aloud.

"Anyways," Coggins said as he tilted onto one hip. He dug in his pants pocket and brought something out in his hand. Rocking up to his feet, he took a step across the room and held out an offering. "I found this in my truck and I think it must've come off your granddaughter. If I remember right, you used to wear this when you were younger. Figured you'd want it back. Chain must've broke."

Vess held her hand out and the sheriff dropped the pendant she'd given Toya that morning into her palm. She immediately closed her fingers around it and felt the glass and silver warm inside her fist from where he'd carried it. When she opened her hand she rubbed her thumb over the glass as one might work a worry stone, a nervous habit she'd had for years any time trouble struck.

She glanced down at the dark lock of her grandmother's hair encased within the pendant. There was something caught beneath the rolled silver edge like dirt trapped under a fingernail, just a thin track of debris that would've gone unnoticed or been dismissed as tarnish by anyone who hadn't held that charm for decades. Vess ran the edge of her fingernail against the curved lip and smeared what came off against her palm. There was a bit of grit, a deep black loam, but scattered about were specks of color, flakes of scarlet red. Whenever she'd butcher meat chickens there was always a bit of blood she'd miss when she washed her hands, tiny specks she'd spot later on and scratch off her skin. That's what this looked like. There was no doubt in her mind it was blood.

"I don't think I ever asked whether Toya got caught up in all of that fighting, whether or not she got hurt."

"No," he said. "Right when everything started, I got to her and we slipped out the back. We left that mess for the town to fool with. That was their jurisdiction. I was hoping my presence might help keep the peace. Sure didn't turn out that way, but to answer your question, no, she didn't get hurt." Coggins slapped his knees and stood up. "You know, I think I'll take you up on a drink of water."

"Help yourself, John," Vess said. "Glasses in the cabinet. Ice in the freezer."

As the sheriff passed in front of her on his way to the kitchen, Vess glared at what lay in the palm of her hand. The details poured over her in a wave that took her breath. Suddenly it struck her why that place on Dicks Creek had seemed so familiar that afternoon when Detective Green drove her out to show her where they'd found the body. Right there in that exact curve was where John, Lonnie, and a group of other men had released the first turkeys on that side of the county back in the mid-eighties, nine birds captured and relocated from Standing Indian. Years later, after the turkeys had laid claim to every field and ridgeline in Jackson County, her husband took her up Dicks Creek and showed her where they'd let them go. She hadn't half believed him.

All of those details—Coggins's having lied about where he dropped her off, the charm, that place—forged together into a certainty that she could not shake. The way he'd looked at Toya that day on the porch, that absolute rage in his eyes. Vess had somehow managed to look past it because of their history, and now that looking past became agony.

On the small end table beside the recliner a cordless house phone stood on its charger, and beside it lay the recorder that Detective Green had given her in case anyone called. Her cell phone rested beside those two things and Vess picked it up to dial Leah's number. She could hear Coggins in the kitchen shoveling ice from the freezer into his glass. When Leah picked up the phone, Vess whispered into the receiver, "I need you to get over to my house." She heard Leah scramble with questions, but Vess had no time to listen and spoke over her. "I'm going to leave this call going and you just keep listening. You understand me? Don't hang up. Whatever you do, don't hang up. And get over here just as fast as you can. You hear me?"

"You say something, Vess?" Coggins hollered from the kitchen.

"Yeah, I'm sorry, John. I said go ahead and make me a glass of water while you're in there if you don't mind." When she heard him open the cabinet she set the cell phone on the arm of the recliner and moved for her husband's shotgun, which stood in the corner behind the chair.

When Coggins came through the doorway holding a glass of water in each hand, Vess Jones had her husband's double-barrel laid over the back of the recliner. With her head down on the gun, she settled the bead in the center of his chest and thumbed back both rabbit-ear hammers. Coggins's eyes stretched wide and he dropped the glasses of water against the floor as he jumped back into the kitchen.

"What in the world are you doing, Vess? Put that gun down!"

"Why'd you do it, John?" Her voice broke as she said this. "Why'd you kill my grandbaby?"

"What in the world are you talking about, Vess? I didn't kill nobody. Now, put that gun down and let's talk about this. Let's put some sense in your head."

"I know it was you, John. I know it was you like I know my name. There's not a doubt in my mind. I should've seen it that day I saw where they found her. You killed my Toya, and I want you to tell me why." Vess crouched behind the chair so that she was shielded. Her legs quaked, and despite the gun's being propped on the chair, the thirty-inch barrels were front-heavy and she struggled to hold them steady. "Tell me why you killed her, John!" she screamed with tears filling her eyes and a deep catch in her throat.

Coggins eased around the corner with his service weapon drawn. He held the pistol outstretched and even with the edge of his body, then slowly pulled to center as he stepped through the shattered glass and water into the open. "Put the gun down, Vess, and let's talk. Let's talk about this. You're not making any sense right now."

"I'm sick of the lying, John! I'm so sick of the lying! Tell me what she could've done to make you do that. Tell me, John, or I swear to my Lord and savior, I will end you and let Him sort it out."

"Vess, I've told you. I don't know what you're talking about."

"You're lying," she growled.

"I don't know what you've got fixed in your head, but you need to put that gun down. Put that gun down and we'll talk about this. We'll get this figured out."

"It's figured out, John. I don't need to do no more figuring."

Coggins tried to take a step forward and Vess jabbed the barrels toward him like she was prodding at a snake with a shovel. When she did, that sudden movement stopped him in his tracks.

"Stop lying to me, John. Just stop the lying." Vess's jaw was clenched and her teeth ground on every word. "You took my baby girl, my only grandbaby. You took her out there where you and Lonnie turned them turkeys loose and I don't know why you did that and I don't know what went on out there to make you do what you did, but I know you did it. I know it just as clear as my own name."

Coggins didn't speak now, and there was a shift in the way he looked at her.

"Tell me why you did it, John." Vess repeated that same thing over and over as if that statement alone were the breaths she took. "Tell me why you did it."

The moment stretched out for what seemed unending, and when that spell finally broke between them, what he said came across her neck like the blade of a guillotine.

"She just wouldn't listen," he said.

Everything she'd ever held in her heart severed clean in two. Vess felt the trigger ease back against the tip of her finger, the weight steady and growing, and she had to fight to keep from following that simple pull all the way to its break. She had to will her finger forward to keep from shooting him where he stood. "And so you killed her?" Vess could hardly find enough air for words. What she said now came out a whisper. "You killed her because she wouldn't listen?"

"I tried to tell her this place wasn't what she thought, and she didn't want to hear it. She wanted to paint it all the one way." There was arrogance in his voice now, as if a piece of him still believed he was justified. "I tried to tell her things wasn't as simple as she wanted to make them out to be. But she wouldn't listen. She wouldn't even let me finish a sentence. I told her how much I loved Lon, how much I loved you, and she said it couldn't have ever been how I thought. Said it couldn't have been that way because there'd always been power on one side and not the other. She said that like he couldn't have loved me, like he couldn't have felt the same way I did. I took her up there to tell her how much I loved that man and that's what she said to me. She wouldn't listen. She wouldn't even let me talk . . ."

Vess couldn't believe what he was saying. She couldn't believe something so simple had pushed him to that sort of end, that something so simple had taken her beautiful granddaughter out of this world.

"She didn't have to listen to you, John! Nobody has to listen to you! Nobody in this world owes you anything!" Vess was screaming at the top of her lungs but he was still talking, as if he were in another place altogether.

"Nothing like this ever happened until that girl showed up. Not once in our lifetime. And you look at the times we lived through. You look at what went on all over this country and nothing like this ever happened here until this summer." He seemed to snap back out of that place right then and his eyes stretched far back into her. "We've lived side by side our whole lives. You and Lon like family to me. Like family. And then she shows up here and rips this place open like a goddamn plow."

Vess was shaking harder and harder and she could feel her grip loosening on the gun like she might drop it at any minute. She closed her fists tightly then until her fingers felt as if they would shatter.

"My granddaughter did nothing," she snarled. "It was pride. It's pride, John. And it's power. It's you not wanting to let go of one ounce of what you've had, what you were born with, for fear that the scale might tilt. It's you keeping your hand on that scale and smiling while you done it. Smiling in my face. Coming in my house lying to me. Lying to my face, John. Looking me dead in my eyes like you are right now and lying because you thought you could. You thought you'd just walk away from all this, that there'd be no consequence. That's how delusional you are. That's what living in a world like that does to you."

There was a visible resentment building in him, his body coiling into stone. "I come from nothing. I come from the same place you come from. And you want to talk about privilege and power. Everything I got I made. There wasn't nothing ever given to me. And that's why I'll be damned if I sit back and let somebody lie about where I come from just so they can rip it out from under me."

"Delusion," she said. "You're living in delusion."

Right then she could see in him the very thing that had brought them to this moment. Rage welled up, and his voice came out as if he were possessed. "Put the gun down, Vess." He inched closer and every bit of space that disappeared between them brought him closer to grabbing ahold of the barrels. "You're not going to fucking shoot me. Put that fucking gun down."

Vess was crying now, and her body rattled like a leaf about to break from the tree. She knew she could not let him come any closer. Her finger tightened over the front trigger and when she pulled, she closed her eyes.

When the hammer fell, her body jerked and a deafening crack of sound split through the house. She was surprised to still be standing, surprised to have felt no recoil at all. Vess opened her eyes and he was still there. Coggins was untouched and his pistol was aimed at her chest. As she tried to make sense of what had happened, a voice screamed from the kitchen and all of that madness nearly swept her legs out from under her like a sudden rush of water. She felt as if she were being carried away by a flood.

60

When the back door cracked like a gunshot against the wall, Coggins's upper half twisted, and as his eyes found Leah Green standing there, his shoulders slouched as if he was coming to realize she had him dead to rights.

"Drop the fucking weapon, Sheriff!" Leah screamed again. "Now!"

He moved his left hand away from the gun and raised it before his chest, palm out, as if he were about to take an oath before God. His index finger slid out of the trigger guard and he held the pistol flat toward the ground in his strong hand. "What are you doing, girl?" He slowly knelt until he was hovering just above the ground, and he set his service weapon onto the hardwood floor with his left hand still raised before him.

"Kick it across the floor."

Coggins stood up but that was all. "You're drawn down on the very man that put that badge on your belt."

"I heard everything you said. Every goddamn word of it." She broke that sentence apart so that each syllable fell like the head of a hammer. There were tears in her eyes and she gritted her teeth to keep from breaking. "Now, kick the gun across the floor or I swear to God you won't leave this room."

Coggins still didn't move.

"I said kick the fucking gun, Sheriff! Now!"

Leah bulldozed through the kitchen, and when she reached the threshold into the den the sheriff settled the toe of his boot over his service weapon and shoved the gun forward a few feet, where it spun a slow circle, then stopped with the muzzle pointed at the wall. She looked down to where two glasses had shattered on the floor and a puddle of water rested in front of her feet. Easing a little farther into the room, she peeked around the corner, cutting her eyes back and forth to locate Vess.

"Are you all right, Mrs. Jones?"

"I'm okay," Vess said.

Leah stepped fully into the den and saw that the old woman had a shotgun aimed at Coggins, the fore end of the heavy double barrel rested on the back of the recliner. She was knelt down so that only the tops of her shoulders and her head showed above the bunker she'd taken.

"It's all right, Mrs. Jones. You can put that down now. He's not going to do anything. He's not going to hurt you."

"If it's all the same, I think I'll stay on the gun," Vess said without so much as glancing away from the bead.

Leah was holding her breath without realizing, and when she finally broke she gasped for air. Disbelief and shock rendered what was happening into something that felt like a dream. Until that phone call she'd held on to a tiny speck of hope that it was all coincidence and confusion. Never could she have imagined John Coggins capable of what he'd done, but over the past few minutes she'd listened to every grisly detail straight from his own fucking mouth while she drove as fast as her car would carry her.

"How could you do it?" she said, and when she finally asked that question, she couldn't hold it together any longer. Those words ruined her. "How could you do that to that girl?" Leah sputtered, then ground her teeth as if biting down on a length of rope to endure some unbearable pain. "How could you lie like that? How could you look me in my eyes, look *that woman* in her eyes, and lie like that?"

"Leah—" He started to speak, but she cut him off.

"He doesn't have a soul to save, Mrs. Jones. And there ain't a courtroom on this planet could bring a punishment upon him that would amount to any sort of justice."

Her face wrenched and she tilted her head to the side. The tears in her eyes blurred her vision of him.

"I used to believe all this meant something. I used to believe that. But looking at what passes for law anymore, I don't think this badge means anything. It's never meant anything at all." Leah dropped her weak hand and pulled the shield she wore from her belt and dropped it onto the floor. "If you want to kill him, Mrs. Jones, you go ahead and do it. I won't blame you. You go ahead and I'll tell them any story you feel like telling."

"I don't—"

She didn't allow Vess to finish her thought. "If you don't want to dirty your floors we can tote him off somewhere. I know plenty of places in this country they won't find a hair off his head."

"He's done killed himself," Vess said.

The statement caught Leah by surprise. "What do you mean?"

"That recorder. That tape's been running since the second I called."

Leah looked at her there in the corner and the old woman cut her eyes toward a small end table just beside the chair. There was a cordless phone there and she could see the red light glowing on the top of the recorder, hear the slow turn of the wheels rolling through that fitful silence. Coggins made a sudden move and the old woman welded her cheek to the gun. Leah snapped onto him and would not make the same mistake twice.

"He's killed himself, honey. And I can't think of a punishment worse for a man as prideful as that one standing there than having to watch his name leave nothing but a sour taste in people's mouths."

For a few moments they all just stood there saying nothing. What Vess Jones proposed didn't seem like enough. Leah had a headful of questions she wanted answered, but right then she didn't feel that it was her place to ask anything of a woman who'd already given more than she ever deserved to lose. Leah knew her own suffering was weightless by comparison.

"I need to go outside and get some air," Vess said. "I feel like I'm suffocating."

The old woman came from around the back of the chair and she held the shotgun with one hand at her side, the heavy barrels tilting the balance so that the muzzle angled to the floor. Leah stepped aside to let her pass and in a second she heard the screen door creak open, then slap closed behind her. Now it was just the two of them.

61

Vess walked to the center of the backyard and stared straight above at what little was left of heaven. The grass was damp and cold against her feet, and a breeze pulled the duster she wore tight to her body. She closed her eyes and took a deep breath through her nose, exhaled slowly from her lips, and when she opened her eyes she felt betrayed to find the stars exactly how she'd left them. There was a verse from the Bible beating inside her heart. *The sun and the moon shall be dark, and the stars shall withdraw their shining.*

That's what the Book said, and it was a lie. There they were, blinking and constant and piercing through her like needles. For the first time in her life, she wondered if God existed at all. If He was there, then how could she not hate Him for what He'd allowed? If He'd been standing there right then, she would've buried the blade of a lockback knife in the side of His throat and bled Him out like a hog.

Vess looked at the gun she held, the left hammer down, the right still cocked and ready. She thumbed the hammer spur to rest, cracked open the chambers, and the ejectors spit both shells to the ground at her feet. Bending over, she took them into her hand and examined their brass faces. The primer on the one was dented where the firing pin had hit, but evidently there hadn't been enough force. A light strike had been the thing that kept Coggins alive, and that seemed to confirm what she was already thinking. How could a man like that be so damned lucky and her have had to endure so much loss and suffering? Vess slid both shells back into the chambers and folded the action closed.

She could hear Leah and Coggins barking and snarling like dogs, then out of nowhere the yard flashed bright around her in a quick strobe as three shots clapped from inside the house. Vess spun and rushed for the door. As she came into the kitchen with the shotgun shouldered, she saw Leah kneeling over the sheriff's body in the den, the soles of his boots facing her like two crooked tombstones.

When she came into the room, Coggins was still conscious, but his neck and face were trembling and what little bit of air he held gurgled from the back of his throat, his tongue lapping at the blood that filled his mouth. The way he'd fallen, his head had come to rest against the stacked-cobble hearth, his face tilted up with his chin flush to his chest. Sweat beaded his forehead. His eyes stretched wide and pulled back, stretched wide again as he stared at what stood before him, then off at something beyond.

Vess watched as the last of his breath escaped him.

"He—he went for the gun," Leah stuttered. "I . . . I didn't have a choice."

The old woman came forward and hovered above where he lay. All three shots had caught him in the center of the chest over an area about the size of a tomato. Blood soaked through the front of his shirt, but most seemed to seep from beneath him, spreading over the hardwood floor, leaching into the cracks between slats, and reaching farther until it touched the tips of her toes. She took a step back and Leah watched her with some bewildered look about her face. Neither spoke a word.

Still kneeling beside the body, Leah held the slide of Coggins's service weapon in her left hand, her index finger slid through the trigger guard so that he could not have pulled if he'd tried. His fist was clenched tightly around the grip, but there was this feeling that swept over Vess right then, a question really that she'd never be able to answer. Did he truly have the gun in that moment she fired or was Leah placing the weapon in his hand when Vess came into the house? That was a question she would take to her grave, never once so much as speak it aloud.

In the months that would come, Vess Jones would replay the events of that night through her mind. She would listen to the tape again and again and try to discern exactly what had happened once she left the room. The only thing that was certain was that there was a loud crash and the recording went dead. At trial, Leah's defense would argue that this was the moment Coggins made his move for the gun. The prosecution would point back to what Leah'd said a few minutes before in order to argue she'd simply cut the tape and killed him.

In the end, Vess would never know what to believe or if the truth really mattered at all. Either way, the results were the same, and fully believing one way or the other offered neither solace nor satisfaction. She was the last thing he ever saw of this world.

62

The church is empty like always and she sits alone. Her hands have aged and she folds them over one knee, her legs crossed and her eyes long adjusted to the dark. Time runs quicker now, and she can feel that water building and rising against the dam. She knows that the day moves nearer when that wall shall not hold and she will finally know the after for herself.

A part of her longs for this moment, though she refuses to pray that prayer and will never make the choice her own. She waits, for that is all there is, but make no mistake, she is ready. She locks the door of the sanctuary and goes home, where she crawls into bed and lies with things she cannot stop from thinking. As she drifts off, she hears him. Her eyes open and she rolls onto her side, fully believing for one split second that she will find the man she loves beside her.

The thought is like smoke, and as it fades, she remembers the morning she woke up to find him not breathing. Lon died in his sleep from a heart attack. He was flat on his back with his head tilted on the pillow and his mouth hung open like a mackerel. Her first thought wasn't to reach for the phone and call for help, for she knew it was far too late. She remembers how instead she snuggled close and threw her leg across him one last time, her hand resting on his chest as she stared at him and tried to pretend for a few seconds longer that she did not know the future.

She climbs out of bed and goes to the den. She sits in his chair and stares at the floor where the hardwood slats run beneath the cobblestone hearth. She opens the doors of the potbelly stove, taps the log with the cast iron poker, and what had seemed whole crumbles into cinders that glow and spark an orange deep as jewelweed. The room smells of wood smoke but the place feels cold, and she stares down at her bare feet on the floor knowing well what has lain there and the blood that has touched her toes.

A pleading look swept across those wicked eyes as the light pulled back and gone. She remembers that desperation on his face, that moment just before the fire snuffed out, as if she might offer something that would save him, and there is a strange emotion that wrenches her heart, a feeling caught somewhere between gratefulness and guilt. When she glances up to the mantel and catches her reflection in the glass of the clock, she realizes that she is smiling.

Sometimes she thinks about what he said. She thinks about the excuses he made. She thinks about the lies he told himself right up to the end and she knows good and well he believed them. What he was too blind to see was that it wasn't anything the girl did, but rather the questions she raised and his own inability to sit with or answer them. There were people in this world so privileged that the notion of enduring any discomfort at all, even for a second, struck them as trauma. He was soft. He was as fragile as a trout. And that was why the anger took him so easily. That's what it's like to sit in the shade of that tree, she thinks, and in some ways she is thankful to have never known that privilege for herself.

She wanders into the kitchen for a drink. While she stands there at the sink she thinks about that last moment with the girl, that morning it had felt like they were dancing. She remembers knowing in that moment she'd never feel that way again, and it breaks her to know she was right. She remembers how hot their bodies felt pressed together, and that warmth is what she has come to miss most. Sometimes she can't remember all that has happened, and she welcomes that forgetting as an act of mercy.

Year after year, the summer's heat beats down on her shoulders. She wipes the sweat from her brow and dusts the dirt from her hands. She goes inside and puts a cool rag across her neck, and when she returns to the yard the leaves burn quick with color, fade and crisp until they cannot hold. Season renders to season. She blinks and it is winter again. Once more the house is cold and there is no amount of fire that can keep her warm. This is always hardest. The days are short and the darkness long. She stays in bed and curses the dreams that somehow never find her.

There are moments she cannot carry what has been allotted, and on those nights she goes to Lula's and stays in the guest room, but sleep rarely comes. Lula asks her to move in and she asks where she will keep the chickens. Lula points to a place in the yard and tells her she can till the garden there, but the woman knows how long it takes to amend soil. She knows that neither of them has enough time to make an honest go of anything anymore. What she does not know is that Lula will go first and that she will be last. For a while, she will sit alone on that pew.

Her daughter asks her to move. There are apartments close to her town house in Buckhead. She can sell the house and land. Prices in the mountains have risen to more than ten thousand an acre, and houses like hers bring three times what they did a few years before. People are abandoning cities and escaping to the country. She could do the opposite and move closer, be closer to hospitals and doctors and all of the things she will surely need soon enough. Dayna makes good money and can cover whatever she can't. Her daughter gives this same spiel every time they talk. Her daughter begs her to think it over and she does, she truly does, but in the end her answer is always the same.

The woman will never leave this place. She cannot leave this mountain.

On the trail to the river, she notices the trout lilies first, the marbled leaves piercing green through the leaf litter. Poplar coves blush gold midmountain and soon spring turns on like a faucet. The woods are spotted white with trillium. A neighbor comes to till the plot, something she can no longer do herself. She thanks him and tries to pay him but he will not take her money, and when he is gone she crawls on her hands and knees through the dirt, raking the weeds and grass with her fingers and tossing them by the handful into the woods. This is the one place she is happy, and for a moment she turns her face to the sun and is thankful for one more season. There is something in the air around her that feels like the turn of a song.

She sets her onions and buries her seed potatoes. She plants beds of lettuce and soon enough it is nightfall, so she goes into the house, where a large crock sits on the stove. She pulls off the lid and smells the pot liquor, what's left from a head of cabbage. Her grandmother's cast iron skillet, a Wagner seasoned slick as glass, hangs from a nail on the side of the cabinet. She pulls the pan down and bakes a pone of corn bread with meal from a grist stone in Cherokee, and when the cake is done she flips it onto a checkered cloth to cool.

As she eats she thinks of her mother. She holds the bowl of broth to her face and smells the cabbage and carrots and onions, the rosemary and thyme, and she's transported back to her mother's kitchen. She can feel the sting on the top of her hand from the wooden spoon when she steals a bite of heavy cream that has floated to the top of the milk her mother will churn to butter. Her mother swats and screams, "I've done told you with my mouth," as she stands there and licks her fingers clean. She can see her mother's lips and that great big smile, she can hear that belly laugh, and all of those memories seem to be rising out of the steam from that bowl, all of it conjured by nothing more than a smell that has filled her nose.

In a few more weeks, she plants the beans. When she walks the garden the morning after they've sprouted, white stems lifting green heads through black soil, she knows that she's almost there, and this thought fills her with joy. Soon there will be tomatoes and okra and cucumbers and peppers and squash and zucchini, greasy cut-shorts and sweet corn, ears of Peaches & Cream that will hit her tongue like candy.

The outer edges of the garden are lined with river rock that Lon carried stone by stone from the stream decades before. On the edge, though, facing the house sit ten plaster casts that have not been here long. The boy from the college brought them that first winter and she has kept them in the shed until now, for she was not sure what to do with them, unable to confront them. They are glazed and fired a deep black, and when the sun strikes them they shine like obsidian. She picks one up in her hands and stares at her granddaughter's face. She traces her fingers over the girl's face with one hand, and when she sits the cast back onto the ground, she runs her fingers over her own, feeling her nose and lips, her eyes and cheekbones.

She looks at the expressions captured across those faces and each one takes her someplace different. She remembers a card game when she and Lula went nil. She remembers the looks on their husbands' faces when they lost every trick. She remembers how Lula's husband, Marvin, lost his temper and slammed his cards against the table and screamed goddamn and how the two of them broke out laughing so hard they cried.

Her mind drifts back to Lon and she can see the two of them standing up on the parkway leaned against the front bumper of an old C10 pickup he used to drive. She's pregnant and wearing an emerald-green dress with a fake pearl necklace and big gold earrings, and he's got his hand resting on her stomach. She remembers Dayna in an Easter dress. She remembers Dayna in a prom dress. She remembers Dayna hating dresses so much she used to rip her clothes off and storm out into the yard and roll around in the mud like a hog. All of these memories fill her eyes with tears of joy, and in those moments she can't help but find it a blessing. In those moments, she regrets having ever wished the remembering away.

When she looks at the face now, she sees the girl. She sees her dancing there in the dirt barefooted and glowing, her dress spinning around her like a parasol. She remembers the way she looked in that sunlight. She remembers the way her hair whipped about her body, her hips twisting and arms raised to the sky as if she could've reached up and touched the hands of God. The old woman holds on to this. She grips it in her hand like a stone and soon it is all she will see, the only thing she'll remember.

On that night the music finds her and the voices sing her to sleep. This is how the everlasting comes.

ACKNOWLEDGMENTS

To Marie Cochran, to whom this novel is dedicated. Your smile and spirit, your compassion and hope, have always been a light in the darkness. To Victoria Casey McDonald, who worked tirelessly to preserve a story and a people. May that work serve eternal. To the dog, woods, and woman who sustained me while I tried. To my editor, Gaby Mongelli, and my agent, Julia. And above all, to those who swing the axe.